MYSTERIES
OF THE DEEP

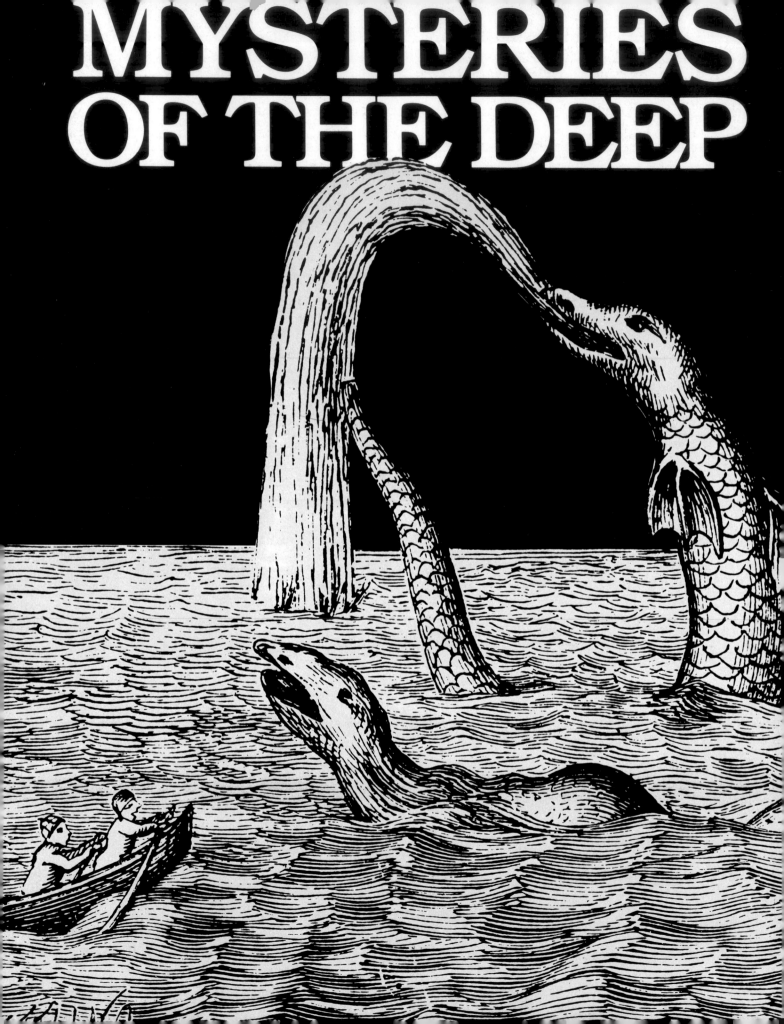

Edited by
JOSEPH J. THORNDIKE, JR.

Published by
AMERICAN HERITAGE
PUBLISHING CO., INC.,
New York

Book Trade Distribution by
Charles Scribner's Sons

Library of Congress Cataloging in
Publication Data
Main entry under title:
Mysteries of the deep.
  Includes index.
  1. Ocean. I. Thorndike, Joseph Jacobs,
1913—
GC21.M97   909′.0962   80-7804
ISBN 0-8281-0407-7
ISBN 0-8281-0408-5 (deluxe)

EDITOR
Joseph J. Thorndike, Jr.

ASSOCIATE EDITOR
Constance R. Roosevelt

ART DIRECTOR
Marleen Adlerblum

MANAGING EDITOR
Brenda Niemand

PICTURE EDITOR
Jane Colihan

ANTHOLOGY EDITOR
Ormonde de Kay, Jr.

ASSISTANT EDITOR
Donna Whiteman

RESEARCH LIBRARIANS
Laura Lane
Marian Weston

FOREIGN PICTURE RESEARCHERS
Rosemary L. Klein, London
Maria Terese Hirschkoff, Paris

AMERICAN HERITAGE
PUBLISHING CO., INC.

CHAIRMAN AND PRESIDENT
Samuel P. Reed

PUBLISHER
Beverley Hilowitz

CORPORATE ART DIRECTOR
Murray Belsky

PRODUCTION DIRECTOR
Elbert Burr

INTRODUCTION

As he lay in the Tower of London, awaiting his executioners, the duke of Clarence dreamed that he was drowning:

> Methought I saw a thousand fearful wrecks;
> A thousand men that fishes gnaw'd upon;
> Wedges of gold, great anchors, heaps of pearl,
> Inestimable stones, unvalu'd jewels,
> All scatter'd in the bottom of the sea.

Shakespeare's duke (in *Richard III*) dreamed of riches and horrors together. And so have others on every coast where men have loved and feared the sea. For every bar of Spanish gold, a lurking shark. For every sweet-singing mermaid, a tentacled monster.

Where knowledge leaves a vacuum, men's minds fill the unknown with imaginings. The Norwegians, who knew the sudden changes of the ocean better than most, believed in a god called Njord, who protected sailors, and another god named Aegir, who ruled the deep with his insatiable wife, Ran. Ran liked to capsize ships, catch the drowning sailors in a net, and take them to an undersea palace where she gave them endless banquets—but only if they paid her in gold. In the Greek world Poseidon held court beneath the sea in a mother-of-pearl palace, from which he rose in golden splendor to ride the waves or, when angry, stir them into tempest.

Even learned men repeated the most preposterous tales. In the pages of Pliny's massive Roman encyclopedia we read that sailors crossing the Indian Ocean saw whales whose backs measured four acres. Erik Pontoppidan, bishop of Bergen, described the giant kraken "which seems to be in appearance about an English mile and a half in circumference (some say more, but I chuse the least for greater certainty)." Even Carolus Linnaeus, the father of modern scientific classification, included the kraken among his species as late as 1735.

Outlandish notions lingered into modern times because the sea remained a realm of mystery. Long after the remotest land areas had been explored and mapped, none but a handful of divers had seen what lay beneath the surface of the sea, and they had seen it only with blurred vision, for a few minutes, for a few feet around them. Otherwise, the surface of the sea was a universal barrier, sometimes fearsome, sometimes seductive, but always impenetrable.

Most of what we now know about the undersea world we have learned in the last century, and the greater part of that in the last third of a century. In this short time of revelation, one milestone was the development of the Aqua-Lung by Jacques-Yves Cousteau and a colleague. With that simple invention men were enabled to swim and glide through the shallow seas and see the bottom as fishes see it. The other, more complex development was the rapid growth of oceanographic technology, especially since World War II. By the use of sophisticated instruments and submersible craft, scientists have been able to study the ocean floor itself and the creatures who inhabit the greatest deeps.

Among those who have put the new technology to use are the treasure hunters. "There is no getting away from a treasure," said Joseph Conrad, "that once fastens upon your mind." The Caribbean is the hunting ground for seekers after sunken treasure, and the mystery they face is simply this: Where is it? In our first chapter, Walter Karp explains in fascinating detail why the Spanish galleons sank where they did and how some of them have been found. Any reader who would like to brave the formidable odds in this adventurous quest would do well to study the methods of the two men who found perhaps the richest galleon of them all, the *Nuestra Señora de la Concepción:* William Phips, a Maine sea captain who partially plundered it in the seventeenth century, and Burt Webber, who found it all over again and is recovering even more treasure from it today.

More important than gold or silver and equally exciting is the knowledge to be recovered from ancient wrecks. In this pursuit the field of search is the Mediterranean, and the searcher is the underwater archaeologist. In our second chapter Peter Throckmorton, one of the pioneers in this work, tells what has been learned and what has yet to be learned of ancient

ships and cargoes and routes of trade. "History," said Francis Bacon, "is the plunder of a shipwreck." More literally, the plunder of an actual shipwreck may fill gaps in known history.

The literature and folklore of every seafaring people is replete with tales of ancient voyages. Dimly, through the mists of time and oceans, we can make out seafarers, first exploring the inland seas and then venturing onto the vast deep, perhaps even to the opposite shores. In Chapter 3 Francis Russell sorts fact from the volumes of speculation about early voyagers.

Sometimes a ship fails to reach its destination. The ancients would have said that Poseidon had claimed it. More recently the cause may be put down as storm or reef or iceberg, piracy, mutiny, or a skipper's madness. In Chapter 4 Ormonde de Kay, Jr., examines some of the mysterious disappearances that defy explanation.

Of all the tales of the sea, the most lurid are those of monstrous creatures that inhabit the depths. In Chapter 5 William MacLeish, editor of *Oceanus,* the journal of the Woods Hole Oceanographic Institution, tells what marine biologists have discovered about the strange and wonderful creatures that do exist in the seas. Though the kraken, the mermaid, and the bishop fish may be dismissed as imaginary, there is solid evidence of giant squid, super-eels, and other mysterious creatures yet unseen by human eyes.

Finally, in Chapter 6 William Wertenbaker, author of *The Floor of the Sea,* takes us into the world of the oceanographer. Here are the mysteries of submarine volcanoes and earthquakes, shifting plates of the earth's crust, rising and sinking land masses, currents and waves, and tsunamis one hundred feet tall.

In this century's great burst of oceanic exploration, many mysteries have been dispelled. Many more remain. And perhaps the most important mystery of all is whether man will find within himself the wisdom to meet the challenge of the next century: to understand the sea and to use its great resources but not to squander and despoil them for all time.

—JOSEPH J. THORNDIKE, JR.

1

SUNKEN TREASURE

For generations the very words inspired daydreams and romance: Spanish galleons, pieces of eight, gold doubloons, corsairs, buccaneers, sunken treasure—the Spanish Main. Shrouded in legend, that cockpit of greed and adventure has become over the long years a part of our folklore, a fable of the New World when that world was young, like El Dorado and the Fountain of Youth. Unlike El Dorado, however, the Main is no fable and its lost treasure no fantasy, for men in our own time have begun to recover that treasure and to rediscover in the process the historic reality of the Spanish Main.

The Spaniards called it, in the lordly style of their heyday, *La Carrera de Indias*, the Route to the Indies, the sea path worked out by Columbus in his three epoch-making voyages to the New World. During the early decades of the sixteenth century, however, the Carrera chiefly guided a humdrum, straightforward commerce. Spanish merchants sailed with manufactured goods for the New World colonists and returned home with raw materials, a profitable enterprise but by no means as profitable as Portugal's spice trade with the Orient. In 1545 the Carrera abruptly ceased to be humdrum when the Spanish conquerors of Peru stumbled on an extraordinary natural bonanza—a mountain composed of silver ore located at an Andean site called Potosí. Spain's good fortune doubled in 1548 when the Spanish in Mexico found the great silver lode of Zacatecas. In the space of three years the Spanish had discovered the richest mines known to man, mines that could produce—and produce with ease—several million ounces of silver a year and thousands of ounces of gold, more precious metal than all Europe possessed when Columbus first sailed for the Indies. Already a great power, Spain became overnight the richest of nations.

More important, the Spanish king became the richest of monarchs, for twenty per cent of the New

LOST GALLEONS OF THE SPANISH MAIN

by Walter Karp

Slave divers, portrayed opposite in a seventeenth-century engraving, were sent down by the Spanish to recover precious cargo from their sunken ships.
PRECEDING PAGES: *Twenty feet down in Bermudian waters, a porgy visits a diver on the remains of a seventeenth-century Spanish treasure ship.*

World's immense and unparalleled treasure production belonged to him personally to use as he alone saw fit. It was known as the *quinto*, the royal fifth, and it worked like a drug on its royal recipients. Like a drug it inspired impossible dreams and unattainable ambitions. It encouraged Spain's Habsburg kings to cling with lunatic tenacity to every jot and tittle of their far-flung dynastic possessions, regardless of their worth and the cost. It inspired their fanatic determination to root out and destroy Protestantism wherever Spain's armies could reach. The treasure of the Indies was to be the sinew of Spain's incomparable infantry, the fuel of her assault on religious heresy, and it lay across a broad ocean, months of sailing time away. From the moment the treasure began flowing, the Spanish crown staked everything on the safety of the shipments: its financial credit, its domestic power, its international prestige, and, above all, its self-imposed duty of restoring the sundered unity of Catholic Christendom. Like a drug the royal fifth was a luxury that swiftly became an addiction.

As the lifeline of a bellicose monarchy, the Carrera was put on a permanent war footing. By the 1560's Spanish officials had worked out the system down to the minutest detail, and for the next two centuries Spain clung to

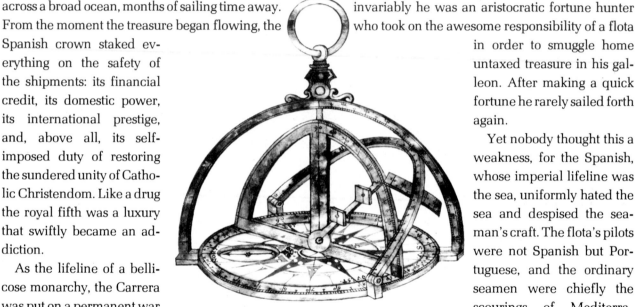

Improved navigational instruments made ocean crossings less haphazard. Illustrations from a pilot's handbook of 1583 show a marine hemisphere, above, and on the opposite page, early devices used for making celestial observations to determine latitude and tell time.

that system in defiance of ferocious enemies, in the teeth of terrifying tempests, through all the vicissitudes of its national fortunes. All Spanish shipping to the New World was concentrated in two annual sailings from the upriver port of Seville. Each May a merchant fleet would sail for Vera Cruz in the Gulf of Mexico. This was known as the New Spain, or Mexican, *flota*. Each August a second merchant fleet would set sail for the port of Cartagena on the northern coast of the South American mainland—the "Main" in the strict sense of the word. This was the Tierra Firme, or mainland, *flota*.

Two galleons bristling with cannons—fifty or more—escorted each merchant fleet. One was the flagship of the captain-general, overall commander of the flota. The second, sailing in the rear, carried the admiral, who took over the fleet's command during combat. Only the galleons were allowed to carry the royal fifth. Private merchant vessels might bring home private treasure, but the galleons, each laden with hundreds of tons of royal silver, were always the treasure ships par excellence. On the success of the galleons the annual hopes of the Spanish crown rested. Yet neither the captain-general nor the admiral was a trained naval officer. Often he had never even been to sea until he took command of a flota. Almost invariably he was an aristocratic fortune hunter who took on the awesome responsibility of a flota in order to smuggle home untaxed treasure in his galleon. After making a quick fortune he rarely sailed forth again.

Yet nobody thought this a weakness, for the Spanish, whose imperial lifeline was the sea, uniformly hated the sea and despised the seaman's craft. The flota's pilots were not Spanish but Portuguese, and the ordinary seamen were chiefly the scourings of Mediterranean quaysides. The galleons themselves had been designed by Venetians, but Spain did little to improve them except to make them bigger and bigger. Essentially freight ships adapted for warfare, they were tubby, top-heavy, and extremely hard to maneuver. The galleon's mighty tiller could turn the ship only five degrees either way; when the seas were rough it took twelve men to move it. The galleon's huge, clumsy squares of canvas made sailing close to the wind impossible and the need for a favoring wind imperative. Far too heavy for their crude rigging, the galleons could not be hove to in a storm. They could only run with the wind and pray for sea room to run in. Unfortunately, sea room was just what the Carrera did not provide for the lumbering galleons.

The essential problem was not Spanish but universal and would not be solved until the mid-eighteenth century. Out of sight of land, a ship's pilot could not determine the longitude of his ship, which is to say, his east-west position at sea. The longer he sailed without landmarks the less certain, in general, he was about his ship's location. The only recourse was to sail, as much as possible, from one charted landmark to the next—a cape, an island, a headland, or even a dangerous reef. Throughout the history of the flotas Spain's pilots avoided reefs by sailing in sight of them. Anything was preferable to getting entirely lost. In consequence, the route to the Indies, straightforward in outline, was in fact an intricate zigzag punctuated by scores of rigidly prescribed turns and menaced at a dozen different points by the landmarks themselves. They were life-savers that storms would time and again turn into deathtraps.

The Atlantic crossing from Spain was the easiest part of the voyage. Following the route discovered by Columbus on his second voyage to the New World, the flotas headed south past the Canary Islands, strung out in line behind the gilded galleon of the captain-general and moving at a stately four knots an hour.

They continued south until they caught the brisk, reliable southeast trade winds, which carried the flotas with little trouble to a Caribbean landfall at Martinique or Guadalupe, "to wash our foul clothes and take in fresh water, whereof we stood in great need" (so wrote one Thomas Gage, an English Dominican monk who sailed on the Carrera in 1625). After six or more weeks at sea, "foul" was always the operative word for a Spanish galleon. With 600 people crowded together on a deck perhaps 125 feet long, with food grown rotten and maggoty, with the below decks so stench-ridden and vermin-infested that passengers spent the entire voyage soaking wet on deck, wretched discomfort was the plight of all but the very wealthiest passengers. Foul conditions, however, were taken for granted. Gage himself recalled his Atlantic crossing as an agreeable one, "without any storms, with pleasant gales, many calms, daily sports and pastimes," including skits, dances, concerts, cockfights, and watching crewmen being flogged with a cat-o'-nine-tails.

Once inside the coral-rich waters of the Caribbean, the piloting became more exacting. Not for nothing did the Spanish give Caribbean landmarks such telltale names as Abreojos ("eyes open") Reef and Quita Sueña ("stop dreaming") Shoals. From Guadalupe the New Spain fleet sailed for Vera Cruz by coasting along the south shores of Puerto Rico, Hispaniola, and Cuba. Not until the pilots sighted Cape San Antonio, on Cuba's westernmost tip, did the fleet come about and cross the Yucatán Channel. Not until they sighted Cabo Catoche at the tip of the Yucatán Peninsula did they sail into the Gulf of Mexico. From then on the lead line was constantly thrown to sound the shifting depths of treacherous shoal waters. The flotas made certain to reach Vera Cruz during daylight. Piloting through the harbor's reefs while benighted spelled swift disaster and possibly death for the pilots, whom captains-general were prone to hang from the yard-arm whenever mischance occurred. Executing the pilot not only provided the Spanish crown with a scapegoat, it eliminated a witness who might have some awkward things to say about the captain-general when the fleet returned to Seville. The practice did not encourage navigational innovation on the Carrera de Indias.

Anchored outside the shabby hamlet of Vera Cruz, the galleons of the flota loaded the royal treasure, which mule trains had transported from the Mexico City mint, where gold was coined into escudos and doubloons, and silver into one-ounce coins known as pieces of eight, or merely molded into loaves and wedges of bullion. The New Spain fleet usually wintered at Vera Cruz to avoid the season of the *nortes*, fierce winds that swept down the Gulf of Mexico and so terrified the Spanish, reported Gage, that even the mildest shift of wind to the north would set crew and passengers fervently praying for divine intercession. Not until February did the New Spain fleet sail for Havana and its all-important rendezvous with the Tierra Firme fleet, which had reached Cartagena in late summer or early fall.

Treasure collecting on the Main put ponderous machinery in motion. As soon as the Tierra Firme fleet reached Cartagena's fine harbor, couriers were dispatched to distant Lima, capital of the viceroyalty of Peru. From there a third fleet, known as the Armada of the South Seas, was ordered to begin visiting the Pacific ports of Peru where treasure from Potosí and other Andean mines lay piled up on the docksides. Coasting from one port to the next while the Tierra

Firme fleet stayed in Cartagena loading gold from Colombia and diamonds from Venezuela, the armada carried the accumulated Andean treasure to the town of Panama. From there long mule trains—Gage counted 200 mules in one of them—carried the treasure across the hot, fetid Isthmus to a disease-ridden Caribbean harbor called Nombre de Dios. (After Sir Frances Drake sacked the place in 1595 Spain abandoned Nombre de Dios for an equally unhealthy place called Porto Bello). There, if everything went according to schedule, the Tierra Firme fleet would be waiting to pick up the treasure and sail in January for Havana. This was an easy reach with favoring winds and just one tricky bit of piloting, passing through a mid-Caribbean channel between Serranilla Bank and the Pedro Shoals, several hours of tense sailing with danger to port and starboard.

Havana was the fulcrum of the Carrera, the pivot of the entire flota system. It stood guard over the Spanish exit from the Indies. Its massive forts protected the royal treasure while the combined fleets were repaired and victualed for the long journey home to Spain. It was not a commercial center but a fortress-base, an impregnable one, the Spanish believed, and so it was. Not until 1762 did the British finally succeed in taking it. Because Havana was Spain's chosen exit point from the Indies, their ships for two hundred years were forced to negotiate the perilous Florida Straits, which confronted the combined flotas with heavy seas, strong headwinds, deadly reefs, and the looming menace of the hurricane. Havana was the worst possible exit from the Indies, but it was the only one which ships from Vera Cruz could reach, and they had difficulty even doing that. Unable to sail against the easterly winds of the Gulf, the treasure-laden New

The rich silver mines at Potosí (seen here in 1584) yielded much of the wealth carried home annually by the Spanish flotas; the Andean refinery tripled Europe's silver supply in the first 160 years of its operation.

Spain fleets had to proceed as far north as the Texas coast before tacking south along the Gulf coast of Florida to Havana.

Leaving Havana for home, the combined flotas entered the Florida Straits by an intricate and devious route. Using as many landmarks as they could muster, the fleets first sailed due east along the Cuban coast, then northward past four separate Bahamian landmarks, then west across the straits until they sighted the white waters of Cape Reef just south of Key Largo. With the jagged reefs of the Florida Keys on their portside, the mighty convoys beat slowly northward for a week until they sighted present-day Cape Canaveral. During that dangerous week of sailing the Spanish had one consolation: no enemy fleet could ambush them. The Gulf Stream's current made it impossible for hostile warships to maintain a blockading formation.

Once past Cape Canaveral the flotas altered course northeast for the most dangerous landmark of all, the reef-protected, mist-shrouded "Isle of Devils"—Bermuda—where ships came to grief so regularly that "wracking," the salvaging of shipwrecks, supplied the principal occupation of its seventeenth-century English settlers. Only after sighting Bermuda, however, did flota pilots feel that it was safe to swing east across the Atlantic with the prevailing westerlies filling their sails. From Havana to Spain the voyage home took two months or more. Given the perils of the Carrera and the Spanish stake in the outcome of a single voyage, little wonder that Philip II once disbursed a small fortune to the churches of Spain so that they might all pray together for the safety of a late-arriving fleet. Little wonder, too, that a captain-general who disappointed the crown's bottomless appetite for treasure stood a fair chance of losing his head in Seville.

Such was the Carrera de Indias, which inspired more greed and hatred, perhaps, than any institution in modern history. The greed was universal. The hatred burned in the hearts of seagoing Protestants—Englishmen, Dutchmen, and French Huguenots—who believed, understandably enough, that by plundering the treasure ships of popery they were serving both Mammon and God. The potent combination of hatred and greed hurled men and ships against the Carrera with extraordinary fury and, during the late seventeenth-century heyday of the buccaneers, with

blood-chilling cruelty as well.

It was Drake—the dreaded El Draque to the Spanish—who led the first serious assault on the flota system. Adroitly putting his finger on the Carrera's weakest link, young Drake in 1572 swooped down on the Isthmus and ambushed three mule trains on route to Nombre de Dios, a feat the buccaneer Henry Morgan would try to duplicate nearly a century later. With the treasure of the Andes in hand, every one of Drake's small crew of tip-and-run raiders was rewarded with wealth enough to last a lifetime. The temptations of the Carrera, however, had an unerring faculty for inspiring dreams more grandiose than mere personal wealth. Thirteen years after his Isthmian raid, Drake returned to the Indies with twenty warships and an elaborate scheme for capturing the

entire Carrera from Spain, a scheme that was to obsess British leaders for the next 175 years. Drake planned to seize for England the three critical junctures of the Carrera: Cartagena, the Isthmus, and Havana. The Carrera proved tougher than Drake had supposed. Cartagena fell to his men, but Drake's troops were too few to hold it; the Isthmus eluded his raiders; and Havana proved too heavily fortified even to risk an assault.

Nevertheless, Drake's impudent attack on the mightiest power in Europe had vast and immediate consequences. It profoundly humiliated the Spanish king at the very height of his pride and zealotry. In the aftermath of Drake's assault Philip II decided to wipe out Britain's pestiferous Protestants once and for all with an invading host from the Lowlands and the "Invincible Armada." The failure of that plan was the first bitter fruit that the Carrera was to reap for Spain.

The Dutch took up where Drake left off and almost put finish to the route to the Indies. To the Dutch, who had shed blood winning independence from Spain, the destruction of the treasure fleets was at one and the same time a patriotic cause, a religious crusade, and a

A swarm of Dutch squadron ships easily overcame two cumbersome Spanish galleons off the north coast of Cuba in July 1628. The Dutch were so bold and persistent in their attacks on Spanish ships that the term "Hollander" came to mean "pirate" or "corsair." Their successful raids destroyed the Spanish monopoly on trade and settlement in the West Indies and cost the crown heavily in lost treasure.

This melodramatic view of a Caribbean hurricane was engraved by Théodore de Bry in 1594. Throughout the West Indies these storms claimed more ships, lives, and treasure than all the pirates on the seven seas.

dividend might have been greater had not Heyn himself lost two treasure ships on his homeward voyage. They fell victim to a menace that was to take far greater toll of Spanish galleons than all the assaults of Spain's enemies combined: the awesome power of a Caribbean hurricane.

Against the hurricane's hundred-mile-an-hour winds the Spanish were helpless, for a hurricane struck by surprise. It simply traveled faster than any ship could sail bearing news of its terrifying appearance. Time and again Spanish fleets sailed right into a hurricane's path. In 1606, for example, a combined fleet was struck by a hurricane just one day after clearing Havana—four ships were lost in the tempest.

Warning of coming hurricanes was often supplied. As early as 1526 a Spanish manual advised pilots to watch for swelling seas, oppressive air, flying fish, and aching rheumatoid joints. Unfortunately, such signs usually appeared too late, especially for slow-sailing galleons. In 1733 a flota of twenty-two ships was tacking in the Florida Straits near Key Biscayne when hurricane signs became all too apparent. Alarmed, the captain-general signaled the fleet to turn about at once and sail back to Havana. Before they could make any headway the hurricane struck with full force. Between sunup and nightfall every single ship was wrecked on the Florida Keys, which, in tandem with hurricanes, put finish to more Spanish treasure than any other stretch of the Carrera. The Spanish name for the Keys was grimly appropriate: Martyrs' Bank.

The unfortunate 1622 fleet left Havana on September 4, despite one veteran pilot's warning that a hurricane was imminent. Three days later the hurricane duly struck the fleet in the Florida Straits, wrecking nine ships against the reefs of the Florida Keys. Three treasure galleons were lost in the storm, along with some two million ounces of royal treasure and unknown quantities of contraband silver—the first major disaster along the Carrera. The other ships of the 1622 fleet managed to limp back to Havana "without rigging or sails and making much water," the unlucky captain-general reported to the king. Two of the wrecked galleons had been lost on a sandbank and could be readily located, he reassured his sovereign, because their masts still obtruded from the water.

This was a quite common fate. Sailing as they did close to landmarks, most storm-tossed galleons

superbly organized business enterprise run by the famed Dutch West India Company. Founded in 1621, the company not only sold stock to investors; it operated the finest war fleets of the age. Nothing could withstand their skill, their fury, and their tenacity. Within a few years the company's ships swept Spanish merchants completely out of the Caribbean, opened up the islands of the Lesser Antilles to settlers of all nations (including the future buccaneers), and destroyed forever Spain's territorial monopoly in the Indies. Only the treasure galleons managed to fight their way through, but the price for trying almost brought Spain to its knees.

The price was exacted in 1628 when the company's great admiral, Piet Heyn, realized a dream that men had vainly cherished for decades and were to cherish vainly for many decades more: He captured an entire Spanish treasure fleet outward-bound from Havana. Heyn returned home with so much Spanish loot that the Dutch West India Company declared a fifty per cent dividend for their fortunate stockholders. The

grounded on shoals or scraped over reefs, often coming to rest in the shallows beyond, in thirty feet of water or less. Some ships snagged on reefs and stayed there, like the treasure ship that sailed from Cartagena in 1730 and came to rest on the teeth of the Serranilla Bank. Survivors were rescued by a passing ship. Year after year, too, the deadly nortes smashed ships right in the overcrowded harbor of Vera Cruz, grounded them on the shoals of the Yucatán Peninsula, wrecked them on deserted islets of the Gulf or on minute scraps of land called cays. The shipwrecked treasure of Spain came to rest in clear, shallow water.

To recover such treasure the Spanish made Herculean efforts. In every major Caribbean seaport they kept salvage vessels ready at a moment's notice to sail for a wreck site before pirates and wrackers got there first. Slaves did the salvage work, and they were skilled and experienced divers. Many of them were Indian pearl divers whom crown officials put to work on the far more urgent task of lugging seventy-pound bars of silver out of sunken holds. Although the divers could work underwater for only a minute or two, Spanish salvors were quite prepared to work them to death to regain the royal treasure, forcing them to dive from morning until night, day after day, for months at a stretch.

Despite the salvors' grim determination, however, time and the sea inevitably kept for themselves a goodly portion of the treasure. Storms and strong currents could silt over a shattered hull in a matter of months; mighty keels weighed down with hundreds of tons of treasure would inevitably subside beneath the sea bottom. Once buried, the wrecked ship and its treasure were beyond reach of divers with only their bursting lungs to aid them. Spain's treasure salvors often had to abandon their operations with much of a ship's freight still undersea. Whatever part of the vessel remained unburied, the teredo worms consumed or coral encrusted. Over the years, what was left of a once-proud galleon would become almost invisible even in shallow water.

For all practical purposes the wrecked ships had ceased to exist. Their whereabouts became vague rumors and eventually faded from the memory of men, their names, their cargoes, and their unfortunate fates recorded only in the voluminous files of the House of Trade in Seville. One hundred fifty years after the last Spanish fleet sailed for Vera Cruz,

precious few sensible people seriously believed that Spain's lost treasure was not lost to the sea forever. By then, shipwrecked galleons and sunken doubloons had become part of the golden lore of the fabulous Main, stuff for tales with which to amuse children. Then, with the invention of the Aqua-Lung in 1943, the treasure of the Carrera de Indias once more began captivating men's minds.

Treasure fever started rising in the early 1950's when American skin divers began hearing about one Art McKee, a Floridian who had recovered three seventy-pound silver bars from a wreck sunk in the hurricane of 1733. So the first modern treasure hunters, spiritual heirs of the wrackers of old, began searching Florida's waters with visions of gold and glory dancing in their heads. Their enthusiasm availed them nothing, since they labored under an insuperable handicap: they did not know what to look for. What they sought no longer existed except in illustrated tales of adventure, namely, a submerged galleon "with a skeleton at the helm and an octopus sitting on a treasure chest," as one veteran treasure hunter wryly recalled. If they came upon a rusted Spanish anchor or a coral-encrusted cannon resting on the sea floor, they would swim eagerly onward in search of "the ship," which shipworms had long since consumed.

Nobody knew better except McKee, and he was not giving lectures in marine archaeology. When Teddy Tucker recovered a sizable fortune off a Bermuda reef in 1955—the first major salvage of Spanish treasure since the days of the Carrera—he, too, announced that he had yet to locate "the ship." Treasure fever dampened considerably when divers finally realized that there were no wrecks, only wreck sites: rusty cannons, anchors, and mounds of ballast stone might be the only visible remains of a long-lost galleon. If there was treasure, it lay beneath the sea bottom or imprisoned in coral. There might be no visible remains at all except, perhaps, for a dark patch of sand discolored by the rust from a buried cannon.

In addition to pluck, luck, and boundless optimism, the modern wracker who hoped to wax fat on the Spanish Main needed equipment to detect buried metal, and machinery to suck up sand or blast away coral. Above all he needed to know fairly precisely where a galleon went down. Because he had all these, a Floridian named Kip Wagner stunned the world in

1965 when he announced the salvage of a fortune in treasure from one of the greatest disasters in the history of the Carrera, the wreck of the 1715 fleet, which Spanish salvors and British pirates had fought over some 250 years before.

Without precise knowledge of a wreck site's location, even the finest salvage gear is often useless. That knowledge, too, is buried treasure of a sort. It lies concealed among the millions of documents produced over nearly four centuries by the scribes of the Carrera de Indias. The bulk of the archives lies in the 400-year-old House of Trade building in Seville, tied up in bundles stacked from floor to ceiling. Unlocking that archival treasure, scarcely touched until the modern age of treasure hunting, is a daunting task. The documents' Spanish is archaic, the bureaucrats' script obsolete, the documents worm-eaten and faded. The bundles, each containing several thousand sheets frugally used on both sides, are indexed poorly, if at all. The archival treasure hunter may need a saint's patience to piece together scattered accounts of a particular shipwreck and a cryptographer's skill to

decipher the modern meaning of obsolete Spanish place names.

The archive can be as misleading as a legendary pirate's treasure map. For years treasure hunters sought in vain the site of *Nuestra Señora de Atocha*, a galleon wrecked in the disaster of 1622. Yet they searched exactly where the Spanish records plainly indicated—on a sandbank "on the west side of the last of the Matecumbe Keys," a group of islets, so named today, in the upper Florida Keys. In 1970 an experienced American archivist named Eugene Lyon began to suspect that the treasure hunters had misinterpreted the 348-year-old directions. Spurred on by an ebullient treasure hunter named Mel Fisher, Lyon began investigating his own guess that in 1622 the "Matecumbe Keys" might have meant the entire Florida Keys. After a year of scholarly detective work in Seville, Lyon was convinced he was right. The *Atocha*, he believed, had been wrecked off the last of the Florida Keys, the uninhabited scraps of land called the Marquesas, one hundred miles from where the treasure hunters were searching. Boldly following

Lyon's advice, Fisher eventually salvaged millions of dollars' worth of *Atocha* treasure.

"There is no getting away from a treasure that once fastens upon your mind," Joseph Conrad rightly observed. The treasure hunters now plying the Spanish Main are often obsessive. Fisher himself spent five million dollars and twelve years of his life in his quest for the elusive treasure of the *Atocha*. Yet even for those who refuse to give up, success is by no means common. Treasure hunters fail and fail expensively. Even success often turns to ashes. The salvor who discovered off the Grand Bahamas the rich wreck site of one of Piet Heyn's lost galleons came away happy to escape bankruptcy after tax collectors, coin auctioneers, and lawyers took their share of his

gain. In 1969 the men who located a New Spain galleon wrecked off a Texas sand dune in 1553 were foiled when poachers raided the site and made off with the treasure. Art McKee was driven off a wreck site at gunpoint, thereby reliving in miniature one of the perils of wracking in the heyday of the Carrera.

Yet the treasure hunters persist, despite danger, frustration, mounting costs, and the long odds against them, for sunken treasure has the special sweetness of stolen fruit. It is not merely wealth in dollars and cents but wealth snatched from the grip of time. In their obsessive efforts to snatch it, the treasure seekers have done much to bring the dead past to life. Modern marine archaeologists understandably deplore their smash-and-grab tactics, yet it is the treasure hunters who have discovered most of the wreck sites of the Carrera, who have brought up most of the historic relics which museums now proudly display, and who have dusted off the musty archives of the House of Trade in Seville. In their quest for real doubloons and historic galleons, they have salvaged the Spanish Main from the realm of legend.

Seville, painted at the height of its power and prosperity in the sixteenth century, grew fat on revenues from arriving and departing fleets. New World treasure was stored in the fortress-like Tower of Gold (far right).

THE LOST FLOTA OF 1715

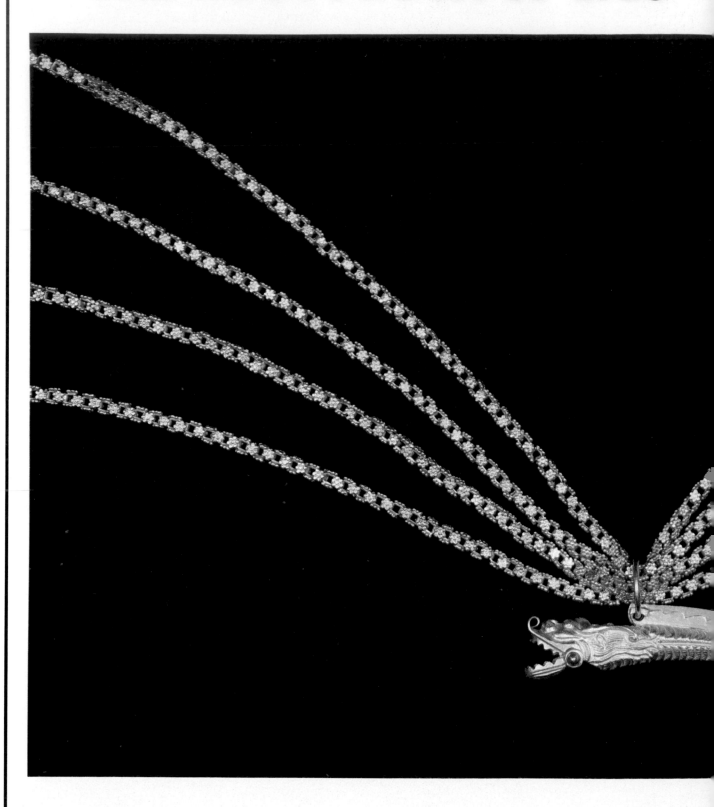

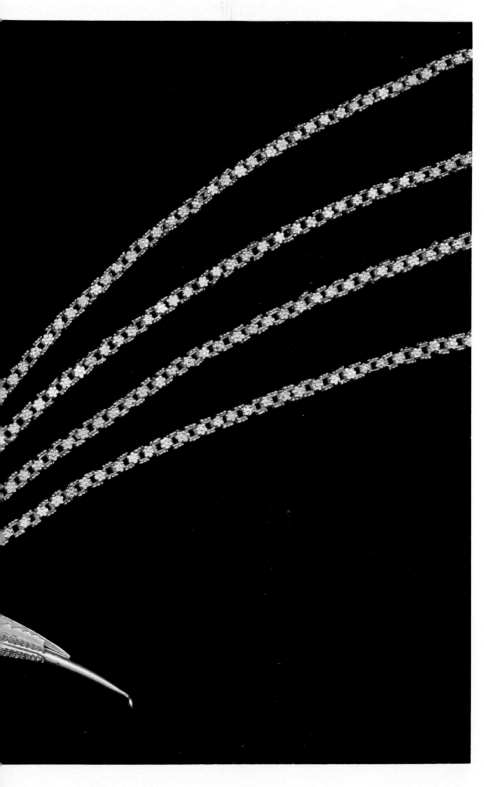

For Kip Wagner, the first person to grow rich in modern times on the lost treasure of Spain, the quest began in 1950 when he discovered a Spanish coin on the barrier beach near his home in Wabasso, Florida. Smitten with a mild dose of treasure fever, Wagner, a building contractor from Ohio, began combing the local beaches in his spare afternoons. Over the years he acquired a modest trove of old coins and a determination to discover why none of them had been struck later than 1715. Wagner began scouring local libraries, paid a visit to the Library of Congress, and finally found the answer when he wrote a letter to the curator of an institution whose name kept cropping up in his research: the General Archive of the Indies in Seville. Did the records reveal anything about a Spanish ship that might have been lost in Florida waters in 1715? The answer from Seville took a year to decipher. It was three thousand feet of micro-filmed documents describing in vivid detail one of the worst disasters in the history of the flotas.

On July 30, 1715, Wagner learned, a much-delayed Spanish treasure fleet had been struck by a hurricane in the Florida Straits. Seventy-five-knot winds drove the ships toward the pounding surf of the very beaches

The prize find from the doomed fleet is this exquisitely worked gold chain and pendant whistle in the form of a dragon. Worn as a badge of office by the captain-general, the chain is eleven feet long, and each of its 2,176 links is embossed with a tiny flower. The dragon hides ear and tooth picks.

that Wagner had come to know so well. Some ships were smashed to bits by mountainous breakers; others hit the shoals so hard that the lower half of their hulls sheared away, while the superstructures floated to shore. Debris, dead bodies, and stunned survivors were strewn over a thirty-mile stretch of uninhabited beach some one hundred miles south of St. Augustine, the nearest civilized settlement. The Spanish documents told how the admiral of the ill-fated fleet built a campsite for the castaways and sent longboats to Havana and St. Augustine with urgent pleas to come at once and rescue the treasure lying offshore and so ''ease the heavy burdens of the crown.'' The documents told, too, of the Spaniards' prolonged efforts to salvage the sunken treasure from a churning surf, of the diver devoured by a shark, and of Captain Henry Jennings, a Jamaica pirate, who raided the salvage camp three times and made off at gunpoint with whatever salvaged treasure the Spanish had accumulated. The 1715 disaster was of such magnitude that when Governor Alexander Spotswood of Virginia heard news of it he wrote a letter to the king of England, advising him ''of this accident which may be improved to the advantage of His Majesty's subjects by encouraging them to attempt the recovery of some of that immense wealth.''

Two and a half centuries later Kip Wagner fully shared the sentiment. Armed with the Spanish records, he not only found the old Spanish campsite (some rusty cutlasses were still there), he discovered two wreck sites simply by paddling around on a surfboard peering into the shallow water. Convinced that a mighty trea-

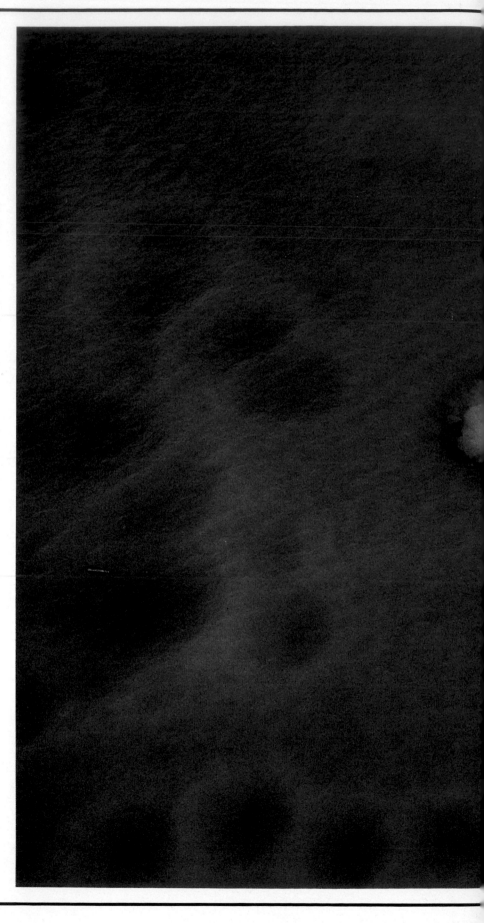

Mel Fisher invented a short cut to treasure when he diverted the propeller wash from his boat downward to blow craters in the sandy sea floor. Divers could then harvest huge quantities of newly revealed coins and artifacts spread across acres underwater.

A silver piece of eight (top) and a gold doubloon, both actual size

sure lay within his grasp, Wagner put together a small team of amateur treasure hunters and began underwater salvage operations in January 1961. On the very first day of diving they made their first find: a blackish lump of coral containing some 1,500 eight-real coins, pieces of eight in English parlance. Filled with optimism, Wagner turned his team into a corporation and named it, appropriately enough, the Real Eight Company.

The wreck sites, however, did not yield up their treasure at once. The treasure hunters soon discovered that their wreck sites' relics were not concentrated in a convenient heap. They lay widely scattered under the sea bottom, chiefly because the ships of the 1715 fleet had spewed out their cargoes as the storm drove them shoreward to destruction. Sifting through acres of sea-bottom sand was slow and laborious work, especially since Wagner and his colleagues were still only weekend treasure hunters. In late 1963, however, Wagner teamed up with Mel Fisher, a treasure-hunting professional, who concocted an ingenious apparatus that could blow enormous holes in the sea bed in a matter of minutes. Fisher's device, which drove a salvage ship's propeller wash straight down to the sea bottom, soon paid sensational dividends. On May 24, 1964, it opened an undersea trench six feet wide and fifteen feet long and revealed a breathtaking spectacle. At the bottom of the trench lay a carpet of gold coins, gleaming, untarnished, impervious to the elements—1,033 doubloons, the greatest one-day haul in the annals of modern treasure hunting. Some months later the Wagner-Fisher team surpassed even that mark when they uncovered a second golden cache of 1,128 doubloons, each of them the size of a fifty-cent piece and worth from $500 to $2,000

each. On yet another red-letter day they hauled up some 10,000 pieces of eight, and within six more days a full ton of silver coins. The world had seen nothing like this since the flotas had plied the seas. A treasure hunt that had begun fifteen years before with a washed-up coin had made Kip Wagner a millionaire. As the treasure began to pile up and the newspapers to churn out stories, beachcombers and scuba divers began swarming over the local beaches, which the city fathers of Fort Pierce, keeping an eye on the treasures of the tourist trade, promptly dubbed the "Gold Coast." Considerably later than Governor Spotswood had envisioned, Americans indeed "improved" the "accident" to Spain's 1715 fleet.

Masses of pieces of eight are often found embedded in coral growth, from which they must be painstakingly extracted. The coral in fact preserves the silver coins, which if left unprotected in sea water will turn to black sulphide and dissolve on touch.

BERMUDA WRACKERS

Edward Bolton Tucker, a descendant of the third governor of Bermuda, was pursuing a time-honored Bermuda occupation when he salvaged a substantial treasure from an old Spanish wreck site. Like the island's first settlers, Tucker, a onetime British navy diver, was a wracker by trade. The wrecks were modern; the salvage was scrap brass, copper, and lead, which he and his brother-in-law retrieved from the crystalline waters around the reefs of Bermuda.

The island's seventeenth-century wrackers had fared better, for in those days Bermuda was the deadliest landmark along the Carrera de Indias, "a mountainous island which it is difficult to approach on account of the dangers that surround it," according to the great French explorer Samuel de Champlain, who sailed with a Spanish flota around 1600. "The sea," noted Champlain, "is very tempestuous around the said island and the waves high as mountains." For three centuries Bermuda's reefs, storms, and seas claimed an average of two ships a year with remarkable regularity. The Spanish hated the very sight of the "Isle of Devils" and doubly so after 1619, when Bermuda's first English governor encouraged his little colony to make wracking a serious occupation. Any ships that shattered on Bermuda's outlying coral reefs the vigilant settlers stripped clean of their cargoes. Survivors they robbed of everything except their lives.

Since Bermuda's natural hazards were the island's chief economic asset, the settlers made certain not to blunt their grim efficiency, making it a strict rule never to keep a light burning anywhere on the island at night. This policy of withholding help from benighted ships they piously described as noninterference with the will of God. The Spanish, understandably, held a contrary theological view. According to Thomas Gage, when his Spanish fellow passengers sailed past the island in 1637 they stood on deck railing bitterly against the British, who, they said, "did still with the Devil raise storms in these seas when the Spanish fleet passed by." As one exasperated Spanish monarch openly complained, the English only settled in Bermuda in order to steal his treasure.

Perhaps because his forebears had salvaged wrecks so thoroughly, Teddy Tucker worked the Bermuda reefs untroubled by daydreams of lost Spanish gold. Once he and his partner had actually salvaged six old Spanish cannon. Yet they were perfectly content to sell them for the goodly sum of one hundred dollars and return to the serious business of stripping twentieth-century wrecks of their metal. Nevertheless, Tucker had not entirely forgotten those cannon when in the late summer of 1955 he found himself by chance sailing right over the spot

The magnificent emerald-studded gold cross above was found on a Spanish galleon that sank in 1595. A more fanciful find was the water jug below, decorated with a caricature of a contemporary cardinal.

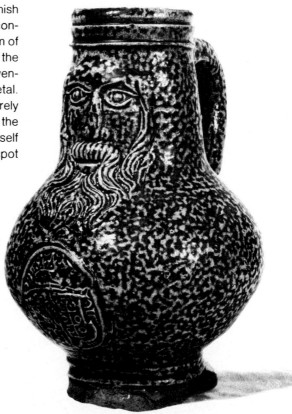

Teddy Tucker uses a magnetometer to locate metals buried beneath the sand.

where he had found them five years before. Noticing that a recent storm had shifted the sea-bottom sand, the sharp-eyed Tucker put on a face mask and dove twenty-five feet down to the wreck site, a side pocket of sand along a reef of Bermuda's Northern Breakers. Luck was with Tucker that day, for he saw at once a piece of metal sticking out of the sand. It was a bronze apothecary mortar with the astonishing date of 1561 clearly stamped on it. Excited, Tucker swam up to his boat, donned scuba gear, and hurriedly returned to the underwater site. This time he uncovered a tiny fragment of the wealth of the West Indies—a two-ounce cube of gold which was to alter his life completely.

The next day, armed with a Ping-Pong paddle to fan away the sand, Tucker found other tantalizing relics: some pearl-studded gold buttons. All thoughts of brass and lead vanished as Tucker toiled away underwater, pursuing his slender trail of gold. Five more days of fanning the sand produced, in addition to a fine array of Spanish weapons, an eighteen-ounce gold disk, a thirty-six-ounce gold bar, and a gold crucifix inlaid with seven large emeralds.

For a time Tucker anxiously hid his cache in an underwater cave, but rumors of treasure soon spread around Bermuda. Every time Tucker put to sea his neighbors jumped in their boats and followed in his wake, hoping to discover the secret source of his mysterious good fortune. In January 1956 Tucker's celebrity spread far beyond Bermuda, when *Life* published a story about the skin diver who had discovered "a sunken bonanza 300 years old." Here, lifted from Bermuda's sand, was the first modern proof that Spain's ship-wrecked gold was more than a yarn-spinner's figment. In fact, as Tucker himself later showed, the source of his gold could be identified precisely. It came from the *San Pedro,* a merchant ship of the Tierra Firme

fleet "lost at Bermuda" in 1595, according to Spanish records. Eager to get back to the sea, Tucker sold his entire treasure trove to the Bermuda government for the bargain price of $100,000 and a grateful government's understanding that henceforth he would enjoy a free hand salvaging relics from Bermuda's reefs.

The treasure hunters who followed in Teddy Tucker's footsteps have far exceeded his original bonanza, but the true treasure hunter's obsession never gripped the man who discovered Spanish gold with a Ping-Pong paddle. Tucker has enriched not himself but the archives of marine archaeology. Working every summer under the aegis of the Smithsonian Institution, Tucker has discovered and excavated more historically valuable wreck sites than any other modern salvager. For Bermuda's only successful wracker, one of those finds is curiously fitting. It is the remains of the *San Antonio,* a rich Spanish merchant ship whose misfortune in Bermuda waters got the islanders started in the wracking trade back in 1621.

Tucker peers into the boiler of a sunken steamship. Before he was struck with treasure fever, he made a living salvaging scrap metal from modern wrecks. OPPOSITE PAGE: *A cannon is hoisted from the bottom, where it has lain for more than 350 years.*

THE YANKEE CAPTAIN'S FIND

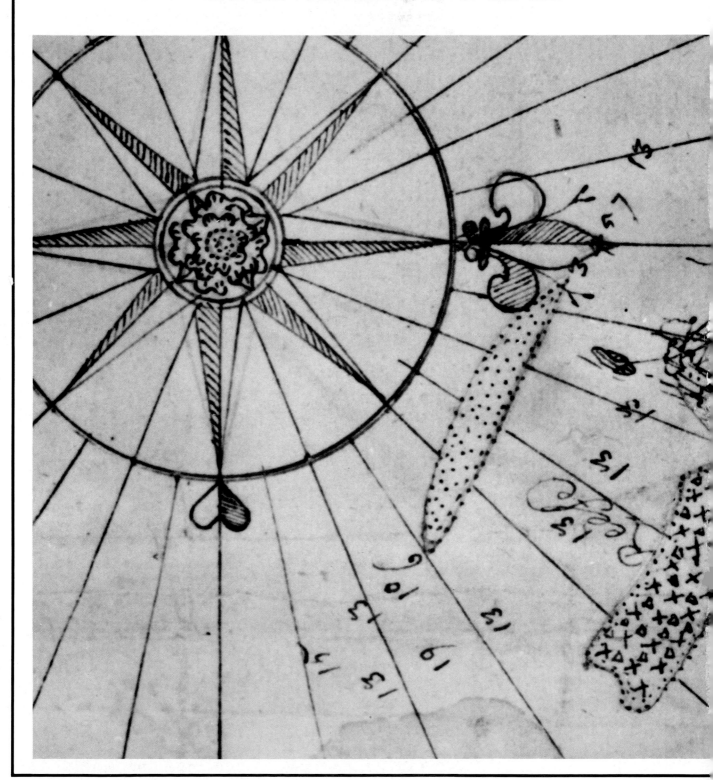

In the year 1683 a tall, burly New England sea captain showed up at the court of King Charles II to confide that he knew where to find the richest Spanish wreck in the Caribbean. The captain was William Phips, who had begun life as the twenty-first child of a Maine gunsmith. Starting off as an apprentice to a ship's carpenter, he had worked himself up to the command of his own ship in trade with the West Indies, where he learned about the sunken treasure ship. At the time Phips reached London to raise money for a salvage venture, the king had just commissioned a group of English treasure hunters to find the same wreck. But Charles could not resist an adventurous gamble, and he gave Phips his backing, along with the loan of a ship, in return for a share of the profits.

Captain Phips sailed to Hispaniola, hired Indian divers, and searched the coral reefs north of the island. He came back empty-handed, as did the other treasure hunters, but unlike them he had lost none of his confidence. By that time, however, King Charles was dead and his glum brother James II lacked any taste for adventurous risk. Undaunted, Phips found new backers in the Duke of Albemarle and other noble patrons. In the fall of 1686 he was off again, with a bigger ship, named the *James and Mary,* as well as a shallow-draft sloop

A genuine treasure map, this seventeenth-century chart of the Silver Bank helped Burt Webber rediscover Phips's galleon in 1979.

for work among the reefs. This time he seemingly knew just where to look. Some say that on his first trip he had met a survivor of the sunken ship who gave him its location. More likely he had realized, from study of the reefs and survivors' stories, that he and the other wrackers had been looking on the wrong reef. Now all he needed was a lucky break, and after only three days of searching, he had it. According to the story told by Phips's biographer, Cotton Mather, one of his men looked over the side of his search boat, spotted a particularly pretty coral "sea feather," and sent a diver down to bring it up as a souvenir. As the diver wrenched it loose he saw beneath it the gleam of a bronze cannon.

The ship thus found, though Phips never knew its name, was the *Nuestra Señora de la Concepción,* the *Almiranta* (admiral's galleon) of the 1641 flota. She had run up on the Ambrosian Bank some sixty miles north of Hispaniola. Before the survivors left the wreck, it was told, they had piled silver ingots on the reef to mark the site. If so, the ingots had long since been salvaged by local wrackers, leaving only the name Silver Bank.

The treasure was richer than even Phips had imagined. His four native divers were driven so hard that they sometimes came up coughing blood. In two months of dawn-to-dusk work they brought up bags and chests of coin, bars and plates of silver. At the end of that time they had retrieved about as much as they could by picking silver off the bottom, prying it loose with crowbars, and breaking into the forward storerooms. Still untouched was the after hold of the vessel, wedged between two rocks and heavily encrusted with new coral growth. Phips, a bold but prudent man, was worried that French war-

This improved version of the diving bell was invented shortly after Phips's successful salvage efforts.

ships or pirates might seize his treasure or that storms might wreck his ship. In May of 1687 he set sail for England.

When the silver was taken in charge by officials of the royal mint, it weighed out at a total of 68,511 pounds troy and seven ounces. Counting in a small quantity of gold and precious stones, and seven cannon, the total value of the treasure came to about £210,000; at 1980 prices it would exceed $10 million. After taking ten per cent off the top for the king and awarding bonuses to the officers and crew, the duke of Albemarle got two sevenths of the remainder, each of the other five backers one seventh—a return of more than 5,000 per cent on their investment. Captain Phips, the entrepreneur of the venture, received only his sixteenth share, £11,043.

But there were other rewards for Phips. The poor boy from Maine was lionized in London society, acclaimed as the mastermind of the most successful business venture since Drake brought home the *Golden Hind*. The duke of Albemarle, it was said, gave him a golden cup worth £1,000 to take home to his wife. Moreover, he was knighted and appointed provost-marshal of New England.

On Phips's assurance that there was an even greater treasure still to be had from the *Concepción,* another and greater expedition was mounted. Five ships, one of them captained by Phips, sailed from London under the overall command of Sir John Narborough, one of the investors in the previous venture. But when they reached the Silver Bank in December 1687, they found a fleet of some thirty vessels from the West Indies and the American colonies clustered at the site. The secret had leaked out and the wreck had been picked nearly clean of all the treasure within reach. Narborough died of a fever and his body was consigned to the waters over the wreck. The expedition returned to London to report a loss.

The rather stodgy portrait of Sir William Phips (above) belies his adventuresome career. A medal struck in honor of his successful voyage bears James II and Queen Mary on one side and Phips's treasure-hunting expedition on the other (below).

Burt Webber (seated) and a colleague pore over a chart of the wreck site in the cabin of their salvage ship. Gold chains, tens of thousands of silver coins, and bars of silver are among the treasure recovered so far.

Phips sailed directly to Boston, never to hunt for treasure again. As Sir William Phips he commanded the expeditionary force that captured the French stronghold of Port Royal in Acadia (now Nova Scotia) in 1690, and after that victory he was appointed royal governor of Massachusetts.

In all their plunder of the *Concepción*, neither Phips nor the English adventurers nor the local wrackers had been able to break into the stern of the ship. Locked fast in the ever-growing coral, the remaining treasure lay untouched for almost three centuries, while its exact location once more faded from memory. Then in January 1979 *The New York Times* carried this headline: "A Treasure Galleon That Sank in 1641 Is Found by American." The new Phips was a Pennsylvanian named Burt Webber who had located the *Concepción* with the help of Phips's log and a cesium magnetometer that can detect bits of ferrous metal, such as nails or anchors, even under many feet of coral. Early in 1980 Webber and his treasure-hunting outfit, Seaquest International, was attacking the stern of the *Concepción* with drills, hydraulic jacks, suction pumps, and all the paraphernalia of modern marine salvors. Relying on Phips's own judgment, they hoped to find a treasure as great or greater than the one that Phips brought up.

A diver brings artifacts to the collecting basket poised near the wreck. When the basket is full, the balloon will be inflated and will lift the load to the surface.

CARGO OF QUICKSILVER

The galleons that brought back gold and silver from the New World to Spain did not go out empty. On the westward voyage they carried a mixed cargo of supplies: guns and ammunition for the armies, tools and machinery for the mines, robes and medals for the church, and all the furnishings required by aristocratic households far from home.

In 1724 two such galleons, the *Conde de Tolosa* and the *Nuestra Señora de Guadalupe,* outward-bound from Cádiz, were driven by a hurricane onto the sandbars and coral reefs of Samaná Bay on the northeast coast of Hispaniola. Their principal cargo was mercury—four hundred tons of it—consigned to Vera Cruz, Mexico, for use in the refining of gold and silver by the amalgamation process. They also carried some 1,200 passengers and crew, including—to judge by the personal possessions they lost—a good number of highborn travelers.

The wrecks of the *Tolosa* and the *Guadalupe* have been found and explored since 1976 by Tracy Bowden, a treasure diver who works with a group called Caribe Salvage. It was no surprise to find that most of the mercury had leaked out of the casks that held it, leaving behind only small pools and globules. But Bowden and his team were rewarded by a dazzling collection of pearls, jewels, glassware, religious tokens, and other valuables, including those shown on these pages.

A cargo of mercury stored in wooden casks (left) led to the positive identification of this wreck as the long-sought Tolosa. *Its discoverer, Tracy Bowden, here triumphantly pours the precious quicksilver into a bowl under forty feet of water.*

The wreck site of the Tolosa yielded an astonishing variety and quantity of goods, ranging from a diamond- and emerald-studded medallion to a pewter chamber pot—most in near-perfect condition. The delicately engraved hunting scene above adorns a glass beaker intended for the table of a Spanish colonialist. A special camera enabled the entire circular scene to be photographed as a frieze.

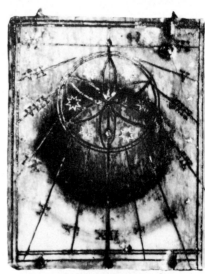

The four ivory plaques at right folded together into an invaluable aid for the ocean-going traveler. The set comprised (clockwise, from top left) a horizontal sundial, a vertical sundial, a compass, and a moon dial, in a compact package the size of a deck of cards.

OPPOSITE PAGE: A quantity of clay vessels, here being cleaned and stored, once held pine pitch, olives, wine, or water.

THE ARMADA WRECKS

On the morning of August 9, 1588, the duke of Medina Sidonia, commander of the Spanish Armada, stood on the poop of his flagship the *San Martín,* just off the Zeeland banks in the North Sea. For nine days he had scarcely left his post except for sleep and for councils with his captains, while the great fleet, sailing in the shape of a crescent, made its majestic way up the English Channel. The nimbler English ships had kept the weather gauge, now coming close to pump cannon balls into a logy galleon or picking off a straggler, but never allowing the Spanish to grapple and board. One night the English had broken up the Spanish formation by sending fireboats into it, but at dawn the Armada reformed its crescent.

In the running battle with the English the Armada had lost only seven of its 130 vessels. But the duke could see that many of the rest were floating low and moving slowly because of the damage inflicted by superior English gunnery. And in the fierce, sporadic cannon duels they had used up most of their ammunition.

Moreover, the grand strategy of the operation had collapsed. Medina Sidonia's orders had been to rendezvous off the Dutch coast with the Spanish army of the Netherlands, commanded by the duke of Parma, and in combination with those forces to make a landing on the English coast. But Parma's forces were bottled up in port by the flyboats of the Dutch "Sea Beggars," and in those

An imaginative contemporary painting shows the defeat of the Spanish Armada by the English in the summer of 1588.

shallow waters the Spanish ships could not approach the shore. Only by minutes and a providential change of wind had the Armada escaped going fast aground on the Zeeland banks.

Before he ever left Spain, Medina Sidonia had foreseen this fate. He had advised his master, Philip II, to give up or postpone the "Enterprise of England" and, when Philip persisted, had begged to be spared the command. Now the royal dream was ended and the duke would be its scapegoat.

Medina Sidonia knew that his last service to the king must be to get as many ships as possible back to Spain, perchance to fight another day. That meant taking the harsh "north-about route," up the North Sea, over the top of Scotland and Ireland, and back down the Atlantic coast to Spain. Accordingly, the Armada turned north, followed by the English fleet. Three days later, off the Firth of Forth, the English gave up the chase. Like the Spanish, they were almost out of food and cannon balls.

Even on the day of its sailing from Spain, the Armada had looked more formidable than it was. The great galleons of Castile and Portugal were mighty ships of war, heavily armed with the finest cannon of the age but meant for closing with the enemy and fighting deck to deck. Many of the other vessels were slow, unwieldy merchantmen, commandeered from Venice and Sicily and other Mediterranean powers and given makeshift armament. Twenty-three of the vessels were "hulks," or cargo carriers, lightly armed and meant to be sheltered within the crescent formation. To get this fleet, in its crippled condition, safely back to Spain was the duke's last challenge. He might have done it—given faithful captains, favoring winds, and a bit of luck.

Philip II (top) and Queen Elizabeth clashed in a struggle for naval supremacy that had far-reaching implications for the New World.

A map by Richard Adams shows the course of the ill-fated Armada through the various battles off the coast of England, the flight around Scotland, the calamitous shipwrecks on the coast of Ireland, and the survivors' run for home.

Medina Sidonia had none of these. Even before he rounded the Orkney Islands, north of Scotland, ships were dropping away, singly or in twos and threes, in hope of finding some closer haven. Three great Levantine carracks turned east, perhaps heading for Norway, and were never seen again. Others fell behind, filling with water or unable to steer against the wind with their damaged rudders and broken masts. When the Armada was off the western coast of Ireland a storm struck the fleet, driving it back on the coast. The duke had warned his captains to give Ireland a wide berth, "for fear of the harm that may happen to you upon that coast." But many of the captains, desperate in their broken ships, loaded with sick and wounded, almost out of food and water, took their separate courses. One by one they headed toward shore, sometimes finding an anchorage, more often running aground on reefs or piling up on rocky headlands. At least seventeen ships met their end on the Irish coast, while those that followed the duke's lead—forty-four in all—limped back to Spain.

Few of the Spaniards whose ships were wrecked on the Irish coast survived. Of the 1,300 souls aboard the *Girona*, only five reached shore. Of some 500 who landed safely from *La Trinidad Valencera* and surrendered to the local lord, more than half were massacred, the officers being held for ransom. A few of the Spaniards were given refuge by Catholic sympathizers and smuggled back to Spain; perhaps a handful lived out their lives in Ireland. But the order of the queen's lord deputy for Ireland, Sir William Fitzwilliam, was to kill every Spaniard, and generally the order was

Two ships founder in stormy seas: Cornelisz Vroom painted this scene a few years after Armada galleons ran into foul weather and wrecked off the coast of Ireland. Below is an aerial view of the treacherous rocks that claimed the Girona.

In frigid waters off western Ireland two divers (above) inspect a bronze cannon from the Girona, the first Armada wreck excavated. Robert Sténuit, leader of the expedition, spent six hundred hours researching the Girona in the archives of five countries and was able to locate the wreck in just one hour of diving. Among the jewelry he found was a winged salamander (right), crafted in gold with a spine of rubies.

carried out. So much for the legend that the "black Irish" owe their coloration to an admixture of Spanish blood.

All of the Spanish ships that ran ashore or sank in very shallow water were soon looted by the poor local people. Some of the cannon were salvaged and melted down. But most of the ships that were wrecked in deeper water lay untouched, breaking up on rocks or sinking slowly into the sand, until the coming of scuba divers in the twentieth century.

In the summer of 1967 a Belgian diver named Robert Sténuit began searching for the wreck of the *Girona*, on the northern coast of Ireland near Portballintrae. When she struck a rocky ledge not far from the Giant's Causeway, the *Girona* was carrying the survivors of five Armada ships that had come to grief on the same coast. Don Alonso Martínez de Leiva, one of the Armada's ablest captains, had rounded them up and put them aboard the *Girona,* the only seaworthy ship among the five, and set sail for Scotland, hoping that the Stuart court would give them asylum. The rock where the *Girona* ran aground for the second time was almost in the front yard of an Irish lord known as Sorley Boy McDonnell. In short order the McDonnells had helped themselves to several bronze cannon from the wreck and, according to report, "three chests of treasure."

When Sténuit went over the side of his salvage dinghy in 1967 he did not know whether he could locate the wreck or whether, if he did, he would find any treasure the McDonnells had missed. By luck, after swimming through an underwater forest of kelp, he came upon a clear stretch of sand where he found first a three-foot ingot of lead and farther on a bronze cannon. Among those who had sailed with Don Alonso were *aventureros*, sons of Spain's noblest families, who

had thought to bring with them the adornments they would need to make a proper show when they entered London. From the wreck of the *Girona* Sténuit and his fellow divers brought up coins, rings, bracelets, necklaces, jewels, even a golden toothpick. Some of these trinkets were lodged in crannies of rocks, some locked with guns and navigational instruments in hard, concretelike masses formed by the chemical reaction of rust, gunpowder, and the lime of seashells.

In the same year, Sydney Wignall, a Welsh underwater archaeologist, began a search for the *Santa María de la Rosa,* a large merchant vessel that had come scudding into Blasket Sound on the western coast of Ireland and sunk in 110 feet of water. Upon advice from the Irish government that the wreck was still a Spanish possession, Wignall put up a £1,000 bond against payment of twenty per cent (the old royal fifth) of the value of anything he recovered.

The tidal race in Blasket Sound is so swift that Wignall's divers could work for only half an hour at slack tide. Believing that the *Santa María* had run onto an underwater reef called Stromboli, they searched that area first— without result. Then they made a grid of the entire bay and, swimming in a line of eight or more divers, methodically scanned every yard of the four-square-mile bay—still without success. After they had already decided to give up and look for another Armada ship, they made one more search of the Stromboli area and discovered a pile of rocks that turned out to be ballast from the *Santa María*. Under the stones the divers found cannon balls, sows of lead for making into bullets, and a set of pewter plates with the word "Matute" inscribed on each. Presumably these had belonged to Francisco Ruiz Matute, commander of the troops who had shipped on the *Santa María*

to carry out the landing in England.

Two years after the salvage of the *Santa María de la Rosa,* Wignall and Colin Martin located the wreck of *El Gran Grifón,* the flagship of the hulks, or supply ships, which had gone aground on Fair Isle, a desolate island halfway between the Shetlands and the Orkneys. The vessel had driven into a rocky gully called Stroms Hellier or Cave of the Tide Race, and the 300 survivors had clambered up the masts to safety on the cliff above. At the bottom of the gully the divers found bronze cannon, lead ingots, cannon balls, and scraps of the ship's gear, but no gold or silver. The next summer Martin joined in the salvage of *La Trinidad Valencera,* one of the Armada's greatest ships, that had been found by members of a diving club in a bay off the northern coast of County Donegal. The site yielded a variety of armament, ship's gear, and personal possessions, along with the biggest and finest bronze cannon yet recovered from an Armada wreck, a fifty-pounder bearing the arms of Philip II and the mark of Remigy de Halut, the master founder of the Spanish royal gun foundry at Malines in the Spanish Netherlands.

None of these wrecks has yielded any such treasure as old reports promised (unless Sorley Boy McDonnell took some off the *Girona*). But treasure hunters never give up hope. Visions of gold ducats still shimmer above the so-called Tobermory Galleon, sunk in a bay off the island of Mull and claimed as the personal property of the dukes of Argyll. Since the seventeenth century successive dukes have been trying to raise its precious freight. Several great guns have been brought up, along with "strange and pleasing relics," but no gold. If nothing comes of that search, there are still as many as thirteen other wrecks to be found and salvaged on the Irish coast.

THE SUNKEN PORT OF THE PIRATES

The town of Port Royal, built on a sandy cay off the coast of Jamaica, was renowned in its heyday as the toughest, wickedest port in the western hemisphere. Jamaica had been part of New Spain, but in 1655 the English captured the island and fortified Port Royal to protect the harbor of Kingston. Fearing a Spanish attempt to recapture the island, the English sought to bolster their own naval strength by offering sanctuary at Port Royal for the buccaneers who roamed the Spanish Main.

The buccaneers were somewhat to the evil side of privateers, for they did not necessarily operate under legitimate commissions. But they were on the godly side of pirates, for they preyed—or so they claimed—only on the ships of England's great maritime rival, Spain. In the face of temptation these distinctions were often blurred, but the buccaneers maintained enough kinship with the English cause to enjoy the hero worship of the English public, as well as the protection of their base at Port Royal. The most successful of them, Henry Morgan, was even knighted by the king and made lieutenant governor of Jamaica, with orders to police the seas and keep his old comrades in line.

In the gray zone between piracy and legal privateering, Port Royal prospered so famously that a waterfront lot on the island went for as much as a lot in central London. The narrow streets were lined with merchants' warehouses, slave markets, barrooms, and brothels. "Everywhere abideth ye lazy strumpets," one clergyman reported in despair. God, the ministers prophesied, would destroy the Sodom of the West.

And so, in the ministers' view, it turned out. Just before noon on the

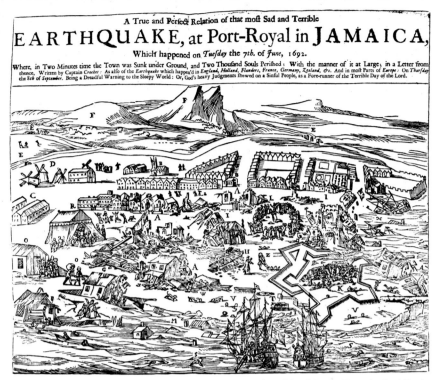

This contemporary announcement of the "most sad and terrible earthquake" at Port Royal appeared in a London paper. The disaster was regarded as a fitting end to "a sink of all filthiness, a mere Sodom."

morning of June 7, 1692, three strong earthquakes struck Port Royal in the space of a few minutes. The sands shifted, buildings crumbled, and the whole shorefront of the town slid underwater.

Port Royal was devastated but its legend lived on, exaggerated and embroidered by romantic writers. Some forty years ago one such imaginative account reached the eyes of a ten-year-old boy named Robert Marx who lived in Brooklyn. He decided that what he wanted to do more than anything else in life was to dive into the harbor of Port Royal and find the sunken city that the writer described, complete with the church where the skeletons of the congregation still sat in their pews and the bells in the steeple tolled when the tide was running strong.

Ten years later Marx arrived on the scene, equipped with mask and fins. He dived into the murky water

and swam out to a buoy, called the Church Beacon because it supposedly marked the site of the sunken structure. Here is his account:

"Reaching the beacon, I gulped air into my lungs and jackknifed down. I felt something all right: the sea floor. My head and arms were embedded in the soft silt before I saw it coming. Extracting myself, I found I could see nothing except my own face: the combination of muddy water on the bottom and the glass of my own face mask acted like a mirror. Still determined to find the cathedral, I groped in the darkness for a wall, any wall. Suddenly it felt as though a thousand needles were being driven into my hand: I had caught hold of a large, black, spiny sea urchin."

When his hand had recovered, Marx returned to the harbor, diving repeatedly, feeling his way along the bottom, straining to see in the swirling murk. His total salvage: one nine-

The infamous Henry Morgan and his privateers carouse on the deck of their ship, surrounded by the fruits of their labor, in this nineteenth-century French illustration.

teenth-century whiskey bottle.

Eleven years later Marx returned to Port Royal to begin excavation of the site. In the meantime he had become a trained marine archaeologist with experience in the Caribbean and Mediterranean. By then others had explored the bottom of the harbor, most notably Edwin Link, the inventor of the Link Trainer, who had used his marine salvage vessel, the *Sea Diver,* to recover a small cannon and other artifacts. Now, with reduced hopes but increased professional skill, Marx was able to map the sunken city, most of it under mud or encrusted with coral. The building below the Church Beacon was in fact a fort, while the church itself had been covered by so much mud that its site had again become dry land. The excavation was slow work, the visibility so minimal that Marx and his Jamaican divers had to grope through the mud with bare hands, suffering frequent, slow-healing cuts from the coral and the sea urchin spines.

Since the city had sunk in shallow water, native divers had long ago scavenged the site for any precious objects. Only by digging under walls that had collapsed in the earthquake did Marx discover a large musket, a silver pocket watch, and a goodly number of pieces of eight found amid the remnants of a strongbox. But he filled many barrels with everyday objects. A concentration of pewter tankards, wineglasses, and clay smoking pipes marked the site of a tavern; a chest of medicine bottles and an apothecary's pestle identified a druggist's shop; stores of ship's rigging and fittings located a shipyard. After two and a half years of hard and risky work, Marx turned his last finds over to the Jamaica government and departed for more rewarding sites.

In the murky harbor waters a diver, above, extracts a wine bottle from a heap of rubble. Below, archaeologist Robert Marx displays a wealth of pewter tableware retrieved from the underwater ruins of the port.

Pirates demand loot from a kneeling prisoner in this Howard Pyle illustration.

INTO THE DEEP

Throughout recorded history man has tried to devise ways to extend his domain into the deep. Spurred by the search for sponges and oysters, lost artillery and treasure, he has considered every imaginable scheme that might allow him to see and breathe under the surface of the oceans.

According to legend at least, Alexander the Great was the first to make an extended dive. In the fourth century B.C., at great risk to himself and his empire, he descended to the bottom of the sea in a glass barrel. No contemporary historians recorded the event, but according to a fifteenth-century French account, illustrated at right,

Alexander . . . had all the glass makers of the continent come to him and he proposed that they make for him a glass barrel which would be ample enough to move around in and transparent enough to see everything through it.

When the barrel was made he had it very well attached with good iron chains to a big metal circle and to this he had strong cords attached. . . . He had himself brought in the high sea by boat, and lowered by the cords which held the barrel. Afterwards he could not make anybody believe what he had seen . . . because he saw fishes of such different kinds and colors. . . . He said that he had seen men, women, or fishes, in that order, which were walking on their feet running after the fish to eat, as on the earth one runs after animals. When he had looked at all the marvels of the sea as long as he wanted, he signalled to those above who pulled him up. . . .

In this upbeat version of the legend, Alexander sees small fish eluding larger ones, and concludes that ingenuity is more important than strength. In another account, when he reaches the surface he announces, "That world is damned and lost. The large and powerful fish devour the smaller fry." This rather somber pronouncement was later used by some chroniclers to explain the long hiatus between Alexander's dive and the seventeenth and eighteenth centuries, when underwater technology made its next leaps forward. Some innovative diving gear from that period and an early attempt at salvaging a sunken ship are illustrated on the following pages.

Fish, a mermaid, and men "walking on their feet" crowd around to pay homage to Alexander in his glass barrel in this illustration from The History of Alexander.

The scene at left was part of a salvage operation mounted between 1839 and 1842 to raise the British ship Royal George. The 108-gun warship had been lost on a calm day in 1782 when engineers, trying to heel the ship to repair a leak, moved many of the guns to one side. The strain caused some timbers to give way and the ship sank, drowning eight hundred people. Attempting to recover the lost artillery and to remove the hazard to navigation, divers made repeated trips to the rotting hulk. Wearing metal helmets hermetically sealed to heavy canvas suits, the invention of a German named Augustus Siebe, they were able to salvage many of the guns and other articles of value. Unable to raise the hull in one piece, they blasted it with explosives, placed slings around parts of the hull, and raised it in sections.

Leonardo da Vinci sketched a number of diving suits, including the design above, intended for submarine warfare. The diver breathes air from a wineskin connected by tubes to his helmet. Tied over his shoulders are sandbags to carry him to the bottom.

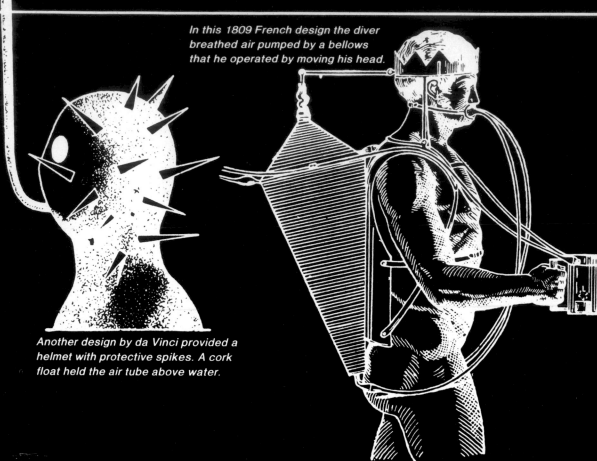

In this 1809 French design the diver breathed air pumped by a bellows that he operated by moving his head.

Another design by da Vinci provided a helmet with protective spikes. A cork float held the air tube above water.

This barrel-shaped suit with leather shorts and sleeves was successfully tried out in the Oder River.

Divers in Jules Verne's Twenty Thousand Leagues Under the Sea *(1870) hunted the forests of Crespo carrying compressed-air guns that fired electric bullets.*

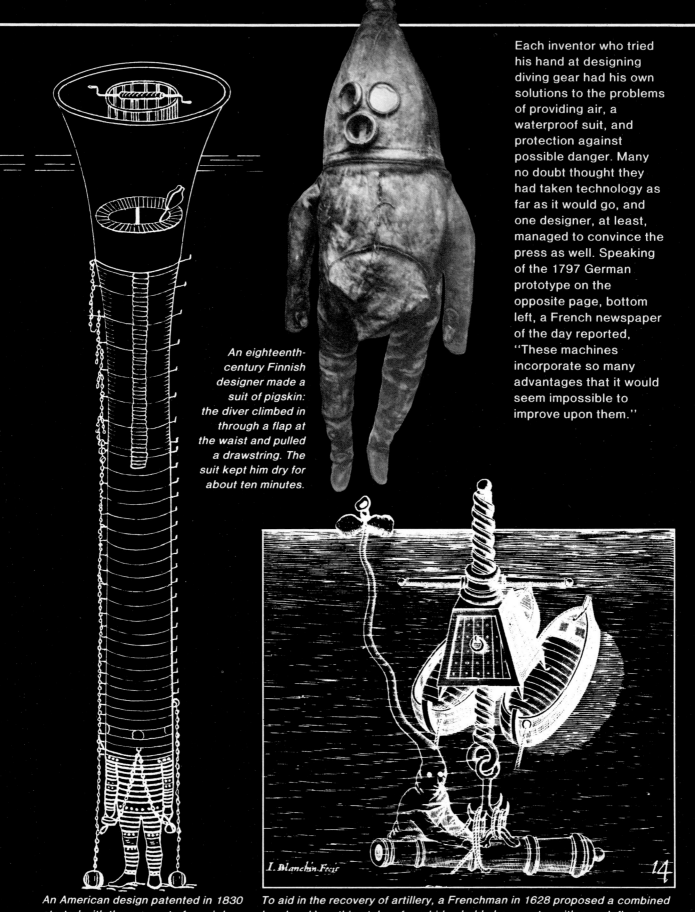

Each inventor who tried his hand at designing diving gear had his own solutions to the problems of providing air, a waterproof suit, and protection against possible danger. Many no doubt thought they had taken technology as far as it would go, and one designer, at least, managed to convince the press as well. Speaking of the 1797 German prototype on the opposite page, bottom left, a French newspaper of the day reported, "These machines incorporate so many advantages that it would seem impossible to improve upon them."

An eighteenth-century Finnish designer made a suit of pigskin: the diver climbed in through a flap at the waist and pulled a drawstring. The suit kept him dry for about ten minutes.

I. Blanchin Fecit

14

An American design patented in 1830 started with the concept of an air hose and built a suit around it.

To aid in the recovery of artillery, a Frenchman in 1628 proposed a combined hood and breathing tube of cowhide, held above water with a cork float.

1 Man that manages the vessel with oars.
2 Men supplying the diver No. 1 with air.
3 Man holding the signal rope.
4 Man in diving dress.
5 Man managing small boat.
6 Man getting sponges with a staff.
7 Man looking through water glass.
8 Man resting himself to dive.
9 Man holding rope for No. 10 to dive.
10 Man diving after No. 14.
11 Man holding rope for No. 15.
12 Man helping No. 13 to get in the vessel.
13 Man getting in vessel.
14 He lost his senses and fell back and was drowned.
15 A man tries to pull out by the roots a big sponge.
16 He signals for the man in the boat to pull him up.
17 A man dressing.
18 Holding rope for No. 23.
19 Pulling up No. 25.
20 Pulling up No. 25.
21 Fixing rope to dive.
22 Lost the rope and tries to get up by himself.
23 Man diving with a rock in his hand.
24 A man tries to pull a sponge out by the roots.

SPONG

None of the preceding designs seems to have caught on with the West Indian
sponge divers pictured in this lithograph, which was distributed by a St. Louis

ISHING.

by the rope.	31	Catching No. 32 by the hair as he comes up from diving.	37	Man managing small boat.	43	Man that steers the vessel.
	32	He has just gotten up from diving.	38	Waiting to help No. 39 with staff.	44	Sponge drag.
ag rope to the head of the	33	Helping No. 32 to get in the boat.	39	Man getting sponges with a staff and looking through water glass.	45	Net bag for man in diving dress to put sponges in.
hand, ready to dive.	34	A man coming up from diving.	40	Men pulling up the anchor.	46	White marble rock, the divers use in diving, weighing
o. 29.	35	Is trying to get away from shark.	41	Man undressing to dive.		40 lbs., to carry them down quickly.
	36	A man destroyed by a shark.	42	Men taking out the oars.	47	Net bag to put sponges in.

*sponge dealer in 1897. Only one diver, at far left, has been outfitted with special
gear, and nothing he can do, it appears, will save his colleagues No. 14 and No. 36.*

UNDER ANCIENT SEAS

The pursuit of underwater archaeology in the eastern Mediterranean involves a great deal of sitting around waterfront cafés, talking to the sponge divers who work at the bottom of the sea. I remember one old diver who used to tell me about a tower that stood forty fathoms deep, somewhere off the Turkish coast. Its height increased in direct proportion to the diver's consumption of raki, the anise-flavored, hundred-proof apéritif of the Levant. The drinkers in the little gaslit restaurant smiled as Ahmet described the great doors, the stone lintels of the first story, and the fish swimming in and out of the windows of the second. A huge grouper, "big as a Volkswagen," lived downstairs. The sponges that he harvested from the roof of the tower, said Ahmet, made his daughter's dowry.

When Ahmet told the tower story his friends would buy him another quarter-liter of raki and send for his ten-year-old grandson to lead him home. Ahmet's limbs were twisted like gnarled apple-tree limbs from diving too deep, too long, too many times. When he left, we heard the click-clack of his stick on the cobbles and the tired voice still mumbling about the tower and all those sponges, and all that money.

Ahmet never got around to showing me the tower because it existed only in his imagination. No one has ever seen such a tower, anywhere. Yet Ahmet believed in the tower, as dwellers on seacoasts have believed in many strange and wonderful things beneath the waters. And some of these things do exist. I myself have seen groupers as huge as the one that Ahmet described and have met divers who were attacked and barely escaped being swallowed by them.

The ancient Greeks believed that Poseidon, lord of the sea, lived at the bottom of the Aegean in a palace with walls of mother-of-pearl and gardens of coral. When he rose above the waves he was riding in a chariot drawn by spirited horses, holding the reins in one hand and a trident in the other. Like all the

ARCHAEOLOGY OF THE MEDITERRANEAN

by Peter Throckmorton

The busy maritime trade of Rhodes was protected by the bronze Colossus that stood near (though not astride) its harbor mouth. Nevertheless, the storms and reefs of the Mediterranean, if not the monster shown in this fifteenth-century engraving, took a heavy toll of the little Hellenistic ships. PRECEDING PAGES: A diver scans a mound of amphorae, off the coast of Cyprus, marking a third-century B.C. shipwreck.

Olympian gods, Poseidon was ruled by human moods on a superhuman scale. In benign mood he was the protector of sailors against the perils of the sea, but in anger he was capable of raising storms with his trident that would send vessels down to his kingdom. Poseidon was followed by a train of marine creatures both real and imaginary: dolphins, hippocampi, sea dragons, centaurs, bare-breasted Nereids, and the Tritons—half man, half fish—who calmed the waves with the music of conch shells.

The combination of beauty and peril that the ancients saw in the sea found embodiment in the sweet-singing Sirens, who stretched out their lovely arms and lured sailors to their doom. Jason escaped them only because Orpheus, his shipmate, sang more sweetly than they. Ulysses had himself lashed to the mast and stopped up the ears of his crew.

Imagination had free rein among seagoing peoples because all of Poseidon's realm was *mare incognitum.* To humans the sea was a liquid plain, sometimes smooth as glass, sometimes roiled by storms and waves, but always and everywhere impenetrable. In a clear body of water like the Mediterranean, boatmen could see a few fathoms below the surface, and divers could descend a hundred feet or more but could see only a few yards around them. All else was darkness.

The failure to explore the sea beneath its surface was not for lack of trying. Medieval chroniclers from Persia to France told and embroidered the tale that Alexander the Great had descended into the deep in a glass diving cage (see page 54), from which he witnessed such marvels as a fish so big that it took three days to pass the submerged conqueror. If the tale did not reflect fact it certainly reflected a fascination with the underwater realm. Medieval writers told also of an ancient diver called Nicholas the Fish, who spent so much time below the surface that he learned the secret of how the forces of the sea stirred up storms. On a more practical level, Leonardo da Vinci designed on paper a diving helmet, breathing tube, and webbed footgear—everything that later divers used except scuba tanks.

Off the coast of Greece, a helmeted sponge diver is helped to his boat. Most of the known wrecks in the Mediterranean were discovered by sponge divers in the course of their work.

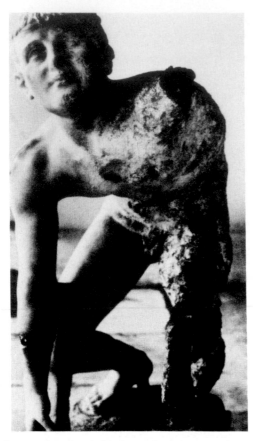

The damage done to marble by marine borers can be seen on this marble statue of a discus thrower. The right side of the figure had been covered by sand, the left side exposed to the sea for two thousand years. At right, some of the badly eroded marbles from the Antikýthēra wreck were piled in a courtyard after their recovery in 1901.

None of these attempts to penetrate the mysteries of the deep yielded much solid information. But men's curiosity was kept alive by things that the sea periodically cast up or fishermen found. Pearls from the Indian Ocean, amber from the Baltic Sea, and the purple dye extracted from mollusks at Tyre were gifts of the sea to the Roman luxury trade. The wooden head of a god, which the oracle at Delphi seemed to identify as Dionysus, was pulled up by fishermen of Lesbos in the second century; the bronze Marathon Boy (see page 106), a fine piece of sculpture, came up in a trawler's net in 1925.

During all those centuries, from the time of the Minoans and Phoenicians, the only humans who saw the undersea world with their own eyes were the sponge divers. Without suit or mask or helmet they leaped into the sea, carrying a stone to help them descend quickly. "No ordeal," wrote the Greek poet Oppian, "is more terrible than that of the sponge divers and no labor is more arduous for men." They worked at depths of seventy-five to a hundred feet, where the best sponges grew, and sometimes went down as far as two hundred feet, holding their breath for minutes at a time. After a few years of work most of them suffered some loss of hearing because of the pressure of the

water on eardrums.

Since Greek times or earlier, men had been trying to invent some apparatus that would enable divers to breathe underwater. But not until 1819 did Augustus Siebe invent the first practical helmeted diving suit, in which a diver was supplied with air by a tube and pump. This cumbersome gear afforded him extended vision and a longer stay underwater. It also exposed him to excruciating pains (and sometimes death) from the bends, a condition caused by the formation of nitrogen bubbles in the blood when a diver comes up too fast. By the latter half of the nineteenth century most of the Mediterranean sponge divers were using helmets, though "naked" pearl divers still operate to-

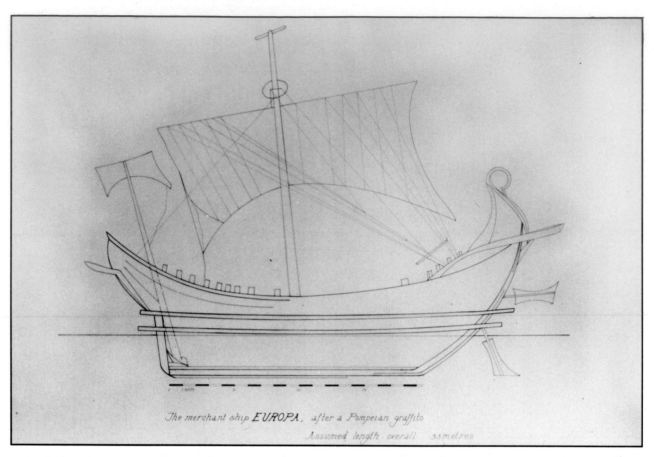

The merchant ship EUROPA, after a Pompeian graffito
Assumed length overall 33 metres

This drawing is a copy of a graffito scratched on a wall at Pompeii before that city was buried in the first century A.D. It shows a large merchant ship, the Europa, probably comparable to those wrecked at Mahdia and Antikýthēra.

day in the Persian Gulf, Japan, and the South Pacific.

Three great discoveries, all made by sponge divers, opened the eyes of archaeologists to the treasures hidden beneath the seas. The first occurred in 1900 off the little island of Antikýthēra, lying at the western entrance to the Aegean Sea between the Peloponnesus and Crete. Captain Dimitrios Kondos and his crew had spent the summer harvesting sponges off the coast of North Africa and were returning to their home port of Symē in the Dodecanese, islands famed since antiquity for their sponge fleets. At Antikýthēra he was forced to take refuge from a storm and, while waiting for it to abate, decided to send a diver down to look for more sponges.

Elias Stadiatis, the diver, got into his suit and helmet, slipped over the side, and landed on a sandy shelf of rock at 180 feet. Minutes later he came up rapidly with a wild report of arms, legs, and a horse's head, all

sticking out of the sand. Captain Kondos then descended to the site, recognized an ancient shipload of sculpture, and retrieved the bronze arm of a man as evidence. He carried the arm back to Symē, where he was persuaded to take his find to the Greek government's archaeological office in Athens. Soon he was on his way back to the site, with more divers and an archaeologist, to conduct a full salvage job.

The cargo consisted mainly of marble statues—how many we will never know because they were so corroded by marine borers and so encrusted with coralline limestone accretion that the divers thought at first they were boulders, fallen from the overhanging cliff. Dozens of these huge chunks were dragged off the rocky shelf into deep water in order to retrieve the statues buried in the sand below. When one of them was finally raised, it turned out to be a marble Hercules. Among the pieces that were raised in good condition were a bronze statue of a youth and a head dubbed The Philosopher. Other figures were perfectly preserved on the side covered by sand, badly eaten away on the other.

The ship had gone down in the first quarter of the first century B.C., at a time when Greece was a

FARNACES AVGISTER

ARASCANTVS

ISISGI MINIA NA

RES

PEL

A smaller Roman ship, the Isis Giminiana *(Farnaces, master), is depicted in this wall painting. Grain from Egypt was unloaded from large freighters at the port of Ostia and taken aboard boats like this one for the run up the Tiber to Rome.*

province of Rome. While the bronze statues were originals, most of the marbles were copies of Greek works from earlier centuries. The ship was in all probability headed for Rome, where enthusiasm for classical Greek art was at a peak.

Historians recalled that the great Roman general, Lucius Cornelius Sulla, had put down a rebellion in Greece at about that time and in 83 B.C. had sent back from Athens several shiploads of Greek art, one of which had sunk on the way. Could this be Sulla's ship?

Some light on that conjecture was provided years later by another object from the Antikýthēra wreck. This was an odd-looking mechanism, made up of wheels and gears but so badly corroded and encrusted that for decades no one could make much of it. At first it was identified as an astrolabe or a clock (mostly by people who knew nothing about astrolabes and little

about clocks). Some fifty years passed before Derek de Solla Price, a physicist and mathematician, traveled to Athens and made a thorough study of the curious object. He found, astonishingly, that it was an orrery, a primitive computer used for calculating the movements of the heavenly bodies—a mechanism far in advance of anything known to have existed in the ancient world. When new it had looked like the working part of a small grandfather clock, with brass gear wheels inside a wooden case and dials outside.

Price argues, convincingly, that the computer was made in Rhodes about 82 B.C. and was last adjusted two years later. Assuming that this adjustment took place shortly before the ship sank, the year of the disaster can be fixed at 80 B.C. That was three years after Sulla had left Greece. Further support for the dating was provided recently when Jacques Cousteau, returning to the site with a diving team, salvaged a coin that had been minted at Pergamum in Asia Minor in 86 B.C.

Seven years after the Antikýthēra discovery, Greek sponge divers found another shipload of antique art, this time off the coast of North Africa near the port of Mahdia in Tunisia. The Mahdia ship was as old as the

Antikýthēra ship, or perhaps a little older. It too had come from a Greek port and was headed for Rome or possibly one of the Roman cities in North Africa. Laid out on its deck at the time it sank were forty marble columns with their capitals, enough to build a small temple or a fine villa. In its hold were bronze and marble statues, vases and candelabra, fine furniture, and other decorative objects that rich Romans imported from Greece. These treasures now fill five rooms of the Bardo Museum in Tunis.

Both the Mahdia and the Antikýthēra ships were big, able to carry perhaps as much as three hundred tons of cargo. They must have looked much like the ship named *Europa* that is depicted on a wall at Pompeii: such a vessel would have been more than one hundred feet long, with a breadth amidships of thirty feet, rather bluff-bowed, with fine lines aft; it usually had a high poop, with a tile-roofed cabin on it, and two steering oars in place of a rudder.

The rig of an ancient ship would seem clumsy to a modern sailor, consisting as it did of one tall mainmast carrying a big square sail in the center of the ship and a foremast carrying a much smaller sail, which the ancients called the *artemon*, or steering sail. Experiments with a scale model have shown that this rig worked better than a modern sailor might expect.

One other, smaller ship bearing sculptures came to light in 1928 off Cape Artemisium in Greece. A trawler had snagged her nets on an underwater obstruction 140 feet below. When a diver went down to free the nets he found them caught on a larger-than-life-size bronze arm stretching out of the mud. A salvage expedition, sent out by archaeologists in Athens, brought up the rest of the heroic statue, as well as a bronze jockey and about half of the horse he was riding. The heroic sculpture, regarded as the finest surviving bronze sculpture of the Greek classical age, was made in the fifth century B.C. and represents, according to differing authorities, either Zeus or Poseidon. A copy stands in the lobby of the General Assembly building of the United Nations in New York.

Until after World War II the bottom of the sea remained the exclusive domain of the professional diver. When ancient wrecks were found, it was generally because the ships had happened to sink at places where sponges grew. Students of antiquity could only hope that the divers would not destroy more than they retrieved and would not sell it all in the market for cash.

The device that changed all that was developed in 1943 by Jacques-Yves Cousteau, then a young French naval officer, and Emile Gagnan, an engineer. During the wartime gasoline shortage Gagnan had designed a diaphragm regulator for use in cars and trucks fueled with pressurized coal gas. At Cousteau's urging he adapted the regulator to feed compressed air from small tanks to a diver's mask. The invention was soon named the Aqua-Lung, or SCUBA (Self-Contained Underwater Breathing Apparatus).

The Aqua-Lung found its first and most widespread use soon after the war in the shallow waters of the Mediterranean shore. With only a few days of training, an amateur diver could swim underwater, scan the bottom, poke into coral reefs, and glide down a rocky slope like a bird over a mountain cliff. The Mediterranean is ideal territory for the skin diver. It is warm, generally shallow along the shore, and, because of the paucity of plankton, clear to a depth of many feet. And there was much to find, because this had been the center of western civilization for thousands of years, and the waterway of ancient shipping.

The proliferation of scuba divers in the Mediterranean in the 1950's brought a rash of discoveries of ancient shipwrecks scattered along the littoral from Spain to Italy. Most of the ships were not the bearers of art objects or other treasure. They were simply coastwise trading vessels, freighted with such staples as grain, wine, and olive oil, much of it in clay containers called amphorae, the jerrycans of the ancient world. Generally the timbers of the ship had been eaten away by shipworms or covered by sand; what the divers found typically was a mound of amphorae, indicating the site and sometimes the shape of the sunken vessel.

For the science of archaeology the sudden opening up of this underwater world to amateurs was a mixed blessing. Many of the scuba divers were primarily sportsmen, armed with camera and spear gun. After they had virtually wiped out the population of big fishes to a depth of two hundred feet, they turned their

In a rocky cove near Cape Gelidonya on the coast of Turkey, a sponge boat anchors above the site of a Bronze Age wreck. Here George Bass and Peter Throckmorton carried out the first scientific underwater archaeological "dig" in 1960.

This narrow beach, thirty minutes away by boat, was the archaeologists' campsite during the work off Cape Gelidonya. Mrs. Bass stands in the surf at the foot of a cliff from which rocks frequently fell onto the tents.

attention to the ancient wrecks. An amphora was a trophy second only to a marlin over the mantelpiece. The rest was junk.

Indeed, a heap of such junk on the bottom remains junk unless it is properly excavated, studied, preserved, and imaginatively exhibited in a museum. Among the scuba divers were some who had a serious interest in the shipping and trade of antiquity and understood what they saw. But they, like the simple sponge divers before them, failed to make themselves understood to land-bound archaeologists. The first conference on underwater archaeology was held at Cannes, under the sponsorship of the Club Alpin Sous-Marin, in 1955. On rereading the reports of the conference, and articles published at the time, one is struck by the lack of communication between divers

and archaeologists. Articles by archaeologists pay little attention to the ships themselves and concentrate on the objects found. No one talks about even attempting to practice archaeology as such underwater.

By 1955 land archaeology had come a long way from the heady times when Heinrich Schliemann had "gazed upon the face of Agamemnon" at Mycenae and parties of Edwardian English gentlemen had employed farm laborers to look for golden cups in burial mounds between lunch and tea. Field archaeology on land had become a serious discipline, with its rules and recognized techniques. A modern excavation produces a series of carefully made drawings, notes, and photographs. The resulting report is an exquisitely boring document, laboriously compiled, rather like a homicide detective's report. If historians are to use archaeological evidence it must be of the same quality as the evidence a judge requires before delivering a verdict. By 1955 archaeologists no longer dug primarily for treasure or art objects; they excavated in order to recreate the history of the site that they were destroying by their digging.

The first effort to excavate a wreck by scientific methods was made by Cousteau and his crew in 1952. Cousteau had learned of an untouched wreck lying off a craggy islet called Grand Congloué, a few miles from Marseilles. The excavation was carried out over a period of five years by more than one hundred divers who made more than five thousand dives to a depth of 140 feet. Grand Congloué yielded some six thousand pieces of pottery, of forty different types, along with a collection of copper and bronze objects, a warehouse full of amphorae, and pieces of the sunken ship.

Cousteau is an oceanographer, not an archaeologist, and his work at Grand Congloué fell under some criticism. Some archaeologists complained of a lack of site drawings, technical photographs, and scholarly records. There are archaeologists who, as I write this a generation later, still believe that the Congloué was not one wreck but two.

But at that time there were no archaeologists who had learned to work underwater. The best epitaph on Grand Congloué comes from one of its principal participants, Frédéric Dumas, who wrote:

If we hadn't opened up this sunken ship, would anybody have been willing to undertake the task on a scientific basis? Even after our demonstration of the importance of ancient wrecks, it is still difficult to get science on the move. . . . Certain journalists, taking their cue from a few archaeologists, have condemned us for our mistakes at Grand Congloué. But to us the essential thing was to get the project under way, and you can't do that by just sitting around and thinking about it.

Cousteau and his associate Philippe Tailliez, who went on to excavate another wreck on the French coast, faced the problem of preserving what they recovered. Clay pots and some metals, including gold and sometimes bronze, are impervious to water or air. But iron cannon balls, which looked perfect when the sea growth was knocked off them, turned into a heap of crystalline fragments if left to dry out in the air. A shipwreck is in effect a giant galvanic battery, with the seawater acting as the electrolyte and the several kinds of metal on board as the plates. Silver coins, for instance, are often preserved intact if there is a lot of iron around them, because the iron corrodes before the silver.

Wood that was so well preserved underwater that the ancient carpenter's tool marks could still be seen, dried out to a shrunken ruin of its former self. The first great breakthrough in the conservation of waterlogged wood was made by the Swedish chemist Lars Barkman, who conducted his studies on the seventeenth-century warship *Vasa* before she was raised from Stockholm Harbor in 1961. Barkman found that the water in the wood could be replaced by polyethylene glycol, which would prevent the wood from collapsing as the water evaporated from its cells. But the process is costly and takes a year or more for large pieces.

Most of the ancient wrecks found in the western Mediterranean dated from Roman times. But the eastern Mediterranean was a commercial waterway for two thousand years or more before the Roman Empire. Along the coasts of Greece and Turkey and the Aegean Islands, sponge divers had seen and worked among many very early wrecks and had brought up whatever seemed of value to them, especially lead anchor stocks and ingots of copper. At least two cargoes of copper ingots from the Middle Bronze Age were salvaged and sold for scrap before the First World War. One of the wrecks was found off Kýmē in Euboea, and a few ingots from it survive in the Numismatic Museum at Athens. A much larger cargo turned up off the Manavgat River in Turkish Asia Minor; the last ingot escaped scrapping until World War II because it served as a doorstop in a sponge dealer's office in Kalymnos. But few people outside the sponge ports ever heard of the divers' finds and fewer paid attention. The divers were a clannish people who spoke a dialect that was unintelligible to most educated Greeks.

In 1958, the year after Cousteau and Tailliez had completed their pioneering work on the French wrecks, I was in Turkey with the late Mustafa Kapkin, making a film about sponge divers. From them we learned of the numerous shipwrecks that lay scattered along the Anatolian coast and especially off Yassi Ada, an island west of Bodrum. At one of these wrecks about five years earlier, a sponge boat's net had pulled up a bronze bust of the Greek goddess Demeter. More recently a trawler captain, catching amphorae in his nets, had smashed them up as a menace to fishing.

We made friends with a sponge captain named Kemâl Aras, who agreed to take us to Yassi Ada. The island lies directly on the route that has been used by coastal shipping since prehistoric times. Unlike all the other islands in the Karabaglar group, it does not drop

Under a nylon canopy at their base camp, George and Ann Bass work on the preservation of artifacts from the wreck. At right, a diver inspects two "ox hide" copper ingots, so called because of their shape, on the deck of the expedition ship.

to deep water but is bordered by a reef whose jagged rocks reach almost to the surface. It is a natural trap for unsuspecting mariners coming down the coast from the north with the prevailing wind behind them.

On my first dive at Yassi Ada I landed in a field of broken amphorae. Scattered over the reef we counted, during the next few days, more than a dozen wrecks. The earliest victim of the reef dated from the fourth century B.C.; the latest was a schooner of the 1920's, which had come to rest almost on top of the ancient vessel. Mixed with debris from both of them were cannon balls from an eighteenth-century frigate and pottery that spanned the centuries of Roman and Arab shipping.

Two ships, one from the fourth and the other from the seventh century A.D., had hit the reef and gone over it to land on a muddy bottom in deep water. Because their timbers would be preserved by the mud, these looked like the best candidates for excavation. When one of these Byzantine wrecks was excavated a few years later, a third wreck, from the Crusader period, was found between the earlier ones.

Captain Kemâl told us of another wreck, at Cape Gelidonya to the north, where a ship had sunk with a cargo of copper. I paid little attention, for copper might be found on a ship of any period, until one of his divers recalled that he had salvaged a couple of bronze knives from the wreck and given them to his children to play with. Bronze has not been used for knives since

the Iron Age began. When we got back to port I scrabbled in the diver's yard for the knives but never found them.

A year passed before I was able to arrange a cruise to Cape Gelidonya. But then, in July 1959, after three days of searching, we found the site. The ship had indeed carried a cargo of copper ingots from Cyprus, cast in the shape of ox hides. With the ingots were

bronze tools and pieces of pottery dating from the Late Bronze Age. It was the oldest wreck that had ever been found.

Here, it seemed to me, was the opportunity to apply the principles of archaeology to an underwater excavation. Having no resources of my own for such an operation, I wrote to the late Professor Rodney Young, who was establishing the University of Pennsylvania Museum as the leading center of marine archaeology. He adopted the project and assigned a young classical archaeologist, George Bass, to represent the university. Bass had never dived before but he learned fast. The guiding principle was that we were carrying out a job of field archaeology. The ninety feet of clear water that lay over the wreck was considered to be simply a special impediment which would not

The two-man Asherah *was the first submersible built for underwater archaeology. It was used to locate and photograph wreck sites.*

affect the step-by-step excavation. We were not to be a diving expedition but a scientific enterprise that happened to take place underwater.

The expedition arrived at Cape Gelidonya in Captain Kemâl's boat in June of 1960, anchored another boat over the wreck to serve as a diving barge, and set up camp on the nearest beach. The first step was to survey, map, and photograph the site, tagging every visible object with a number on plastic. The thirty-four copper ingots that we eventually raised were compacted together in lumps as if they had been dumped in heaps on the ocean floor and then covered by a truckload of cement. The lumps had to be broken away from the bottom with a hydraulic auto jack, raised, and then carefully taken apart on the beach.

Under the ingots lay the remnants of what had been the ship: some planks and a bit of what might have been the keel, together with ropes, matting, and scattered brushwood. There were hundreds of bronze tools: adzes, axes, hoes, picks, spatulas, spear points, and knives—most of which, curiously, seemed to have been broken before the ship went down. Also, there was a jar of glass beads that had to be kept wet lest they explode to dust. There were four scarabs, a scarab plaque, and a Syrian cylinder seal that was hundreds of years older than the date of the wreck.

It soon became clear that the ship had carried a seaborne metalsmith, who plied the coast of Asia Minor fashioning tools from his supply of copper and taking broken tools in part payment. Bass's conclusion that the ship was a Phoenician or Syrian trader, which sank about 1200 B.C. while on its way to the Aegean, was startling and controversial, because the conventional view of most archaeologists at the time was that such trading was carried on mainly by Greeks. Bass believes that Semitic trading in later Mycenaean times was much more important than anyone has recognized and that perhaps most of the ingots found on Mediterranean sites were traded by Semites rather than Greeks.

The beach at Cape Gelidonya was furnace-hot in the daytime and filled with mosquitoes at night. We rarely had enough to eat because we were twenty miles from the nearest market and a boat could seldom be spared for the trip; each of us lost about twenty pounds. But it was exciting to handle objects that had not been touched for so long, and a new discovery every day or so kept our spirits up. We were

A diver guides a vacuum pipe called an airlift on the floor of the Mediterranean. It sucks up sand covering the remains of a Roman ship that carried the amphorae in the foreground.

An unusual underwater telephone booth allowed divers at Yassi Ada to communicate with the ship 125 feet above.

Even after we had finished at Cape Gelidonya, the first site to be excavated completely on the seabed, I read a statement by some of the pioneers emphasizing that only professional divers could work properly underwater, that it required many years of diving experience to understand ancient wrecks: that no archaeologist could possibly learn in just a few years to dive well enough to excavate underwater: some even said that only men who had been reared in the Mediterranean were qualified for the job—immediately excluding all divers from England, Scandinavia, and the Americas! . . . In underwater archaeology if those whose skills were limited to diving were to admit that architects and photographers and archaeologists could learn to excavate wrecks together, what role would they have left for themselves? . . . The divers had now had their day, and scientific results were limited.

Cape Gelidonya set the pattern for other excavations in the Mediterranean and elsewhere. While Bass went on to excavate the Byzantine wreck which we had found at Yassi Ada, I formed a new group that surveyed a series of Roman wrecks on the route between Rome and the Aegean, finding several shiploads of columns, marble sarcophagi, and other Roman imports. Meanwhile, Michael Katzev, an alumnus of Yassi Ada, and his wife, Susan, went to work on a Greek ship that sank off Kyrenia in Cyprus, while carrying a cargo of almonds and other produce. Radiocarbon tests and bronze coins found on the site agree that she went down about 300 B.C. The hull was so well preserved that the Katzevs were able to raise it, plank by plank, and after soaking the wood in preservative solution, reassemble it in the hall of the medieval castle at Kyrenia.

The Kyrenian ship provides a graphic demonstration of the difference between an ancient's way of shipbuilding and the method used by western shipwrights ever since the Middle Ages. In the West we build frame first, that is, the skeleton is erected on the ways and the hull is then planked. Ancient technology was just the opposite: after laying the keel and stem and stern posts, the ancient shipwright built the hull, joining the planks edge to edge with mortise and tenons. Into the shell so made he then inserted the ribs. Thus the shape of the ship came from the hull itself; the frame buttressed the sides and supported the deck.

especially pleased to find the first archaeological evidence to explain a phrase that had long puzzled translators of the *Odyssey*. The phrase related to the use of brushwood in the fitting out of a ship. It was now clear that the brushwood had been strewn inside the hull as dunnage to protect the cargo against damage.

We also had the satisfaction of knowing that we were in at the beginning of truly scientific archaeology underwater. Frédéric Dumas and I were the most experienced divers in the group and, like all professional divers, were obsessed with the time-money equation. Since at that depth a diver could spend only about an hour a day underwater without risking the bends, we felt impelled to get down and do the job fast. We were always squabbling with Bass, who was capable of suspending all operations while he studied some significant find. He was right and we were wrong, and we both admitted it.

Bass wrote the epilogue to Gelidonya in *Archaeology Beneath the Sea*:

Archaeologists uncover the hull timbers of a Greek merchant ship that sank off Kyrenia, Cyprus, in the third century B.C. Working amid the plastic rods of a grid that has been erected to aid in mapping the site, the divers at left and right are operating airlift suction hoses.

The earliest example of a ship built in the standard western manner, completely frame first, came to light in 1977 when George Bass began the exploration of a wreck on the southwest coast of Turkey. Bass was led to the cove of Serçe Liman by sponge divers who had found the sandy bottom strewn with bright bits of glass. The wreck, Bass discovered, was that of an Islamic ship that had gone down in the eleventh century A.D. while carrying a cargo of bottles, vases, and other glassware, as well as a mass of cullet, the chunks of glass from which a glass blower makes his finished pieces. To maritime historians the surprising discovery was that the ship had been built frame first, in the manner that became standard before the Age of Exploration.

In its brief span, underwater archaeology has enlarged our knowledge in many ways. We know much more than we did a generation ago about ancient ships—how they were built, where they sailed, and what they carried. The history of art and technology has been enriched by objects retrieved from the sea. In the last decade the pace of discovery in the Mediterranean has been slowed, partly because the known wrecks on the western shores have been looted by amateur scuba divers, partly because the governments of Greece and Turkey have closed their waters to most foreign archaeologists. But many of those who got their training in the Mediterranean have gone on to other promising though more difficult fields. Donald Keith, a specialist in oriental maritime history, is excavating the wreck of a fourteenth-century Chinese junk in the Yellow Sea. I am engaged in a project for the National Maritime Association to preserve some of the nineteenth-century sailing ships that were wrecked at Cape Horn. Others are retrieving bits of American history from the warships that sank in Lakes Champlain and Erie during the American Revolution and the War of 1812, and from the freight canoes of the voyageurs that foundered in the rapids of midwestern rivers. There is even a project to raise the Civil War ironclad *Monitor* from its resting place in the turbulent waters off Cape Hatteras.

Meanwhile, technology is opening up new fields of underwater exploration. Small submersible ships, equipped with powerful lights, can now take archaeologists into deep waters. Increasingly sensitive magnetometers can detect tiny bits of metal such as nails. In the calm deeps, untouched beneath a cover of sand and mud, a ship might be much better preserved than in shallow seas. There, some archaeologist may yet discover the ancient ship of his dreams, intact and waiting to be raised.

In the great hall of the Crusader castle at Kyrenia (opposite) the hull of the ancient ship is partially assembled from the fragments brought up from the shipwreck site. The larger pieces had to be soaked in a bath of polyethylene glycol for more than a year to prevent deterioration. The construction of the hull is illustrated in the cross section below.

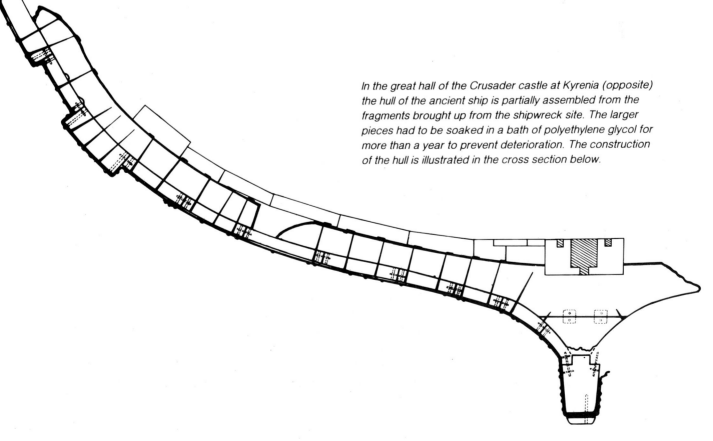

SUNKEN SHORES

PHAROS

Around the shores of the Mediterranean, on its European, Asian, and African coasts, are sunken structures, often visible when the sea is smooth. Some are the remains of ancient harbor works, as at Sidon and Tyre and Alexandria. Some are villas or the floors of temples, as at Posilipo on the Bay of Naples or at Kenchreai on the Gulf of Corinth. Some are entire waterfronts of lost cities, with roads leading into the water and stairways descending out of sight.

It is to Gaston Jondet, chief engineer of ports and lights in Egypt, that we owe the first real survey of an ancient harbor, carried out at Alexandria just before World War I. Alexandria was one of the greatest harbors of antiquity, continuously used and rebuilt under Egyptian, Greek, Roman, Byzantine, and Arab rule, from before 2000 B.C. to the present day. The harbor was extended out from the island of Pharos where Ptolemy II had built the lighthouse that was one of the Seven Wonders of the World. Jondet's purpose, in the years between 1910 and 1915, was to make a record of the ancient harbor works before they were covered up by modern buildings. Under his direction free swimmers and helmet divers mapped the breakwaters that had formed an outer and inner harbor. The moles, stretching for more than one and a half miles, enclosed a roadstead of 300 acres. Having little help from archaeologists, Jondet was unable to determine the age or history of the harbor works, but the presump-

The Pharos or lighthouse of Alexandria, drawn from imagination in this sixteenth-century engraving, guided mariners to one of the largest and busiest harbors of the ancient world.

tion is that most of them were Roman, very likely built on older foundations.

Twenty years later another Frenchman, Father Antoine Poidebard, made the first use of aerial photography to study underwater archaeological sites. Mounting his cameras on a plane lent him by the French air force, Father Poidebard made a survey of the coast of Lebanon, focusing especially on the ancient Phoenician ports of Tyre and Sidon. Tyre was a maritime stronghold from the time of the Phoenicians, who built it on an offshore island in the fifteenth century B.C., until it was destroyed by the Muslims during the Crusades, almost three thousand years later. It withstood sieges by Shalmaneser IV, king of Assyria, and Nebuchadnezzar, king of Babylon, the latter lasting thirteen years. Alexander the Great was the first to capture it. He did so in 332 B.C. by building a mole to connect the island with the mainland and then mounting a combined attack by land and sea.

Guided by Father Poidebard's photographs, divers found that the harbor installations were much more massive than anyone had imagined. Building on earlier Phoenician breakwaters, later engineers, presumably Roman, had used stone blocks bound with iron and reinforced by concrete.

Father Poidebard's underwater surveys at Tyre and its sister port Sidon had practical value for the French administration of Lebanon. In 1939 the French had built a new breakwater for Sidon, but it silted up almost immediately. Poidebard's surveys showed why: the ancient breakwaters had sophisticated systems of sluice gates that allowed the silt to wash through. In the 1960's, when French and Israeli engineers constructed the new Israeli port of Ashdod for ocean-going ships, they used a design which incorporated the wash-through features used three thousand years earlier on the same coast.

Since the invention of scuba gear, divers have explored many other ancient ports. In 1960 Dr. Edwin Link took his research ship *Sea Diver* to Caesarea, once the chief Roman naval base in the eastern Mediterranean. The city and harbor of Caesarea were built just before the time of Christ by King Herod the Great on what is now the coast of Israel. It was the seat of the Roman procurator Pontius Pilate, and a thousand years later the place where, some say, Crusaders found the green crystal chalice they called the Holy Grail. Among the artifacts that the Link expedition recovered was a medal showing the towers at the entrance of the ancient port.

Kenneth MacLeish, a *Life* editor who accompanied the Link team, caught the excitement of the underwater search in his description of one dive, made in company with Professor John Bullitt of Harvard:

"We go over the side together, feet first, hands to masks. Our momentum carries us down into the blood-warm water. We hang in a jade mist, bright above, dark below. . . .

"As we approach the crumbling ruin of the jetty it looms dark and formless. At six or seven feet it comes into clear focus. . . .

"We move on, following the sea-changed ruin toward its end at the harbor mouth. . . . We are precisely at the point which Josephus had in mind and perhaps in sight when he described towering structures flanking the harbor's mouth, topped by 'colossi'—statues, probably, gleaming white and so tall as to beckon to ships far off shore. . . .

"A sharp tug on my right fin brings me up short. I turn to see Bullitt pointing at a spot on the 20-ton block beside us. He draws his knife from its leg sheath and pokes at it. Turning, I see an odd lump on the block near me. It juts out a few inches from the stone and has an unnatural-looking hole in its center. I tear the moss away and brush it clean with my fingers, fending off a small fierce crab which menaces me with fragile claws from the doorway of its strange home. The hole is perfectly rectangular, a few inches deep. Its sides do not feel like stone. I move over to where Bullitt is working with his knife. He has found a similar hole. Its edges glow like silver where the blade has scraped them. We swarm all over the block and find that there are seven lumps in parallel lines, all with rectangular holes. On the sandy bottom lies an eighth lump, apparently washed out of the stone by wave action. . . . I grab it up and sink instantly to the sea floor. It is pure lead, about 20 pounds of it.

"We surface, signal for the outboard and return to *Sea Diver* with our unglamorous prize. An archaeologist explains it. 'This is very important,' he says. 'It's a lead socket for a peg of iron or bronze. The Romans assembled their statues in this manner, using the pegs to lock blocks together so that they could not slide out of place. Perhaps you have found part of one of the great colossi.' "

The earliest harbor works in the Mediterranean seem to have been built primarily for the use of warships. The small merchant ships of the period customarily ran up on a beach, threw out a gangplank, and unloaded their cargo, or else they unloaded at simple docks in protected bays. But warships required harbor works, sheds to keep them dry when not in use, for they were in effect oversized racing shells. This was especially the case after the earlier type of ship with a single bank of rowers gave way to

The remains of ancient breakwaters have been found beneath the sea at Alexandria. These divers are exploring what may be the foundation stones of the lighthouse, which stood until the fourteenth century A.D.

At the port of Kenchreai, near Corinth, archaeologists discovered under several feet of water this mosaic floor of a temple. The sanctuary was evidently dedicated to Isis, the Egyptian goddess whose worship spread through the Mediterranean world in Hellenistic times. Above is a view of the temple floor after it was drained and, at left, building foundations still partly underwater.

the complicated trireme, with its three banks of rowers, around the end of the sixth century B.C.

At the peak of Athenian naval power in the fourth century B.C., the two military harbors of Athens, Munychia and Zea, contained 372 ship sheds where triremes could be stored for the winter and launched directly into the water. The trireme remained the queen of naval warfare until Hellenistic engineers began building larger and heavier war galleys—quadriremes, quinquiremes, and so on—which accommodated many more rowers pulling longer and more powerful oars.

After Octavian (later Augustus) defeated Mark Antony and Cleopatra at Actium in 31 B.C., Mare Nostrum came, for the first and last time in history, under the control of a single power. It was safer for commerce than it had ever been before or would be again until England's navy cleaned the last pirates out of the Aegean a decade after the young American navy had suppressed the Barbary pirates.

With a million people to feed, Rome depended on massive imports of grain from North Africa. And not only grain. In *The Ancient Mariners* Lionel Casson says of the Roman at the time of Augustus:

"He cooked with north African oil in pots and pans of copper mined in Spain, ate off dishes fired in French kilns, drank wine from Spain or France and, if he spilled any of his dinner on his toga, had it cleaned with fuller's earth from the Aegean Islands. The Roman of wealth dressed in garments of wool from Miletus or linen from Egypt; his wife wore silks from China, adorned herself with diamonds and pearls from India, and made up with cosmetics from South Arabia. He seasoned his food with Indian pepper and sweetened it with Athenian honey, had it served in dishes of Spanish silver on tables of African citrus wood, and washed it down with Sicilian wine poured from decanters of Syrian glass. He lived in a house whose walls

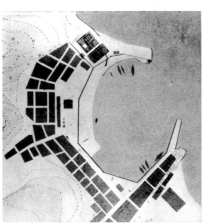

Foundations of the ancient harbor works at Kenchreai can be seen in the water off the modern shorefront. At left is a drawing of the ancient port, based on the findings of archaeologists.

were covered with colored marble veneer quarried in Asia Minor; his furniture was of Indian ebony or teak inlaid with African ivory, and his rooms were filled with statues imported from Greece."

One could add that this Roman walked through porticoes whose tall columns were chiseled from red and gray granite from far up the Nile, and he was buried in a sarcophagus of marble or granite which had been quarried in Asia Minor.

Trade like this required big seagoing ships. These sailing vessels, similar to the one found at Antikýthēra, probably carried from 200 to 400 tons

of cargo. It is reported by ancient writers that some of the grain ships carried as much as 1,000 tons. We have not found such a big commercial vessel yet, but the two pleasure barges excavated at Lake Nemi (see page 100) prove that Roman shipwrights were perfectly capable of building them. One may compare the length of the Nemi ships, 234 and 240 feet, with the length of the square-rigged down-easters, built for the Cape Horn trade in the nineteenth century at the end of the wooden shipbuilding era. The later down-easters averaged 240 feet. Most ocean traders in the heyday of the Atlantic

At Pozzuoli on the Bay of Naples columns still rise (above) from the partially submerged Temple of Serapis. Pozzuoli was the chief port for Roman grain ships until Ostia was built at the mouth of the Tiber. Contemporary descriptions of the port and its arched breakwater match the ancient painting of a Roman port at left.

trade measured less than 150 feet and carried about 500 to 700 tons.

The Roman ships required good harbors, safe in any weather. They were covered on their underwater surface with a sheathing of lead against the marine borer; no doubt they were hauled out periodically to have their bottoms cleaned, and perhaps there were even skidways for this purpose. The ports were manned by an army of clerks and customs officers, insurance agents and lawyers, tugboatmen and stevedores.

In 1958 Nicholas Flemming, at that time a graduate student at Cambridge University, began a survey of North African ports that engaged the efforts of other divers, chiefly Cambridge students, for the next decade. At Apollonia, the ancient port of Cyrene in what is now Libya, Flemming found a mile-long stretch of underwater works, including what seem to have been large, shallow pools for the raising and harvesting of fish and shellfish. Other students, using only inflatable rubber boats and scuba

gear, explored harbors along the coasts of Algeria and Tunisia. The names of the ancient ports on that coast, familiar now only to experts, read like a Roman navigator's portolano: Chulla, Tipasa, Rasguniae, Ruscinona, Saldae, Rusucurru, Rusicada, Igilgilis, Hippo Regius, and a dozen others.

Flemming's central purpose in his underwater survey was to find whether the Mediterranean ports had actually sunk and if so what had caused the sinking. Some, he concluded, had not. Where the remains were primarily harbor works, as at Tyre and Sidon, they had been eroded by the action of the waves and storms over many centuries. But at other places, such as Kenchreai and Apollonia, buildings and plazas had clearly sunk and were still to be seen.

First he ruled out the theory that a drastic change in the level of the Mediterranean had occurred in the time that men had been building on its shores or sailing on it in ships. True, there was once a great rising of the

waters in the Mediterranean, as in all the seas and oceans of the earth. That occurred, over many thousands of years, at the end of the last Ice Age, when the ice caps shrank and poured their locked-up water into the sea. We have plenty of geologic proof of that event. It may be that the postglacial rising of the waters finds an echo in the legends of the Flood that are common to cultures not only in the Near East but in lands throughout the world.

But that was long before the age of any man-made structure now extant. In recent millennia there is no evidence for a rise of more than two feet in the Mediterranean.

The answer to the mystery of the sunken coasts must be sought in that branch of geology known as plate tectonics. The earth's crust is made up of great plates (discussed at length in Chapter 6), and where these grind together, the land is unstable. One of these lines of instability is the Anatolian fault, which runs through northern Turkey into the Aegean. A similar arc runs through Sicily and southern Italy. Along these arcs we find volcanoes: Thera on the Anatolian fault, Vesuvius, Aetna, and Stromboli on the Italian fault. And here, too, we find places that have actually sunk beneath the sea: Kenchreai and Helice and Pheia in Greece, Pozzuoli and Sybaris in Italy. In some few cases coastal cities have been raised, as at Phalasarna, on the western end of Crete.

The most extensive complex of sunken structures lies along the shores of the Bay of Naples. Pozzuoli, with its fine natural harbor, was the chief Italian port of entry for overseas cargoes, which were shipped over-

This mosaic panel, made of bits of colored glass, was found in the submerged Temple of Isis at Kenchreai. The ibis and lotus blossoms are native to the Nile Delta of Egypt.

land to Rome or unloaded onto small vessels for the coastal run to the Tiber. Nearby were the posh resorts of Baiae and Posilipo and beyond them the imperial naval base of Misenum.

Moralists have long drawn lessons from the splendid ruins that can be seen underwater along the shorefront. Here is Guillaume de Villeneuve, writing in 1495:

"From Naples to the port of Baiae, which is a large and excellent port, is a distance of seven miles, and in times gone by there was a great city there. It was the most beautiful city in the kingdom, but because of the wicked sinfulness of the people, and the prevalence of sodomy, the city was destroyed, and sank into the sea."

Baiae and Posilipo, by the testimony of Juvenal and Petronius, were certainly wicked. There are plenty of people today who would argue that they, like Sodom, Gomorrah, and even Atlantis, were destroyed by God's wrath. But if so, tectonic activity was the agency of divine intervention.

In 1750 antiquarians excavated a building at Pozzuoli which is now known as the Temple of Serapis. When they began, only the tops of the temple columns protruded from earth, on an elevation near the shore. When they had dug down forty feet they found that the columns stood on a marble floor which was then two feet below sea level. Seven feet under that floor was another, older mosaic floor. Curiously, the standing columns were smooth to a height of twelve feet; above that level they were deeply perforated with holes from marine borers. The temple, with its puzzling evidence of submersion, was described in a series of scientific letters sent to the Royal Society in 1779 by Sir William Hamilton, the British ambassador to the court of Naples (but probably better known as the husband of Emma, Lord Nelson's mistress.)

The puzzle presented by the Temple of Serapis was resolved at the end of the nineteenth century by the British

geologist Sir Charles Lyell. On geologic evidence he concluded that sometime between A.D. 500 and A.D. 1300 the coast around Pozzuoli had gradually sunk into the sea. At about the same time volcanic eruptions had enveloped the lower third of the temple in ash, thus protecting the bottoms of the columns but leaving the tops exposed to marine borers. Some centuries later another round of volcanic activity raised the land and the temple partly above water. The climactic eruption occurred on September 29, 1538, when flames burst from the ground near the city. Eruptions continued for a week, creating a mountain five hundred feet high.

Professor Lyell's sequence of events was confirmed by an Oxford don named Robert Theodore Günther, who made an exhaustive study of the whole coast before World War I. Between Pozzuoli and Posilipo he traced beneath the bay a Roman road which had been lined with luxurious villas. Work in the Baiae area was continued by Amedeo Maiuri, one of the recent excavators of Pompeii, who explored the bay with divers in 1959.

Because of its complicated geologic history and the riches that lie beneath its waters, the Bay of Naples is a tempting site for exploration. But it is not a pleasant place for divers, being one of the most polluted bays in the world. There is generally no blue water to be seen until one is five miles out of Naples on the way to Capri. Much of the area that Günther could inspect through a glass-bottomed bucket in the early nineteenth century now has zero visibility. Even at Baiae, which lies farthest from the city, visibility is seldom more than ten feet. The ruins are spread over an area of at least 50,000 square meters and reach to depths as great as sixty feet. It is perhaps understandable that Professor Maiuri preferred, after a season with divers, to return to the more agreeable task of digging out the still uncovered quarters of Herculaneum and Pompeii.

SUNKEN CITIES

An archaeologist or a scuba diver who looks for sunken buildings or sunken harbors may dream of finding someday a whole sunken city—a city preserved beneath the sea as Pompeii was preserved by the ashes of Vesuvius. For anyone who cherishes such a dream, a good place to look would be the site of Helice.

The ancient Greek city of Helice, lying west of Corinth on the Peloponnesus, was destroyed by an earthquake in 373 B.C. The land subsided and the entire city was engulfed by the sea. When Eratosthenes, the great Greek geographer, visited the site 150 years later, fishermen told him that a statue of Poseidon was still standing underwater and caught their nets. For more than five hundred years after the earthquake, travelers reported that the ruins were visible on the bottom of the Gulf of Corinth. But no one has seen them in modern times.

Attempts have been made to find the sunken city, one of them by myself and Professor Harold Edgerton of the Massachusetts Institute of Technology in 1971. We found a likely looking mound in deep water bearing shells from A.D. 640, plus or minus 110 years, but no trace of buildings. Our conclusion was that Helice may no longer be under the sea at all. The site of the ancient city may lie beneath the alluvial plain that is constantly being built up by mud washed down from the mountains. The rate of sedimentation is such that, even if Helice was one hundred feet under water two thousand years ago, by now the site may well have been filled in by land.

The best way to explore such an area for buried ruins is by use of the magnetometer, an instrument that registers variations in the magnetic field of the earth, such as those caused by ferrous metal or even pottery (since molecules in the clay line up with the local magnetic field when the pottery is fired, thus creating

When the volcano of Thera erupted about 1500 B.C. it left in its place a deep lagoon, partly enclosed by what was left of the original island—the modern Greek Santoríni. The picture at left, taken from Santoríni, and the air view below show also the small cindery islets thrown up in later eruptions. The original explosion destroyed one of the chief centers of the Minoan civilization.

Buried for more than 3,000 years under the volcanic ash of Thera, this fresco was uncovered in 1974. The landscape (marsh), the fauna (lion and antelope), and the "Afro" hair style suggest to some scholars that the scene depicted may be Libya, where Minoan ships are known to have traded. One puzzling detail is the position of the rowers on the two ships on the opposite page; they seem to be facing forward and pushing, rather than pulling, their oars. The oarsmen in the smaller ship, above, on the other hand, are rowing in the customary fashion.

a detectable anomaly). A practical problem at Helice is that the likely area of search is now a vineyard where the vines hang from wires attached to ferroconcrete posts. To use the magnetometer, it would be necessary to remove and later replace the posts and wires, at a cost that no one has yet been willing to pay.

It is worthy of note that the destruction of Helice occurred not long before the appearance of two dialogues by Plato, the *Timaeus* and *Critias*. The disaster must have been vivid in Plato's mind when he related in those works the story of Atlantis, the fabulous lost continent that supposedly sank beneath the sea. Plato has Critias relate that he heard the tale as a boy of ten from his ninety-year-old grandfather who had heard it from his father who had heard it from Solon who had heard it from some priests in Egypt. Down through this chain of informants had come the story of a vast, prosperous land, with an advanced civilization, that existed in the Atlantic Ocean beyond the Pillars of Hercules (the Strait of Gibraltar). Some 9,000 years before the time of the Egyptian priests it had been swallowed up by earthquakes and floods.

Since there is no geological support for the existence of any such land mass in the Atlantic, at least since the appearance of man on earth, many people have looked elsewhere for some kernel of truth in the legend. In

the nineteenth century a French writer, Louis Figuier, advanced the theory that the basis of the Atlantis tale was the eruption of the volcano on the Aegean island of Thera about 1500 B.C. In that explosion the whole top of Thera was blown sky-high, while the remainder was buried beneath a thick layer of pumice and volcanic ash. What was left—a crescent-shaped island and two smaller fragments—embraced a deep lagoon where the rest of the island used to be.

Whether or not the Thera explosion was the basis of the Atlantis fable, there is no doubt that the island was an important center of Bronze Age civilization, presumably an outpost of

the Minoan culture that had its center on Crete. In 1967 the Greek archaeologist Spyridon Marinatos began to excavate an area at one end of the island. Tunneling under the overlay of volcanic tephra, he found an extensive Minoan city. As at Pompeii, the ash had fallen lightly, filling every crevice and preserving what it covered virtually intact. But the volcano of Thera, unlike Vesuvius, must have given ample warning, for the inhabitants had removed most of their personal possessions before the final eruption and had made their own escape, though no one knows where they went. They could not take with them the wall paintings, fragments of

which have been painstakingly assembled to provide some fine and rare examples of what artists of the age were capable of doing.

Atlantis, according to the fable, sank beneath the sea. But there is little hope of finding any underwater ruins at Thera. Whatever stood near the volcano must have been demolished by the blast. If any parts of the island later slid into the sea, they lie at the bottom of the caldera, a thousand feet deep.

Another Mediterranean site that seems likely to yield a city preserved since ancient times is Sybaris, on the instep of the Italian boot. As it happens, Sybaris was founded about

720 B.C. by colonists from Helice as an outpost of the Greek seaborne empire known as Magna Graecia. It flourished as a port of transshipment for goods exported from Greece and Asia Minor to the Etruscan cities in Italy. With growing wealth, the people of Sybaris indulged themselves in so many luxuries that the word "sybarite" has found a lasting place in western languages. Even Roman writers of the opulent second century A.D., no strangers to luxury, were nevertheless impressed by the stories told of Sybaris. It was said that the Sybarites spent much of their time at banquets, drinking wine that was piped into their homes direct from wineries. They valued their slumber so highly that they barred all noise-producing craftsmen from the city, and even forbade the keeping of a rooster within earshot. Sybarite hostesses issued their party invitations a year in advance to give the guests time to prepare their dresses and jewelry.

The Sybarites were so fond of horses and also of music that they taught their mounts to dance to the pipe. This, according to Athenaeus, a gossipy writer who lived 700 years later, was their undoing. When Sybaris was attacked in 510 B.C. by its neighbor and enemy, Crotona, the Crotoniate musicians played the tunes on which the Sybarite horses had been trained. The beasts broke into dance, the Sybarite army was routed, and the city was captured. The Crotoniates, we are told by Strabo, then diverted the river Crathis to flow over the ruined city.

These Greek temples stand at Paestum, which was a satellite of Sybaris in southern Italy. If such superb examples of Greek architecture were built in the daughter colony, archaeologists wonder what they may find at the mother city.

When archaeologists came to look for buried Sybaris in the 1960's they did not know where to search. In two thousand years great quantities of earth had been washed down from the foothills of the Apennines, behind the city. Earthquakes had periodically shaken the Calabrian plain. The rivers had changed channels many times.

After eight years of work with magnetometers and probes, the site was finally located, under fifteen to twenty feet of sandy mud. At some time in the intervening centuries the coastal dunes on which the ruined city stood had sunk below sea level, forming a lagoon. Then slowly the alluvial runoff filled the lagoon and made the site land again. But the city was still below sea level, and any excavation was immediately filled with water. Thus Sybaris lies where marine archaeology and land archaeology meet. One of the funniest sights I ever saw during my experience in field archaeology was that of a distinguished and very nervous scholar, examining a wall at the bottom of a deep pit with a rope tied around his middle and a gang of workmen at the other end of the rope. The foreman stood at the edge of the excavation with a whistle, so that if the muddy walls started collapsing the scholar could be rescued.

The excavation of Sybaris would be a major undertaking, requiring huge pumps and earth-moving machines. But the likely rewards are tempting. For Sybaris was the richest city of Magna Graecia and may well have been the most splendid.

CALIGULA'S BARGES

The Roman emperor Caligula, we are told by Suetonius, "built two ships with two banks of oars after the Liburnian fashion, the poops of which blazed with jewels and the sails were of various parti colors; they were fitted up with ample baths, galleries, and saloons and supplied with a great variety of vines and fruit trees. In these he would sail in the day along the coast of Campania, feasting amid dancing and concerts of music."

This was at about the same time that Caligula built a bridge of boats across the Bay of Baiae, proposed his favorite horse for consul, and declared himself a god. Caligula was presently murdered by his own Praetorian Guard. What happened to his barges is not known from historical sources, but a tradition dating back at least to the Renaissance holds that they ended up on the bottom of Lake Nemi, fifteen miles southeast of Rome and as far from the coast.

In the fifteenth century a Cardinal Colonna engaged Leon Battista Alberti, the famous architect and humanist, to try to raise the two barges that were known to lie on the lake bottom. Renaissance technology, alas, was not up to the task, and Alberti salvaged only a single statue from the hulks. Later attempts were no more successful. But in 1928 Benito Mussolini, applying his dictatorial powers to his hobby of archaeology, ordered Lake Nemi drained.

The barges that emerged to view were indeed of imperial size, one 234 feet long and the other 240, with bronze fittings and marble baths. The

This vision of an imperial pleasure barge owes something to Suetonius's description but more to the imagination of the Italian artist who drew it before the remains of the vessel were uncovered.

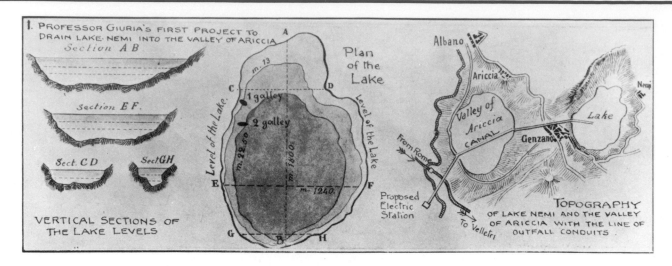

1. PROFESSOR GIURIA'S FIRST PROJECT TO DRAIN LAKE NEMI INTO THE VALLEY OF ARICCIA

Section AB

Section EF

Sect CD   Sect GH

VERTICAL SECTIONS OF THE LAKE LEVELS

Plan of the Lake

1 galley
2 galley

Level of the Lake

Level of the Lake

m. 13
m. 22,60
m. 180.1
m. 1240

Albano
Ariccia
Valley of Ariccia
CANAL
Genzano
From Rome
To Velletri
Proposed Electric Station
Nemi
Lake

TOPOGRAPHY OF LAKE NEMI AND THE VALLEY OF ARICCIA WITH THE LINE OF OUTFALL CONDUITS.

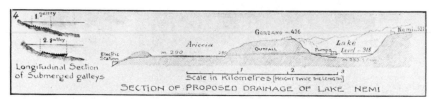

4. 1 galley
2 galley

Longitudinal Section of Submerged galleys

Electric Station

Genzano - 436
Ariccia
m. 290   285
OUTFALL
Pumps
Nemi - 52
Lake
Level - 318
m. 283.5

Scale in Kilometres [HEIGHT TWICE THE LENGTH]
1   2   3

SECTION OF PROPOSED DRAINAGE OF LAKE NEMI

This plan to lay bare the bottom of Lake Nemi by draining its water into the Valley of Ariccia was published in 1906. Seen from the air at lower left is one of the two barges that were revealed when the lake was drained in 1929.

hulls were in good shape, but nothing was left of the superstructures. Modern artists who attempted to depict the vessels as they once looked did not hesitate to draw upon Suetonius's description as well as their own visions of the life style of the mad emperor.

Whether these were really Caligula's barges is not provable. It is quite possible that they were moved overland to Lake Nemi by order of Caligula or one of his successors, Domitian, who had a villa on the lake. In any case they provided archaeologists with their first opportunity to study actual Roman ships. They were built in the same fashion as ancient trading ships, with the hull planks fastened together first and the frame added later. Like seagoing ships they were sheathed in lead, although shipworms are not a problem in fresh water.

After so many centuries underwater, the ships had only a brief existence on dry land. In 1944 they were burned by soldiers of the retreating German army. The museum at Lake Nemi now holds only scale models of the barges and some of the objects found inside them.

One of the barges (top) was photographed after it was cleaned and before it was destroyed by the German army. Among the marble treasures yielded by the barges were the pilaster in the form of a two-faced herma (left), a column (above), and a statue believed to represent Drusilla, the sister and, according to Roman historians, the incestuous lover of the emperor.

THE BLUE MUSEUM

Virtually all we know of classical Greek monumental sculpture we know from pieces that have been recovered from the sea. Ironically, statues that went down in ships have stood the best chance for survival. Large numbers of works by celebrated sculptors were destroyed during wars in the third and fourth centuries B.C. Later, during the Middle Ages, valuable bronzes were routinely melted down and recast into church bells or artillery. The marine environment, hostile as it might seem with its marine borers and corrosive effect on metal, at least protected works of art from casual human destruction. And the deeper the statues sank beneath the sea into mud and slime, the better they were preserved.

Having safeguarded its treasures for two thousand years, it is perhaps fitting that the sea should take its time in returning them to us. So far, sponge divers making chance discoveries have located wrecks and their cargoes of art; trained scientists with their sonar scans have not been able to hurry the pace. But as the writer C. W. Ceram pointed out, "archaeology is a patient discipline. What rests below is quite safe in the blue museum. What has waited for two millennia can wait for another generation, or even for two."

Sponge divers working in bulky helmets and canvas diving suits (opposite page) have been the first to spot many ancient wrecks, including one off Artemisium, where the bronze jockey at left was found in 1928. Further searches also produced fragments of his galloping horse and parts of a wooden ship, but after a diver at the site surfaced too quickly and died, work was suspended. Later expeditions failed to locate the wreck.

UNDER ANCIENT SEAS 105

This bronze youth, found in 1925 by a fisherman in the Bay of Marathon, is a rare original from the fourth century B.C. and may be the work of Praxiteles. The band encircling his head identifies him as one of the competitors in the palaestra, or perhaps their patron, Hermes.

One of only two surviving statues dating from the fifth century B.C., this Zeus or Poseidon ranks among the greatest works of antiquity. The six-foot-ten-inch figure has the lordly bearing of either of the two omnipotent gods, but the thunderbolt or trident that would positively identify him still lies buried where he was found in 1928, under the sea off Cape Artemisium.

A bronze Medusa (left) and a lion's head (below) were among the objects recovered from Caligula's barges at the bottom of Lake Nemi (see pages 100–103). The ring in the lion's mouth was probably used to moor small boats.

The life-sized, staring head on the opposite page, called The Philosopher, was part of a cargo of artwork sunk off the island of Antikýthēra in the first century B.C. Greek sponge divers led archaeologists to the site in 1900.

The winged boy at left was part of a large collection of artworks recovered from the Mahdia wreck, off the coast of North Africa, during an intensive six-year salvage effort. When fishermen in the Adriatic Sea found the figure at right, it was completely encrusted with barnacles. Now that it has been cleaned, scholars believe the bronze to be an original from the fourth century B.C. by the celebrated Lysippus, previously known only from copies and descriptions of his work

A diver in the Blue Grotto on the island of Capri carefully guides his find to the surface. Modern scuba gear makes this part of his job easier, but for the hardest part—finding the sites of ancient wrecks—the diver must still rely on old-fashioned luck.

John P. Holland, inventor of the first widely successful submarine, strikes a jaunty pose in the hatch of his submersible in 1900.

An Anthology of Accounts by
Explorers of the Deep

Undersea Adventure

STEVENSON'S DIVE
Born in Edinburgh, Robert Louis Stevenson, the future novelist and poet, was the son of a civil engineer who specialized in harbor works. He was expected to follow his father's profession, "but indeed," he later wrote, "I had already my own private determination to be an author." In spite of this, however—and in spite of being already handicapped by the delicate health that would be his throughout his comparatively short life (1850–94)—there was one activity associated with his father's work that tempted him, "and that was diving, an experience I burned to taste of."

Into the bay of Wick stretched the dark length of the unfinished breakwater, in its cage of open staging; the travelers (like frames of churches) overplumbing all; and away at the extreme end, the divers toiling unseen on the foundation. On a platform of loose planks, the assistants turned their air-mills; a stone might be swinging between wind and water; underneath the swell ran gaily; and from time to time a mailed dragon with a window-glass snout came dripping up the ladder. To go down in the diving dress, that was my absorbing fancy; and with the countenance of a certain handsome scamp of a diver, Bob Bain by name, I gratified the whim.

It was gray, harsh, easterly weather, the swell ran pretty high, and out in the open there were "skipper's daughters," when I found myself at last on the divers' platform, twenty pounds of lead upon each foot, and my whole person swollen with ply and ply of woolen underclothing. One moment, the salt

wind was whistling round my night-capped head; the next, I was crushed almost double under the weight of the helmet. As that intolerable burthen was laid upon me, I could have found it in my heart (only for shame's sake) to cry off the whole enterprise. But it was too late. The attendants began to turn the hurdy-gurdy, and the air to whistle through the tube; someone screwed in the barred window of the vizor; and I was cut off in a moment from my fellow men; standing there in their midst, but quite divorced from intercourse; a creature deaf and dumb, pathetically looking forth upon them from a climate of his own. Except that I could move and feel, I was like a man fallen in a catalepsy. But time was scarce given me to realize my isolation; the weights were hung upon my back and breast, the signal rope was thrust into my unresisting hand; and setting a twenty-pound foot upon the ladder I began ponderously to descend.

Some twenty rounds below the platform twilight fell. Looking up, I saw a low green heaven mottled with vanishing bells of white; looking around, except for the weedy spokes and shafts of the ladder, nothing but a green gloaming, somewhat opaque but very restful and delicious. Thirty rounds lower, I stepped off on the *pierres perdues* of the foundation; a dumb helmeted figure took me by the hand, and made a gesture (as I read it) of encouragement; and looking in at the creature's window, I beheld the face of Bain. There we were, hand to hand and (when it pleased us) eye to eye; and either might have burst himself with shouting, and not a whisper came to his companion's hearing. . . .

How a man's weight, so far from

being an encumbrance, is the very ground of his agility, was the chief lesson of my submarine experience. The knowledge came upon me by degrees. As I began to go forward with the hand of my estranged companion, a world of tumbled stone was visible, pillared with the weedy uprights of the staging; overhead, a flat roof of green; a little in front, the sea wall, like an unfinished rampart. And presently in our upward progress, Bob motioned me to leap upon a stone; I looked to see if he were possibly in earnest; and he only signed to me the more imperiously. Now the block stood six feet high; it would have been quite a leap for me unencumbered; with the breast and back weights, and the twenty pounds upon each foot, and the staggering load of the helmet, the thing was out of reason. I laughed aloud in my tomb; and to prove to Bob how far he was astray, I gave a little impulse from my toes. Up I soared like a bird, my companion soaring at my side. As high as to the stone, and then higher, I pursued my impotent and empty flight. Even when the strong arm of Bob had checked my shoulders, my heels continued their ascent; so that I blew out sideways like an autumn leaf, and must be hauled in, hand over hand, as sailors haul in the slack of a sail, and propped upon my feet again like an intoxicated sparrow. . . .

There was something strangely exasperating, as well as strangely wearying, in these uncommanded evolutions. It is bitter to return to infancy, to be supported, and directed and perpetually set upon your feet, by the hand of someone else. The air besides, as it is supplied to you by the busy millers on the platform, closes the Eustachian tubes and keeps the neophyte perpetually swallowing, till the throat is grown so dry that he can swallow no longer. And for all these reasons—although I had a fine, dizzy, muddleheaded joy in my surroundings, and longed, and tried, and always failed to lay my hands on the fish that darted here and there about me, swift as hummingbirds—yet I fancy I was rather relieved than otherwise when Bain brought me back to the ladder and signed to me to mount. Of a sudden, my ascending head passed into the trough of a swell. Out of the green, I shot at once into a glory of rosy, almost of sanguine light, the multitudinous seas incarnadined, the heaven above a vault of crimson. And then the glory faded into the hard, ugly daylight of a Caithness autumn, with a low sky, a gray sea, and a whistling wind.

THE SUBMARINE FORETOLD

John Wilkins (1614–72) was the bishop of Chester, England, and a scientist who helped to found the Royal Society. In the remarkable passage below from his *Mathematical Magick* (1648) he contrived to foresee not only combat submarines (paragraph 3) but also (paragraph 5) the specialized craft employed by twentieth-century explorers of the deep. With some slight editing, Wilkins's final paragraph might serve as the abstract of an article in a present-day publication speculating on the possibility of establishing permanent colonies on the ocean floor to exploit its mineral deposits and farm its food resources.

Advantages of a Submarine Vessell:
1. 'Tis *private*; a man may thus go to any coast of the world invisibly, without being discovered or prevented in his journey.
2. 'Tis *safe*; from the uncertainty of *Tides*, and the violence of *Tempests*, which doe never move the sea about five or six paces deep; From *Pirates* and *Robbers* which do so infest other voyages; From ice and great frosts which doe so much endanger the passages towards the Poles.
3. It may be of very great advantage against a Navy of enemies, who by this means may be undermined in the water and blown up.
4. It may be of a special use for the relief of any place that is besieged by water, to convey unto them invisible supplies; and so likewise for the surprisal of any place that is accessible by water.
5. It may be of unspeakable benefit for submarine experiments and discoveries: as,

The deep caverns and subterraneous passages where the sea-water in the course of its circulation doth vent itself into other places and the like. The nature and kinds of fishes, the severall arts of catching them, by alluring them with lights, by placing nets around the sides of this Vessell, shooting the greater sort of them with guns, . . . with like artifices and treacheries, which may be more successively practised by such who live so familiarly together. These fish may serve not only for food, but for fewell likewise, in respect of that oyl which may be extracted from them.

The many fresh springs that may probably be met with in the bottom of the sea, will serve for the supply of drink and other occasions.

But above all, the discovery of submarine treasures is more especially considerable, not only in regard of what hath been drowned by wrecks, but the several precious things that grow there, as Pearl, Coral Mines, with innumerable other things of great value, which may be much more easily found out, and fetcht up by the help of this, than by any other usual way of the Divers.

To which purpose, this great Vessell may have some lesser Cabins tyed

about it, at various distances, wherein several persons, as Scouts, may be lodged for the taking of observations, according as the Admiral shall direct them. . . .

All kinds of arts and manufactures may be exercised in this Vessell. The observations made by it, may be both written, and (if need were) printed here likewise. Severall Colonies may thus inhabit, having their children born and bred up without the knowledge of land, who could not chuse but be amazed with strange conceits upon the discovery of this upper world.

A WORLD OF COLOR

An ornithologist by training and profession, America's William Beebe (1877–1962) became, in his fifties, an investigator of the mysterious domain of the birds' distant relatives, the fish. Thanks to his enthusiasm and his gift for description, he was soon recognized as the leading publicist of the strange and endlessly fascinating world beneath the sea.

Human life is bounded by less than two hundred degrees of temperature, about five miles of altitude, and by the presence of a delicate mixture of gases called atmosphere. To win into a new phase of life outside these realms is to be born again in a new incarnation, and to relive the enthusiasm of far distant aquatic ancestors. Nearly four-fifths of the surface of the earth is covered with water, and although two-thirds of our body consists of the self-same fluid, yet we are so intolerant of this wonderful substance that we can breathe it only as gaseous clouds, paddle about on the surface of the liquid, and skate upon the solid. Five minutes' immersion spells certain death.

I have been fortunate enough to go St. Peter one better, and to walk about on the bottom of the sea during this winter in Haiti. In the course of three hundred odd strolls, one of the most astounding things was the color of this new world. With constant use of the helmet and clear glass windows, there came after a while a forgetfulness of the new medium I had entered. High and low tide came to have no meaning; the shore, as a definite thing, became non-existent, and my mind completely bridged the gap between the last view of the palms and mangroves, which blurred out as I submerged, and the first clear glimpse of the same littoral slope so forever wet that one never thought of it as even damp. . . .

We need a whole new vocabulary, new adjectives, adequately to describe the designs and colors of under sea. The very medium of water prevents any garishness, its pastel perspective compels most exquisite harmony of tints. Filtered through its softness, the harshest, most gaudy parrotfish resolves into the delicacy of an old Chinese print, an age-mellowed tapestry. If one asks for modernist or futuristic designs, no opium dream can compare with a batfish or an angry octopus. The night overhead glories in a single moon; here, whole schools of silvery moonfish rise, pass and set before us, while at our feet rest constellations of starfish—crimson, sepia and mauve.

An unreal, fairy fish of greens and blues and purples appears in the distance, vanishes forever, yet the next moment is close to the glass of our helmet, peering in at us, mouthing soundless Ohs! We try to catch him, with the same success as snatching a sunbeam from the upper air. As he balances calmly, easily, in mid-water, we count the distinct colors on his scales, and stop at the fourteenth, for he has shifted slightly and every single tint and hue has altered.

I walk toward a coral palace in the distance and work more magic. It is of the most delicately tinted lavender, picked out with patches of orange. I lean closer to get the exact shade, when every particle of color vanishes—the feathery-headed worms whose tentacles covered the surface have withdrawn like lightning into their tubes, and I see that the orange was merely reflection and that the coral is actually salmon-pink. My hand now brushes the surface and between winks the thousands of minute polyps disappear within their stony home, revealing at last the beautiful clear ivory of the real coral. Bewildered after this three-ply palimpsest of color, I look aside just in time to see a fish, in brilliant shining blue with three broad, vertical bands of

brown, swim slowly into a fairy cavern. A few minutes later the identical fish emerges clad in brilliant yellow, thickly covered with black polka-dots.

This spirit of astonishing happenings, of exquisite magic, of ineffable, colorful mystery is the theme of this watery world, and should be the chief motif in any writing or painting inspired or influenced by it. For while the roses and peonies of our gardens may look differently in light and in shade, they certainly, when alarmed, do not dash into the ground, and when we see a tortoise-shell tabby disappear into an alley, we can be reasonably sure that it will emerge practically the same color. . . .

Some day, when I can carry a color book in my helmet, I will be able to enumerate an exact color code of distance. Even in our colder, thinner atmosphere the green of mountain slopes softens to purple a long way off, but on the bottom of the sea, still greater changes take place within a few feet or yards. I have walked backward and seen a feathery-crowned sea-worm of dragon's blood alter, in my vision, within a few seconds and steps, to the palest of coral pink; while a sea-weed, deep olive-green when within reach, comes gently to the eye, when five yards away, as faintest glaucous.

An artist of great skill and patience can approximate the oxydized royal purple of a gorgonia, even the pink and ivory sunset of a conch shell,—but the vanishing point of distance beneath the water, where the coral reef ends and the mysteries of the unknown deeps begin—the illusion, too subtle for color, of submarine visual infinity—this is not to be whelmed by man-made brushes nor imprisoned on any terrestrial dimension.

SHARKS

Co-inventor (with Emile Gagnan) of the Aqua-Lung, founder in 1945 of the French navy's undersea research group, director since 1951 of Monaco's famous oceanographic museum, author or coauthor of numerous books, and maker of numerous documentary films, France's Jacques-Yves Cousteau (born 1910) has done

more than any other living person to popularize the still little-known submarine world and to encourage others to join him in exploring it. This passage from _The Silent World_ (1953) relates an encounter, in company with his coauthor, Frédéric Dumas, with some rather unpleasant predators, in the vicinity of a mortally wounded and bleeding whale.

Below the blue sharks there appeared great tunas with long fins. Perhaps they had been there since the beginning, but it was the first time we noticed them. Above us flying fish gamboled, adding a discordant touch of gaiety to what was becoming a tragedy for us. Dumas and I ransacked our memories for advices on how to frighten off sharks. "_Gesticulate wildly,_" _said a lifeguard._ We flailed our arms. The gray did not falter. "_Give 'em a flood of bubbles,_" _said a helmet diver._ Dumas waited until the shark had reached his nearest point and released a heavy exhalation. The shark did not react. "_Shout as loud as you can,_" _said Hans Hass._ We hooted until our voices cracked. The shark appeared deaf. "_Cupric acetate tablets fastened to leg and belt will keep sharks away if you go into the drink,_" _said an Air Force briefing officer._ Our friend swam through the copper-stained water without a wink. His cold, tranquil eye appraised us. He seemed to know what he wanted, and he was in no hurry. . . .

Instinctively I felt my comrade move close to me, and I saw his hand held out clutching his belt knife. Beyond the camera and the knife, the gray shark retreated some distance, turned, and glided at us head-on.

We did not believe in knifing sharks, but the final moment had come, when knife and camera were all we had. I had my hand on the camera button and it was running, without my knowledge that I was filming the oncoming beast. The flat snout grew larger and there was only the head. I was flooded with anger. With all my strength I thrust the camera and banged his muzzle. I felt the wash of a heavy body flashing past and the shark was twelve feet away, circling us as slowly as before, unharmed and expressionless. I thought, _Why in hell doesn't he go to the_ *whale? The nice juicy whale. What did we ever do to him?*

The blue sharks now climbed up and joined us. Dumas and I decided to take a chance on the surface. We swam up and thrust our masks out of the water. The *Elie Monnier* was three hundred yards away, under the wind. We waved wildly and saw no reply from the ship. We believed that floating on the surface with one's head out of the water is the

classic method of being eaten away. Hanging there, one's legs could be plucked like bananas. I looked down. The three sharks were rising toward us in a concerted attack.

We dived and faced them. The sharks resumed the circling maneuver. As long as we were a fathom or two down, they hesitated to approach. It would have been an excellent idea for us to navigate toward the ship. However, without landmarks, or a wrist compass, we could not follow course.

Dumas and I took a position with each man's head watching the other man's flippers, in the theory that the sharks preferred to strike at feet. Dumas made quick spurts to the surface to wave his arms for a few seconds. We evolved a system of taking turns for brief appeals on the surface, while the low man pulled his knees up against his chest and watched the sharks. A blue closed in on Duma's feet while he was above. I yelled. Dumas turned over and resolutely faced the shark. The beast broke off and went back to the circle. When we went up to look we were dizzy and disoriented from spinning around under water, and had to revolve our heads like a lighthouse beacon to find the *Elie Monnier*. . . .

We were nearing exhaustion, and cold was claiming the outer layers of our bodies. I reckoned we had been down over a half hour. Any moment we expected the constriction of air in our

mouthpieces, a sign that the air supply nears exhaustion. When it came, we would reach behind our backs and turn the emergency supply valve. There was five minutes' worth of air in the emergency ration. When that was gone, we could abandon our mouthpieces and make mask dives, holding our breath. That would quicken the pace, redouble the drain on our strength, and leave us facing tireless, indestructible creatures that never needed breath. The movements of the sharks grew agitated. They ran around us, working all their strong propulsive fins, turned down and disappeared. We could not believe it. Dumas and I stared at each other. A shadow fell across us. We looked up and saw the hull of the *Elie Monnier's* launch. Our mates had seen our signals and had located our bubbles. The sharks ran when they saw the launch.

We flopped into the boat, weak and shaken. The crew were as distraught as we were. The ship had lost sight of our bubbles and drifted away. We could not believe what they told us; we had been in the water only twenty minutes. The camera was jammed by contact with the shark's nose.

ATTACKED BY A BIG FISH

Jacques Piccard is the son of the Swiss physicist Auguste Piccard (1884-1962), famous for his balloon ascents into the stratosphere (August 1932: 10.5 miles), who in 1946 turned his attention from the upper air to the ocean depths. With his father, the younger Piccard made several dives in a bathyscaph of the former's design, and in 1960, this time with an American naval officer, he descended to 35,800 feet (6.8 miles) in the Marianas Trench. The excerpt that follows, from his book *The Sun Beneath the Sea* (1971), tells of an attack by a swordfish on the little submarine *Ben Franklin,* then proceeding tranquilly northeast in the Gulf Stream. The improbable incident recalls, inevitably, the attack on the whaler *Essex* mounted a century and a half earlier by a furious whale (see "Oh, My God! Where Is the Ship?" on page 238).

It was while I was asleep—restlessly, because of the cold, the inevitable noise, and perhaps excessive fatigue as well—that the attack took place.

This event seemed to me so important that I wanted immediately to commit every possible detail to paper. At the moment it occurred, Ken Haigh, Frank Busby, and Erwin Aebersold were awake, so I brought them together and tried to get some agreement about the size of the aggressors, their characteristics, and the circumstances of the attack. It is very important to note such impressions promptly, for they change readily, even with the best will in the world and the greatest sincerity and objectivity. The way hunting and fishing stories proliferate and expand is well known. I determined to have this account utterly objective.

The incident occurred at 6:09 A.M. at a depth of 252 meters. No one was at the portholes. An exterior floodlight had been on all night. Frank Busby, working in the section of the stern that we called the laboratory, suddenly saw something glinting through the porthole. He rushed to the window and saw a magnificent swordfish of the kind that is known to live in the depths of the Gulf Stream and is among the handsomest trophies of the Florida fishermen. Frank had time to see that it was unquestionably a broadbill—that is, it had a large "beak" or "nose," unlike the marlin's which is rounded and narrower. The function of the sword is, it is thought, to impale fish the swordfish intends to eat, perhaps holding them in reserve for a few minutes while continuing to hunt and eating them eventually in a protected spot secure from possible rivals. Some swordfish exceed 4 meters in length: in the Gulf Stream fishermen often catch specimens 2 or 3 meters long. The one in question, according to Frank, could not have been more than 1.5 to 1.8 meters, but length is difficult to estimate exactly. Frank observes the swordfish for a few seconds, during which it seems very agitated and comes to take a close look into the porthole through which it itself is being observed. It appears to parade up and down in front of the window, dashing to and fro, not knowing how to interpret our presence, swimming a few meters and then returning, as though fascinated by our great Plexiglas eye. Suddenly it attacks, dashing straight forward and striking the hull of the mesoscaph with the point of the sword, aiming perhaps for the porthole but only hitting the steel of the hull 15 to 20 centimeters beneath the Plexiglas. Frank and Ken Haigh, not far from the porthole, both hear the impact clearly. Frank rushes to the bow of the mesoscaph to get his camera. When he returns the attacker has disappeared, but meanwhile Ken Haigh distinctly sees a second swordfish which, as though directing the attack from a distance, remains at a prudent remove, at the limit of our searchlight range. The whole incident lasted perhaps a minute. Erwin Aebersold, who was breakfasting in the bow of the mesoscaph, did not hear the blow and had seen nothing through the forward porthole.

Listening to this account, I thought of my two cameras which I had had ready at hand an hour before and with which I could have recorded so many details now gone forever. Forever? Who knows? Perhaps the incident will be repeated. Another attack of this sort—and this is not the least interesting part—had been observed in similar circumstances. The *Alvin,* a small submarine mostly designed by the engineer Al Vine of Woods Hole, had been the object of such an attack during the course of one of its numerous dives. That swordfish, less fortunate, had remained wedged in the submarine, his sword caught in the plastic and fiberglass superstructure. The pilot, not knowing whether there had been serious damage, decided to ascend; thus he brought back the fish so that it could be . . . taken to the harbor, shown to the Woods Hole zoologists, and eaten the same evening. . . .

Does an attack like this present any danger for a submarine? To tell the truth, I do not think so, but one can imagine extreme cases in which the situation might become critical. If the submarine, as a result of any cause whatever (errors of calculation, pilot error, enemy action), is at the point of rupture, the violent shock caused by a creature of this size striking at a particular point at a speed of some 10 meters a second, might make just the crucial difference. These are extreme condi-

tions, highly improbable. On the other hand, after the attack on the *Alvin,* specialists (in what field, I do not know) calculated that if the sword had struck at a certain angle exactly at the ring that holds the porthole, ring and porthole could have been removed, causing the destruction of the submarine (and an insoluble problem for investigators even if the vessel were recovered). As for our portholes, each is held in place by a steel ring secured by a sufficient number of high-resistance screws, so I consider that the hypothesis of such a rupture can safely be discarded. Obviously if a porthole were destroyed, the situation aboard would not be comfortable. At a depth of 250 meters the water would rush into the hull at a speed of some 70 meters a second and with a flow exceeding 1 cubic meter a second. In a few moments more water would have entered than could be compensated for with the emergency ballast and the various ballast tanks, and the overweighted hull would rapidly go to the bottom with no chance for its passengers to escape.

GOD'S LITTLE
UNDERWATER ACRE
In an article that appeared in ***Sports Illustrated*** **in September 1957, Clare Boothe Luce described, entertainingly, her recent experience of learning to dive off Bermuda.**

I see myself hauling my heavy tank-burdened body over the side of the *Wally III* and backing down the ladder. I am eager now to shed my weight under the sparkling waters. Happily, I let go. Splash, and down a few feet. I wait for my flippers to be thrown over the side. I tug them on, level off on my face, and look down.

There, twenty feet below, lies the liquid blue jungle of the barrier reef. The world of madrepores and polyps, where everything is endlessly living and endlessly dying to make the fretted vaults and cloistered crannies of the reefs, of rose coral, star coral and brain coral, coral with antlers and horns, coral formed like tree stumps, anemones and sponges; and crustaceans, worms and fishes. . . . And there in the midst of this wild calm jungle, lying ten feet deeper, I see a lovely sandy cave.

Along its walls the waving purple fronds of the sea's fans beckon me in. . . . I glide down to the cave slowly, at a gentle plane. I can see a hundred feet in every direction. As far as I can see, the colors are Gauguin's and Cézanne's and Seurat's. Beyond, the dark blue-green sea belongs to Dufy and Chagall. I'm almost on the cave. I throw back my head and my flippers' tips touch the shining floor. I feel like a bird lighting on a bough. I sink to the bottom of the cave and, lolling, look up at the even feathers of bubbles which fly up from my neck, expanding as they go into shining silver mushrooms, little pearly parachutes, seeking the far sun. Overhead, the bottom of a rowboat is a liquid yellow plate, and on the distant surface, the shadowy silhouette of the *Wally III* is a salver of spinach jade. Circling high, thirty feet above me, looking like little frogs, are a pair of skin divers with spears. They drift slowly along on top of the waters searching out snappers and rockfishes below.

I look around. Park is there. He is pointing a camera in a plastic case at me. His body is the color of polished amber, his short hair is a dandelion going to seed. Jeanne is there, on her knees, head down, fingering through the creamy sand. It flows like gauze through her fingers. Her hair is floating straight above her, a restless golden halo. She looks up as I sink beside her, and her eyes are smiling aquamarines.

She sees something and slides away, beckoning me to follow. We glide to the crannied wall, sink on our elbows and peer under a coral ledge. We see two crimson enameled wires and peer deeper and see an elegant lobster, rich with eggs made of old red Chinese lacquer. Jeanne tickles its antennae and it draws into its dark palace with mandarin dignity. She wishes to tease it more. I don't. I have only an hour to explore my enchanted liquid acre. Only an hour to find an angelfish. . . .

I drift up the crenelated sides of the cave. I begin to see they are deliciously full of mysterious holes. A delicate, slightly open mouth pokes out of one of them. I flipper slowly over to the hole and stop. It is the white beak of a rainbow parrot fish. I see his body, the length of my forearm. It is all purple and red and gold. I swoon softly closer. We eye one another. I, in what delight can he know? . . .

Gently I reach out hoping he will let me scratch his beak. He withdraws, flicks around, shoots out another hole and, squittering delicately, hovers in the clear water ahead. I pursue. He moves and hovers again. We repeat our little ballet.

Three little sergeant majors, gold with black stripes, draw across my chase. They tipple at me. I bubble at them. *Delighted to meet you, young gentlemen.* They pass, and I glide, like a gondola, among waving gorgonians, in and out of madreporic crevices. I am careful to skirt the ginger coral—the poison ivy of the sea. I am cautious with my hands and knees lest they be punctured by the waving black needles of the giant sea urchins, like pincushions in their coral waterpots. . . .

I no longer think whether I am cold or tired, or down too far, or breathing right. I no longer struggle against gravity. How can one struggle against what does not seem to exist? I am living in the sea, outside myself. All but my eyes, which are seeking that angelfish. . . .

Park taps me on the arm, points. Jeanne is examining something on the reef. We swoop down. Park makes a sign of a pistol pointing. Jeanne crawls along the pale pink and green lime-encrusted thing he is pointing at, and I crawl with her. I do not know that I am looking at the barrel of an ancient Spanish cannon from a wreck come to grief in the days of the conquistadors. I swim away. I prefer the great bonito that I see in the distance. (Had I known, I would have swum off anyway. I am definitely allergic to all artifacts, regardless of size, which are even remotely shaped like bobby pins.)

The bonito is a quarter of the size of me, and much prettier. Park follows with his camera, resigned to my disinterest in artifacts. . . .

Near a tiny waterpot, I meet a little fish, no larger than the palm of my hand. He charges my mask furiously. It is a demoiselle fish, spunkily guarding his coral *garconnière*, where his mistress lies sleeping. *If the demoiselles could talk they would talk like sharks, surely.*

Now I see a shimmering cloud moving toward me. It is a large school of small fry, curtaining a spear diver who searches the waters below, his long

steel spear glinting in the blue. I swim deliberately through it. The cloud shatters into a million soft glassy splinters all around my body, and reforms into a silver curtain in my wake. I turn to Park, laughing with glee. My mouth opens. Water rushes past my mouthpiece. I experience a moment of terror. I spit out the water through the tube, breathe slowly, spiral, and drop to the floor of the cave, and rest.

How long have I been here? I do not know. Time, under water, is not a mechanical thing. It is organic. You judge it by the strength and slant of the light, the warmth of your blood, the rhythm of your breathing. But for dark and cold, and weariness and lack of air, you might stay there forever and call it a minute. . . .

Now I notice with delight that a large rockfish weighing about thirty pounds is swimming in a friendly fashion at our flippers' tips. I test his friendship. I spurt away. He spurts after me. *Aha! Monsieur Cousteau! Let me present you Ulysses, Junior!*

Suddenly my rockfish friend whooshes away, toward a rock ledge. Too late. Overhead a skin-diver has been stalking him. The skin-diver comes down in a long powerful diagonal. His steel spear speeds through the water. My friend is impaled and is carried struggling and bleeding to the top.

I am angry. I breathe harder. I lie on a rock to rest.

I know about the feeding cycle. Little fish eat plankton, bigger fish eat the little fish. Why should I care if man then eats the big ones? Have not many fish eaten man down here? I remember Teddy Tucker's gold and emerald pectoral cross. . . . They have even dined on bishops.

I go cruising again in the gorgonian forest. And then—there, in a perforation of the coral maze, I find *my* treasure. I find the jewel of the lapidary sea, the rarest gem of ray serene the bright and fathomed caves of ocean bear. He is as large as two of my fingers. His body is all lapis lazuli; his brow is sprinkled with turquoise. He glows all over. I don't move, for I know now that a teasing movement will drive him away. Oh, to be a Saint Francis of Assisi among the Fish! Poor Saint Francis, born out of time, never to have met Brother Jewel Fish and Sister Sea Fan at their own level! What canticles you would have sung to them! What holy converse held with them about their Maker!

> Immense, of fishy form and mind,
> Squamous, omnipotent and kind:
> And under that Almighty Fin
> The littlest fish may enter in.

The jewel fish sinks, forever, from my eye. Never from my mind. I slide away. I still hope to see an angelfish, a heart-shaped angelfish, a Fra Angelico angelfish, a Queen of the Angelfish, in all her sunlit glory.

I see a shark instead. Out there where the waters grow dim, the ugly gray squaloid form is cruising toward us. My finger shoots like a rifle barrel, pointing it out to Park. Pete sees it, too, and flippers hard toward it. Park snaps its picture. Breathlessly watching, I sink to the floor of the reef. Park swings his camera toward my face to catch my expression. Then he swims after Pete. The shark disappears in the gloom. Overhead the spear divers are still floating and stalking. I remember that the blood of wounded fish sometimes attracts sharks. So does Park. He thumbs everyone up. Only Saint Francis would feel completely safe down here. The day is ended.

DEATH OF A YOUNG DIVER
It is always at their peril that fragile humans penetrate the deep, as we learn anew from this true story recounted by Jacques-Yves Cousteau in *The Living Sea* (1963, written with James Dugan). The occasion for young Serventi's fatal dive was the accidental loss of an anchor belonging to the *Calypso,* from which Cousteau and the others did their diving; the locale, in the Mediterranean off the French coast, was hard by Grand Congloué, site of the wreck of an ancient Greek merchantman loaded with amphorae.

Serventi said, "I observed the end of the chain very closely. It left a deep track in the mud until it caught in the rocks. It would be easy to follow the track back until we came to the break in the anchor chain."

I said, "But the working depth is very difficult—probably 200 to 230 feet."

Serventi said, "*Oui, Commandant.* But we can use three or four divers in succession, planting marker buoys along the chain track when they have to come up. I suggest using a cork float with a reel of fishing line and a small weight that we can drop when one of us becomes over-extended. The next man can go down the fishing line and take up the search. In two or three dives I'm sure we'll find the anchor without trouble."

I liked our new friend's ingenuity. "Okay," I said, "if the weather's right tomorrow, we'll try it."

Serventi said, "I volunteer as first diver."

Overnight we assembled several Serventi marker buoys. Next day,

November 6, the weather was propitious, and *Calypso* sailed for Grand Congloué. Since we were shorthanded and Saôut was on leave, I decided to risk anchoring between Riou and Grand Congloué. Most of the eleven people aboard would be needed on launch operations, leaving too few to maneuver *Calypso* on station.

I went in the launch with Raud, Falco, and the new pair, who had been with us less than a week but were already solid members of the team. At the battleship buoy Serventi put on the triple-pack Aqua-Lung, strapped a depth gauge and chronometer on his wrist, and secured the marker buoy to his belt. I said, "Remember, you are not allowed more than ten minutes at that depth. If you tire sooner, drop the buoy and come up. You must decompress for three minutes at ten feet."

"*Oui, Commandant,*" said Serventi. He molded his lips over the mouth grip, hurdled into the water, showed his flukes, and drove down the chain. The mistral was dying reluctantly; the water was still choppy. I stood at the bow, watching the diver's bubbles. Falco, the next man to go down, checked his lung and joined me in the always anxious scrutiny when an agitated surface threatens to smother the breathing track of a man below.

About three hundred yards from the can buoy we became unsure of distinguishing his bubbles. I called on Raud to look sharp from the helm, glanced at my watch, and said, "He's been down eight minutes." The boat was in line with Serventi's previous course, but we could not find his breathing track. At nine minutes my throat went dry. A half-minute later, I had to hold onto myself firmly to avoid becoming rattled. Something warned me that the worst had happened. At ten minutes I said, "Falco. You understand. Hurry up if you want to bring him back alive." Without a word, Falco went in.

I had too much experience to have any hope for Serventi. Whatever had happened, had happened too deep. He would be very hard to find. I suppressed the dreadful images crossing my mind and took automatic actions. "Raud!" I said. "Go to *Calypso* while he's down. We need more divers." We sped to the ship, and I called on Yves

Girault and Jacques Ertaud to get ready to dive immediately....

Falco surfaced off the side, struggling for breath, and gasped, "He's unconscious. Very deep. I ran out of air. Quick! Quick!"

"Girault," I said, "try to empty his lungs by bringing him up head down, holding his feet." This was his last chance for life. Girault brought him up in that way. We put Serventi into the one-man recompression chamber and rocked it rhythmically to provoke artificial respiration while *Calypso* ran to Marseilles at top speed, radioing for a truck to meet us. We put the chamber onto the truck and raced to a big recompression chamber. There Dr. Nivelleau went in with Serventi and tried every known method of reanimation. After agonizing hours we had to abandon our efforts. Kientzy, Simone, and I drove away to tell Serventi's mother.

The medical examiner gave heart failure as the cause of death. Girault had found the diver 220 feet down, apparently stricken while trying to affix his fishing line to one of the concrete-block anchors laid by *Léonor Fresnel.* Serventi was buried at Hyères with a Grand Congloué amphora on his grave.

A FLASH IN THE DEEP
In the 1930's William Beebe began to make deep-sea dives in a reinforced spherical chamber, lowered by cable from a boat, called a bathysphere. Through its portholes he observed a host of underwater wonders, the first human being ever to do so. Though understandably dazzled by these sights, he was also, as a trained naturalist, eager to interpret their meaning and significance.

I have spoken of the three outstanding moments in the mind of a bathysphere diver, the first flash of animal light, the level of eternal darkness, and the discovery and description of a new species of fish. There is a fourth, lacking definite level or anticipation, a roving moment which might very possibly occur near the surface or at the greatest depth, or even as one lies awake, days after the dive, thinking over and reliving it. It is, to my mind, the most important of all, far more so than the discovery of new species. It is the explanation of some mysterious occurrence, of the display of some inexplicable habit which has taken place before our eyes, but which, like a sublimated trick of some master fakir, evades understanding.

This came to me on this last deep dive at 1,680 feet, and it explained much that had been a complete puzzle. I saw some creature, several inches long, dart toward the window, turn sideways and—explode. This time my eyes were focused and my mind ready, and at the flash, which was so strong that it illumined my face and the inner sill of the window, I saw the great red shrimp and the outpouring fluid of flame. This was a real Fourth Moment, for many "dim gray fish" as I had reported them, now resolved into distant clouds of light, and all the previous "explosions" against the glass became intelligible. At the next occurrence the shrimp showed plainly before and during the phenomenon, illustrating the value in observation of knowing what to look for. The fact that a number of the deep-sea shrimps had this power of defense is well known, and I have had an aquarium aglow with the emanation. It is the abyssal complement of the sepia smoke screen of a squid at the surface.

Before this dive was completed, I had made a still greater refinement in discernment, perceiving that there were two very distinct types of defense clouds emitted, one which instantly diffused into a glowing mist or cloud, and the other which exploded in a burst of individual sparks, for all the world like a diminutive roman candle. Both occurred at the window or near it a number of times, but it was the latter which was the more startling.

HUNTING FOR BODIES
In 1955 a group of French, Belgian, English, and American youths converged on Vigo Bay, on Spain's west coast, to search for galleons sunk there in 1702 by Anglo-Dutch raiders. During three seasons of diving the young treasure seekers came to know the Galician fishing people of the area, and at least once—as recounted in this grisly yet touching excerpt from the book *Treasure Divers of Vigo Bay*, by an American member of the expedition, John S. Potter, Jr.—the visitors were able to render their hosts a grim but greatly appreciated service.

On the stormy morning of November 10, 1957, at low tide, the drowned and battered bodies of two seamen were found at the seaward entrance of the passage between the Cies Islands, where they had been thrown up by waves onto the rocks. Simultaneously a chilling report spread among the closely related families of Moana, on the north shore of Vigo Bay. One of their fishing ships was missing at sea. Aboard were twenty-five men and boys— fathers and sons from nearly every home in the little community.

Newspaper headlines of the next day confirmed the terrible news: "Consternation Throughout the Bay over the Catastrophe of the *Ave del Mar*—1,000 people affected by the great tragedy." Sometime during the night of the ninth, the twenty-ton fishing ship, groping her way back to port through fog and rain, had struck the reefs off Point Galera and been dashed to pieces by heavy seas. Aside from some wood splinters and the two bodies there was no trace of her or her crew. The annual fiesta of Moana had just begun. Sounds of laughter and fireworks abruptly changed into hysterical weeping of widows as a tide of grief rolled over the stunned, bereaved pueblo.

Two helmet divers were sent out to look for the bodies of the victims. They dropped below the surface from their lines and air hoses, landing on a sea bed of jagged rock peaks and twisting ravines, hidden under a submarine jungle of seaweed, undulating in the strong swells. Limited in mobility over the terrain by their cumbersome equipment, they could only rise from the weeds and drop into new spots, again and again, through manipulation of the air volume within their suits. After two days of futile searching they gave up without having found a piece of wreckage. . . .

Our free divers were working a little to the south of Carrumeiro when an unfamiliar fishing launch approached, flag at half-mast. On the stern were two wooden coffins. A rope was thrown to the *Dios te Guarde*. From the launch stepped a short, pale-faced man, dressed entirely in black. He introduced himself: "I am the owner of the *Ave del Mar*, and the father of her captain." In a trembling, exhausted voice, repeating himself frequently, he told our team that he had been in the Cies Islands for three days and nights without sleep, waiting for the ocean to return the body of his son and the other crew members, nearly all of whom were his cousins or nephews. Offering two thousand pesetas for each body that we could recover, he begged, "Won't you help me find my son?"

Robert Sténuit, Florent Ramaugé and John Nathan were moved by the pathetic plea. Turning down the remunerative offer, they agreed immediately. Within an hour the *Dios te Guarde* was going out through the Freo de la Porta—the passage between the two principal Cies Islands. On the ocean end a strange and mildly disagreeable odor was noticed in the air. It grew stronger as the estimated site of the shipwreck was reached. Rough waves were breaking against the nearby rocks, and a slight brownish tinge was visible in the spume. Our local companion, Faustino Otero Lino, stared at the spray for a few moments, then shuddered. "Corpse soup," he muttered.

Robert made the first dive, reaching bottom at fifty feet. The visibility was surprisingly good, but the familiar thick blanket of seaweed lay over the rocks, covering all but a few bare pinnacles. Robert spotted a shredded fishing net tangled on one of these. Then he encountered a splintered wood board. There was no other sign of the boat. Florent and Johnny dived after him and found scattered pieces of wreckage.

For the following two days stormy weather prevented the *Dios te Guarde* from reaching this dangerous site. Then the wind and waves subsided, and a search pattern was set up off the reefs, with the divers combing the bottom at forty-foot intervals. Florent had made six parallel runs when he came across a fuel tank. On the succeeding dive

Robert discovered a water tank jammed into a ravine and nearby a broken section of the propeller shaft. A submarine cliff jutted up on the shoreward side. Reasoning that this would halt the drift of ocean-impelled wreckage, he followed its base to a sunken, sand-floored arena. It was strewn with broken remnants of the *Ave del Mar*— the rudder, twisted iron fragments, wood splinters, and several fishing boots.

A pale apparition caught his eye. Swimming closer, Robert found himself hovering over an alabaster-white cadaver, stripped of clothing, moving gently with the wave motions on the sand. His arms were outstretched limply from a grotesquely swollen trunk, and a faceless ivory skull, with shreds of cheek skin waving gently around hollow eye sockets, grinned up at him. Two more cadavers lay on the sand. Swimming farther, Robert came across another body that looked tiny even in the magnified submarine world. It was that of the ship's boy, only fourteen. He was lying on his back, partly cloaked in seaweed, little arms placed in a cross over his chest. On his sea-floor bed, the child seemed resting in peaceful slumber. When he had finished his tour, Robert had counted eleven bodies. Naked, or clothed in blue trousers and here and there a plaid shirt, the crew had obviously been asleep at the moment of the shipwreck. He had still not found the *Ave del Mar* and wondered why the corpses had assembled in this place. Then he realized that it was the center of an eddy. The currents were assembling here material and bodies which had been swept from the shattered wreck. Robert let himself rise a few yards over the sand and gazed down through the unusually clear water, contemplating the gruesome task at hand. Then he returned to the surface. On the *Dios te Guarde* he told the others, "I have counted eleven."

"Eleven what?"

"Bodies."

"What do they look like?"

"White like marble," replied Robert. "Like statues, only they move sometimes, very small, like children asleep. Some are not entire—the sea has not been gentle with them." Shouts crossed the water to the nearby fishing launch from Moana, crowded with close relatives of the victims. They seemed relieved to hear the news but gave no other sign of emotion.

Robert returned to the submarine graveyard with Florent and Johnny, carrying two lengths of rope. While Johnny searched for the missing ship Robert and Florent gingerly approached the cadavers, then separated, each selecting a group to string together on his rope. The flesh felt soft, and involuntary shudders ran through the divers as they lifted weightless bodies, passing the rope under their arms and knotting it in front.

After attaching four corpses Robert found that the rope would not reach the others, which were some distance away. He tugged at the ones which he had tied. They jumped up from the sand. Swimming hard, Robert pulled his ghastly train across the bottom, watching the cadavers rise to their feet and follow him, arms and legs waving in a macabre dance. He stopped at the next group and bent over the closest body. A footless leg brushed against his cheek. Turning, he saw the first four corpses, still advancing under their momentum, prancing overhead. As quickly as he could he completed the job, trying to avoid looking more than necessary at his cargo. . . .

Florent was on the barge, and his salvage of three corpses floated in the water near the diving ladder. Johnny had found the sunken ship, which had been battered into kindling wood, and attached a sling to the motor, with which to raise it later. A Spanish naval launch from Vigo had arrived on the scene. Faustino, King-of-the-Grapes, and the divers climbed aboard to help load the corpses. There was muttering among the navy crew, then the petty officer told King-of-the-Grapes that the bodies would have to be loaded on the *Dios te Guarde*—that our boat should return them to Moana. They didn't want the navy craft smelling from the bodies. Johnny exploded, "For Christ's sake, what about *our* boat? We brought them up. The least they can do . . ." Turning to Faustino he said angrily, "Tell them that if they want the bodies they'll have to take them back themselves. We'll help with the loading."

The navy crew withdrew into a huddle at the bow of their launch while Faustino, Juan, and King-of-the-Grapes lifted the corpses, smelling of death, from the water and stacked them on the poop. Now they were inert, no longer possessed of their leisurely, wave-given movements. As the last of the bodies were piled on the deck the sound of vomiting was heard from the bow.

On the following day, which was Sunday, a solemn mass interment took place in the Moana cemetery. The entire community, wearing black, had assembled, as well as government and naval officials from Vigo and Pontevedra. Beneath the visible manifestation of heartache in the quietly sobbing women and grim-faced men ran an undercurrent of gratitude to the

hombres-ranas for the return of the eleven bodies being laid to rest. These deeply religious people attached a profound importance to burial of their dead under the sacred soil of a cemetery blessed by the representative of God. Here, through the ages, their departed kinsmen would receive the benefit of future special orations. And on the resurrection before the final judgment they could rise in their entirety to face their Maker. . . .

During succeeding weeks a subtle change was noted in the attitude of people who addressed the members of our team. Beneath the joking "And the water? Isn't it cold?" ran a thread of new intimacy and respect. But the work was not over. There were still twelve unrecovered bodies. The weather prevented resumption of the human salvage for four days, while sheets of spray exploded upward from the rocks adjacent to the wreck site. Then, on Friday, the *Dios te Guarde* was carefully steered out through the passage and anchored a hundred yards from shore with her bow facing the incoming waves which lifted and dropped her in monotonous regularity. During the preceding days the sea had begun in earnest its work of decomposition on the remaining bodies. The sickening sweet smell was noticeable downward for half a mile and over the work site it was nearly overpowering. The ocean reeked with death.

A little pale, Robert lowered himself into the noxious water and hung from the back of the rowboat as Faustino rowed him as close to the sand pocket as he could. Then Robert dived into a maelstrom of opposing currents. Swept to and fro like a leaf in the wind, he fought his way to the graveyard, where he reasoned other bodies would be assembling. He was correct. Five cadavers awaited him, horribly mutilated, rolling and somersaulting across the sand in the wave motions. The water was no longer clear but clouded with thousands of white specks. Biting firmly on his mouthpiece to prevent water seeping in, he swam into the soup of human flesh particles and began chasing the cavorting bodies. With all five tied firmly to his rope, Robert thought he had seen a glimpse of still another chalky cadaver at the limit of his visibility and rose to study the terrain. His eyes were drawn in macabre fascination to the animated forms on his line. He grew philosophical, down there on the ocean bottom, cold and alone in this world of the dead. How sudden, he thought, can be the transition from life.

Something tapped him lightly on the elbow.

His heart stopped. A violent shiver ran down his body as he spun around in a lightning-flash reaction. Then he closed his eyes and drew a deep breath. A piece of broken wood had drifted against him. The five cadavers were delivered to the navy launch, and Robert told the others his unnerving experience. "I turned my head so fast that the mask slipped sideways," he said with a reflective shudder.

Day after day Robert, Florent, Johnny and Owen Lee—who had just returned from a vacation—dived on the underwater assembly point and surfaced with corpses. Finally, when they terminated their efforts, twenty-three of the *Ave del Mar*'s complement had been

returned to Moana and buried. Only two were still lost at sea, voyaging silently through the submarine depths to unknown destinations.

Several days and many hot scrubs after the last dive into the "corpse soup" the clinging sweetish odor was finally washed from the divers' bodies. Often aftereffects lingered on. Nightmares of approaching hordes of cadavers continued for weeks, and so did a weird daytime visual phenomenon. Frequently when interviewing Galician fishermen, Robert or Florent or Johnny had the illusion that the face of the man with whom he was talking had turned into a grinning ivory skull.

On my return to Vigo I realized how deeply the team's deed had been appreciated when a friend handed me an editorial by our newspaper chronicler, Bene. Captioned "Praise for the Amphibious Men," it lauded their work over the *Ave del Mar* and concluded with:

"In this permanent battlefield of the sea, with its evident risks, we have seen how the amphibious men threw themselves forward, not in their accustomed search for treasure, but in the search of their dead brothers of the sea. We saw them go, without awaiting the calm summer days—which for this mission of the deepest human sentiment would be too late—into this difficult and dangerous work, time and again, in search of those lost bodies, abandoned to the whim of the waves and the greed of the fish. These they tenderly raised to the surface to be given Christian burial in their parochial cemeteries. This deed deserves full praise and public gratitude, for it was carried out in the spirit of civic feeling and human solidarity."

LAUGHING SEA COWS
In the late 1950's Clay Blair, Jr., an American editor, led an expedition to Yucatán to salvage treasure from the submerged wreck of an eighteenth-century ship. That the attempt succeeded was thanks in no small measure to the skill of his chief diver, Robert Marx, then considered by many America's foremost diver. In his account of the expedition, *Diving for Pleasure and Treasure* (1960),

Blair describes a bizarre underwater confrontation between Marx and a specimen of a seldom-seen breed, the manatee.

While on one of these scouting expeditions to the Yucatán mainland, Marx had an extraordinary underwater experience.

Passing Punta Soliman with a boatload of tourists, as was his custom, he ordered the boat anchored. Then, alone, he dived over the side with face plate, snorkel, and flippers at a point where he had previously found what appeared to be an ancient grappling hook, believed to date from the Montejo period.

Swimming along the coral reef, Marx was suddenly aware of some strange thing in the water nearby. Taking a deep breath, he submerged and eased

toward it. As Marx closed in, he slowed his pace. He could see that the submerged thing was enormous—seemingly the size of a whale. Marx stared wide-eyed at the "thing" which, according to Marx, "had a very human-like face." It returned the stare and then seemed to laugh. "He—he—he—he—he."

Marx, stupefied by fear and excitement, backed slowly toward the boat and shouted for the Mexican boatman, who could see the huge shape underwater near Marx, to load and pass to him the powerful speargun, which the Meistrells had furnished us for the second expedition. While the awe-struck tourists looked on, Bob grabbed the gun and closed in on the 20-foot beast. He brought the gun to within a foot of the face, noting the monster had whiskers and "arms, hands, and breasts, just like a woman."

In the excitement both the boatman and Marx had forgotten to cock the gun. When Marx nervously pulled the trigger, the released spear simply slid out and lightly touched the monster. When that happened, the beast charged past

Marx "like a freight train" and disappeared in the distance, "laughing" insanely as it went.

By then Marx had regained his senses and realized at once what he had been dealing with: a manatee, sometimes called a "sea cow." These rare, huge, lumbering beasts of the sea, with their humanlike faces and breasts, are believed to have inspired the myth of the mermaid. Few men in recent times have seen one. No diver had ever speared one. Marx was determined not to let it get away. He searched the water for hours. Then he traded his gun for a camera, put on an aqualung, and swam in toward the reef.

Some distance from the anchored boat, Marx noted a slight change in the temperature and visibility of the water, indicating fresh water flowing out to sea. Turning, he followed the flow until, close to the reef, he spied a cave near the ocean bottom. Camera in hand, he dived down and poked his head into the opening. It was an exit point of some underground fresh-water river or spring.

Moved by curiosity, Marx swam cautiously inside the cave. It was pitch-black but he determined to go "another ten feet." Having swum those ten feet he decided to advance another ten. As he slid along in the inky blackness, small fish, panicked by his presence, rushed past, brushing his face plate and body. Then all at once Marx heard a familiar sound in the distance: "He—he—he—he—he." It was unmistakably the manatee. Its "laughter" seemed to come from deep inside the cave.

Marx swam on until, far in the distance, he could see a faint patch of light. Reaching this, he surfaced into a heretofore undiscovered, jungle-ringed, fresh-water lagoon. Marx thought that it must be a home for the manatees who came and went through the underground cave connecting the lagoon and the sea.

Submerging again, Marx explored the bottom of the lagoon. Rounding a corner of a rock, about ten feet down, he came face to face with the manatee. There were two others, smaller in size (no more than twelve or fifteen feet), behind the first. Quickly Marx brought his camera to bear, but when he moved his arms all three manatees, "laughing"

hideously, swam for the bottom and buried themselves in clouds of mud. Marx waited for the water to clear and made one more effort with the camera, but when he approached them the manatees again stirred up the silt. It was then near sunset, so Marx felt his way underwater back to the cave, and swam out to sea.

CAVE DIVING
In his *Silent World* Jacques-Yves Cousteau recounts the gripping story of a dive that took place many miles from the sea and very nearly proved fatal.

Our worst experience in five thousand dives did not come in the sea but in an inland water cave, the famous Fountain of Vaucluse near Avignon. The renowned spring is a quiet pool in a crater under a six-hundred-foot limestone cliff above the River Sorgue. A trickle flows from it the year around, until March comes; then the Fountain of Vaucluse erupts in a rage of water which swells the Sorgue to flood. It pumps furiously for five weeks, then subsides. The phenomenon has occurred every year of recorded history.

The fountain has evoked the fancy of poets since the Middle Ages. Petrarch wrote sonnets to Laura by the Fountain of Vaucluse in the fourteenth century. Frédéric Mistral, our Provençal poet, was another admirer of the spring. Generations of hydrologists have leaned over the fountain, evolving dozens of theories. They have measured the rainfall on the plateau above, mapped the potholes in it, analyzed the water, and determined that it is an invariable fifty-five degrees Fahrenheit the year round. But no one knew what happened to discharge the amazing flood.

One principle of intermittent natural fountains is that of an underground siphon, which taps a pool of water lying higher inside the hill than the water level of the surface pool. Simple overflows of the inner pool by heavy rain seeping through the porous limestone did not explain Vaucluse, because it did not entirely respond to rainfall. There was either a huge inner reservoir or a series of inner caverns and a system of

siphons. Scientific theories had no more validity than Mistral's explanation: "One day the fairy of the Fountain changed herself into a beautiful maiden and took an old strolling minstrel by the hand and led him down through Vaucluse's waters to an underground prairie, where seven huge diamonds plugged seven holes. 'See these diamonds?' said the fairy. 'When I lift the seventh, the fountain rises to the roots of the fig tree that drinks only once a year.'" Mistral's theory, as a matter of fact, possessed one more piece of tangible evidence than the scientific guesses. There is a rachitic hundred-year-old fig tree hooked on the vertical wall at the waterline of the annual flood. Its roots are watered but once a year.

A retired Army officer, Commandant Brunet, who had settled in the nearby village of Apt, became an addict of the Fountain as had Petrarch six hundred years before. The Commandant suggested that the Undersea Research Group dive into the Fountain and learn the secret of the mechanism. In 1946 the Navy gave us permission to try. We journeyed to Vaucluse on the twenty-fourth of August, when the spring was quiescent. . . .

The arrival of uniformed naval officers and sailors in trucks loaded with diving equipment set off a commotion in Vaucluse. We were overwhelmed by boys, vying for the privilege of carrying our air cylinders, portable decompression chamber, aqualungs and diving dresses up the wooded trail to the Fountain. Half the town, led by Mayor Garcin, dropped work and accompanied us. They told us about the formidable dive into the Fountain made by Señor Negri in 1936. What a bold type was this Señor Negri! He had descended in a diving suit with a microphone inside the helmet through which he broadcast a running account of his incredible rigors as he plunged one hundred and twenty feet to the inferior elbow of a siphon. Our friends of Vaucluse recalled with a thrill the dramatic moment when the voice from the depths announced that Señor Negri had found Ottonelli's zinc boat!

We knew about Negri and Ottonelli, the two men who had preceded us into the fountain, Ottonelli in 1878. We greatly admired Ottonelli's dive in the primitive equipment of his era. We were somewhat mystified by Señor Negri, a salvage contractor of Marseilles, who had avoided seeing us on several occasions when we sought firsthand information on the topography of the Fountain. We had read his diving report, but we felt deprived of the details he might have given us personally.

The helmet divers described certain features to be found in the Fountain. Ottonelli's report stated that he had alighted on the bottom of a basin forty-five feet down and reached a depth of ninety feet in a sloping tunnel under a huge triangular stone. During the dive his zinc boat had capsized in the pool and slid down through the shaft. Negri said he had gone to one hundred and twenty feet, to the elbow of a siphon leading uphill, and found the zinc boat. The corrosion-proof metal had, of course, survived sixty years of immersion. Negri reported he could proceed no further because his air pipe was dragging against a great boulder, precariously balanced on a pivot. The slightest move might have toppled the rock and pinned him down to a gruesome death.

We had predicated our tactical planning on the physical features described by the pioneer divers. Dumas and I were to form the first *cordée*—we used the mountain climber's term because we were to be tied together by a thirty-foot cord attached to our belts. Negri's measurements determined the length of our guide rope—four hundred feet—and the weights we carried on our belts, which were unusually heavy to allow us to penetrate the tunnel he had described and to plant ourselves against currents inside the siphon.

What we could not know until we had gone inside the Fountain was that Negri was overimaginative. The topography of the cavern was completely unlike his description. Señor Negri's dramatic broadcast was probably delivered just out of sight of the watchers, about fifty feet down. Dumas and I all but gave our lives to learn that Ottonelli's zinc boat never existed. That misinformation was not all of the burden we carried into the Fountain: the new air compressor with which we filled the

breathing cylinders had prepared a fantastic fate for us.

We adjusted our eyes to the gloom of the crater. Mayor Garcin had lent us a Canadian canoe, which was floated over the throat of the Fountain, to anchor the guide rope. There was a heavy pig-iron weight on the end of the rope, which we wanted lowered beforehand as far as it would go down. The underwater entry was partially blocked by a huge stone buttress, but we managed to lower the pig iron fifty-five feet. Chief Petty Officer Jean Pinard volunteered to dive without a protective suit to attempt to roll the pig iron down as far as it was possible. Pinard returned lobster-red with cold and reported he had shoved the weight down to ninety feet. He did not suspect that he had been down further than Negri.

I donned my constant-volume diving dress over long woolens, under the eyes of an appreciative audience perched around the rocky lip of the crater. My wife was among them, not liking this venture at all. Dumas wore an Italian Navy frogman outfit. We were loaded like donkeys. Each wore a three-cylinder lung, rubber foot fins, heavy dagger and two large waterproof flashlights, one in hand and one on the belt. Over my left arm was coiled three hundred feet of line.... Dumas carried an emergency micro-aqualung on his belt, a depth gauge and a *piolet,* the Alpinist's ice axe. There were rock slopes to be negotiated: with our heavy ballast we might need the *piolet.*

The surface commander was the late Lieutenant Maurice Fargues, our resourceful equipment officer. He was to keep his hand on the guide line as we transported the pig iron down with us. The guide rope was our only communication with the surface. We had memorized a signal code. One tug from below requested Fargues to tighten the rope to clear snags. Three tugs means pay out more line. Six tugs was the emergency signal for Fargues to haul us up as quickly as possible.

When the *cordée* reached Negri's siphon, we planned to station the pig iron, and attach to it one of the lengths of rope I carried over my arm. As we climbed on into the siphon, I would unreel this line behind me. We

believed that our goal would be found past Negri's teetering rock, up a long sloping arm of the siphon, in an air cave, where in some manner unknown the annual outburst of Vaucluse was launched.

Embarrassed by our pendant gadgetry and requiring the support of our comrades, we waded into the pool. We looked around for the last time. I saw the reassuring silhouette of Fargues and the crowd jutting around the amphitheater. In their forefront was a young *abbé,* who had come no doubt to be of service in a certain eventuality.

As we submerged, the water liberated us from weight. We stayed motionless in the pool for a minute to test our ballast and communications system. Under my flexible helmet I had a special mouthpiece which allowed me to articulate under water. Dumas had no speaking facility, but could answer me with nods and gestures.

I turned face down and plunged throught the dark door. I rapidly passed the buttress into the shaft, unworried about Dumas's keeping pace on the thirty-foot cord at my waist. He can outswim me any time. Our dive was a trial run: we were the first *cordée* of a series. We intended to waste no time on details of topography but proceed directly to the pig iron and take it on to the elbow of Negri's siphon, from which we would quickly take up a new thread into the secret of the Fountain. In retrospect I can also find that my subconscious mechanism was anxious to conclude the first dive....

I glanced back and saw Didi gliding easily through the door against a faint green haze. The sky was no longer our business. We belonged now to a world where no light had ever struck. ... A disc of light blinked on and off in the darkness, when my flashlight beam hit rock. I went head down with tigerish speed, sinking by my overballast, unmindful of Dumas. Suddenly I was held by the belt and stones rattled past me. Heavier borne than I, Dumas was trying to brake his fall with his feet. Big limestone blocks came loose and rumbled down around me. A stone bounced off my shoulder. I remotely realized I should try to think. I could not think.

Ninety feet down I found the pig iron standing on a ledge. It did not appear in the torch beam as an object from the world above, but as something germane to this place. Dimly I recalled that I must do something about the pig iron. I shoved it down the slope. It roared down with Dumas's stones. During this blurred effort I did not notice that I lost the lines coiled on my arm. I did not know that I had failed to give Fargues three tugs on the line to pay out the weight. I had forgotten Fargues, and everything behind. The tunnel broke into a sharper decline. I circled my right hand continuously, playing the torch in spirals on the clean and polished walls. I was traveling at two knots. I was in the Paris subway. I met nobody. There was nobody in the Metro, not a single rock bass. No fish at all.

At that time of year our ears are well trained to pressure after a summer's diving. *Why did my ears ache so?* Something was happening. The light no longer ran around the tunnel walls. The beam spread on a flat bottom, covered with pebbles. It was earth, not rock, the detritus of the chasm. I could find no walls. I was on the floor of a vast drowned cave. I found the pig iron, but no zinc boat, no siphon and no teetering rock. My head ached. I was drained of initiative.

I returned to our purpose, to learn the geography of the immensity that had no visible roof or walls, but rolled away down at a forty-five-degree incline. I could not surface without searching the ceiling for the hole that led up to the inner cavern of our theory.

I was attached to something, I remembered. The flashlight picked out a rope which curled off to a strange form floating supine above the pebbles. Dumas hung there in his cumbersome equipment, holding his torch like a ridiculous glowworm. Only his arms were moving. He was sleepily trying to tie his *piolet* to the pig-iron line. His black frogman suit was filling with water. He struggled weakly to inflate it with compressed air. I swam to him and looked at his depth gauge. It read one hundred and fifty feet. The dial was flooded. We were deeper than that. We were at least two hundred feet down, four hundred feet away from the surface at the bottom of a crooked slanting tunnel.

We had rapture of the depths, but not

the familiar drunkenness. We felt heavy and anxious, instead of exuberant. Dumas was stricken worse than I. This is what I thought: *I shouldn't feel this way in this depth. . . . I can't go back until I learn where we are. Why don't I feel a current? The pig-iron line is our only way home. What if we lose it? Where is the rope I had on my arm?* I was able in that instant to recall that I had lost the line somewhere above. I took Dumas's hand and closed it around the guide line. "Stay here," I shouted. "I'll find the shaft." Dumas understood me to mean I had no air and needed the

safety aqualung. I sent the beam of the flashlight around in search of the roof of the cave. I found no ceiling.

Dumas was passing under heavy narcosis. He thought I was the one in danger. He fumbled to release the emergency lung. As he tugged hopelessly at his belt, he scudded across the drowned shingle and abandoned the guide line to the surface. The rope dissolved in the dark. I was swimming above, mulishly seeking for a wall or a ceiling, when I felt his weight tugging me back like a drifting anchor, restraining my search.

Above us somewhere were seventy fathoms of tunnel and crumbling rock. My weakened brain found the power to conjure up our fate. When our air ran out we would grope along the ceiling and suffocate in dulled agony. I shook off this thought and swam down to the ebbing glow of Dumas's flashlight.

He had lost the better part of his consciousness. When I touched him, he grabbed my wrist with awful strength and hauled me toward him for a final experience of life, an embrace that would take me with him. I twisted out of

his hold and backed off. I examined Dumas with the torch. I saw his protruded eyes rolling inside the mask.

The cave was quiet between my gasping breaths. I marshaled all my remaining brain power to consider the situation. Fortunately there was no current to carry Dumas away from the pig iron. If there had been the least current we would have been lost. *The pig iron must be near.* I looked for that rusted metal block, more precious than gold. And suddenly there was the stolid and reassuring pig iron. Its line flew away into the dark. . . .

In his stupor, Didi lost control of his jaws and his mouthpiece slipped from his teeth. He swallowed water and took some in his lungs before he somehow got the grip back into his mouth. Now, with the guide line beckoning, I realized that I could not swim to the surface, carrying the inert Dumas, who weighed at least twenty-five pounds in his waterlogged suit. I was in a state of exhaustion from the mysterious effect of the cave. We had not exercised strenuously, yet Dumas was helpless and I was becoming idiotic.

I would climb the rope, dragging Dumas with me. I grasped the pig-iron rope and started up, hand over hand, with Dumas drifting below, along the smooth vertical rock.

My first three hand holds on the line were interpreted correctly by Fargues as the signal to pay our more rope. He did so, with a will. I regarded with utter dismay the phenomenon of the rope slackening and made superhuman efforts to climb it. Fargues smartly fed me rope when he felt my traction. It took an eternal minute for me to form the tactic that I should continue to haul down rope, until the end of it came into Fagues's hand. He would never let that go. I hauled rope in dull glee.

Four hundred feet of rope passed through my hands and curled into the cavern. And a knot came into my hands. Fargues was giving us more rope to penetrate the ultimate gallery of Vaucluse. He had efficiently tied on another length to encourage us to pass deeper.

I dropped my rope like an enemy. I would have to climb the tunnel slope like an Alpinist. Foot by foot I climbed the fingerholds of rock, stopping when I lost my respiratory rhythm by exertion and was near to fainting. I drove myself on, and felt that I was making progress. I reached for a good hand hold, standing on the tips of my fins. The crag eluded my fingers and I was dragged down by the weight of Dumas.

The shock turned my mind to the rope again and I received a last-minute remembrance of our signals: six tugs meant pull everything up. I grabbed the line and jerked it, confident that I could count to six. The line was slacked and snagged on obstacles in the four hundred feet to Maurice Fargues. *Fargues, do you not understand my situation? I was at the end of my strength. Dumas was hanging on me.*

Why doesn't Dumas understand how bad he is for me? Dumas, you will die, anyway. Maybe you are already gone. Didi, I hate to do it, but you are dead and you will not let me live. Go away, Didi. I reached for my belt dagger and prepared to cut the cord to Dumas.

Even in my incompetence there was something that held the knife in its holster. *Before I cut you off, Didi, I will try again to reach Fargues.* I took the line and repeated the distress signal, again and again. *Didi, I am doing all a man can do. I am dying too.*

On shore, Fargues stood in perplexed concentration. The first *cordée* had not been down for the full period of the plan, but the strange pattern of our signals disturbed him. His hard but sensitive hand on the rope had felt no clear signals since the episode a few minutes back when suddenly we wanted lots of rope. He had given it to us, eagerly adding another length. *They must have found something tremendous down there,* thought Fargues. He was eager to penetrate the mystery himself on a later dive. Yet he was uneasy about the lifelessness of the rope in the last few minutes. . . .

Up from the lag of rope, four hundred feet across the friction of rocks, and through the surface, a faint vibration tickled Fargues's finger. He reacted by standing and grumbling, half to himself, half to the cave watchers, *"Qu'est-ce que je risque? De me faire engueuler?"* (What do I risk? A bawling out?) With a set face he hauled the pig iron in.

I felt the rope tighten. I jerked my hand off the dagger and hung on. Dumas's air cylinders rang on the rocks as we were borne swiftly up. A hundred feet above I saw a faint triangle of green light, where hope lay. In less than a minute Fargues pulled us out into the pool and leaped in the water after the senseless Dumas. Tailliez and Pinard waded in after me. I gathered what strength I had left to control my emotions, not to break down. I managed to walk out of the pool. Dumas lay on his stomach and vomited. Our friends stripped off our rubber suits. I warmed myself around a flaming caldron of gasoline. Fargues and the doctor worked over Dumas. In five minutes he was on his feet, standing by the fire. I handed him a bottle of brandy. He took a drink and said, "I'm going down again." . . .

Dumas's recuperative powers put the color back on him and his mind cleared. He wanted to know why we had been drugged in the cavern. In the afternoon another *cordée,* Tailliez and Guy Morandière, prepared to dive, without the junk we had carried. They wore only long underwear and light ballast, which rendered them slightly buoyant. They planned to go to the cavern and reconnoiter for the passage which led to the secret of Vaucluse. Having found it they would immediately return and sketch the layout for the third *cordée,* which would make the final plunge.

From the diving logs of Captain Tailliez and Morandière, I am able to recount their experience, which was almost as appalling as ours. Certainly it took greater courage than ours to enter the Fountain from which we had been luckily saved. In their familiarization period just under the surface of the pool, Morandière felt intense cold. They entered the tunnel abreast, roped together. Second *cordée* tactics were to swim down side by side along the ceiling.

When they encountered humps sticking down from the roof, they were to duck under and return to follow closely the ceiling contour. Each hump they met promised to level off beyond, but never did. They went down and down. Our only depth gauge had been ruined, but the veteran Tailliez had a sharp physiological sense of depth. At an estimated one hundred and twenty feet he halted the march so they might study their subjective sensations. Tailliez felt the first inviting throbs of rapture of the depths. He knew that to be impossible at a mere twenty fathoms. However, the symptoms were pronounced.

He hooted to Morandière that they should turn back. Morandière maneuvered himself and the rope to facilitate Tailliez's turnabout. As he did so, he heard that Tailliez's respiratory rhythm was disorderly, and faced his partner so that Tailliez could see him give six pulls on the pig-iron rope. Unable to exchange words under water, the team had to depend on errant flashlight beams and understanding, to accomplish the turn. Morandière stationed himself below Tailliez to conduct the Captain to the surface. Tailliez construed these activities to mean that Morandière was in trouble. Both men were slipping into the blank rapture that had almost finished the first *cordée.*

Tailliez carefully climbed the guide line. The rope behind drifted aimlessly in the water and a loop hung around his shoulders. Tailliez felt he had to sever the rope before it entangled him. He whipped out his dagger and cut it away. Morandière, swimming freely below him, was afraid his mate was passing out. The confused second *cordée* ascended to the green hall light of the Fountain. Morandière closed in, took Tailliez's feet and gave him a strong boost through the narrow door. The effort upset Morandière's breathing cycle.

We saw Tailliez emerge in his white underwear, Morandière following through the underwater door. Tailliez broke the surface, found a footing and walked out of the water, erect and wild-eyed. In his right hand he held his dagger, upside down. His fingers were bitten to the bone by the blade and blood flowed down his sodden woolens. He did not feel it.

We resolved to call it a day with a shallow plunge to map the entrance of the Fountain. . . . The final reconnaissance of the entrance shaft passed without incident.

It was an emotional day. That evening in Vaucluse the first and second *cordées* made a subjective comparison of cognac narcosis and rapture of the Fountain. None of us could relax, thinking of the enigmatic stupor that had overtaken us. We knew the berserk intoxication of *l'ivresse des grandes profondeurs* at two hundred and twenty feet in the sea, but why did this clear, lifeless limestone water cheat a man's mind in a different way?

Simone, Didi and I drove back to Toulon that night, thinking hard, despite fatigue and headache. Long silences were spaced by occasional suggestions. Didi said, "Narcotic effects aren't the only cause of diving accidents. There are social and subjective fears, the air you breathe . . ." I jumped at the idea. "The air you breathe!" I said. "Let's run a lab test on the air left in the lungs."

The next morning we sampled the cylinders. The analysis showed 1/2000 of carbon monoxide. At a depth of one hundred and sixty feet the effect of carbon monoxide is sixfold. The amount we were breathing may kill a man in twenty minutes. We started our new Diesel-powered free-piston air compressor. We saw the compressor sucking in its own exhaust fumes. We had all been breathing lethal doses of carbon monoxide.

THE DEEPEST TRENCH

In 1960 Jacques Piccard and Lieutenant Don Walsh of the United States Navy descended in the bathyscaph *Trieste* to the very bottom of the Challenger Deep in the Marianas Trench, the deepest known depression on the earth's surface. Pending the possible discovery of a deeper spot somewhere, their record is virtually guaranteed to stay unbroken.

Thirty-four thousand feet—no bottom . . . 35,000 feet, only water and more water . . . 36,000 feet, descending smoothly at sixty feet per minute. Now we were at the supposed depth of the Challenger Deep. Had we found a new hole or was our depth gauge in error? Then a wry thought—perhaps we'd missed the bottom!

. . . 1256, Walsh's eyes were glued to the echo sounder. I was watching alternately through the port and at the fathometer. Suddenly, we saw black echoes on the graph. "There it is, Jacques! It looks like we have found it!" Yes, we had finally found it, just forty-two fathoms down.

While I peered through the port preparing to touch-down, Walsh called off the soundings. "Thirty-six fathoms, echo coming in weakly—thirty-two—twenty-eight—twenty-five—twenty-four—now we are getting a nice trace. Twenty-two fathoms—still going down—yes, this is it! Twenty—eighteen—fifteen—ten—makes a nice trace now. Going right down. Six fathoms—we're slowing up, very slowly, we may come to a stop. You say you saw a small animal, possibly a red shrimp about one inch long? Wonderful, wonderful! Three fathoms—you can see the bottom through the port? Good—we've made it!"

The bottom appeared light and clear, a waste of snuff-colored ooze. We were landing on a nice, flat bottom of firm diatomaceous ooze. Indifferent to the nearly 200,000 tons of pressure clamped on her metal sphere, the *Trieste* balanced herself delicately on the few pounds of guide rope that lay on the bottom, making token claim, in the name of science and humanity, to the ultimate depths in all our oceans—the Challenger Deep.

The depth gauge read 6,300 fathoms—37,800 feet. The time—1306 hours.

The depth gauge was originally calibrated in Switzerland for pressures in fresh water, considering water a noncompressible fluid as is usual in these cases. After the dive, the gauge was recalibrated by the Naval Weapons Plant in Washington, D. C. Then several oceanographers (especially Dr. John Knauss of Scripps Institution of Oceanography and Dr. John Lyman of the National Science Foundation) applied corrections for salinity, compres-

sibility, temperature, and gravity. Agreement was reached that the depth attained was 35,800 feet—or 5,966 fathoms. This computed depth agrees well with the deepest sonic soundings obtained by American, British and Russian oceanographic ships, all of which had reported the round-trip sounding time in the Challenger Deep at almost precisely fourteen seconds. The corrected figure confirmed that the *Trieste* had indeed attained the *deepest* hole in the trench.

And as we were settling this final fathom, I saw a wonderful thing. Lying on the bottom just beneath us was some type of flatfish, resembling a sole, about one foot long and six inches across. Even as I saw him, his two round eyes on top of his head spied us—a monster of steel—invading his silent realm. Eyes? Why should he have eyes? Merely to see phosphorescence? The floodlight that bathed him was the first real light ever to enter this hadal realm. Here, in an instant, was the answer that biologists had asked for decades. Could life exist in the greatest depths of the ocean? It could! And not only that, here apparently, was a true, bony teleost fish, not a primitive ray or elasmobranch. Yes, a highly evolved vertebrate, in time's arrow very close to man himself.

Slowly, extremely slowly, this flatfish swam away. Moving along the bottom, partly in the ooze and partly in the water, he disappeared into his night. Slowly too—perhaps everything is slow at the bottom of the sea—Walsh and I shook hands.

Walsh keyed the UQC four times, the prearranged signal for "on the bottom." We assumed that we were far beyond the range of voice communication. Simply as a matter of routine and perhaps to enjoy the companionship of his own voice, Walsh called on the voice circuit. "*Wandank, Wandank.* This is the *Trieste.* We are at the bottom of the Challenger Deep at sixty-three hundred fathoms. Over."

To our complete astonishment a voice from nowhere drifted through to us. "*Trieste, Trieste,* this is *Wandank.* I hear you faint but clear. Will you repeat your depth? Over."

Walsh repeated the depth and added, "Our ETA on the surface is seventeen hundred hours. Over."

The voice came back to us charged with excitement, "*Trieste*, this is *Wandank*. Understand. Six three zero zero fathoms. Roger. Out."

A FICTIONAL MAELSTROM
Edgar Allan Poe's short story "A Descent Into the Maelstrom" has inspired chills of terror in generations of readers. The natural phenomenon that excited Poe's imagination was the Moskenstraumen, a tidewater whirlpool in the Lofoten Islands of northwestern Norway. Formed when the strong tidal current flows through an irregular channel south of Moskenesoya Island, it is about two and a half miles wide and may at its center reach a speed of ten feet per second. Although it never resembles the gaping abyss of Poe's imagination, it has claimed many unlucky vessels.

I was now trying to get the better of the stupor which had come over me, and to collect my senses so as to see what was to be done, when I felt somebody grasp my arm. It was my elder brother, and my heart leaped for joy, for I had made sure that he was overboard—but the next moment all this joy was turned to horror—for he put his mouth close to my ear, and screamed out the word "*Moskoe-strom!*"

No-one will ever know what my feelings were at that moment. I shook from head to foot as if I had had the most violent fit of the ague. I knew what he meant by that one word well enough—I knew what he wished to make me understand. With the wind that now drove us on, we were bound for the whirl of the Strom, and nothing could save us.

You perceive that in crossing the Strom *channel*, we always went a long way up above the whirl, even in the calmest weather, and then had to wait and watch carefully for the slack, but now we were driving right upon the pool itself, and in such a hurricane as this! "To be sure," I thought, "we shall get there just about the slack—there is some little hope in that"—but in the next moment I cursed myself for being so great a fool as to dream of hope at all.

By this time the fury of the tempest had spent itself; or perhaps we did not feel it so much, as we scudded before it, but at all events the seas, which had at first been kept down by the wind and lay flat and frothing, now got up into absolute mountains. A singular change, too, had come over the heavens. Around in every direction it was as black as pitch, but nearly overhead there burst out, all at once, a circular rift of clear sky—as clear as I ever saw—and of a deep, bright blue—and through it there blazed forth the full moon with a lustre that I never before knew her to wear. She lit up everything about us with the greatest distinctness—but, oh God, what a scene it was ....

I now made one or two attempts to speak to my brother—but in some manner which I could not understand, the din had so increased that I could not make him hear a single word, although I screamed at the top of my voice in his ear. Presently he shook his head, looking as pale as death, and held up one of his fingers as if to say "*listen!*"

At first I could not make out what he meant—but soon a hideous thought flashed upon me. I dragged my watch from its fob. It was not going. I glanced at its face by the moonlight, and then burst into tears as I flung it far away into the ocean. *It had run down at seven o'clock! We were behind the time of the slack, and the whirl of the Strom was in full fury!*

Well, so far we had ridden the swells very cleverly, but presently a gigantic sea happened to take us right under the counter, and bore us with it as it rose—up—up—as if into the sky. I would not have believed that any wave could rise so high. And then down we came with a sweep, a slide and a plunge that made me feel sick and dizzy, as if I was falling from some lofty mountaintop in a dream. But while we were up I had thrown a quick glance around—and that one glance was all-sufficient. I saw our exact position in an instant. The Moskoe-strom whirlpool was about a quarter of a mile dead ahead—but no more like the every-day Moskoe-strom than the whirl, as you now see it, is like a mill-race. If I had not known where we were, and what we had to expect, I should not have recognised the place at all. As it was I involuntarily closed my eyes in horror. The lids clenched themselves together as if in a spasm.

It could not have been more than two minutes afterwards when we suddenly felt the waves subside, and were enveloped in foam. The boat made a sharp half-turn to larboard, and then shot off in its new direction like a thunderbolt. At the same moment the roaring noise of the water was completely drowned in a kind of shrill shriek—such a sound as you might imagine given out by the water-pipes of many thousand steam-vessels letting off their steam all together. We were now in the belt of surf that always surrounds the whirl, and I thought, of course, that another moment would plunge us into the abyss, down which we could only see indistinctly on account of the amazing velocity with which we were borne along. The boat did not seem to sink into the water at all, but to skim like an air-bubble upon the surface of the surge. Her starboard side was next the whirl, and on the larboard arose the world of ocean we had left. It stood like a huge writhing wall between us and the horizon. . . . Scarcely had I secured myself in my new position, when we gave a wild lurch to starboard, and rushed headlong into the abyss. As I felt the sickening sweep of the descent, I had instinctively tightened my hold upon the barrel, and closed my eyes. For some seconds I dared not open them—while I expected instant destruction. But moment after moment elapsed. I still lived. I took courage and looked once again upon the scene.

Never shall I forget the sensation of awe, horror and admiration with which I gazed about me. The boat appeared to be hanging, as if by magic, midway down, upon the interior surface of a funnel vast in circumference, prodigious in depth, and whose perfectly smooth sides might have been mistaken for ebony, but for the bewildering rapidity with which they spun around, and for the gleaming and ghastly radiance they shot forth, as the rays of the full moon, from that circular rift amid the clouds which I have already described, streamed in a flood of golden glory along the black walls, and far away down into the inmost recesses of the abyss.

In this view of Poe's maelstrom by British illustrator Arthur Rackham, a fisherman clings to a barrel as tree trunks and ships swirl past.

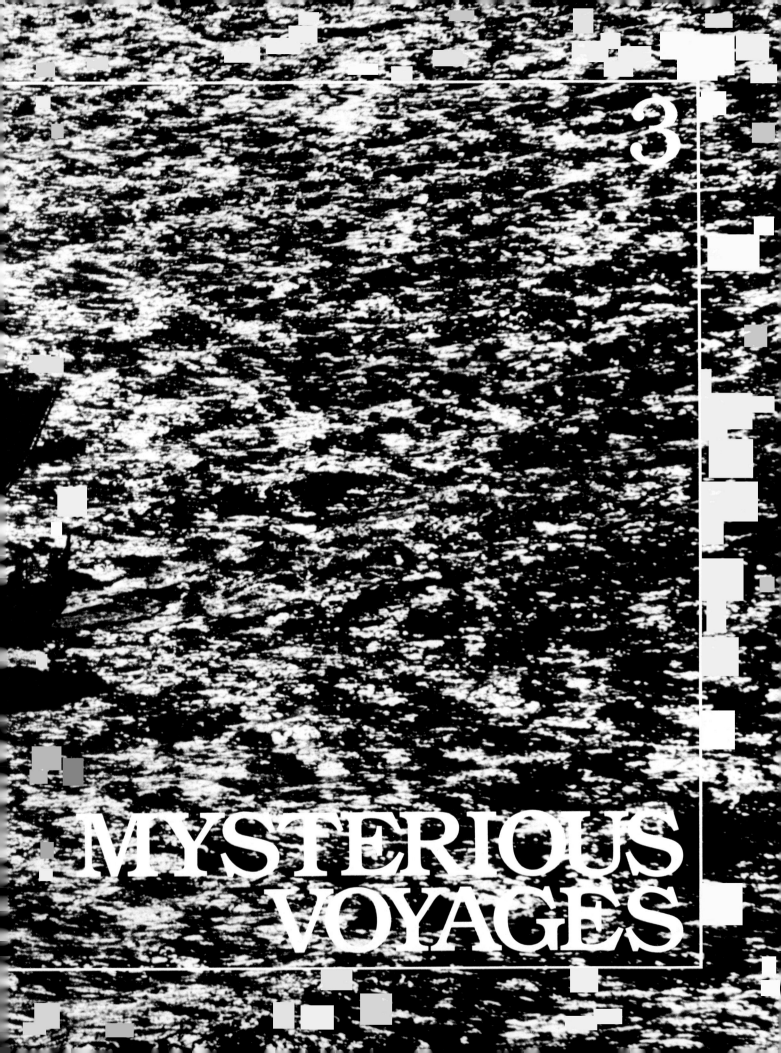

3

MYSTERIOUS VOYAGES

The great scowlike vessel shuddered in the wave trough, its timbers chafing. Breakers curled and crashed down on the flat upper deck, pounding on the wooden hull. By the captain's reckoning the storm had been going on for over a month, though days and nights could be reckoned only roughly in such overwhelming darkness. Scored by waves and winds and sleeting rain, the ship lurched forward on its uncharted voyage.

Inside the cavernous hull the air dripped moisture, an ammoniacal compound of excretions and decay. The thin clay lamps in their brackets flickered, smoked, at times went out. Somewhere in the shadows lions roared, wolves howled, cattle lowed, sheep baaed, men shouted imprecations; a din, a bedlam, the terrified chatter of monkeys, the scream of a macaw, wailing women, the slosh of bilge. And when the rain finally stopped and the men, desperate for air, tentatively opened a few hatches, there was nothing outside but a wild and raging sea from which the sun-ball rose scarlet and ominous. A flood it was beyond all floods.

More months of rudderless drifting followed, the ship still buffeted by winds, though the cloud rack was breaking up now and the waves beginning to subside. Calmer days followed. The captain had the hatches thrown open, offal carted out, stores set right, cages cleaned, and dead and dying animals tossed overboard. As a turn of the wind diminished the waters, the first hilltops emerged. The captain loosed one of his caged ravens. For a while the bird circled, then disappeared. Still hopeful, the captain released a dove, which soared upward, found no place to land, and returned to the ship. A week later another dove was released. This one flew out of sight, eventually to return with an olive leaf in its beak, green sign of the earth's renewal. Being a prudent man the captain waited another week before releasing a third dove. This time the bird flew off and did not return. The ship itself had grounded on a bar or ledge on a mountain. The waters continued to recede. The captain, who was

MYSTERIOUS VOYAGES

TRAVELERS IN ANCIENT TIMES

by Francis Russell

A magisterial Noah watches the descent of the animals from the ark in this anonymous seventeenth-century engraving.
PRECEDING PAGES: *A modern recreation of a Polynesian boat glides over calm seas in an attempt to retrace the route of early voyagers across the Pacific.*

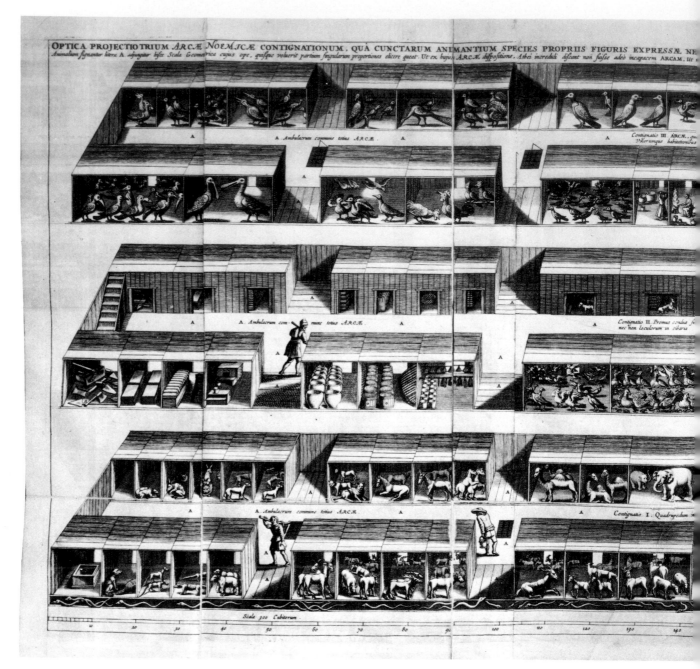

of course Noah, knew then that he could disembark, free his cargo of livestock, and lead his family from the ark's fetid interior. They had been aboard just 371 days.

Such is the legend of Noah's Ark, accepted literally by Jews and Christians through the centuries until quite recent times, accepted even today in the backwaters of fundamentalism. As set down in Genesis, God instructed Noah:

Make thee an ark of gopher wood; rooms shalt thou make in the ark, and shall pitch it within and without with pitch. And this *is the fashion* which thou shalt make it *of*: The length of the ark *shall be* three hundred cubits, the breadth of it fifty cubits, and the height of it thirty cubits. A window shalt thou make in the ark, and in a cubit shalt thou finish it above; and the door of the ark shalt thou set in the side thereof; *with* lower, second, and third *stories* shalt thou make it.

Translated into modern dimensions, the ark was 450 feet long, 75 feet wide, 45 feet in height, with three decks each about 14 feet high. Nothing that size would be seen again until 1885, when the Cunard Line launched the *Etruria*. Technically minded biblicists have determined that the ark's construction required 280,000 cubic feet of timber, or between 9,000 and 13,000 planks. Edged stone or possibly bronze tools were used—for this was before the age of iron—and

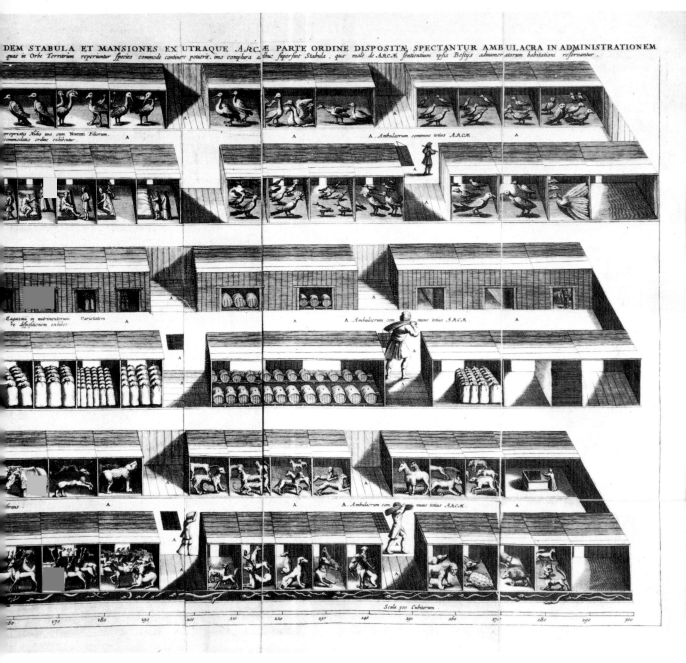

Taking the Bible at its word, a seventeenth-century Dutch artist created this precise plan of the three-tiered ark. Among its passengers he included a pair of unicorns, along with more familiar birds, animals, and reptiles.

since there were no nails, the planks must have been joined in interlocking sections. At the time Noah began his ark he was, according to Genesis, over five hundred years old, and his backyard shipbuilding would take him and his sons eighty-one years.

The ark's capacity was equal to that of about 569 freight cars. As to the number of animals, estimates vary. Fishes, mollusks, most worms, many insects and reptiles, amphibians, whales, and other marine animals could accommodate themselves to deluge conditions indefinitely. But by biblicist estimates there would have been some 25,000 pairs of land animals forced to seek shelter on the ark. To feed and tend such

a menagerie would seem an impossible task for only eight people—Noah, his wife, and their three sons and daughters-in-law—unless animals had, as biblicists have suggested, conveniently hibernated. Not all the animals, however, slept through that long voyage. According to a Mohammedan version, Noah neglected to bring cats on board. Soon the mice started multiplying, mice being able to breed when they are

In this medieval bronze bas-relief from a cathedral in Sicily, Noah welcomes two sheep to the ark. In another panel (opposite page) he and his wife look out from a tiny ark perched precariously on two pinnacles of Mount Ararat.

less than a month old; in a year's time the ark would have been overrun. Just as the mice began to get underfoot and overwhelming, the lion sneezed and two cats came out of his nostrils to take care of the mice!

The ark legend of a life-preserving voyage above a drowned earth was formed in Mesopotamia, that cradle of history between the Euphrates and Tigris rivers. Elaborated through generations of oral repetition, as is the way with legends, it holds a core of fact. Folk memories tenaciously retained the image of a great flood, a primeval catastrophe that engulfed the ancient Tigro-Euphrates plain. Some men survived it, floating on rafts or wattle boats, until in centuries of telling the men became one man and his family, the flood world-encompassing. The ancient world was believed to float like a saucer on the vast waters of the deep. About 4250 B.C.—if one can fix the date by Sumerian dynasties recorded as having reigned since the flood—a cataclysm upset the saucer.

In 1929 Sir Leonard Woolley, the archaeologist, while excavating the successive layers of the Sumerian civilization of Ur of the Chaldees, came on a bank of clay at the 150-foot level. That packed clay, six feet thick, sharply divided the Sumerian civilization above

it from the relics of an earlier people below. The clay's texture showed by its thickness that an unparalleled inundation had occurred, the biblical Flood, no less.

Such a flood in that extended alluvial plain might well have seemed to drown the world. In Genesis "all the fountains of the great deep [were] broken up, and the windows of heaven were opened." An Austrian geologist Eduard Suess at the beginning of this century was of the opinion that the deluge was a disastrous combination of a hurricane at the height of the annual Tigro-Euphrates inundation and a violent earthquake in the Persian Gulf that produced gigantic waves to add to subterranean waters bursting through the fissured Mesopotamian plain. "The rising of great quantities of water from the depths," Suess wrote, "is a phenomenon which is the characteristic accompaniment of earthquakes in the alluvial districts of great rivers."

From this devastating flood the legends developed—Sumerian, Babylonian, Hebrew, Greek. Cuneiform inscriptions on clay tablets recovered from buried Sumerian cities give the earliest, if fragmentary, versions of the legend. These are absorbed and reconstructed in the Babylonian Gilgamesh epic of about 2000 B.C. A version of the epic inscribed on twelve large tablets was discovered toward the middle of the last century among the ruins of the palace library of the Assyrian king Ashurbanipal at Nineveh.

The young ruler Gilgamesh hears the story of the Deluge from Utnapishtim, the Babylonian Noah, who was warned by Ea, the god of the ocean: "Man of Shuruppak, tear down your house, build a ship! Abandon your possessions, save your life. Bring into the ship the seed of all living creatures."

On the fifth day I laid its framework [Utnapishtim told Gilgamesh]. One acre was its floor space. One hundred and twenty cubits each was the height of its walls; one hundred and twenty cubits measured each side of its deck. I laid the shape of the outside and fashioned it. Six lower decks I built into it, dividing it into seven stories. . . .

Whatever I had of silver I loaded aboard her. Whatever I had of gold I loaded aboard her. Whatever I had of the seed of all living creatures I loaded aboard her. After I had brought all my family and relatives into the ship, I brought in the game of the field, the beasts of the field, and all the craftsmen to go into it. . . .

As soon as the first shimmer of morning beamed a black cloud came up. By evening a destructive rain was falling. The weather was frightful to behold. The raging of Adad [the god of storm and rain] reached to heaven and turned all light to darkness. He broke the land like a pot. For a day the

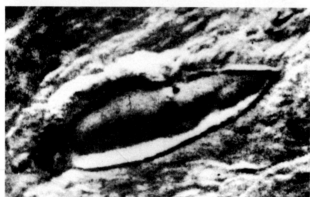

Turkish soldiers (top) take part in one of the searches for the ark on Mount Ararat, in 1959. The detail from an aerial photograph (bottom) shows what some true believers identified as the ark. In the picture at right, the snow-capped mountain top is seen across a cloud-filled valley.

tempest blew, swept over the people like a battle. No man could see his fellow. . . . Six days and six nights the wind blew, the rain poured down, the tempest and the flood overwhelmed the land.

When the seventh day arrived, the tempest, the invading flood subsided. The sea grew quiet, the storm abated, the flood ceased. I opened a window and light fell upon my face. I looked upon the sea. All was silent and all mankind had turned to mud. The land was as level as a flat roof. I bowed and sat down and wept. I looked in all directions for the boundaries of the sea. At a distance of twelve double-hours a stretch of land emerged. On Mount Nisir the ship landed. Two days Mount Nisir held the ship fast and did not it move. . . . When the seventh day arrived I sent forth a dove and let her go. The dove flew away and came back to me; there was no resting place, and so she returned. Then I sent a swallow and let her go. The swallow flew away and came back to me; there was no resting place and so she returned. Then I sent

forth a raven and let her go. The raven flew away, and when she saw that the waters had abated she ate, she flew about, she cawed, and did not return. Then I sent forth all to the four winds and offered a sacrifice. I poured out a libation on the peak of the mountain.

The parallels between the Genesis account, written down about 550 B.C. during the Babylonian Captivity, and Tablet Eleven, dating a century earlier, show clearly enough that the biblical Deluge derives from earlier Babylonian epics. Utnapishtim's ark, in the shape of a cube, is twice the size of Noah's rectangular vessel and approximates the bulk of the *Queen Mary*. But aside from the impossible size and shape of the

In these depictions of the biblical story, Jonah is being delivered directly into the mouth of the "great fish." The gilt-enamel panel above is from a twelfth-century Viennese altarpiece; the bas-relief at right is on a fourth-century Italian reliquary.

ark, some of the details in both the Sumerian and biblical texts ring true to the practices of the time. Both ships are described as coated with pitch, a substance used to waterproof the earliest wattle-built vessels, of which the original ark was no doubt one. Both captains released birds, this being a common method in extended voyages for determining by their flight the direction of the nearest shore. Both captains after disembarking proceeded to sacrifice to their deities.

Turkey's snow-capped Ararat, 17,000 feet high and taller than any mountain in Europe, was early identified as the landing place of the ark and became a sacred mountain. God, it was believed, did not wish man to climb it. Travelers' tales held that the ark was still perched on the summit. Josephus, the Jewish historian of the first Christian era, mentioned Ararat three times in his *Antiquities of the Jews.* "The Armenians call the spot the Landing Place," he wrote, "for it was there that the Ark came safe to land, and they show relics of it to this day." Isidore of Seville in his *Etymologies,* compiled about 610, said that "even to this day wood remains of it are to be seen there." During and after the Crusades, when the relics craze swept Europe, enterprising Armenians did a brisk trade in slivers of wood from the ark. Sir John Mandeville, after visiting the Ararat region in 1356, wrote in his *Travels:* "And some men say that they have seen and touched the Ark, and put their fingers in the parts where the fiend went out when Noah said 'Benedicte.' " In medieval times it was so commonly accepted that the ark was still on Ararat that merchants used the expression "under Noah's Ark" as a synonym for Armenia.

The first to climb Ararat's peak was a German doctor, J. J. Friedrich von Parrot, who in 1829 placed a cross on the summit. On the way he visited two monasteries and was shown pieces of the ark but saw no sign of it on the mountain. His ascent brought more climbers, a plethora by the century's end, and hearsay tales multiplied of those who had seen the ark, touched it, and even gone aboard and seen the still-intact animal stalls and cages. Perhaps the most bizarre of these "arkivists" was a Persian who styled himself "His Chaldean Excellency, the Venerable Monsignor, the Zamorrian, Earl of the Great House of Nouri," and who in addition claimed to be a prince of Nouri and the patriarchal archdeacon of Babylon. He said that on an 1887 climb up Ararat he had "found the Ark

wedged in the rocks and half filled with snow and ice . . . that it was made of dark beams of very thick wood." A decade earlier Sir James Bryce, devoutly convinced of the Bible's historical accuracy, had conducted his own ark explorations on Ararat. At the mountain's 13,000-foot level he found a piece of frozen wood that he believed was from the ark, though it was probably a fragment of some cross a pilgrim had planted there.

In this century a number of expeditions have been launched to find the ark that Bible literalists, mostly from small American fundamentalist sects, insist still exists. About two hundred people have claimed at various times to have seen it, though the claims when examined closely dissolve in Ararat mists. After the Second World War a Frenchman, Fernand Navarra, led three Ararat expeditions and in 1955 brought back a piece of wood he said he cut from the ark, which he had seen through the ice. His two books, *The Forbidden Mountain* and *Noah's Ark: I Touched It,* made his fortune. A piously earnest American who had climbed Ararat half a dozen times in fruitless search of the ark accused Navarra of bringing ancient pieces of wood secretly from France and burying them where they could be "discovered" later. The Holy Ground Changing Center of Texas displayed a photograph of the ark that they had made on Ararat with a telescopic lens. It showed the prow of the ark and even the planking, but on careful examination it turned out to be no more than a crudely retouched picture of a rock. And so the will-o'-the-wisp of the ark continues to entice the pious. Meanwhile, Ararat has become a challenge to secular mountaineers, three of whom died on its summit slopes in the 1960's.

Another biblical voyage, rivaling Noah's in its enduring imaginative qualities, was that of Jonah. Despite Noah, the Jews were never a seafaring people. Indeed, they had no word for "mariner" until they borrowed it from the Babylonian. Jonah's voyage is that of a passenger. Fleeing from God's command to denounce the wickedness of Nineveh, the renegade prophet took passage on a ship going to Tarshish. "But the Lord sent out a great wind into the sea, and there was a mighty tempest in the sea, so that the ship was like to be broken." The mariners fixed on their alien passenger as a man who must have angered the gods. "Then said they unto him, What shall we do unto thee, that the sea may be calm unto us?" Jonah, guilt-

Poseidon (below, in a bronze statuette from the second century B.C.) delayed Ulysses' return home because he was angry with him for blinding the sea god's son, the Cyclops Polyphemus. Ulysses is depicted in a Roman bronze statue (opposite page) as a weary wanderer, frustrated at every port of call.

tormented, told them to cast him into the sea. Reluctant at first to drown the stranger, the mariners tried to row their boat to land, but when they could make no headway "they took up Jonah, and cast him forth into the sea: and the sea ceased from her raging." Propitiation of Heaven through human sacrifice was commonplace enough, but Jonah before he could drown was swallowed by a "great fish." "And Jonah was in the belly of the fish three days and three nights" until it vomited him out on land. Jonah and the great fish derived from popular mythology. Parallels exist in Egyptian, Indian, and late Greek legends. The great fish itself is a variety of a Babylonian sea monster called in the Old Testament by such names as Rahab, the Dragon, the Serpent. "Three days and three nights" is merely the conventional expression for a short time. It may well be that beyond these great fish legends there lies some ancient actuality, a man swallowed or at least dragged under by a sea monster. Whatever the fact behind the legend, something of the kind has happened at least twice in modern times.

In 1863 a Cape Cod whaler, Peleg Nye, fell from a longboat directly into the mouth of a harpooned sperm whale. He struggled to escape, but the whale's jaws caught him just below the knees. The whale sounded, dragging the man so deep that he lost consciousness. Then the mortally wounded whale relesed Nye, who bobbed to the surface and was picked up still alive by his fellow sailors.

The most singular instance on record of a whale's swallowing a man—or so we are soberly informed—occurred in 1891 when the whaling ship *Star of the East* came upon a great school of sperm whales. One whale, wounded by a bomb lance thrown from a whaleboat, turned on the boat and crushed it in his jaws. The sailors flung themselves into the sea. But just as the steersman, James Bartley, struck the water the whale lunged, opened its mouth, and swallowed him.

Later that day a dead whale floated to the surface and the whalers spent the next two days removing its blubber. When they cut open the stomach they could see a man's body outlined through the membranes. Carefully slicing away the muscles, they uncovered Bartley, still alive though unconscious, smeared with the whale's blood and his body a lurid purple. After they had washed him and forced brandy down his throat, he regained partial consciousness, but kept thinking he was being consumed in a fiery furnace. On the voyage home he recovered completely. Later he described his underwater voyage:

I remember very well from the moment that I jumped from the boat and felt my feet strike some soft substance. I looked up and saw a big ribbed canopy of light pink and white descending over me, and the next moment I felt myself drawn downward, feet first, and I realized that I was being swallowed by a whale. I was drawn lower and lower; a wall of flesh surrounded me and hemmed me in on every side, yet the pressure was not painful, and the flesh easily gave way like soft India-rubber before my slightest movement.

Suddenly I found myself in a sack much larger than my body but completely dark; and my hand came in contact with several fishes, some of which seemed to be still alive, for they squirmed in my fingers, and slipped back to my feet. Soon I felt a great pain in my head, and my breathing became more and more difficult. At the same time I felt a terrible heat; it seemed to consume me, growing hotter and hotter. My eyes became coals of fire in my head, and I believed every moment that I was condemned to perish in the belly of a whale. It tormented me beyond all endurance, while at the same time the awful silence of the terrible prison weighed me down. I tried to rise, to move my arms and legs, to cry out. All action was now impossible, but my brain seemed abnormally clear; and with a full comprehension of my awful fate, I finally lost consciousness.

This very nearly incredible account came to the attention of the editor of the prestigious *Journal des Debats*, Henri de Parville, in Paris. So uncertain of its authenticity was de Parville that he held the account for four years, but when it stood up to scrupulous checking, he published it in 1896.

Second only to the Bible in the imagery of Western man are the *Iliad* and the *Odyssey*, the tale of Troy and the tale of Ulysses' years of voyaging. Ever since the oral tales of the *Odyssey* were written down by Homer, readers have been asking what seabound actuality is concealed in the episodic poem. How much is based on real voyages? Are the places to which Ulysses traveled real or the poem a pure myth? Even in classical times the matter was much debated. The geographer and astronomer Eratosthenes, of so exact a mind that in 250 B.C. he was able to estimate the earth's circumference with surprising accuracy, considered the Odysseyan voyages to be as mythic as the bag of winds that Aeolus gave Ulysses. A century later the grammarian Crates thought that the itinerary of

Ulysses took him to the unknown Baths of Ocean beyond the Straits of Gibraltar. But Strabo, the much-traveled Greek geographer of the first century B.C., accepted the widespread tradition that Ulysses' sea wanderings took place in the western Mediterranean along the shorelines of southern Italy and Sicily. "It is not Homer's way," he wrote, "to present a mere recital of marvels in no way related to reality."

Sagas and legends from the end of the Age of Bronze together with Mycenaean seafaring lore were undercurrents to bear Ulysses and his ships from sacked Troy. The *Odyssey*, memorized and overlaid by generations of commentators, elucidated, allegorized, translated (in English alone there are more than thirty translations), is so much a literary landmark that it obscures the timeless immediacy of the present when it all began. There was such a moment, tangible, living, and unshadowed, between the shadowed past and the shadowy future: ships gliding through the waves on a bright morning, the sunlight glittering against the sea spray; the cheerful sound of men's voices, the hard cry of gulls, slight hiss of water against the prows. That scene: sails, sun and wind and sea and shadow, the green and golden shoreline, the whole breath of life that in such a poised moment seems as if it would never pass. The words alone remain—and centuries later one wonders.

The wanderings of Ulysses of the barren isle of Ithaca echo the folk migrations after the Trojan War. The little ships of the time put to sea at all hazard, enduring storms and wrecks and, in some cases at least, finding the fair fortune of a safe haven.

There lies the port: the vessel puffs her sail:
There glow the dark broad seas.

Ulysses begins his "calamitous homeward journey" by crossing the Aegean and beaching his ships on the coast of Thrace, the land of the Cicones.

From Ilion the wind served me to near Ismarus of the Cicones. I sacked the city and slew them.

This has the bloody ring of inherent truth, for the Cicones as allies of the Trojans were foreordained enemies, and it was common custom to put the inhabitants of a conquered city to the sword. In the same period Joshua in capturing Jericho "utterly destroyed all that was in the city, both man and woman, young and old, and ox, and sheep, and ass, with the edge of the sword."

The Greeks had planned to skirt the Peloponnesus and sail homeward to Ithaca, but as they rounded Cape Maleia the currents and a ravening wind drove them for nine days across the Libyan Sea.

On the tenth day we made the land of the Lotos-eaters, men who browse on a food of flowers.

According to Strabo this was the North African island of Meninx, the Jerba of today. From Alexandrian times there was much debate as to what the lotos really was. Polybius described it as a purplish olive-sized berry. Herodotus found it sweet as a date. Yet Homer calls it a flower and not a fruit. The most obvious meaning is of course the opium poppy.

Leaving the land of the Lotos-eaters, Ulysses and his men came at night to the land of the Cyclops. No one has identified this place, though its aspects suggest the hill country of the Sicilian and southern Italian cave dwellers. This fierce landscape was the home of the one-eyed giant Polyphemus, whom Ulysses blinds with a burning stake to escape his ravenous clutches. The enraged ogre, hurling rocks at the ships of the fleeing Greeks, may have a volcanic origin.

Modern elucidators such as Victor Bérard echo Strabo in maintaining that the places Homer describes are real and that he gives us sufficient detail to recognize them. But there is much diversity in this recognition. Ulysses' next port of call, Aeolia with its sheer cliffs and encompassing wall of bronze, the home of Aeolus, who can tie up the bursting winds in a bag, has been surmised to be Madeira. Ancient writers considered it to be one of the Lipari Islands, most probably Stromboli.

The site of the Greeks' next adventure, where Ulysses loses all the other ships and their crews, retains the folk memory of some Baltic region. Crates thought it in northern Europe during the white nights of summer, for Homer said a shepherd could earn his wages there twice over by working double time in the unfading light. The geographic conundrums remain. Where was the enchantress Circe's magic Aeaea, the isle of Sunrise, so puzzling to Ulysses that he did not know "where is west and where is east"? Northern regions are again suggested when Ulysses sets sail from Aeaea to consult the Theban prophet Tiresias in the Land of the Dead.

We had attained the Earth's verge and its girdling river of Ocean where are the cloud-wrapped and misty confines of the Cimmerian men.

Homer's description of the Land of the Dead, the House of Hades, superimposed on Cimmeria, may well derive from the Oracle of the Dead overlooking the River Acheron in Thesprotia. Some later interpreters have even suggested that the Cimmerians were the Cymry, the people of Wales.

An ancient belief that Circe lived in Latium is preserved today in Cape Circeo, halfway between Rome and Naples. Scylla and Charybdis are generally accepted as the rocks and whirlpools of the Messina Strait, between Italy and Sicily. Scylla's rock still juts out from Italy near the village of Scilla. It has been ingeniously suggested that the six-headed monster was a giant squid, its yelps the wind whistling through the rock fissures. Thrinacia, where Ulysses and his

crew were delayed a month by contrary winds, was believed by later Greeks to be Sicily. When they again set sail a sudden tempest wrecks their ship and all are drowned except Ulysses. Clinging to a piece of wood, he drifts for nine days until he comes to Ogygia, the island of the sea-nymph Calypso.

Ogygia, "at the navel of the world," is an enchanted place, like Prospero's island not to be located in any man's domain. There in an everlasting summer Ulysses lives in Calypso's gracious cavern and shares her bed for seven years. But when he continues to long for his rocky Ithaca, she lets him go, giving him a raft and provisions. Once more a storm overwhelms him, and his raft is broken to pieces. He swims to shore and collapses on the beach at Scheria, the land of the

In one version of his quest for the golden fleece, depicted on this Greek plate, Jason was swallowed by a dragon who was guarding it and was then disgorged under the watchful eyes of Athena, at the right. The fleece hangs from a tree in the background.

Phaeacians, thought to be the modern island of Corfu. There his real voyaging and adventures come to an end, for the Phaeacian king sends him by ship to Ithaca. On that peaceful journey of a hundred miles south the seafarer

who had in the past suffered heartbreak as the common sport of man's wars and the troublous waves, now slept in tranquil forgetfulness of all he had endured.

Myth, fact, and fancy intertwining in Ulysses' voyages have given rise to endless speculations. But beyond the adventures, the floating islands, the one-eyed monsters, the enchanting nymphs and foul winged creatures, there are the sight and taste of salt water, the pungent scent of wrack, the drifting fog, the spume and bubble of breakers, the billowing turbulence, the rush and retreat of waves on the shingle, the varied instant presence of the "wine-dark" sea itself. And at the core is a real voyage.

Real, too, is the voyage of the Argonauts, however embroidered with myth and folk tale. Sometime in the late fourteenth century B.C., several generations before the Trojan War, a band of Minyan raiders from Thessaly crossed the Aegean, passed through the Hellespont and the Bosporus, and entered the Black Sea, then as forbiddingly unknown as the Baths of Ocean of the West would be to later generations of Greeks. Their sea-bark, to the neolithic men of Thessaly a wonder of construction, was built by the Bronze Age craftsmen of Argos, the royal city of Argolis. From that birthplace the ship took the name Argo, "the swift," her captain being Jason, "the healer," a prince who had been deprived by an uncle of his father's throne.

But Jason before he became a hero was flesh and blood, a hirsute adventurer with enormous shoulders, hardy, piratical, and daring enough to lead his violent crew of Argonauts on their voyage across that hostile northern sea to golden Aea, identified by later Greeks as Colchis. Jason's mission was to recover from Aeetes, the king of Colchis, a golden fleece that would enable him to gain his rightful kingship. The voyage stuck in the folk memory, and over generations it gathered in extraneous legends, absorbed other myths.

Before the fifth century B.C. there are various accounts of the Argonauts. In the twelfth book of the Odyssey, the "world-famed" Argo is recorded as the only ship to maneuver safely between the Clashing

Rocks. Hesiod in the eighth century B.C., in one of the earliest accounts of the Argo's voyage, makes the first mention of the fleece being golden. In the fifth century B.C. Aeschylus, Sophocles, and Euripides all wrote plays about Jason and the voyage to Colchis, though only Euripides' horror-tinged Medea has survived. It was left to Pindar in his fourth Pythian ode, written in 466 B.C., to take the various and varying legends and combine them in the first consecutive narrative of the Argonaut saga.

When three centuries later Apollonius of Rhodes, the director of the Alexandrian library, wrote the four books of his Argonautica, he intended to immortalize himself by creating an epic about Jason and his quest that would in its four books rival Homer. Though the overwrought Alexandrian-age poem lacks the vernal strength of the earlier epic, nevertheless the Argonautica has come down as the final embodiment of the story of Jason and his Argo voyage and the quest for the golden fleece.

Beyond Jason's complicated family interrelationships as elaborated by Apollonius—kings, cousins, uncles, and usurpers, all fastened like barnacles to the Argo—what is the "thick-fleeced pelt of the ram," the golden fleece of Colchis, guarded by its sleepless dragon? What is the quest? The Argonautica is a curious mixture of things that could have happened and things that can be explained symbolically or mythologically. One German commentator of the last century saw the fleece as a "rain cloud brought by the east wind in the spring. Jason the healer travels east toward the dawn in search of the golden clouds that would heal his parched land. Or the fleece radiates the sunlight itself, from the realm of Aeetes, child of the sun." In other interpretations the ram becomes the setting sun that rises again and returns from the east.

For the Greeks, Colchis or Aea was a fabled land of gold. Strabo thought that the fleece was the gold of Colchis washed down by the mountain torrents of the Phasis and caught by the Colchians in the "ram's pelt." Aea—in Greek "the land"—was also a rich source of wheat for the Greeks, whose thin native soil was insufficient to feed them. The quest for the fleece may have been the quest for golden grain.

Apollonius's Argo, a ship of fifty oars, with a "speaking bow" carved from a branch of the sacred oak at the oracle of Dodona, is a vessel that no men of Jason's day could have built. In size and construction it

The bow of a Phoenician war galley, carved in bas-relief, was found in the ruins of the palace of the Assyrian king Sennacherib, who reigned in the seventh century B.C. On the lower deck, rowers grasp the upper bank of oars; on the upper deck, soldiers stand ready with spears.

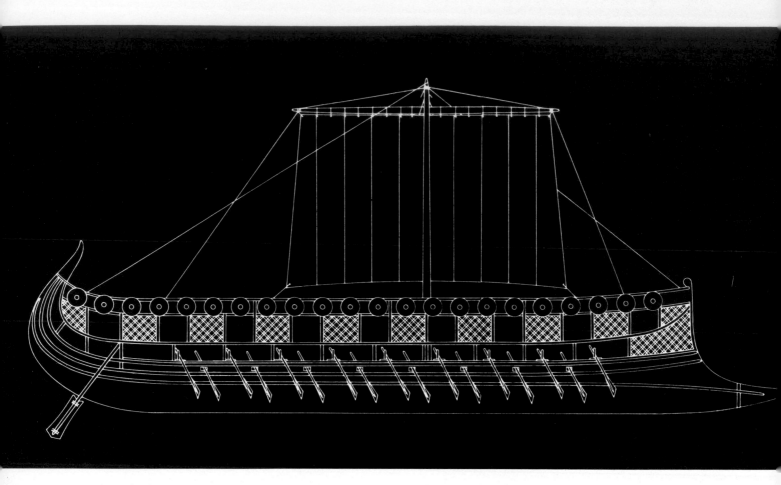

This drawing, based on the carving that appears on the preceding page, shows a Phoenician warship with two banks of oars, a single square sail, and a sharp, armored ram bow, designed to penetrate an enemy ship and then break off, leaving the Phoenician vessel free to maneuver.

is almost as anachronistic as the ark. The heroes that Jason summoned to his great adventure are themselves embodiments of myths: Hercules; Theseus; Peleus, the grandson of Zeus; Mopsus, who knew the augury of birds; Zetes and Calais, the winged sons of the North Wind; the keen-sighted Lynceus; Castor and his boxer brother Pollux; Idas, "the strongest man on earth"; Autolycus, the master thief; Idmon the seer; the pilot Tiphys; Orpheus. Hercules in his search for Hylas in Mysia is a late interpolation into the Argonaut story, and the abandonment of Hercules in Magnesia is explained in Apollodorus's handbook of mythology as brought about by the speaking bow having declared that the *Argo* could not bear his weight."

Whatever the actuality underlying their adventurous course through the Hellespont and across the Black Sea, the places they visited are identifiable enough. Lemnos, where the island women who had killed their husbands received the Argonauts as lovers, echoes an ancient gynocracy with its sacrificial rites. The Deliones who welcomed them so warmly may have been Thessalian settlers, kinsmen of Jason.

So the names follow sequentially. Bithynia on the Asiatic side of the Bosporus is the country of the Bebryces, whose king compelled all strangers to box with him—again an echo of sacrificial rites. Though Apollodorus places the foul, winged Harpies in Salmydessus in Thrace, others locate them in Bithynia. The Harpies are really wind demons, and in the earlier argonautic versions the blind King Phineus, so tormented by them, is actually a sorcerer and their ruler. Strabo identified the Clashing Rocks as two islands in the Hellespont.

On the return voyage, after Jason with the help of the king's daughter Medea, "the cunning one," has drugged the dragon, stolen the fleece, and fled Colchis, the Argonauts' pursuers forced them to change course, to go far to the north. According to Sophocles, they sailed to Colchis along the south coast of the Black Sea and followed the shoreline north on their return. Jason left Thessaly in the spring. Not until late in the year did the returning Argonauts reach the South Russian coast, where in that wintry season they would have run into ice floes, a phenomenon quite new to them and a grave peril to their fragile *Argo*. The menace of floating ice, moving with such crushing force, seems the most likely explanation for the Clashing Rocks that Homer later incorporated into the *Odyssey*. Their last adventure was with the bronze man of Crete, who went round the island every day and is probably a representation of the sun. From Crete the remaining Argonauts returned to Thessaly.

Not until Pindar was the haunting Orpheus myth transposed into the Argonaut legend. A strange extraneous beauty, bound up in the Orphic mystery cult, flickers in those passages in which Orpheus appears. To calm the strife of two Argonauts he sings of the creation of the world; when he sings of Artemis, schools of fish follow the ship like sheep after a shepherd; his lyre drowns out the fatal song of the Sirens; he persuades the Hesperid nymphs to give his companions fresh water; he guides the Argonauts to the mysteries at Samothrace. Musician, guardian of mysteries, he would scarcely have been accepted by the original horny-handed Argonauts.

Janet Baker in *The Voyage of the Argonauts,* her scholarly summing-up of the Argonaut legend, asks the double-edged final question. Does Argo stand for

a concentration of world-history, a single embodiment of all the pioneers who went out to seek a distant treasure, who followed a road that led past Colchis to the riches of a vast continent; and the Golden Fleece becomes a type of all those riches? . . . Was *Argo* a symbol of anything so large and so world-wide? Or does her story reflect, not a whole process of historic or prehistoric development, but a single fact—that a Thessalian ship of the Bronze Age sailed the Euxine Sea?

In the *Odyssey* and the *Argonautica* the Greeks had their epics of voyage. The greatest voyagers of the ancient world, the Phoenicians, left no literary traces. Yet they were the Mediterranean's most skilled and venturesome mariners, exceeding even those pioneers of seamanship, sailors of the island kingdom of Crete. From the time of Jason to the fall of Carthage a thousand years later, their solid, tubby vessels dominated the sea lanes. Most of the world's goods traveled in Phoenician bottoms—gold from Ophir, copper from Cyprus, silver from Ethiopia, tin from Spain, ivory and black slaves from Libya [Africa].

An elusive people to whom the Greeks gave the name they themselves never used, the Phoenicians derived from the Canaanites, whose trading posts along the eastern Mediterranean littoral grew into commercial cities with ports of call around the Mediterranean's rim and beyond. All the towns along the North African coast, except for the single Greek colony of Cyrene, were settled by Phoenicians. Carthage, founded by Phoenicians from Tyre, became the greatest sea power in antiquity.

Phoenician navigators were the first to sail into the unknown sea west of Sicily, the first to venture beyond the Pillars of Hercules into the boundless waters the Greeks called River Ocean and believed encompassed the world. None equaled them in skill and daring. So it was natural for the Egyptian pharaoh Necho II (610–594 B.C.), when he wanted to learn more about Africa, to turn to them. Necho considered Africa to be virtually an island, though he had no idea of its extent. Out of Egypt caravan tracks faded into the desert, and after months or even years the caravans came back from undetermined regions with gold and ivory and black slaves. Necho engaged a Phoenician fleet to sail along the coast and explore this unknown land. He sent his Phoenicians from the Red Sea into the Indian Ocean with instructions to return by way of the Pillars of Hercules. According to Herodotus, who heard the story when he was in Egypt, their voyage lasted three years. Each autumn they went ashore wherever they might be and sowed wheat, waiting until harvest time before they set sail again. Not until the third year did they pass through the Pillars of Hercules. "On their return," Herodotus wrote, "they declared—I for my part do not believe them, but perhaps others may—that in sailing round Libya they had the sun upon their right hand." Herodotus's doubts are of course singular confirmation of their having circumnavigated Africa, for when they sailed down the Red Sea the sun rose on their left, but after they rounded the Cape of Good Hope it rose on their right. Not until A.D. 1497 would another mariner repeat that voyage, when Vasco da Gama edged his fleet around the cape from the west on his voyage to India.

Another attempt a century later to circumnavigate Africa—also recorded by Herodotus—was that of a Carthaginian crew under the Persian Sataspes, a cousin of King Xerxes. Sataspes had violated a lady of the court, and Xerxes was about to have him impaled when his mother begged that instead he be allowed to make a voyage of exploration round Africa. Xerxes agreed, no doubt feeling that the result would be the same for Sataspes in any case. After obtaining a ship and gathering a crew together in Egypt, Sataspes sailed through the Pillars of Hercules, doubled Cape Spartel, and headed south.

Following this course for many months [Herodotus wrote] over a vast stretch of sea, and finding more water than he had crossed still lay before him, he put about and came back to Egypt. Then proceeding to the court, he reported to Xerxes that at the farthest point he reached, the coast was occupied by a dwarfish race that, whenever he landed, left their towns and fled to the mountains. The reason why he had not sailed quite round Libya was, he said, because the ship stopped and would not go any farther. Xerxes, however, did not believe this; and so Sataspes, as he had failed to accomplish the task set him, was impaled by the king's order.

Although Sataspes never rounded Africa's great bend at Cape Palmas, he probably reached at least as far as Senegal, and the tribes that fled from him may have been Bushmen, living then farther north than they did later.

At about the same time that Sataspes was making his doomed voyage, the Carthaginian admiral Hanno sailed over roughly the same course with a fleet of sixty warships followed by merchant vessels containing several thousand colonists, whom he left here and there in settlements along the coast. Hanno's is the most authenticated voyage of antiquity, for he kept a log which he had inscribed in bronze when he returned, some 650 words that a Greek scribe later copied. According to his narrative, he followed the shoreline to a deep easterly gulf at the head of which he founded the island-colony of Cerne. Whether Cerne was Herne Island, just to the north of the Tropic of Cancer, or one at the mouth of the Senegal River has been much debated. From Cerne, Hanno wrote, "we sailed through the delta of a big river, named the Chretes, and came to a lake containing three islands larger than Cerne. . . . Sailing on from that point we came to another deep and wide river, which was infested with crocodiles and hippopotamuses. From there we turned back to Cerne."

Hanno's river with its crocodiles and hippopotamuses is obviously the Senegal, wherever Cerne may be. Sailing farther south he, like Sataspes, encoun-

tered Negro tribesmen who fled at his approach. Landing on a small island for the night—there were no sleeping quarters on those narrow warships—the admiral and his men could see the glow of many fires on the mainland, hear shouts and the noise of pipes and cymbals and the beat of tom-toms. On following nights they continued to see pinpoints of fire and leaping flames. One flaring bonfire on a mountain called the Chariot of the Gods "seemed to reach the sky." Three days they continued, their path marked by flames, until they reached a gulf called the Southern Horn, where according to Hanno there was an island "full of wild people. By far the greater number were women with hairy bodies. Our interpreters called them gorillas. . . . We secured three women, who bit and scratched and resisted their captors. But we killed and flayed them, and brought the hides to Carthage. This was the end of our journey, owing to lack of provisions."

Here in this brief narrative Africa emerges into history for the first time, fearful and enigmatic: the jungle; the tropical night with its throbbing tom-toms; skin-clad savages showering the intruders with rocks from the heights; fires as warning beacons; herds of elephants; river creatures; apes like men. Geographers have debated whether Hanno turned back at Sierra Leone or went on to Cameroon, whether the Chariot of the Gods is Mount Kakulima in Guinea or Mount Cameroon, the highest peak in West Africa. In any case, spending less than two months on his outward leg, the Carthaginian admiral made one of the extraordinary voyages of antiquity. Even the colonies that he so hastily set up lasted for centuries.

There is no cast-bronze record of the journey of Hanno's brother admiral, Himilco, who may actually have been his real brother. Historians have preserved the tradition that Himilco sailed north out of the Pillars of Hercules and up the coast of Spain and France as far as Britain. Whether he actually reached the British Isles remains uncertain, but it is at least certain that voyages from Carthaginian Spain were made there during the Iron Age, voyages significant or disastrous at the time and which wind and water and the passing years have long obliterated. Tradition also has it that the Phoenicians first reached the Canary Islands, Madeira, and the Azores, as they might well have done when gales relentlessly blew their vessels off course.

Even vaguer than the accounts of Himilco's northern expedition were the stories bruited about the Greek Mediterranean world of Phoenician voyages across the Atlantic. But however vague, the stories persisted. Aristotle heard of an island discovered by the Carthaginians—the masters of the western ocean, he called them—sailing far beyond the Pillars of Hercules toward the western horizon. Fearful that knowledge of this new and bountiful land might encourage alien adventurers and imperil the Carthaginian sea dominion, the Carthaginian senate decreed that no one, under penalty of death, should from then on sail there.

Enlarging on Aristotle, Diodorus of Sicily in the first century B.C. told of

a very great island in the vast Ocean, many days' sail from Libya westward. The soil there is very fruitful, a great part whereof is mountainous, but much likewise a plain, which is the most sweet and pleasant part, for it is watered with several navigable rivers. . . . This island seems rather to be the residence of some of the gods, than of men.

Anciently by reason of its remote location it was altogether unknown, but afterwards discovered upon this occasion: the Phoenicians in ancient times undertook frequent voyages by sea, in way of traffic as merchants, so that they planted many colonies both in Africa and in these western parts of Europe. These merchants succeeding in their undertaking and thereupon growing very rich, passed at length beyond the Pillars of Hercules, into the sea called the Ocean. And first they built the city called Gades [Cádiz]. The Phoenicians, having found out the coasts beyond the Pillars, and sailing along by the shore of Africa, were on a sudden driven by a furious storm off into the main ocean, and after they had lain under this violent tempest for many days, they at length arrived at this island, and so they were the first that discovered it.

Strabo wrote that some time around 1200 B.C. a fleet of Phoenician ships exploring the west coast of Africa was suddenly blown across the Atlantic in a storm and there discovered new lands. In the second century A.D. the historian Claudius Aelianus said that the discovery of a western land was "a definite tradition of the Carthaginians or Phoenicians of Gades." It was a tradition that persisted in Cádiz through the centuries.

As late as the seventeenth century the Spanish historian Marianus de Orscelar wrote that a Carthaginian fleet had sailed from Cádiz early in the fourth century B.C.: "Taking the course between the setting sun and the meridian, they surmounted the waves of the ocean, and after many days' sail discovered a very extensive 'island.'"

But did they? Archaeological enthusiasts of this century have found stones with markings that they claim to be Phoenician linear script in places as far apart as New England, West Virginia, Oklahoma, and Pennsylvania. A professor of zoology at Harvard, Barry Fell, maintains that he has identified and transcribed inscriptions proving that Phoenicians and Iberian Celts not only crossed the Atlantic but established "far-flung settlements at the edge of the world in a land that lay behind the Irish sunset." Monhegan Island off the coast of Maine was, he writes with scholarly insistence, a trading station used by Phoenician captains, and he has translated an inscription attesting to the "periodic arrival of Phoenician ships on the New England coast." A physicist collected several hundred rune stones near Mechanicsburg, Pennsylvania, with odd markings he recognized as letters of the North Phoenician alphabet. The head curator of the Smithsonian Institution's department of geology, however, declared these allegedly cuneiform characters to be "natural in origins and due to the shrinkage of finely crystalline material." Inscriptions found earlier in Paraíba, Brazil, are held by adherents of Professor Cyrus Gordon to be Phoenician, by others to be a fraud. Nothing as yet has been found in North or South America, no artifacts or cache of coins (as was uncovered in the Azores), no Phoenician glass or Iberian pottery fragments, that would convince the doubters. Phoenician sailors were tough, able, and venturesome. Perhaps some may have been blown off course across the Atlantic. But if they had seen the New World, could they have managed to return home to tell about it? A mystery.

THE ROUTE OF ULYSSES

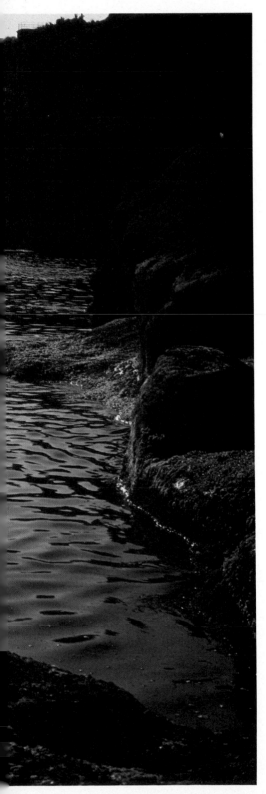

For more than two thousand years readers of the *Odyssey* have wondered whether it is the story of a real voyage and, if so, just where Ulysses went. By general agreement Scylla and Charybdis are the rocks and the whirlpool on opposite sides of the Strait of Messina. But other ports of call are not so easy to identify. At least thirty Italian caves go by the name of the Cave of Polyphemus.

In modern times several scholarly sailors, including Victor Bérard and Ernle Bradford, have made serious attempts to retrace Ulysses' voyage, matching passages in the *Odyssey* and ancient tradition with physical landscapes in the Mediterranean. The legendary places still cast a spell. Bradford wrote that while cruising off the Galli Islands, long identified as the home of the Sirens:

"I suddenly heard something that sounded like a song. I cannot describe it exactly, but it was low and far away. It resembled the waves and the wind. Yet it certainly was not produced by either of them because it had a human quality, disturbing and evocative . . . and for some reason that I cannot explain, I felt afraid."

Following the routes of Bérard and Bradford, Erich Lessing made an odyssey of his own in 1964 to photograph the landscapes that appear on these pages.

The land of the Cyclops, where Ulysses and his companions drove a staff into the eye of Polyphemus (as shown on the vase below), is located by scholars somewhere on the coast of Sicily or southern Italy. Lessing photographed the rocky harbor at left at the foot of Italy's Mount Posilipo.

Mount Circe on the Italian coast (opposite page), halfway between Rome and Naples, has long been regarded as the home of the enchantress Circe. In ancient times it was an island, but a rise of the sea floor has made it a cape in the Gulf of Gaeta. At Circe's bidding, Ulysses descended to Hades, where the soul of his dead comrade Elpenor (below, at right) begged him to find his unburied body. The map at right shows Ulysses' landfalls as plotted by Ernle Bradford.

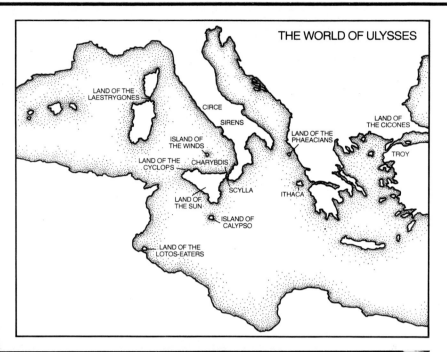

THE WORLD OF ULYSSES

LAND OF THE LAESTRYGONES

CIRCE

SIRENS

ISLAND OF THE WINDS

LAND OF THE CYCLOPS

CHARYBDIS

SCYLLA

LAND OF THE SUN

ISLAND OF CALYPSO

LAND OF THE LOTOS-EATERS

LAND OF THE PHAEACIANS

ITHACA

LAND OF THE CICONES

TROY

In this Roman terra cotta, Ulysses, lashed to the mast of his ship, listens to the song of the Sirens, while his companions, their ears stuffed with wax, row the ship out of hearing. In a Greek vase painting of the same scene (left), one of the Sirens dives upon the ship.

The Galli Islands (opposite page) in the Gulf of Salerno are often identified as the home of the Sirens.

Ulysses landed on the coast of Ithaca (opposite page) at the end of his nine-year journey. At right is the plateau of Marathia, where he took refuge with his faithful swineherd.

Disguised as a beggar, Ulysses rejoices to discover that his wife, Penelope, has been faithful to him.

ACROSS THE WIDE PACIFIC

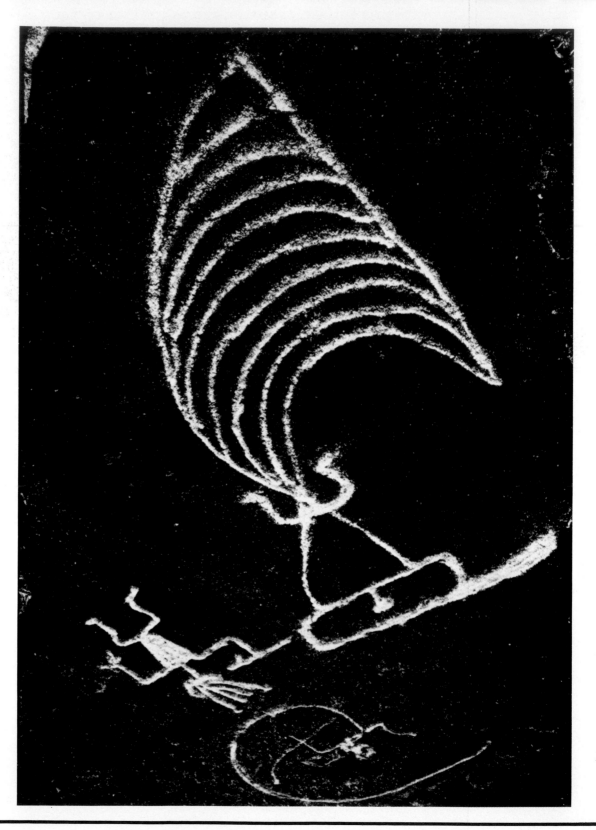

From the Atlantic to the Pacific, east of the sun and west of the moon, fable or fact—what lies in the voyage of the Buddhist monk Hui-Shen and four companions from China to the Land of Fu-Sang in the fifth century A.D.? According to imperial records of about A.D. 629, Hui-Shen appeared before the emperor Liang Wu Ti in 499 to give his account of a voyage to a land 20,000 li (6,600 miles) east of Ta-Han, that is, Kamchatka. He called the land Fu-Sang, the fabled land long a motif of Chinese literature, the Oriental equivalent of the Hesperides and the Western Islands of the Blessed. Was Fu-Sang the American continent, and had Chinese voyagers reached America even before this? According to a third-century poem,

East of the Eastern Ocean lie
The shores of the Land of Fu-Sang.
If, after landing there you travel
East for ten thousand li
You will come to another ocean,
  blue,
Vast, huge, boundless.

This Fu-Sang has the dimensions of North America, a surprisingly accurate 3,300 miles from coast to coast with the blue Atlantic beyond.

If Hui-Shen had been carried along across the Pacific by the Kuroshio, the great Japan Current, and had then caught the Pacific Current to drift along the coast from Alaska to California, he would after traveling 20,000 li have reached the neighborhood of Acapulco, Mexico, a semitropical region much like the one he describes as Fu-Sang.

Joseph de Guignes, the eigh-

A Hawaiian rock carving depicts a prehistoric canoe with a crab-claw sail. The incised lines were chalked in for clarity before it was photographed.

teenth-century French Orientalist, a man given to speculative fancies, published in 1761 a memoir derived from the Records of the Liang Dynasty, in which he made known Hui-Shen's story for the first time to the West. He claimed that the records were evidence of Chinese voyages to America a thousand years before Columbus, and he appended to the memoir copper-plate maps showing routes to Alaska and California, regions which, he said, the Chinese knew as Fu-Sang.

In the last century his evidence became the subject of much acrimonious dispute. The great naturalist and explorer Alexander von Humboldt accepted it, calling Hui-Shen the Leif Ericson of China and Fu-Sang the Vinland of the West. Charles Godfrey Leland, the American humorist and Gypsy scholar, wrote a defending monograph, *Fusang,* and in 1885 one E. P. Vining produced an 800-page tome about the man he considered *An Inglorious Columbus.* And so on.

As recorded by Guignes, Hui-Shen's new land "has many Fu-Sang trees and these give it its name. The tree's first sprouts are like bamboo shoots. The people of the country eat them. The fruit is like a pear but reddish. They spin thread from the bark and make coarse cloth from which they make clothing and from it they also make a finer fabric. The wood is used to build houses and they use Fu-Sang bark to make paper." According to Hui-Shen the natives had no fortresses or walled cities, but they did have oxen and horses and they drank deer milk. He describes their marriage and funeral and other customs, the appearance of their rulers, the curious fact that they cared little about gold, their other folkways. Added to Hui-Shen's tale is an account of a country of women,

This rubbing, taken from the engraved back of a Chinese mirror (ninth to twelfth century) shows a ship sailing in strong winds and heavy seas.

creatures completely covered with hair, who walk erect and chatter among themselves.

A German scholar of the last century, Karl Friedrich Neumann, identified Hui-Shen's Fu-Sang as Mexico. Elucidators have pursued the parallels, explaining the Fu-Sang tree as the century plant, which grows thirty feet high and branches out like a tree. Its trunk has been used in Mexico for the framework of buildings, and its flat rubbery leaves have served as shingles. Its shoots are edible, and its bark supplies a coarse thread from which a kind of hemp cloth is woven, while the finer fibers produce a linen-like thread as well as paper. The reddish fruit may be the prickly pear. As for the hairy, chattering women, they could be monkeys.

Such explanations are ingenious, but they do not hold. Hui-Shen said he returned to China with 300 pounds of native silk after forty years in Fu-Sang. His tale faces the same obstacle that any theory of Phoenician transatlantic voyages faces. Ocean current patterns were still relatively unknown. There would have been no viable way for him and his aged companions to get back. Most Sinologists of this century have dismissed Hui-Shen's American voyage as a fable.

And yet, and yet. The Kuroshio, the Black Stream, sweeps northeastward, and there could have been other, unrecorded voyages to America, voluntary or otherwise. Prehistorians have long been intrigued by parallels between the art, architecture, customs, and beliefs of Asia and those of Central America. Botanists speculate on how peanuts, which originated in Brazil, reached China before 1500 B.C., and how the sweet potato, which is native to South America and is known in Peru as *kumar,* reached Polynesia, where it is called *kumara.* There are no artifacts of undisputed provenance to prove that voyages were made in either direction. But during the eighteenth and nineteenth centuries, East Asian junks were so frequently driven off their course by storms and wrecked on the Pacific coast of North America that they provided the Indians of British Columbia with their chief source of iron and copper. If so many crossings occurred in historic times, it is reasonable to suppose that voyages in one or both directions were made in the long centuries before records existed.

The *Shih Chi,* the oldest of the Chinese dynastic accounts, relates that in 219 B.C. Hsü Fu asked the emperor Ch'in Shih Huang Ti permission to launch an expedition into the Pacific to search out three magic mountain islands. The emperor acceded, with the stipulation that Hsü Fu also search for those drugs that prolong life. "Bring me young men of good breeding, together with apt virgins, and workmen of all the trades; then you will get your drugs," Hsü Fu told the emperor. Ch'in Shih Huang Ti, said the chronicle, "very pleased, set three thousand young men and girls at Hsü Fu's disposal, gave him ample supplies of the seeds of five grains, and artisans of every sort, after which his fleet set sail. Hsü Fu must have found some calm and fertile plain, with broad forests and rich marshes, where he made himself king—at any rate, he never came back to China." Whether the Kuroshio bore them across the Pacific, whether their traces endured in South America's Indian culture, remains a mystery. Yet some Chinese may have made that voyage and survived.

Among the unrecorded voyages can certainly be put those of the Polynesians, for the obscure settlers of the mid-Pacific are Asiatic in origin, and there beyond memory they have lived in their scattering of islands thousands of miles from the mainland. How did they get there and when? In their double-hulled voyaging canoes and outriggers they must have made some of the longest voyages in history. Did they follow the Kuroshio and the Pacific Current and come to Oceania from the east? Or did they angle east against trade winds and currents? The questions will never be finally resolved. Their stupendous achievement remains.

The ancestors of the Polynesians came first as rovers from Indonesia and the shores of the South China Sea. Sometime between 5000 and 3000 B.C. they reached New Guinea and the Philippines, pausing there as if to gather strength for a thrust into the vast emptiness of the Pacific. Sea people, they absorbed the subtleties of navigation, the meaning of cloud formations, of wave patterns and currents, of bird flight, the indications of the rising and setting stars. By 1500 B.C. they had penetrated into Micronesia, a thousand miles beyond the Philippines, and in the south their canoes and outriggers had crossed 400 blank miles of water to Fiji.

A few centuries later they had reached Tonga and Samoa, where for

The route of Hui-Shen (or Hwui Shan), based on his fifth-century account, is traced on the map below. He may have sailed in a simpler version of the elaborate junks shown in the seventh-century painting on the opposite page.

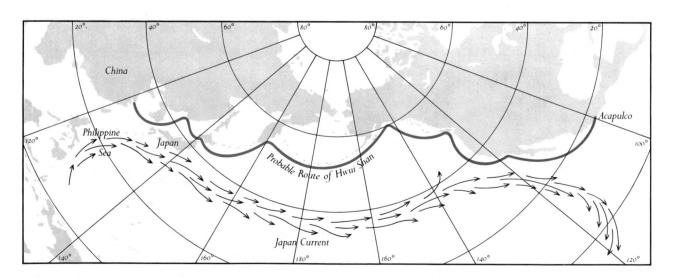

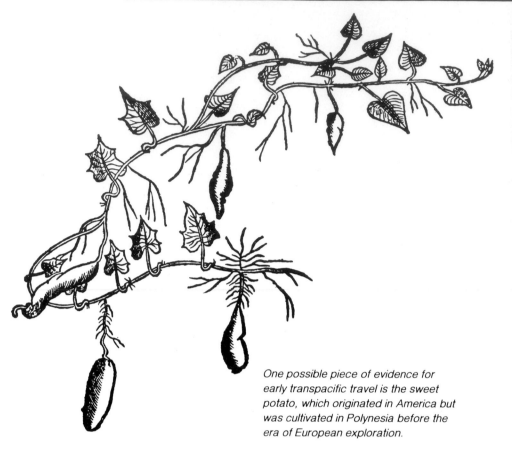

One possible piece of evidence for early transpacific travel is the sweet potato, which originated in America but was cultivated in Polynesia before the era of European exploration.

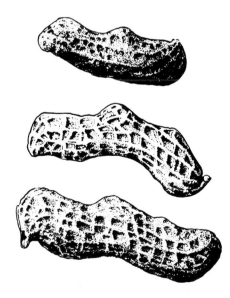

Peanuts, native to South America, reached China as early as 1500 B.C. The top and bottom peanuts shown above are prehistoric Peruvian types similar to the present Chinese variety, center; all differ from the modern American type.

a millennium they remained, evolving into the homogeneous Polynesians, who in time came to believe that their true origins were in the Samoa Islands. In the first century A.D. Samoans and Tongans probed the sea limits again, exploring in successive voyages eastward until they reached mid-Pacific islands then unknown to mankind. Sometime in that century, according to the analysis of potsherds by archaeologists, Polynesians arrived in the Marquesas, two thousand miles upwind from Samoa. Their twin-hulled canoes, up to seventy feet long, were constructed of planks lashed together with sennit on wooden frames and caulked with coconut fiber and breadfruit sap. The crab-claw sails were of plaited leaves. Early the Polynesians had learned the technique of drying foods. Such vessels could carry thirty or forty passengers hundreds of miles.

A legend has persisted among the Nuku Hiva islanders in the Marquesas that their ancestors were Tongans and Samoans who had left their native islands in search of a new home. On their eastward voyage they reached eight islands in turn, none of which they considered suitable. But in the next island they found at last what they had been looking for, and gave it the name Ninth Island, Nuku Hiva.

The Society Islands, a thousand miles south of the Marquesas, re-

mained uninhabited until about A.D. 500. Then a group of Polynesians from the Marquesas—the Land of Men—urged on by drought or crop failure or possibly sheer restlessness, crossed the seas from their homeland to occupy Tahiti and Raiatea. For such sea venturers even those islands did not suffice. Generation after generation set out on tremendous voyages, exploring a vast triangle bounded by Hawaii, Easter Island, and New Zealand. The Pacific must have become an anonymous grave-yard for many a canoe convoy shat-tered by storms or blown by adverse winds to empty horizon. In the begin-ning the majority of these venturers may have perished. Yet enough sur-vived to discover new islands.

Memories of the voyages grew to sagas, passing from generation to

Sailors of the Caroline Islands travel hundreds of miles across open sea in these light outrigger canoes.

generation. Raiatea still preserves the memory of the high priest Pa'Ao, who thirty generations ago sailed to Hawaii. Dismayed that these more recently settled islands lacked a strong ruler, he returned to Raiatea to bring back to Hawaii the high chief Pili, founder of a dynasty to which Kamehameha, the great Hawaiian king, would belong. In turn, a Hawaiian legend tells of Mo'Ikena, who voyaged from Hawaii to "Tahiti of the Golden Haze" and returned to wed the daughter of the ruling chief of the Kauhi.

New Zealand, the Land of the Long White Cloud, so Polynesian folktellers relate, was accidentally discovered by the Raiatean fisherman Kupe in pursuit of an octopus that had stolen his bait. For over two thousand miles the enraged Kupe followed the octopus's trail, finally killing it in New Zealand's Cook Strait. When he came back to Raiatea he told of the great island that he had found "to the left of the setting sun in November."

When Raiatea itself grew overpopulated, the chief navigator of the island, Ru, announced to his family and relatives that he had selected a star beneath which lay a "larger and better land." He gathered his people together—including twenty young women chosen for their beauty, strength, and virtue—and set out in an oversize canoe. A three-day storm of unusual violence overtook them and so terrified the crew and passengers that they appealed to Ru. He invoked the aid of the sea god, Tangaroa. As he did so, the clouds parted to reveal his guiding star. According to legend the voyagers landed safely three days later at Aitutaki, one of the Cook Islands, whose inhabitants still hold an annual festival in Ru's honor.

Such long expeditions in frail canoes were always perilous, and as settled and self-sufficient societies developed in the larger islands, seafaring was less impelling and the tradition itself withered, to be finally disrupted by the coming of the Spanish. As the islanders grew more self-contained they also grew more xenophobic and, oblivious of a common ancestry, raided or made war on other islands. Particularly in the smaller and more vulnerable atolls, distrust of any stranger from the sea became general. Storm-beaten survivors drifting ashore could expect to be killed. Cannibalism in the South Seas was not uncommon, surviving even into the last century.

Present-day efforts in Polynesia to revive the ancient construction crafts and navigation skills, to repeat the ancient voyages, have been picturesquely successful. Such recreated voyages are always a little self-conscious and never quite bold enough to dispense with two-way radio communication. Yet they have been sufficient at least to demonstrate the enduring truth behind the Polynesian sea legends.

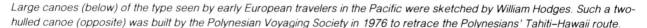

Large canoes (below) of the type seen by early European travelers in the Pacific were sketched by William Hodges. Such a two-hulled canoe (opposite) was built by the Polynesian Voyaging Society in 1976 to retrace the Polynesians' Tahiti–Hawaii route.

THROUGH ATLANTIC MISTS

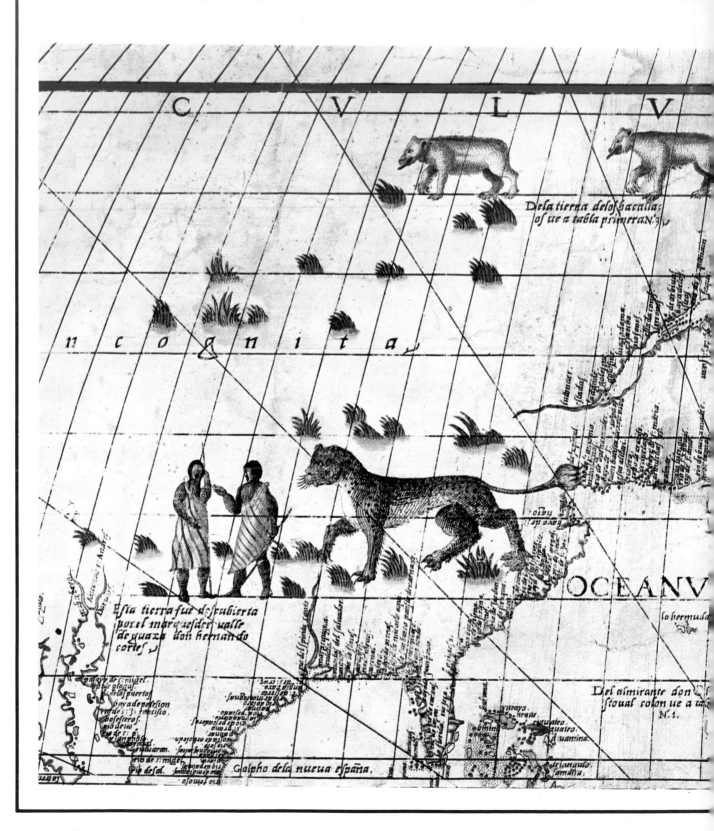

Whatever transatlantic traffic may have existed in earlier times faded under the Roman Empire. Though Roman war galleys ruled the Mediterranean after the defeat of Carthage and ranged as far as Britain, Rome was not a maritime nation. For some centuries there was a hiatus in voyages beyond the Pillars of Hercules. Nowhere is there any legend of Roman explorations in America.

The first post-Roman account of a voyage westward into the Atlantic is the *Navigatio Sancti Brendani Abbatis*, the voyage of the Irish monk Saint Brendan the Navigator, which may or may not have taken him as far as the shores of North America. Brendan himself, born about 486 near Tralee, County Kerry, was a real enough person, and his voyage has been documented, indeed overdocumented, for there are at least 120 manuscripts of his *Navigatio*, thirteen dating from the early eleventh century. A contemporary account of his life mentions the voyage but gives few details.

As abbot of the monastery of Clonfert in Galway, "on the verge of the ocean," Brendan like most Irish and many a monastic had a love of salt water. The words of his contemporary, Saint Columba, echoed his own thoughts: "What joy to sail the crested sea!" When Brendan was seventy, a fellow abbot persuaded him to undertake a voyage out into the

Atlantic in search of the Promised Land of the Saints—mankind's recurring dream of a sea-girt paradise. Brendan engaged his monks to build a "very little vessel, ribbed and sided with wood, but covered with oak-tanned ox-hides and caulked with ox-tallow." What they built was a traditional Irish curragh, a wicker frame covered with skins, theirs large enough to carry eighteen men.

So Brendan and his pious companions set out, making their way from one island to another through calm and storm, voyaging for seven years until they finally reached their ultimate island. Like all prescientific accounts, the *Navigatio* is a mixture of fact and fantasy; monkish scribes were not averse to tacking a sustaining fable onto the narrative or inserting a good tale worth the retelling. The first island Brendan and his monks reached seems tangible enough, high and rocky, dashed by breakers, not an easy place to make a landing. But once ashore they pass into a region of Celtic legend. Led by a friendly dog, they come to a towering castle devoid of people. Inside the castle they find a huge banqueting hall where unseen hands have set places for them and arranged platters of bread and fish. Only lacking is a vision of the Holy Grail. Not until the following morning do they see anyone. Then a young man appears, bringing them baskets of bread and an amphora of water for their further voyage. The island is by all indications one of the Faeroes, as are the subsequent islands of their visiting: the Island of Sheep and the Paradise of Birds, where birds talk in Latin and sing hymns.

On other islands they find friendly monasteries. Indeed, there were settlements of Irish monks on many

isolated islands. When the wind drops they are becalmed in a sea so smooth that it seems coagulated. At last a breeze from the east speeds them on their way. They are pursued by sea monsters. Fog envelops them. From three days' distance they sight a pillar of crystal, sparkling and translucent in the sunlight. They first pass the Fiery Mountain, then the Island of the Smiths, whose monstrous inhabitants throw lumps of molten slag at them. They even meet a dozing great fish with the genial name of Jasconius, so large that they first think him an island, land on his back, and begin to cook a meal. To this Jasconius objects and shakes them off, but on second thought he lets them return if they promise to kindle no more fires. On one bleak island, says the *Navigatio*, they encounter Judas sitting on a rock, he being allowed out on holy days as a respite from Hell.

Finally they reach the shores of the promised land, guided by a great light that shines through the fog perpetually surrounding it. For forty days—a conventional term for time—they explore a wide land of ripe fruit trees without ever coming to the end of it. They reach a river too wide to cross. A

Saint Brendan and his monks (opposite page) find themselves in the embrace of a large but friendly fish. In the fifteenth-century German woodcuts below, they meet a Siren and a holy man, and do battle with a sea monster.

young man at last approaches them, offers them fruit and precious stones, and tells Brendan that he must return to Ireland, as his death day is approaching.

Could the Promised Land of the Saints be fogbound Nova Scotia? The river too wide to cross, the St. Lawrence? Samuel Eliot Morison did not believe it possible, although he found the *Navigatio* an enchanting narrative that "reflects all seafarers' experiences in northern waters—the translucent sea swarming with fish, the sporting of whales, icebergs melting in the summer sunlight, dungeon fogs, rocky isles covered with trees and grass, pinnacle rocks."

Stripped of the adventitious supernatural, many of the islands can be identified. The sea monsters are whales, as is the amiable Jasconius. The Fiery Mountain and the Island of the Smiths may well be volcanic eruptions in southern Iceland. Obviously the pillar of bright crystal is an iceberg, and the coagulated sea that once held up the voyagers is probably an ice pack.

In 1976 and 1977 an adventurous Irishman, Tim Severin, carefully arranged for the construction of a curragh on ancient models. Then, with a crew of five—later reduced to four—he made a two-part voyage across the Atlantic, following Saint Brendan's watery path in his leather-sheathed ship, named after the saint, until he reached Peckford Island, Newfoundland. He wrote that his Brendan voyage "established the

basic fact that it is entirely possible to sail from one side of the North Atlantic to the other in a skin boat built to medieval specifications, and by a rugged northerly route." Saint Brendan may well have done so.

We know when Brendan was born, where he lived, where and when he died. Nothing so specific can be said of the Welsh Prince Madoc, who, popular tradition claims, brought over a cargo of Welsh settlers to unnamed America in the twelfth century. What is specific is a memorial erected to him by the Daughters of the American Revolution at Fort Morgan, Mobile Bay, Alabama. The bronze tablet reads: "In memory of Prince Madoc, a Welsh explorer, who landed on the shores of Mobile Bay in 1170 and left behind, with the Indians, the Welsh language."

The Madoc story first appeared in print in London in 1583, and over the years, with the assistance of Welsh nationalists, it accumulated material like a rolling snowball. Basing his claim on undisclosed records of the fourteenth century, Sir Thomas Herbert in 1634 related how Madoc, on the death of his father, Owen Gwyneth, king of North Wales, fled with a boatload of colonists to a southern region of North America, fortified a settlement there, and after some years returned home. Subsequently he led a second expedition of seven ships overseas to his old colony. Most of his original settlers had been killed by the Indians, and he decided to make a new settlement of the survi-

Leif Ericson, bearing his spear and shield, inspects the grapes found in "Vinland." Historians were long baffled by the idea of grapes in the northern lands that Leif visited, but climatologists say that the area was warmer in Viking times.

vors and those new colonists he had brought with him from Wales. In this settlement he stayed until he died.

Richard Hakluyt in his *Voyages* (1589) repeated the story and even sent Madoc as far afield as Mexico. Almost a century later a Welsh clergyman traveling through the Carolinas claimed that he had encountered a Welsh-speaking Indian tribe, descendants of Madoc's intermarrying settlers. The legend continued to grow. In 1805 Robert Southey published his *Madoc,* an epic poem of thirty-seven extended cantos on which he had been working for seven years. As late as 1966 enthusiasts

reported the discovery of a twelfth-century portrait of Madoc carved on a rock near Old Oraibi, Arizona.

Unfortunately for the legend, for Southey, for still persisting investigators and legendists, Madoc never existed. There is no mention of any such person in Welsh annals. Madoc is, like the Irish hero Ossian, a literary creation. Late in the eighteenth century a London society sent David Williams, a Welsh clergyman, to America to seek out any Welsh-speaking Indians. He visited many of the tribes, spent a winter with one of them, but found no trace of Welsh speakers. "I think you may safely

inform my friends," he wrote back to London, "that they have no existence."

There is no doubt about the existence of Leif Ericson, the Viking chief who led his beaked ships across the seas to the New World five hundred years before Columbus, as recorded in the sagas *Eric the Red* and *The Tale of the Greenlanders*, though there has been considerable doubt as to just where he landed and where these Norse newcomers set up their ephemeral colonies in the place they called Vinland. Many communities have laid claim to them. In the latter half of the last century a Viking fever swept academic circles in New England. "*Skoal!* to the Northland! *Skoal!*" Longfellow intoned, with triple exclamations, in his *Skeleton in Armor,* over the bones of an Indian with his poor metal trinkets dug up in Fall River in 1831. The Cambridge archpoet presumed the Indian to be a Viking chief and even ascribed the Newport Stone Tower as his grave marker, though later the tower was proved to be the remains of a windmill built by a colonial governor. Graffiti on Dighton Rock, a sandstone boulder on the Taunton River in Massachusetts, have been claimed to be a picture record of the Norse colony. An excavated wall demonstrated that the Vikings had come to Provincetown.

And where there were no towers, they were built. Norumbega Tower, a massive stone structure edging the Charles River in Waltham, Massachusetts, was ordered by a Harvard professor who had made a fortune in patent medicine. He named it Norumbega, claiming that here was the site of the town mentioned in *Eric the Red.* Local pride demanded the Viking presence. Yet no artifacts, no real traces of any settlements, were found until 1960, when the Norwegian archaeologist, Dr. Helge Ingstad, in making excavations at L'Anse aux Meadows in northern Newfoundland, uncovered the foundations of two great houses similar to Norse houses uncovered earlier in Greenland. Here, if belatedly, was corroboration of the accounts in the sagas.

It is not surprising that Norsemen in their formidable ships reached the New World. It would be more surprising if they had not. For they were the most skilled, most intrepid sailors of Europe, ranging far out to sea when other Europeans still timidly hugged the shore. Before A.D. 800 they had reached the Faeroes, before 900 Iceland, and before the end of the tenth century Greenland, said to have been discovered by Eric the Red, Leif's father. From the colony the Vikings established in Greenland it is only a watery hop and step to Newfoundland, a jump to Nova Scotia and the wild grapes and "self-sown wheat" (lyme grass) mentioned in the sagas. But that the Vikings built their Norumbega farther south is an academic will-o'-the-wisp.

Not until five years after Columbus touched land in the Bahamas did John Cabot reach the New Found Land, the first European to set foot on North America since the Vikings. Cabot, Caboto, Chiabotto, Savoto, however his name may be spelled or pronounced, remains a man of the shadows, mysterious in his beginnings, mysterious in his aspect (no portrait of him exists), mysterious in his end. Most of what is known about him is hearsay. We do know he was an Italian, of about Columbus's age, and probably, like Columbus, from Genoa.

In 1484 he was living with his wife and three sons in Venice and dealing in real estate. When Columbus made his astounding voyage to what everyone believed was the Orient, Cabot became obsessed with the belief that there must be a shorter northern route to the fabled Spice Islands. In 1495 he went to England and settled in Bristol. There he tried to organize an expedition to search out this northern route. He found a willing listener to his scheme in King Henry VII, already chagrined by Span-

ish maritime successes. The king granted him letters patent "to sayle to all partes, countreys, and seas, of the East, of the West, and of the North, under our banners and ensignes." Although the king had agreed to allow him five ships, Cabot was only able to purchase and outfit one, a small but seaworthy craft called the *Mathew*.

Cabot considered his first voyage chiefly a reconnaissance in the hope of finding the northern passage to Cathay. He took departure from Dursey Head, Ireland, on May 22, 1497, a quick and easy voyage, for he made landfall on the morning of June 24. Where he landed was most probably Cape Dégrat, at the northern tip of Newfoundland. There he and his company went ashore with a crucifix and banners bearing the arms of the pope and King Henry. They found a land "rich in pastorage," with towering trees suitable for ship masts. The only signs of any natives were a few snares and fish nets and the embers of a campfire. Nevertheless, they did not venture inland farther than a crossbow shot.

Cabot then sailed southward along the coast of Nova Scotia to the vicinity of Cape Race, where he thought he had discovered a passage to the Spice Islands. There, short of supplies, he turned back. His return voyage with westering winds lasted a mere fifteen days, and by mid-August he was back in Bristol. Brief though his voyage had been, it gave England her American title. King Henry in recognition granted "our trusty and well-beloved John Kaboto" the right to impress six English ships for a second voyage. This time Cabot planned to sail through to Cipango (Japan), that equinoctial region where he believed all the spices of the world had their origin. There he would set up a trading depot to by-pass all other entrepôts and middlemen.

Henry sponsored one ship, and four more were subsidized and stocked by Bristol merchants. Cabot's little fleet sailed at the begin-

ning of May 1498. One ship was disabled and had to put in at an Irish port. John Cabot with his four remaining ships continued out into the Atlantic. They were never seen or heard of again.

If Cabot is a man of the shadows, Amerigo Vespucci is a man in the light, so written about that the light itself becomes a blur. Did he make four voyages to his New World? Did he make two? Did he make any? His achievements have been denigrated, his voyages denied, but his name has remained, covering north and south a quarter of the globe. Was he a discoverer or a conniving thief who robbed Columbus of his rightful glory? His almost-contemporary, the priestly historian Bartolemé de Las Casas, wrote that "it is well to give thought here to the injustice and offense that Amerigo Vespucci seems to have done the Admiral [Columbus], attributing to himself, or alluding only to him, the discovery of this mainland." Three centuries later Ralph Waldo Emerson was writing indignantly: "Strange that broad America must wear the name of a thief. Amerigo Vespucci, the pickle-dealer at Seville whose highest rank was a boatswain's mate in an expedition that never sailed, managed in this lying world to supplant Columbus and baptize half of the earth with his own dishonest name." And even as late as 1931 the Portuguese historian Duarte Leite could denounce "this fatuous personage" as a "lying novelist, a navigator of the caliber of hosts of others, a cosmographer who repeated the ideas of others, a false discoverer who appropriated the glory of others."

Vespucci was no parvenu adventurer but the respected younger member of a well-known Florentine family associated with the Medici. By circumstance an agent, a trader, partner in a Spanish shipping firm, by nature he was more a scholar and armchair explorer, intrigued by the world he lived in rather than acquisitive. He recounted four voyages to the land

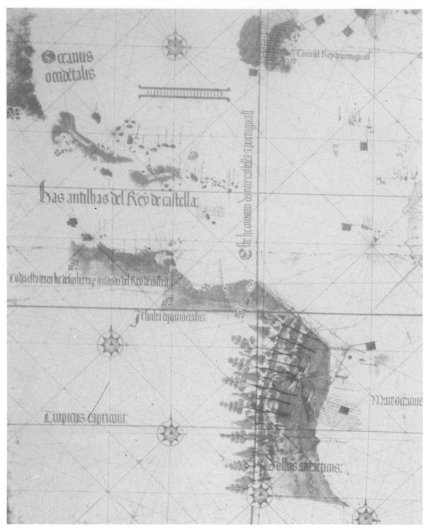

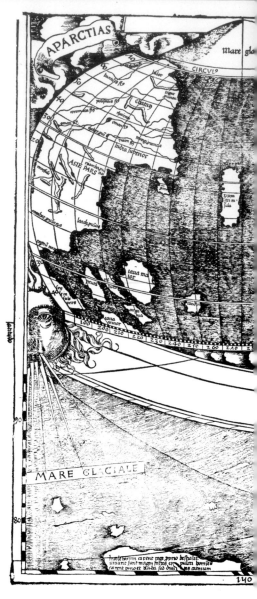

The Cantino map of 1502 (above) shows parrots on the coast of Brazil, which Vespucci called The Land of Parrots. Five years later Vespucci himself appears in a border on Waldseemüller's map (left), which first labeled the New World "America."

which was to bear his name, and unlike Columbus he came to realize that this region in the west was no extension of India or Japan but a fourth continent.

Coming to Seville from Florence on Medici affairs, he became a partner of the Florentine merchant-trader Gianetto Berardi in a firm that put up a fifth of the money for Columbus's first voyage and chartered ships and made provisioning arrangements for his second colonizing expedition. After the anticlimax of his second return, Columbus was no longer the lordly and triumphant admiral but a

prematurely aged man in the brown cassock of the Third Order of Saint Francis, broken by quarrels with the adventurers he had taken with him as colonists. King Ferdinand grew so weary of complaints about the high-handed Columbus that he held up permission for a third voyage until he could send a fact-finding expedition across the Atlantic to determine what was happening there. To get an impartial report the king relied chiefly on Amerigo Vespucci.

"The reason for my coming to this Kingdom of Spain was to engage in trade [Amerigo wrote], and during the

four years I pursued this purpose I had occasion to observe and experience the vicissitudes of fortune, which alters these perishable and transitory worldly goods. And so, knowing the unremitting effort man puts into securing such goods, suffering so many distresses and dangers, I decided to give up trade and devote myself to more praiseworthy and firmer things. I prepared myself to go and observe a part of the world and its wonders. The opportunity to do so was afforded me at a most timely moment and conjunction, for the King, Don Ferdinand of Castile, needing to send out four ships

was no record of Vespucci's having been in Spain from 1496 to 1498 and that there was no reason to doubt he had been at sea during that time. Nor does there seem to be any adequate reason to doubt the Vespucci account, even granting that it may have been altered in some details by later scribes. Unfortunately, doubts about the first voyage have cast doubts on the remaining three. More recent scholarship tends to bear out Vespucci's authenticity. Harvard's professor of oceanic history, John Parry, though conceding that other hands may have added to the account of the first voyage, has no doubts about the next two, the most important voyages. Whatever doubts may still linger, it seems reasonable to accept Amerigo Vespucci as an honorable man and a skilled navigator who made no great claims for himself and whose voyages were all that he claimed.

According to Amerigo's account he was forty-three when he sailed from Cádiz, and never before had he been on the Atlantic. He kept two things in mind: to acquire the navigator's art, and to satisfy his scientific curiosity. It took the expedition a little over a month to cross the ocean, the ships sailing south of Columbus's Hispaniola and Cuba. Somewhere near Costa Rica they sighted land, the first Spanish ships to reach the American mainland. For the next year they edged north, following the shoreline along the Gulf of Mexico, circling the Florida peninsula, making brief intrusions inland, continuing north to the vicinity of Cape Hatteras before heading home. In those months Amerigo sharpened his cosmographic skills, learned practical navigation, became deft in the use of the quadrant and the astrolabe. Later he would write nostalgically of the white beaches, the opulent green foliage, the natives who once their fear wore off swam round the ships like fish. Gold, the obsession of most Spanish voyagers, did not particularly interest him. He was not a

to discover new lands to the west, I was chosen by His Highness to go with the fleet and help in the discovery. We set out from Cádiz on the 10th of May 1497.''

From Father Las Casas on, Amerigo Vespucci has had what would later be called a bad press. To praise Columbus has been to dispraise Vespucci. The crown historian Antonio de Herrera (1559–1625), not finding Amerigo's name in a suit by Columbus's heirs over the discovery of the mainland, doubted the account of the first voyage, although since Amerigo went merely as an observer there is no reason why he should have been mentioned. Two hundred years later Martín Fernández de Navarrete claimed that Amerigo could not have made the voyage because he was in Spain at the time, in charge of outfitting fleets. Humboldt and others accepted his thesis, and it was repeated again and again that the voyage was a fiction designed to rob Columbus of the fact of discovering mainland North America.

Then in 1895 the English scholar Henry Harrisse, after delving through mountains of documents in the Spanish archives, demonstrated that there fortune-hunter but an observer, observing for himself and the king.

After Columbus had gone on his third expedition the king sent Amerigo on another follow-up voyage. This time Amerigo went not only as an observer but as a pilot. His three or four caravels were the first to cross the equator in the New World sea, making landfall near what is now Recife, at that point where Brazil juts closest to Africa. To him it seemed a fabulous country. The Land of Parrots he called it, marveling at the brilliance of their plumage—scarlet, green and scarlet, yellow, iridescent green, black and red.

"What shall I say [he wrote] of the number of birds, and their plumage, colors, and songs, the manifold species and their beauty? I shall not extend myself, because you will not believe me. Who could enumerate the myriad wild animals, the abundance of lions and ounces and cats, not those of Spain any longer, but of the antipodes? All the wolves, baboons, monkeys of many kinds, some of them so large? Such a variety of animals we saw that I think it would have been hard to get them all in the ark. And the wild boar, the goats, and deer, and stags, and hares, and rabbits. We did not see any domestic animals."

Sailing north he passed the mouths of the Amazon but made no attempt to enter the river. To a settlement of reed huts perched above the water on poles he gave the name of Venezuela—Little Venice—and the name stuck. For the first time he saw the Southern Cross, although its four stars looked to him like a mandolin. The greatest profit from this voyage was his study of the heavens. On a midnight in August 1499, he made an extraordinary discovery bearing on the co-ordinates of longitude. Professor J. W. Stein of the Vatican Observatory wrote in 1950 that Vespucci was the inventor of the method of lunar distance. "He was the first to employ it, measuring the distance between the moon and Mars."

Amerigo's second voyage was practically useful in developing a general policy for the discoveries. He returned to Seville with a high reputation. The king of Portugal sent to ask him to undertake a voyage across the Atlantic on behalf of Portugal. He agreed to go, undaunted by the hardships of his earlier voyages, the sea still in his blood. "I consider this voyage I am now undertaking," he wrote, "dangerous from the point of view of this our human existence. Nevertheless I set out upon it with resolute heart to serve God and the world."

This was his most spectacular voyage, the one that gave his name to the New World. Three caravels were dispatched by the king from Lisbon in May 1501, with the goal of searching out Atlantic routes below the Tropic of Capricorn to the Moluccas. Again Amerigo sailed merely as an adviser and observer, although he was the only one of the party who had made the voyage before, the only one who knew cosmography and could use the quadrant and astrolabe.

They took a more southern course than that of Columbus, and what with bad weather and the ignorance of the pilots it was two months before they made landfall. But to Amerigo it was familiar territory, the jutting edge of Brazil. For the next four months they sailed south along the coast. They encountered various tribes, some friendly, some hostile, all curious. Once a group of women enticed a young sailor ashore with lascivious gestures, then bludgeoned, killed, and ate him. As the ships held to their southward course, the lush tropical landscape faded. Strange stars appeared in the night sky. The pole star and the bear had vanished.

In May 1493 Pope Alexander had issued a bull dividing any newly discovered land between Spain and Portugal. The pope drew a line a hundred leagues west of the Azores. To the east of this all would be Portugal's, to the west, Spain's. When the fleet reached the point where the coast veered west beyond the demarcation line, the Portuguese commander resigned. He and the two other captains decided to give over command to Amerigo, and for the first and only time he became a commander. Almost 4,000 miles they sailed, along the coast of Argentina and barren Patagonia to 52 degrees latitude, the farthest south any European navigator had ever sailed. They all but reached the strait leading into the Pacific. Cold encompassed them.

"The nights were very long [Amerigo wrote] and we had one, that of April 7, which lasted fifteen hours, because the sun was just emerging from Aries, and in this region it was winter. In the midst of the storm on April 7 we sighted a new land along which we sailed for twenty leagues; the coast was rough, and we saw no harbor or people, because of the cold, I think, which was so intense that none of the men could defend themselves from it or endure it. Finding ourselves in such a peril with such a storm that we could hardly see from one boat to another because of the huge waves and the fog, we decided, after consulting the captain major, to signal the fleet to assemble and set its course for Portugal. And this was a wise decision, for if we had kept on that night we would all have been surely lost."

The months he had spent following the coastline from Brazil to Patagonia, the leagues he had sailed, the vast virgin regions he had seen, convinced him utterly that this land was no outpost of Asia. Whatever Columbus might think, this was a new world. Shortly after Amerigo's return he wrote that "we reached a new land which we discovered to be the mainland. . . . I reached the region of the antipodes, which according to my navigation is the fourth part of the world."

Later he wrote the more considered *Mundus Novus* which would become one of the most famous letters in history. In it he introduced the phrase "New World," setting apart the land he had seen from Europe, Asia, and Africa. "We learned," he wrote, "that the land is not an island but a continent, because it extends along far-stretching shores that do not encompass it and it is populated by innumerable inhabitants." Amerigo's letter destroyed the hypothesis of Columbus, the hypothesis from which John Cabot never freed himself, that the land mass they had discovered was an extension of Asia. *Mundus Novus* circulated rapidly among European scholars. Its very title was as significant as the text. In Paris it was printed in a Latin translation and quickly went into three editions. Translations into German, Dutch, and other languages followed.

Amerigo was still possessed by the idea of finding a southern passage to the Indies. He made a fourth voyage, but this was an anticlimax. Although he reached the coast of Brazil and built a fort there, after leaving several dozen settlers behind he sailed for home. "We could not continue farther," he explained, "because we were short of men, and much of our gear was gone."

Three months after his return he composed a thirty-two-page letter to the new gonfalonier of Florence, Piero Soderini, giving an account of his four voyages. This letter circulated as rapidly and as far as had *Mundus Novus.* Amerigo's name became a household word, at least among scholars. Favored by King Ferdinand, he became a Spanish subject and remained in Seville the rest of his life. The king made him pilot major of Spain, and with this office he established a maritime academy for training

The *Brendan, the curragh in which Tim Severin retraced the Irish saint's legendary voyage, was made of ox hides stretched over a frame of ash.*

pilots which included a library for maps. He died in 1512.

Amerigo's two letters reached the printing shop of the monastery of Saint-Dié in Lorraine's Vosges Mountains at a time when the monks were preparing a new geography of the world. In April 1507 they printed their *Cosmographiae Introductio,* consisting of a prologue, an epilogue, and nine brief chapters, followed by Amerigo's letter to Soderini (in Latin) and maps and a planisphere designed by the priest Martin Waldseemüller. The first eight chapters concern themselves with mathematics, and only the last deals with the earth. But in this ninth chapter the name America appears for the first time. In the margin is written: "It is fitting that this fourth part of the world, inasmuch as Americus discovered it, be called Amerige, or

let us say, land of Americi, that is: AMERICA." Nine lines of Latin verse expand the suggestion: "But now these parts of the world have been widely examined and another fourth part has been discovered by Americu Vesputiu (as will be seen in the following), I see no reason why we should not call it America, that is to say, land of Americus, for Americus its discoverer, man of sagacious wit, just as Europe and Asia received in days gone by their names from Women."

When Waldseemüller drew his map, he lettered in the word AMERICA. And so it has remained on maps and in minds ever since. Pilot Major Vespucci in Seville was all unaware that his Christian name was being immortalized. But his was the conception of a new world, and "America" is not unfitting for it.

CAPE HORN GHOSTS

The fiercest place on all the seven seas, in the judgment of sailing men, was the tip of South America. Whether they rounded Cape Horn or fought their way through the Strait of Magellan, ships faced violent storms, towering seas, and rocky coasts. Until 1848 the traffic consisted mainly of whalers and vessels in the China trade. But the discovery of gold in California led hundreds of ships, ranging from unseaworthy tubs to splendid new clippers, to attempt the passage.

Many did not make it. Some ran aground on reefs, shoals, and rocky shores. Many limped into harbor at the Falkland Islands, three hundred miles to the east, for repairs or scuttling. The wrecks of ships that never left those waters now make up the most remarkable maritime graveyard to be seen anywhere.

Historians have long seen these hulks as priceless relics of seafaring history. The *Great Britain*, first of the famous Atlantic ocean liners, which was dismasted and condemned at Port Stanley in 1886, has been refloated and returned to her home port of Bristol, England. Plans are afoot to save others, including some of the relics shown on these pages.

FALKLAND ISLANDS

CAPE HORN

Violent seas off Cape Horn (above) damaged the Ambassador (right) so badly that eventually she was beached. Her iron skeleton, stripped of its planking, now lies on a shore of the Strait of Magellan, offering a unique exhibit of composite hull construction. Except for the Cutty Sark, now a museum at Greenwich, England, she is the last surviving example of the extreme clipper

The short, inglorious career of the Saint Mary began
when she was launched at Phippsburg, Maine, on March
20, 1890. A wood-hulled square-rigger, 242 feet long,
she was one of the last of the ships that have come to
be known as down-easters. During the month of May she
lay at dock in New York (opposite page), taking on a
cargo that included 500 tons of iron rails for San
Francisco. Two months of smooth sailing, with skysails
set all the way, took her to the tip of South America,
where she found herself in close company with other
ships rounding the Horn. In the early morning hours of
August 7, while Captain Jesse Carver was in his cabin
and the mate unaccountably absent, the Saint Mary was
rammed by another ship. An untimely storm then drove
the damaged vessel onto a rocky shore of the Falklands,
where her broken hull still rests (above), the largest
surviving remnant of a down-easter. The crew was saved
but Captain Carver refused to leave the Saint Mary. The
ship's stewardess, who went to help him off, found him
holding "a glass of reddish mixture" and threatening to
shoot any crewman who came near. "Three times
I have been in trouble," he said, "and this is my last."
The next day he was dead.

Port Stanley, the chief harbor of the Falkland Islands (seen above in an 1876 sketch and at left in a modern photograph, is the last resting place of more than a dozen ships. The Jhelum (opposite page) was a British bark that reached Port Stanley in sinking condition after an attempted passage around the Horn in 1870.

The bow of the Charles Cooper rises from the harbor at Port Stanley where she lies aground. Built at Black Rock, Connecticut, in 1856, the Charles Cooper was a packet ship that sailed on a fixed schedule, carrying immigrants from Europe to New York. Though she has been a hulk for more than a century, she is more nearly intact below decks than any other American-built, square-rigged merchant ship. She is owned by New York's South Street Seaport Museum, which hopes to have her repaired and returned on a barge to New York as a museum piece. The author of Chapter 2, Peter Throckmorton, is an active participant in the project. Of the Charles Cooper he says: "She is the most complicated piece of American nineteenth-century craftsmanship in wood that exists today—and probably the most beautiful."

The British bark Marjory Glen, *carrying a cargo of coal, caught fire and burned out (top) in 1911. Her twisted metal hull (center and bottom) now lies beached on the coast of Argentina.*

The paddle wheels of the steamer Olympian *lie stranded, like a child giant's broken toy, on a sandy coast of the Strait of Magellan.*

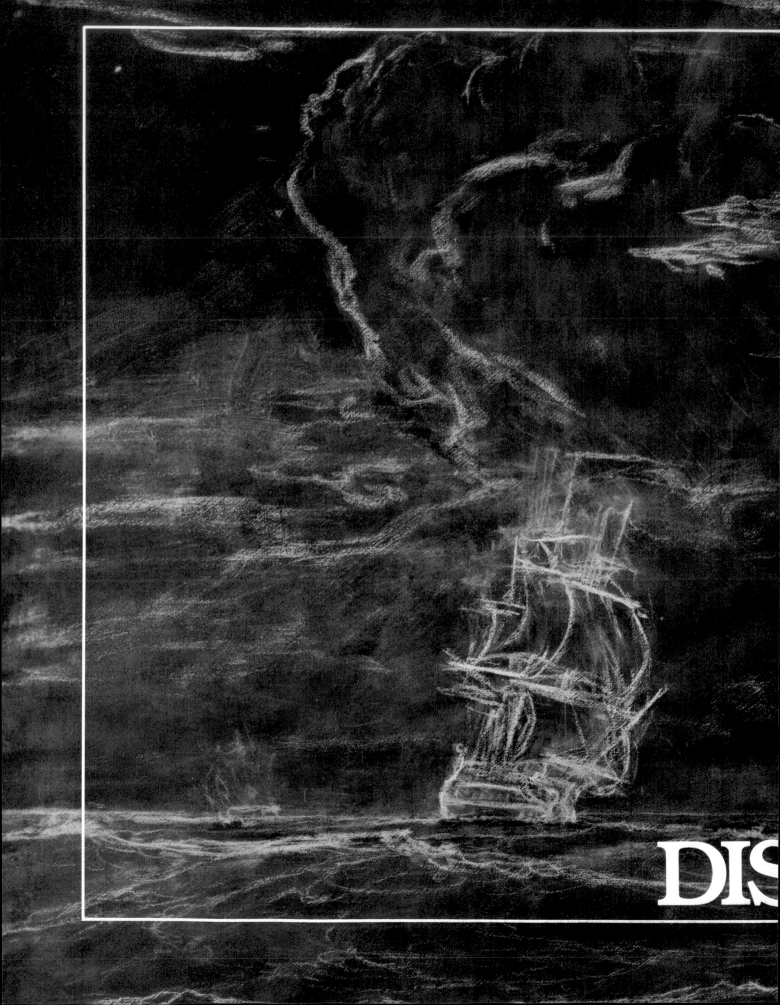

DIS

4

MYSTERIOUS APPEARANCES

Early in the afternoon of December 4, 1872, at a point about midway between the Azores and Portugal, the Nova Scotian brigantine *Dei Gratia* was proceeding on a southeasterly course when her master, David Reed Morehouse, sighted a sailing ship on his port bow, to windward. Through a glass he perceived that she was another brigantine, beating northwest on the opposite or starboard tack under very short canvas. As the gap between the ships narrowed, he was unable to make out any people on the stranger. Concluding that she was in some difficulty, he gave orders to haul wind and, on approaching closer, hailed her. There was no response. He then ordered a boat lowered, and sent First Mate Oliver Deveau, with Second Mate John Wright and a seaman, to investigate.

Rowing up to the silent hulk, the men read the name *Mary Celeste* on her bow, and on reaching her, Deveau and Wright clambered onto her deck, leaving the seaman in the boat alongside. The investigators soon confirmed that there was not a soul on board. The brigantine's one boat was gone. Both her fore and lazarette hatches were uncovered, and her hold, containing hundreds of wooden barrels marked "alcohol," held water to the depth of three and a half feet. The ship's jib and fore-top staysail were set, but the foresail and upper fore-topsail had been blown away, the lower fore-topsail was flapping loose, and the main staysail lay sprawled atop the forward house; all the other sails were furled. The masts and spars were sound and the standing rigging in fair condition, but some of the running rigging was carried away. In the forward house, awash to the coaming, the binnacle had been knocked down and the compass in it destroyed, but the wheel, though not lashed, was undamaged.

More interesting to Deveau and Wright than the disorder wrought by the elements were the many evidences of human order to be seen. The captain's chronometer and sextant, the navigation book, and the ship's register were missing, but the log book lay on the

VANISHED SHIPS AND VANISHED CREWS

by Ormonde de Kay, Jr.

OPPOSITE PAGE: Juno hurls a storm at Aeneas's fleet, smashing it. This pictorial evocation of the ancient belief that deities cause shipwrecks contrasts with Washington Allston's eerie and mysterious Ship in a Squall *on the preceding pages. The Lutine Bell, right, in the office of the marine insurance firm Lloyd's of London, is rung when ships are posted missing.*

desk in the mate's cabin and the log slate, or running log, on the cabin table; the final entry on the latter gave the *Celeste's* position at 8 A.M. November 25 as six miles northeast of Santa Maria, easternmost of the Azores. Contrary to accounts that are still credited, there was nothing in the cabin to eat or drink and no cooked food in the galley, but the ship's stores contained provisions for six months and ample drinking water. There were clean pots and kettles in the galley and clean knives, forks, and dishes in the pantry. In the seamen's quarters forward, and by the berths amidships occupied until recently by the *Celeste's* cook and two mates, were sea chests packed with clothing; among the men's visible effects were oilskins, boots, and even pipes and tobacco—"as if," Deveau was to testify, "they had left in a great haste or hurry." The captain's cabin likewise contained clothing, stowed in boxes and hanging from hooks, including, besides masculine attire, dresses, a pair of women's overshoes, and "articles of child's wearing apparel; also child's toys." A melodeon, or small reed organ, stood opposite the captain's bed, which had been slept in—by a child, Deveau guessed—but not made. Under the bed, finally, Deveau found a sheathed sword with faint discolorations on its blade.

At the end of half an hour the *Dei Gratia's* mates returned to their ship, where Deveau reported their findings. Captain Morehouse was particularly concerned about the fate of the *Mary Celeste's* people since her master, Benjamin Briggs, was a friend: Morehouse may, indeed, have dined with Captain Briggs and his pretty wife at New York's Astor House the night before they and their two-year-old daughter Sophia started down the East River to sea. (The *Mary Celeste*, bound for Genoa, had cleared New York on November 7, and the *Dei Gratia*, bound for Gibraltar and further orders with a cargo of petroleum, on the fifteenth.)

Mate Deveau now proposed that he and two men sail the derelict to Gibraltar. Morehouse hesitated to expose his ship and valuable cargo to the unpredictable hazards of the sea short-handed, but the prospect of earning salvage money overcame his reservations: he detailed two seamen to go with the mate in a small

The Mary Celeste *is shown as she appeared when sighted by the* Dei Gratia *in this wood engraving by Rudolph Ruzicka.*

boat, lending Deveau a barometer, a compass, and a watch. That evening the *Mary Celeste's* skeleton crew pumped her dry, set her sails, and got underway; next day they set a spare trysail in place of the missing foresail, and thereafter managed to keep up with the *Dei Gratia*. After a week, a storm separated the two vessels; the *Dei Gratia* reached Gibraltar on the evening of December 12, and the *Mary Celeste* the following morning.

On December 18 the vice-admiralty court met at Gibraltar to consider Captain Morehouse's claim for a salvage award. The queen's proctor, acting as attorney for the crown, promptly convinced himself that the *Mary Celeste's* second mate, cook, and four seamen had broken into the alcohol below decks and gotten drunk, murdered the Briggses and the chief mate, and escaped in the boat to a passing vessel bound for a North or South American port. This picture of foul play accorded oddly, however, with Captain Briggs's reputation as a firm but fair master, or with the near certainty that, having his wife and child on board, he would have made sure that his crew included only men of upright character. A survey of the 1,701 barrels of alcohol in the *Celeste's* hold, moreover, showed that none had been tampered with, while chemical tests would establish that the supposed bloodstains on Briggs's sword were, in reality, nothing of the sort.

The *Dei Gratia* sailed for Genoa two days before Christmas, but it was not until late February 1873 that the court—yielding to the importunings of the United States consul on behalf of the *Celeste's* owners—released that vessel to proceed to the same Italian port, under a master sent over from New York, and so earn her freight at last. Only in mid-March, after recalling Deveau for further testimony, did the court render judgment, awarding £1,700 to the *Dei Gratia's* master and crew as salvors. By then, lingering hopes that the *Celeste's* people might still turn up somewhere were fading, and before long they would glimmer out altogether.

But why had those people abandoned a vessel "fit to go round the world," in the words of a seaman who helped sail her to Gibraltar, for a small boat affording no protection from the elements and little enough from the sea itself? A fatal miscalculation seemed indicated—but about what? Was Deveau correct in believing that Briggs, finding his hold awash, had concluded that his ship was taking water too rapidly

for the pumps and would at any moment founder? Had something happened to make him think his highly volatile cargo was about to go up in flames? Was some other threat of danger involved? The court had no answers.

Eleven years later an English magazine published an anonymous short story based loosely on the discovery of the derelict *Celeste*. A well written if barely credible tale of wholesale murder for motives of racial vengeance, "J. Habakuk Jephson's Statement" included several embellishments that were absorbed into the evolving legend of the vessel, notably the spelling of her name as *Marie Celeste* and the circumstance of her "boats"—two of them—having been found on board her, neatly slung in davits. (In 1892 the story's author would be revealed to be Arthur Conan Doyle, the creator of Sherlock Holmes.)

Other romancers added their own "improvements" to the story: thus, in one frequently repeated version, the derelict was encountered sailing under a full spread of canvas, and the *Dei Gratia's* boarding party found a partly consumed breakfast on the cabin table, including cups of tea that were *still lukewarm.* Authors variously conjectured that the *Celeste's* people had been carried off by a giant octopus and by pirates; another, that Captain Briggs, overcome by religious mania, had butchered his family and everyone else before flinging himself into the sea; yet another, that fumes from a submarine volcanic eruption had driven the ship's company mad with thirst, causing them to jump overboard. Eventually, "survivors" turned up, ancient mariners apparently too shy to show their grizzled countenances, who left it to Fleet Street journalists and Sunday supplement by-liners to relate their sensational accounts. A nadir of sorts was reached in 1929 when an Englishman named Laurence J. Keating published *The Great Mary Celeste Hoax,* purporting to disclose the whole truth at last; the book was more aptly titled than he perhaps intended, being a pastiche of misstatements, easily demonstrable inaccuracies, and startling accusations, imputing fraud, notably, to that honorable seadog the late Captain Morehouse, and lubricous behavior to the blameless Mrs. Briggs, a clergyman's daughter.

Further errors and inventions continued to proliferate until 1942, seventy years after the event, when, by coincidence, two American writers laid out all the known facts in two carefully researched books: George S. Bryan's *Mystery Ship: The Mary Celeste in Fancy and in Fact* and Charles Edey Fay's *Mary Celeste: The Odyssey of an Abandoned Ship.*

That the *Celeste's* people perished there can be no doubt. As to why they abandoned her, the best published authorities, Messrs. Bryan and Fay, incline to the theory of Dr. Oliver Cobb, a younger cousin of both Captain Briggs and Mrs. Briggs, who shipped on board a brig as a boy and thereafter spent many hours of his long life pondering what could have happened on the morning of November 25, 1872, and afterward. Dr. Cobb ascribed the captain's sudden alarm to the threat of explosion posed by fumes of alcohol that had escaped from the porous red-oak barrels and been warmed by the surrounding waters while being kept confined in the hold. Did these gases rumble menacingly, as Captain Morehouse believed? Or did spontaneous combustion actually occur, blowing off the fore hatch cover, as the *Celeste's* then principal owner, Captain J. H. Winchester, afterward maintained? Dr. Cobb could not say. He felt certain, however, that the presence of Mrs. Briggs and Sophia had hastened the captain's decision to remove everybody from possible harm until the danger was past.

According to Dr. Cobb's hypothesis, Captain Briggs ordered the light sails furled and the mainsail lowered, then had the vessel hove to on the starboard tack. A section of the rail on the port side was taken out and the ship's boat lowered; simultaneously, the main peak halyard, an inch-thick rope, was readied for use as a towline, one end being left attached to the gaff and the other bent on the boat's painter. Gathering up chronometer, sextant, and ship's papers, Captain Briggs ordered everyone into the boat and followed them; they cast off, and within a minute or so the ten people were well astern of the ship, linked to it by four hundred feet of slack halyard and falling rapidly farther astern. All at once a strong northerly breeze unexpectedly filled the *Celeste's* square sails; the halyard leaped out of the water to snap taut, and as the ship gathered headway the straining line was drawn at an angle over the side. It parted—and the little boat was adrift.

No doubt the men rowed desperately, trying to overtake the ship, but it was hopeless: in no more than an hour or so the *Celeste*, a fast sailer, was out of

The lost family: top, Benjamin Briggs, the Celeste's *master; above, his wife (with their son Arthur, not on the voyage); and right, their daughter Sophia, aged two.*

sight. Her people were alone on the vast ocean, Santa Maria somewhere over the horizon. They were done for unless some vessel happened by to rescue them; but none did.

As for the *Mary Celeste*, she drifted on, mile after mile, encountered a squall and lost her foresail and upper fore-topsail. After no one can say how long, she came about to head west and shipped a sea, water cascading into her forward house and cabin and pouring into the hold through the open fore hatch. Hours or days later she again came about and headed east, only, in time, to reverse course once more. When the *Dei Gratia* met her, just over nine days after the last entry was recorded on her log slate, she was holding a reasonably straight course northwest by north.

But whether or not the foregoing scenario describes what actually happened will never be known. More than a century later the disappearance of the eight men, woman, and little girl in the brigantine *Mary Celeste* remains, as an American naval officer who inspected the derelict at Gibraltar wrote, a "sad and silent mystery of the sea," the most baffling of all and one of the most poignant.

Since before the dawn of history countless individuals and vessels have vanished on the world's watery wastes. Until two or three generations before the *Mary Celeste* mystery, however, their disappearance occasioned little wonder, being viewed as unavoidable, like the deaths periodically visited on humankind by pestilence, drought, famine, flood, and other natural calamities. Whether a ship was destroyed by wind and weather, by some mishap such as running aground on a submerged reef, or by faulty navigation and poor seamanship, its loss was nearly always laid to malevolent forces outside human control, forces which at an early stage took the form of deities associated specifically with the sea.

In ancient Greece, sailors whose ships did not return to port might be presumed to have been claimed by Poseidon, or his wife Amphitrite, or his son Triton; alternatively, they could have been lured to their doom by the Sirens, mythical beings, half bird and half woman, whose sweet singing drove all other thoughts out of their minds, leaving them helpless. Similarly, whether or not the proximate cause of a disappearance was known, the Phoenicians, Romans, and other Mediterranean seafarers habitually blamed it on the caprices of their own sea deities, as did maritime peoples living on the shores of far distant seas and oceans.

When Christianity displaced the old pagan gods and goddesses of Europe, belief in the surveillance and frequent intervention of supernatural powers survived intact: Christian seamen prospered under the protection of the Holy Mother and the saints, notably Saints Christopher and Nicholas, but were undone if the Devil outwitted their protectors. With the growth of ocean traffic that followed the discoveries of the New World and the sea route around Africa to India, the Spice Islands, and China, the number of vanishing ships increased, but fatalism regarding them prevailed: even after the Protestant sea powers of northwestern Europe came to dominate intercontinental trade, a vessel's unexplained disappearance was routinely ascribed to the workings of an inscrutable Providence. Americans, in their turn, adopted this attitude. Given the constant uncertainty and manifold perils of the deep, ships were bound to vanish from time to time; such incidents were customarily put down as acts of God, and in due course forgotten.

More appealing to most people in most epochs were sea mysteries of another kind: stories of survival, miraculous and otherwise, like the Biblical account of Jonah. A recurrent theme of ancient epic and legend was that of the sailor-hero—Odysseus, for example, or Sinbad—shipwrecked and cast ashore on an island. Such tales no doubt mirrored actual marine disasters and maroonings, just as Shakespeare, in writing *The Tempest*, is thought to have had in mind a party of Virginia-bound English colonists, stranded on a reef in 1609, who found refuge on uninhabited Bermuda. But the most famous modern "castaway," the eponymous hero of Daniel Defoe's *Robinson Crusoe*, was modeled on a Scottish shipmaster who, far from being wrecked, deliberately opted to remain on a desolate island 300 miles west of Chile when his companions departed. Still, Alexander Selkirk's lonely struggle to sustain existence during the four years and more he spent on Más a Tierra was sufficiently compelling to be converted into a best seller that became a classic.

Defoe's book was not an isolated phenomenon but rather, thanks to his journalist's skill, a conspicuously successful example of a flourishing literary genre. From the onset of the Age of Exploration ships had ventured ever farther out into unknown waters; many

Captain David Reed Morehouse of the Dei Gratia *discovered the* Mary Celeste *abandoned and had her sailed to Gibraltar.*

had come to grief, and the accounts of those survivors of disaster who managed to get to dry land had long held stay-at-homes in thrall. Most latter-day Odysseuses and Sinbads fetched up, it seems, on rocks or barren patches of sand offering little to sustain life; once rescued, sometimes after years, these men became the objects of keen public interest, and their stories were eagerly devoured. Those who perished before succor arrived, like the Dutchman who in 1725 was put ashore on Ascension Island, in the South Atlantic, for the crime of sodomy, sometimes left journals that were later published—in his case, anonymously, as *The Just Vengeance of Heaven Exemplified.* The sufferings of these unfortunates aroused pity, and their courage and enterprise in coping with their unpromising circumstances, admiration; clergymen drew on their experiences for sermons, and writers, for didactic and "improving" tales such as Johann Rudolf Wyss's *Swiss Family Robinson.*

But what happened to some castaways was neither grim nor particularly exemplary: thus Philip Ashton, a young Salem man captured by pirates in 1722 and pressed into their service, escaped to a wooded island off the coast of Honduras teeming with game and rich in fruits and edible plants; he hid out there in comparative comfort until, after sixteen months, he was taken on board an English ship bound for Jamaica. And when vessels, including American vessels, began calling at paradisiacal South Sea islands for water and produce, many a seaman found life there preferable to his harsh existence at sea and jumped ship. Perhaps the most memorable of all such voluntary castaways were the British petty officers and sailors who in April 1789 seized their ship, H.M.S. *Bounty,* and set her captain adrift: after sundry adventures at sea and on nearby Tahiti, they sailed, with women and a few men from that lush island, to remote Pitcairn Island, where, burning the *Bounty,* they set up a pioneer racially integrated community.

Meanwhile, the *Bounty's* autocratic commander, Captain William Bligh, and the eighteen loyal crewmen with him in the ship's boat, suffered horribly from thirst, hunger, and exposure, yet managed, by dint of remarkable seamanship and even more remarkable discipline and determination, to sail, row, and drift 3,618 miles, reaching Timor Island, in the East Indies, in June. Few voyages in open boats have lasted anything like as long, and many have ended less happily. The explorer Henry Hudson, to cite another celebrated victim of mutiny, was set adrift in a shallop in 1611 with his son and seven men, in the immense subarctic bay named for him, and was never seen again. Even today lifeboats loaded with the survivors of a sinking in high latitudes and in high seas have been known to capsize, and their life-jacketed occupants to drown in the icy water, within minutes of launching. In the days before air and sea searches mercifully shortened their ordeal, survivors in boats sometimes threw fellow passengers overboard to make their craft more seaworthy and to stretch scarce provisions further; sometimes, too, they were driven by unbrookable cravings to drink the blood and eat the flesh of dead comrades. It even happened that famished men, instead of waiting for a fellow passenger to die, killed one so that the rest might feed off his carcass; this took place, for example, in a boat holding crewmen from the Nantucket whaler *Essex,* which in 1820 was twice rammed by an implacable and determined whale and sent to the bottom of the Pacific.

Perhaps the most horrifying instance of murder and cannibalism at sea began on July 2, 1816, when the

The sea god Poseidon, here pictured on a vase from the fifth century B.C., struck fear into the hearts of Greek sailors.

French frigate *Medusa* went aground on a sandbank off the coast of present-day Mauritania in West Africa. This mishap was due, incidentally, to the incompetence of her captain, an aristocratic supporter of the restored Bourbon monarchy named Duroys de Chaumareix, who had not been to sea in twenty-five years.

When the *Medusa* shuddered to a sudden halt, she was carrying four hundred passengers and crew members, the former mostly soldiers and civilians, including twenty-one women, en route to Senegal to reoccupy that colony, newly returned to France by the British, who had seized it from Napoleon. That was many more people than her lifeboats could accommodate, and as waves battered the stranded frigate the colonial governor sketched a plan for a raft to be constructed out of her spars and timbers, lashed together. By July 5 the makeshift platform, fitted with a stubby mast and sail, was ready, and the order was given to abandon ship. The ladies and gentlemen of station embarked in the captain's and governor's barges, while most of the *Medusa's* officers, petty officers, and enlisted men found places in the four smaller boats. That left 149 men and one woman, a sergeant's wife, to crowd onto the sixty-five-by-twenty-three-foot raft, provisioned only with a single bag of sea-soaked biscuit, two casks of water, and six barrels of red table wine. Of the four officers who had refused seats in the lifeboats, two would be heard from: Alexandre Corréard, a civil engineer who declined to abandon the twelve construction workers in his charge, and Henri Savigny, a ship's surgeon.

Loaded with 150 people, the raft almost sank; everyone stood in water up to his waist, with little room to move. Supposedly, they were to be towed to shore, but their submerged craft proved too cumbersome for easy towing; as they watched in horror, the boats, one by one, slipped their towlines and sailed off, leaving them helplessly adrift.

That night, several men on the edges of the crowd were swept away, while others were crushed to death by the raft's constantly shifting timbers; next day, though the sea was calm, some in despair flung themselves off the raft. When a severe storm broke that night, a dozen men lost their footing and were drowned. Then many of the soldiers and sailors mutinied; one group broached a wine barrel and in drunken fury attacked the officers and the men who stood by them—among them Corréard and his band of workmen—with knives, sabers, bayonets, and carbines, which they wielded as clubs. In the melee the mutineers actually threw both of the water casks and two of the wine barrels into the sea. By the time peace was restored more than sixty men had been killed or washed overboard—and the survivors were only knee-deep in water.

Now hunger took over: falling on the corpses, men hacked off chunks, chewed the raw meat, and gulped it down. On the fourth day, even the officers learned to savor sun-dried human flesh. The soldiers, feeling their strength revive, stirred themselves to new violence, and before long the raft was strewn with more dead bodies. By the fifth day only thirty were left alive, but a kind of esprit de corps had sprung up among them, so that when, two days later, a pair of soldiers bored a hole in the last barrel of wine, they were summarily pushed overboard. Of those who remained, however, all but fifteen were ill or wounded, and clearly doomed; these individuals were consuming too much of the precious wine supply, and the healthy ones, consulting together, decided that they, too, must be jettisoned, among them the sergeant's wife.

Somehow, the raft's fifteen surviving passengers clung to life through another six days and nights, and on July 17 were picked up at last by the *Argus*, an escort of the *Medusa* which, had that flagship and the convoy been commanded by someone abler than de Chaumareix, would have been on hand to rescue the raft's original company instead of somewhere over the horizon. Arriving feeble and exhausted at Saint-Louis, Senegal, the last survivors were hailed as heroes by the governor, the captain, and the other officers who had set them adrift, but within days five more died.

For about a year the French government succeeded in suppressing newspaper accounts of the disaster, but in 1817 Corréard and his fellow survivor Savigny published an eyewitness account of their own. The national uproar that resulted forced the authorities to bring de Chaumareix to trial; he was sentenced to three years in prison, but the public persisted in pinning responsibility on the reactionaries in the government who entrusted people's lives to unqualified noblemen like him solely on the strength of their family connections and fealty to the king.

At about that time, twenty-six-year-old Théodore Géricault conceived the idea of painting a monumental picture based on the incident. In a few months he completed his colossal masterpiece, sixteen feet high and—like the raft—twenty-three feet wide. Exhibited at the Paris Salon of 1819, the painting was listed in the catalogue, in deference to the government censor, simply as *Shipwreck Scene*, but no viewer had to be told who these sufferers were or how they had arrived in their predicament. The newspapers condemned or praised it in accordance with their sentiments for or against the monarchy. But Géricault's *Raft of the Medusa* (reproduced on pages 222–223) profoundly impressed the throngs that came to see it, and today, when the sordid story behind it is forgotten, it remains perhaps the best-known representation of victims of shipwreck at the mercy of the sea.

Among the many ships that met disaster over the centuries, most went to the bottom or ran ashore. But a certain number of abandoned wrecks kept drifting helplessly around the seas. In 1894 a seven-year survey found a total of 1,628 hulks floating in the North Atlantic alone, many bottom-up, and only

then was a concerted international effort mounted to get rid of them. It was high time, for derelicts were a serious menace to navigation, especially at night. They had an unsettling effect, too, on seamen, a superstitious lot, and it may well have been the occasional sight of them that gave rise to the legends of ghost ships that were told and retold, until two or three generations ago, by sailors everywhere. In the West the most celebrated of these phantom vessels was the *Flying Dutchman*, supposedly seen in stormy weather off the Cape of Good Hope but now and then reported in other latitudes. Her Dutch captain, struggling to round the Cape in the teeth of a gale, is said to have sworn a blasphemous oath, whereupon the Almighty laid a curse on him, condemning him to sail forever with a ghostly crew of dead men, and never make port or know a moment's peace.

Down the ages and around the world, seafarers

Robinson Crusoe sports homemade finery in this illustration from the first edition of Daniel Defoe's 1719 book about him.

have used many names for the evil spirit of the deep, but the one most widely remembered today is Davy Jones, probably a corruption of the West Indian term "Duffy Jonah," a "duffy" being a ghost and Jonah, of course, the prophet who was thrown into the sea. A person who drowns or is buried at sea is said to have gone to Davy Jones's locker.

Sometimes, when a ship founders and its people—or some of them—go to Davy Jones's locker, the reason is evident, as in the *Titanic*'s collision with an iceberg; sometimes, again, it can be determined from survivors and/or witnesses on other vessels or on shore. Even if a sinking occurs in isolation, with the loss of all hands, the stricken vessel's calls for help may have pinpointed the trouble. In the absence of either survivors or witnesses or a clarifying radio message, the event must be counted a mystery; but even then the probable cause can often be deduced from what is known about the ship, its cargo, and its company, and about the sea and weather in the area. Yet today good-sized vessels of modern construction, manned by experienced people and equipped not only with radio but with loran, radar, and sonar, still occasionally disappear for no apparent reason.

That a logical explanation nevertheless exists for every such mystery is, however, firmly assumed by all concerned, in particular the ones who are financially liable, the insurers of the lost vessel and its cargo. And more often than not the pertinent clause in the policy or policies will be found to follow a form that has remained practically unchanged since it was drawn up in 1779 by members of that famous association of independent insurers, Lloyd's of London:

Touching the adventures and perils which we the assurers are contented to bear and do take upon us in this voyage: they are of the seas, men-of-war, fire, enemies, pirates, rovers, thieves, jettisons, letters of mart and countermart, surprisals, takings at sea, arrests, restraints and detainments of all kings, princes, and people, of what nation, condition, or quality soever, barratry of the master and mariners, and of all other perils, losses, and misfortunes, that have or shall come to the hurt, detriment, or damage of the said goods and merchandises, and ship, etc., or any part thereof.

In spite of its mention of men-of-war, enemies, and detention by foreign governments, this so-called perils clause does not now cover losses from war; essentially, it guarantees a shipowner or shipper against loss from "perils of the sea," a phrase broad enough to take in a

Under the bell salvaged from the 1799 wreck of the French ship Lutine, *underwriters at Lloyd's go about their business.*

virtually unlimited range of hazards and circumstances yet well and widely enough understood to have served for over two centuries. The clause itself covers every contingency—excluding acts of war but including acts of folly and/or mischief—that could cause a vessel to sink or suffer shipwreck or incur any kind of injury, and the fact that it does not except ships that vanish without explanation or trace shows that its framers rejected prevailing notions about mysterious acts of God in favor of a rational view. But those framers, successors to the merchants and bankers who a hundred years earlier had begun to drop by at the coffee house of a certain Mr. Lloyd to exchange news of ship movements, commodity prices, and the like, were, of course, men of business, hardheaded underwriters of marine insurance concerned with facts and figures rather than popular fancies; many years would elapse before their outlook would become general.

Precisely when it was that a ship's disappearance ceased to elicit fatalistic shrugs and became instead a subject of lively conjecture is impossible to say, as the change came about sooner in some places than in others. In the United States, a bustling new maritime nation less bound than some, perhaps, to old beliefs, the process seems to have been accomplished shortly after the end of the War of 1812, for it was then, as historian David Stick points out in his book about shipwrecks off the North Carolina coast, *Graveyard of the Atlantic,* that American newspapers, which had previously accorded scant space to ship losses, began instead to treat them in detail as news stories. Only a few years earlier an incident had occurred which has never been fully explained: the disappearance of the schooner *Patriot* with its crew and passengers, among the latter Theodosia Burr Alston, the twenty-nine-year-old daughter of former Vice President Aaron Burr and the wife of Governor Joseph Alston of South Carolina.

The *Patriot* left Georgetown, South Carolina, on December 30, 1812, bound for New York. When she failed to arrive there early the next year inquiries were made at most of the Atlantic seaports between, and even at Nassau in the Bahamas, but although a severe storm was known to have raged at Cape Hatteras just when the schooner was due to pass it, no one seems to have thought to look for her in that most likely of locales, where shifting sandbars had claimed numberless ships and lives over the three preceding centuries. And, indeed, it was near Nags Head on North Carolina's isolated Outer Banks that the *Patriot* apparently came ashore that January, with not a soul on board.

Well before spring, Theodosia and her shipmates were presumed to have been lost at sea, and the search

for them was given up. There matters stood until 1833, when a man in Alabama confessed on his deathbed that he had helped to capture the *Patriot* and murder everyone on board for her silver and other valuables. Fifteen years later another dying man told a similar tale, adding that a woman passenger named "Odessa Burr Alston," offered a chance by the pirate's leader to share his cabin, had opted to die instead.

In 1869, finally, a doctor vacationing at Nags Head was summoned to the dilapidated cottage of an old woman; noticing an expertly painted portrait of a young woman on the wall, he asked her about it and was told it had come from a vessel that had been found beached nearby one winter morning "when we were fighting the British." Since his patient was very poor, the doctor charged her no fee but accepted the picture in lieu of payment and took it home to the mainland. Years later someone who saw it suggested that the portrait might be of Theodosia; word of this theory spread, and in 1888 a descendant of the Burrs, a Mrs. Drake, visited the doctor to inspect the painting. "We were startled," the editor of the local newspaper wrote, "by her close resemblance to the portrait in question." And Mrs. Drake, in a letter to the Washington *Post*, recalled her first glimpse of it: " 'This is the picture,' I exclaimed. 'I know it is, because it bears a strong resemblance to my sister.' "

For some, the pirates' confessions, the old woman's story, and the Burr descendant's intuition about the portrait add up to a convincing and sufficiently complete account of what happened, but for those who insist on firmer evidence, the fate of Theodosia Burr Alston and her fellow voyagers in the *Patriot* will probably remain a mystery for all time.

The decades following the War of 1812 saw the appearance on the seas, especially the North Atlantic, of the first ocean-going steamships and of sailing ships fleeter than any previously built. Although these vessels were generally bigger and sturdier than their predecessors, they proved to be not appreciably less vulnerable to the perils of the sea; a number foundered, some, as always, in unknown circumstances. One mysterious disappearance that aroused much concern in both Britain and America was that of the Royal Mail Packet Service steamship *President*, a side-wheeler, in March 1841. In addition to her captain, an experienced seaman named

Roberts, the *President* was carrying 120 persons, including 27 passengers, among the latter Lord Fitzroy Lennox, son of the duke of Richmond, and the popular Irish comedian Tyrone Power, two of whose descendants and namesakes were to win fame as American actors, one on the stage and the other, his son, in the movies.

Standing out of New York harbor on March 11, the *President* steamed northeastward on the great circle track leading by the shortest path to her home port of Liverpool, perhaps (since she was, like practically all steamers of the time, a hybrid) under canvas as well, making use of the prevailing westerly winds to attain added speed. The next day, however, she encountered a furious gale, which was not to blow itself out until the evening of the thirteenth. So much can be confidently inferred of her final voyage, and no more.

On April 2 the *Orpheus*, which had left New York two days after the *President*, reached Liverpool; her captain said he had not seen the missing ship but suggested that she might have been disabled by the gale and run south or started working east under sail. The same day another steam packet, the *Virginia*, also arrived in Liverpool, having accomplished the crossing from New York, despite bad weather on the seventeenth through nineteenth, in a mere fifteen days; her people, too, had no news of the *President*, but their talk of large and numerous icebergs on the track filled seafaring men with foreboding.

When the rest of April passed with no news, it had to be assumed that the *President* had sunk. Perhaps she had gone down off the coast of Newfoundland in the terrible gale of March 12-13. Or perhaps she had struck an iceberg. Or even an abandoned hulk. But if she did sink, for whatever cause, why was no wreckage of her largely wooden hull and superstructure ever found, or any boat, spar, mast, life belt, or piece of ship's furniture?

In the absence of all clues, the cause of the *President's* disappearance could not be determined. But at least one writer—Elliott O'Donnell, in his book *Strange Sea Mysteries*—has proposed another and grim alternative ending for the ship: mutiny followed by scuttling. Citing rumors circulating at the time of a disabled steamship having been sighted making her way south, O'Donnell points out that in those days seamen were so ill-used that they sometimes turned on their oppressors. Might not the *President*, he asks,

"have been actually taken . . . south by the usurpers of authority, to be plundered and finally destroyed— destroyed in such a manner as to leave no possible telltale trace behind?"

When a ship becomes overdue at her destination long enough to cause comment, she is cited as such in *Lloyd's List*, published daily. If more time then goes by without news of her, Lloyd's solicits information about her under the rubric "Vessels for Inquiry." And if this fails to produce results—as it sometimes used to but rarely does any longer—the committee of Lloyd's may decide to have her posted missing.

Since October 1873 Lloyd's has kept records of all ships posted missing—in large books, each of which contains space for data on about 225 vessels. Every one of the several thousand entries therein represents an unsolved mystery. These records testify eloquently to the effectiveness of improvements in nautical technology and procedures in lessening the toll of life and property exacted by the sea. Whereas the first volume in the series covers just two years and two months, the fourteenth, commencing in July 1929 and running to the end of 1954, covers almost twenty years (the World War II years, 1939-45, being excluded), during which, on average, eleven vessels vanished annually—as opposed to nine *every month* in the first book.

Only once since 1873 has a ship reported missing subsequently turned up. This was the square-rigged freighter *Red Rock*, which on February 20, 1899, left Townsville, on Australia's northeast coast, for Nouméa in New Caledonia, just over a thousand miles east across the Coral Sea. On June 7, having been first reported overdue and then advertised for inquiry, she was posted missing—only to arrive at Nouméa five days later. There was nothing wrong with her; it was just that she was in ballast, high out of the water and hard to handle, and had had to beat to windward all the way. Then, too, she had had to steer clear of coral reefs, the locations of which were only sketchily known. And the spring months her voyage spanned (fall months in those southerly latitudes) coincided with the cyclone season.

The missing vessels book at Lloyd's containing the facts about the *Red Rock* covers four full years, 1897 through 1900 inclusive, which means that at the end of the nineteenth century ships were disappearing only

Is this portrait, purportedly found in a beached ship, that of Aaron Burr's daughter, Theodosia, who disappeared at sea?

half as frequently as they had been just a quarter century earlier. One reason was that engine-powered steel vessels, being sturdier, faster, and more maneuverable than wooden craft powered by the wind, stood up better to some hazards of the sea and more easily outran or evaded others. In this century sundry developments have further tipped the odds in favor of a ship's survival, notably the introduction of radio communications, the subdividing of hulls into watertight compartments, the publication of more accurate and detailed charts, and the establishment of a worldwide network of meteorological stations to collect and disseminate weather information on a continuous basis. Yet experience would show that human fallibility could still doom a ship and her company: a naval architect's miscalculation in placing her center of gravity; an officer's failure to make sure that her cargo was properly stowed and secured against shifting in heavy weather; or an untried young deck officer's fatal error of judgment in a crisis.

One type of modern ocean carrier that is hardly ever posted missing or even listed as overdue is the passenger liner, but in 1909 one was: the Blue Anchor Line's almost brand-new *Waratah*. On her maiden voyage from London to Australia and back, between November 1908 and April 1909, the *Waratah* encountered no bad blows, but a few crew members were unhappy about the way she rolled, and left her. Homeward bound from Australia on her second voyage, she left Durban, South Africa, on July 26 for Capetown and was never seen again. A clairvoyant declared that she had struck an uncharted rock, and it was rumored that some children had been cast up on a seldom-visited coast, where they were being cared for by tribeswomen, but in fact no trace of the liner or her 211 people was ever found. At the inquiry that finally convened at the end of 1910, the missing steamer's owners staunchly defended her stability. With direct evidence lacking and the indirect evidence conflicting, the court could not say how the ship was lost but inclined to the opinion that she had capsized two days out of Durban in her first bad storm. Officially, however, her fate remains undetermined.

There has never been the slightest doubt, on the other hand, about what caused the sinkings of the *Titanic* in 1912 and the *Lusitania* in 1915, apart from the charge, raised some years ago, that the latter ship, torpedoed off the Irish coast by a German submarine, had been purposely exposed to destruction on orders of First Lord of the Admiralty Winston Churchill, with the aim of shocking American opinion and hastening this country's entrance into World War I. But an aura of mystery still surrounds the sinking, off the Orkney Islands in July 1916, of the cruiser carrying Lord Kitchener, then secretary of state for war, to Petrograd. H.M.S. *Hampshire* evidently struck a mine, but was this an accident? It was rumored at the time and acknowledged later that Kitchener's cabinet colleagues bitterly opposed his measures for pursuing the war yet dared not openly challenge so popular a figure: could they have taken this means to get rid of him? This theory, which was promptly credited by some, has its proponents to this day.

In March 1918 the U.S.S. *Cyclops*, a collier, vanished somewhere between Barbados and Norfolk, Virginia, with 288 men; she was the first large radio-equipped vessel to disappear without sending an S O S, and the largest navy ship ever to disappear. It

The President *is being driven before "the terrific gale of March the 13th 1841" in this depiction of her final agony as imagined by a young lithographer named Nathaniel Currier.*

was assumed that she had been destroyed by a U-boat, but an inspection of German naval records after the war revealed that this was not the case. Had she been scuttled, then, by her German-born commander? To disaster buffs who reject this explanation—the great majority—the *Cyclops* affair remains totally baffling. Two recent developments, however, suggest that the conundrum may one day be solved. In 1968 a navy diver reported seeing a large steel vessel of unusual shape on the ocean bottom seventy miles east of Norfolk; he was sure it was the long-missing collier. Years later, researcher Lawrence D. Kusche followed up this clue by checking Norfolk weather records for the day the *Cyclops* would have approached that port, and found that the area had been battered by a severe

and showing no sign of life. Because of the tremendous surf crashing around her, no one could approach her until February 4, by which time the breakers had forced her seams apart and filled her hold. The boarding party found food set out in the galley and on the stove, suggesting a hurried flight by the crew.

What had happened? Speculation centered on three possible explanations: mutiny, piracy, and abandonment.

Investigation revealed that the *Deering*'s captain, a retired mariner who had replaced her ailing master on short notice, had told a friend at the schooner's last port of call, Barbados, that he was in poor health and that his crew was a drunken and shiftless lot, quite capable of treachery. It was further revealed that the day before the ship stranded, as she passed the Cape Lookout light vessel, a crew member—not the captain—had shouted that they had lost their anchors and needed help. Why hadn't the captain done the hailing? Had he been murdered?

The piracy theory appears to have owed much to the postwar "red scare" that had recently convulsed the country, for the *Deering*'s supposed abductors were Bolsheviks intent on sailing her halfway around the world to Vladivostok. Their evil plan had, it seems, miscarried, but the schooner's captive crewmen might even then be en route to Cape Horn or the Cape of Good Hope. A note found in a bottle on a beach told of Russians seizing the vessel and slaughtering most of her crew, but its author was soon revealed to be the same individual—a resident of a nearby village—who had chanced upon it.

The most likely possibility, and the one that gained most support, was that the eleven men in the schooner, convinced that she was going on the dreaded shoals, had taken to the boats—and certain death in the churning waves. Yet doubt persisted, and though new theories are still being put forward and supposedly new evidence uncovered, the fate of the *Deering*'s people is today as much of a puzzle as it ever was.

In 1955, readers of Morris K. Jessup's *The Case for the UFO* were treated to a supposed sea mystery of truly awesome magnitude: the disappearance, not on just one occasion but intermittently over centuries, of uncounted ships and, latterly, airplanes in the western Atlantic. Linking newspaper stories of recent unexplained disappearances with similar incidents in the past, Jessup proposed a single cause for all of them, a

storm. But confirmation that the collier foundered in that storm must await the rediscovery and identification of the sunken hulk.

South of Norfolk, the Diamond Shoals that project seaward from Cape Hatteras became, on the night of January 30–31, 1921, the scene of an intriguing mystery—after that of the *Mary Celeste*, the greatest, perhaps, in American marine annals. This was the stranding there of the schooner *Carroll A. Deering*, with all sails set on her five masts, stripped of her boats, mysterious force he associated with the periodic reappearances of unidentified flying objects. Other writers took up the theme, and in February 1964 Vincent H. Gaddis, in an article in *Argosy*, defined the zone in which the force operated as that bordered by imaginary lines connecting Bermuda, Florida, and Puerto Rico—the Bermuda Triangle. Like the *Mary Celeste* mystery, the mystery of the Bermuda Triangle appealed irresistibly to the popular imagination, the more so in that it afforded unlimited scope for speculation; in books and articles and on radio and television talk shows the solutions to it that were offered covered an extraordinary range, including magnetic and/or gravitational anomalies, time warps, astrological influences, black holes, and death rays from Atlantis. As awareness of the mystery spread, the public's appetite for material about it increased. In 1974 Charles Berlitz and J. Manson Valentine, having absorbed the literature on it and carried out on-the-scene investigations for themselves, published *The Bermuda Triangle*, a comprehensive work that brought the subject to the attention of millions, figuratively putting the oceanic region of the title on the map—or rather, chart.

But could that stretch of ocean really be a pitiless wholesale devourer of human lives? Many doubted it. Although most of the disappearances mentioned thus far in this account are well known to students of marine disasters, not one of them, significantly, occurred within the Triangle. To be sure, a good many ships and planes have in fact vanished there, some in unknown circumstances, but it would be astonishing if they had not, considering that the region has been continuously traversed by craft of all descriptions since the time of Columbus. As for the alleged sinister force or forces, it is worth noting that the Bermuda Triangle takes in at least three natural features affecting navigation: on the east, the Sargasso Sea; to the north and south, Bermuda and the Bahamas, with their beautiful but often treacherous shoals and coral reefs; and on the west, the swift-running Gulf Stream, which can instantly obliterate every trace of a sunken ship or downed plane. And much of the region, finally, is regularly devastated by hurricanes.

Like many other American librarians in the early 1970's, Lawrence D. Kusche of Arizona State University found himself besieged by requests for information about the Bermuda Triangle. With a colleague, he compiled a bibliography on it, but then, his curiosity aroused, he began collecting data on the incidents of disappearance that the writers had reported. By letter, teletype, and telephone he sought assistance from Lloyd's, the National Climatic Center, the United States Air Force, Navy, and Coast Guard, and a host of agencies public and private, national and local, American and foreign; he obtained transcripts or microfilm copies of the London *Times*, *The New York Times*, and newspapers in Miami, Norfolk, Nassau, San Juan, and other cities where the incidents had been reported; and he consulted various individuals with firsthand knowledge of the incidents. For most of the disappearances, he discovered, logical explanations automatically emerged once sufficient information was brought to light, and most of the mysteries that remained unsolved were those about which such information could not be obtained. He also found, among other things, that

• many incidents were not considered mysterious at the time they occurred but only became so when writers seeking new material on the Triangle resurrected them and presented them as such, deliberately or inadvertently omitting contradictory details;

• commentators regularly misrepresented the facts, stating, for instance, that a vessel had vanished in a calm sea under a clear sky when in fact a hurricane had been blowing;

• numerous incidents in the Bermuda Triangle canon occurred hundreds or even thousands of miles from that region;

• many or most publicizers of the incidents did no original research but simply rephrased the work of previous writers, perpetuating the latter's errors and embellishments;

• key details of several incidents and some entire incidents were fictitious.

In 1975 Kusche published his documented findings and conclusions in *The Bermuda Triangle Mystery—Solved*. He acknowledged that a small number of the puzzling events chronicled by writers—the disappearance in 1909 of the solitary circumnavigator Joshua Slocum (see page 210), for one—remained, for want of sufficient information, authentic mysteries; but he left the impression that these exceptions were no more numerous or remarkable than those that might occur in any equally well-traveled region of comparable size. He concluded that the much-publicized Bermu-

Launched only two years before she met her perplexing end, the Carroll A. Deering *was a fine, big five-masted schooner.*

da Triangle mystery was in fact nothing more than a latter-day legend created by several collaborators, some of whom, presumably, believed in it. Because a love of mystery is ingrained in many people, Kusche's book was less than welcome in some quarters, and its sales were modest compared to those of the books it refuted.

Kusche's killjoy conclusions, recalling the no-nonsense attitude of the eighteenth-century Lloyd's underwriters, illustrate once again a truth which more thoughtful seamen may well have recognized—and prudently kept to themselves—through the ages: that ships and men are not sent to their doom by supernatural (or extraterrestrial) beings and forces but by the fury of nature, abetted by the follies and failings of human beings.

Today, in spite of weather-scanning by satellites, the containerization of cargoes, the institution of higher educational standards for officers, the requirement of more frequent inspection of vessels, and the increased attention to all factors affecting a ship's safety, the danger of collision or stranding remains alarmingly high, particularly as regards those new monsters of the deep, the supertankers. But if accidents involving these behemoths inflict harm to oceans and coasts on a scale hitherto unknown, the toll of all mishaps, in terms of human life, is now much reduced from what it was. Even so, it would take a bold prophet to predict that in the future mariners will cease to vanish inexplicably from the face of the deep, if only because, as Joseph Conrad wrote, the sea has always been "the irreconcilable enemy of ships and men ever since ships and men had the unheard-of audacity to go afloat together in the face of its frown."

THE LOST TRAINING SHIPS

Seagoing tradition yields only gradually and grudgingly to change. Long after the leading cargo fleets and navies had converted from wood and canvas to steel and engines, their chiefs still insisted that apprentice officers learn to handle ships under sail; hence the majestic if anachronistic square-rigged school ships in service to this day. The fact that these vessels have been manned in the main by adolescent boys lends a special poignancy to the stories of three that disappeared—one British, one Danish, and one German.

The first, H.M.S. *Atalanta,* was a third of a century old and had been moored for a decade in Portsmouth Harbor, doing double duty as a naval prison and Royal Marine barracks, when in 1878 she was picked to replace the *Eurydice,* lost in a squall—in view of helpless watchers on the Isle of Wight—with her entire complement of three hundred midshipmen and crew members. The following year, in October, the refitted frigate, under command of a veteran officer with the reassuring name of Stirling, took on provisions for a voyage to the West Indies and back. By November the ship's company comprised 290 souls, more than 270 of them midshipmen between the ages of twelve and seventeen. And on the seventh, to the cheers of the boys' families assembled on the quay and the strains of "Rule Britannia" played by a band, the aging three-master moved slowly toward the channel, towed by a tug.

Cadets of the training ship Kobenhavn *gather around the figurehead of* Absalon, *the Danish warrior-priest who founded the ship's name town and home port, Copenhagen.*

The British frigate Atalanta *disappeared en route from Bermuda to Portsmouth in 1880. The Admiralty responded to reports of wreckage near the Azores by sending a six-vessel search party to comb the area, but no trace was ever found.*

On the stormy outward passage via Tenerife, in the Canaries, the *Atalanta* revealed herself to be a sluggish sailer with an alarming tendency to roll in a sea; much of the time some of the middies were too seasick to go aloft. At Barbados Captain Stirling put five seamen ashore, two to be tried for refusing to obey orders and three because they had contracted yellow fever. After a week, on January 9, 1880, the *Atalanta* sailed north to Nova Scotia. From frigid Halifax she was hurled south by northerly gales, to arrive at Bermuda on the twenty-ninth. And on the last day of January she set out on the final leg of her voyage, with everyone in her doubtless eager for home and surcease from the cramped discomfort of life aboard ship.

The *Atalanta* was expected in

Portsmouth around the beginning of April. That winter and early spring the weather over the North Atlantic was even fouler than usual, particularly in the Azores region, and the officers at the Admiralty, who had heard numerous reports of sightings of dismasted ships and of miscellaneous flotsam strewn over the waves, must have felt more anxiety about the training ship than they chose to show, when the midshipmen's relatives began asking, ever more insistently, for news of her. On April 13 a navy spokesman conceded that she was overdue and allowed that she might have been disabled by storms, but he expressed confidence in her "unusual stability." Two days later, however, the Admiralty admitted to "grave apprehensions," and on the sixteenth more than two hundred men and women

At the time of her mysterious disappearance in antarctic waters in late 1928 or early 1929, the Kobenhavn *was, Alan Villiers writes, "the largest and finest sailing-vessel in the world."*

with sons, grandsons, or nephews on the *Atalanta* converged on Whitehall to demand that something be done to find out what had become of her. In response, the sea lords dispatched a stores ship to the Azores to make inquiries.

By then the newspapers were carrying daily reports of developments in the story, and the fate of the missing school ship was becoming a national preoccupation. Soon, aroused public opinion would force the sea lords to commit the entire Channel squadron to the search. Before that, however, on April 27, one of the *Atalanta*'s seamen who had been put ashore at Barbados arrived in Portsmouth, cured of yellow fever; his name was John Verling, and what he had to say made interesting copy. He told reporters that the supposedly stable vessel rolled as much as thirty-two degrees; that Captain Stirling, out of fear for her safety, stayed

on deck at all hours; and that he had heard the captain say the ship would surely founder if she rolled one more degree. Presumably at the instigation of his superiors in Whitehall, a flag captain called on the talkative seaman, then announced that Verling was a simple fellow, not really aware of what he said; but the press and public were not persuaded.

On May 18 the Admiralty abandoned hope for the *Atalanta* and announced an inquiry. Then on June 14, while a select committee was holding hearings in Westminster, the skipper of a trawler off Rockport, Massachusetts, scooped from the sea a bottle containing a hastily written message that read, in part, "April 17, 1880, training ship *Atalanta*. We are sinking in L. 27° Lat. 32°"—a position south of Fayal in the Azores. Two days later children playing on a Nova Scotian beach found a barrel stave half buried in the sand with some words scrawled on it in pencil: "Atalanta: going down, April 15, 1880. No hope. Send this to Mrs. Mary White, Sussex. James White."

Though the select committee reached no firm conclusion, it seems probable that the top-heavy old training ship finally did roll that extra degree or two in a great storm around the Azores, with precisely the result her captain had feared.

More puzzling was the disappearance, half a century later, of the Danish East Asiatic Company school ship Kobenhavn. Launched in 1921, the Kobenhavn, 430 feet overall and capable of spreading 56,000 square feet of canvas, was in 1928 the largest sailing vessel in the world—the only five-masted bark still in service—and by practically any standard the finest. She was also one of the safest, prepared to meet just about any emergency. Her steel hull was strongly built, and her below-decks space was divided athwartships by watertight bulkheads, which enhanced both her structural strength and her capacity to maintain buoyancy if breached. She had an auxiliary diesel motor, long-range radio equipment, and generators providing electricity for lighting and heating; she had ample pumps and all the boats and lifesaving gear she could ever need. In the preceding seven years she had made half a dozen very long voyages, including a circumnavigation of the globe.

Yet this magnificent vessel vanished utterly in late 1928 or early 1929, without an SOS or any other warning of impending disaster, leaving nothing behind to hint at the fate of her fifteen regular crewmen—experienced seafarers who had all sailed in her before—or her forty-five cadets, who unlike the somewhat younger midshipmen on the Atalanta had every one previously been to sea, on the average for more than two and a half years.

The Kobenhavn left Buenos Aires in ballast on December 14, 1928, bound, via the Cape of Good Hope, for Australia, where she was to load grain and proceed home, around Cape Horn, to Denmark. On the twenty-first she exchanged radio signals with a Norwegian steamer a thousand miles out of Buenos Aires, but after that nothing more was ever heard from her. At first her failure to report her position caused no great concern, since her radio could have broken down, but as weeks passed with no news of her, apprehensions mounted. By mid-February, when she was overdue in Australia, her owners were in contact with all the few ships plying the subantarctic reaches of the Atlantic and Indian oceans. None could tell them anything.

In March searchers started visiting the bleak subpolar islands and rocks south of her presumed track in the hope of finding survivors: nowhere did they meet any sign of human life; everywhere the caches left for castaways were untouched. But the owners refused to give up hope. They chartered a ship, the Mexico, which for months combed the southern ocean and its islands and coasts as thoroughly as any vessel ever had before. Meanwhile, other ships were scouting more limited areas. The search, involving dozens of vessels, continued for over a year without coming upon so much as an identifiable splinter or length of cord from the missing ship.

What had happened to the Kobenhavn? The court of inquiry's best guess was that the projecting spur of a low-lying iceberg had ripped her open as she raced past in darkness, driven by a strong west wind; she would then have gone down in seconds, too quickly for anyone to get off an SOS, and since everything topside was lashed down there would have been nothing on deck to float away except the watch: two officers and perhaps fifteen boys. But that was only conjecture, and unless her corpse is one day located and brought up from the ocean bottom—

an unlikely prospect—the cause of her disappearance will never be known.

The demise, in 1938, of the last square-rigger to vanish without a trace was almost a replay of the Kobenhavn tragedy. Built three decades earlier as the Belgian training ship L'Avenir, the four-masted bark had been acquired the previous year by the Hamburg-America Line, extensively refitted, renamed the Admiral Karpfanger, and sent out to South Australia with a crew of sixty that included thirty-three cadets aged fifteen to eighteen. On February 8, 1938, laden with 42,549 bags of wheat for an Irish or English destination, the stately vessel sailed out of Port Germein and Spencer Gulf; days later, at approximately 50 degrees south latitude, she commenced to run due east across the Pacific to Cape Horn. On March 1 she reported her position as longitude 172 degrees east, south of New Zealand, and on March 12 acknowledged a radio signal. After that, all was silence.

When months passed with no news of the Admiral Karpfanger, her owners asked all ships traversing the lonely South Pacific lanes to look out for her—or signs of her. At their request, units of the Argentine navy scoured the bleak bays, straits, and beaches of the island cluster making up South America's southern extremity, but found nothing. At last, the search was given up. But later—much later—wreckage was discovered among the Cape Horn islands, which, since the Argentine searchers had not spotted it, must have recently drifted there: timbers with brass fastenings, ship's doors bearing German inscriptions, a broken-off length of a mast or spar. These objects were identified, tentatively, as pieces of the Admiral Karpfanger; if they were such, that ship had been smashed open, either by rocks or—more likely, in the opinion of the world-famous authority on sailing ships Alan Villiers—by an antarctic iceberg.

JOSHUA SLOCUM'S LAST VOYAGE

On November 14, 1909, eleven years after becoming the first person in history to sail alone around the world, Joshua Slocum, aged sixty-five, boarded the battered old sloop *Spray* in which he had accomplished that feat, hoisted her mainsail and jib, steered her out of the harbor of West Tisbury, on Martha's Vineyard, and headed south into the Atlantic. According to Bermuda Triangle legend he was never seen again, but some people say he turned up later in the West Indies, and others that he was seen sailing up Venezuela's Orinoco River long after he had been declared missing. Whatever the facts of the matter, Slocum did not return, and in time almost everyone agreed that at some point he and his boat had vanished, in or near the Bermuda Triangle, forever.

The disappearance of Joshua Slocum and the *Spray* is, if anything, more baffling than most such incidents. It is also less tragic, since it claimed only one victim, an aging man; given that man's formidable reputation as a seaman, moreover, many people couldn't help but suspect that he had somehow contrived his own fate or at least consented to it. There were whispers that he had secretly been bent on suicide, or that he was seeking a remote haven in which to live out his remaining years in peace. But regardless of what caused

Seated in his boat, deep in thought, old Joshua Slocum seems a figure carved from oak, a Yankee-seafarer version of Rodin's famous statue, The Thinker.

it, Slocum's disappearance at sea struck many people at the time as a curiously appropriate finale to a remarkable life spent almost entirely on salt water or beside it.

Born in Nova Scotia in 1844 to a lighthouse keeper's daughter who had married a farmer, Slocum went to sea at sixteen, was a second mate at eighteen, and at twenty-five accepted command of an American coastal schooner and took steps to become a United States citizen. In 1871, the captain of a San Francisco bark, Slocum married an Australian girl, Virginia Walker, who would accompany him on many voyages in a succession of trading vessels and would bear him seven children. Over the years the couple shared various adventures: quelling a mutiny off New London, Connecticut, rescuing some Gilbert Islanders in the Pacific, narrowly escaping catastrophe near the Cape of Good Hope when a rudder head twisted off.

In July 1884, off Brazil's southeast coast, Virginia fell seriously ill and expressed a wish to see her homeland one last time. Slocum anchored his ship, the bark *Aquidneck,* in the Río de la Plata and went ashore to seek a cargo for Sydney, but seeing a signal flag of distress flying at the yardarm of his vessel, he hurried back on board; his wife was still alive, but that night she died. He buried her in the English cemetery at Buenos Aires. Days later, in a frenzy of grief, he deliberately ran the *Aquidneck* ashore, but then, regaining command of himself, he got her off the beach and sailed her to Boston, where he commended his children to the care of married sisters.

After almost two years of lonely sailing on his little freighter, Slocum, ashore in a Massachusetts port, met

and fell in love with a pretty young seamstress, Henrietta Elliott, and on Washington's Birthday, 1886, married her in Boston. Six days later the couple set out on a wedding trip, with Slocum's sons Victor and Garfield aboard. At the entrance to Paranaguá Bay in southern Brazil the *Aquidneck* became stranded on a sandbar, where Atlantic swells soon smashed her to bits. Her crew drifted away, and Slocum, with his family's help, began salvaging timbers from the wreck; from these, and from logs roughhewn from local hardwood trees, he constructed a craft he called a canoe. It was launched on the day the slaves of Brazil received their freedom, or *liberdade,* so he named it the *Liberdade.* The Slocums then sailed the thirty-five foot vessel north, covering the approximately 5,500 miles to Washington, D.C., in fifty-three days. That was enough for Hettie Slocum: she announced that she would henceforth stay ashore, and she never, in fact, went to sea again.

In 1890 Slocum wrote *The Voyage of the Liberdade* and had it printed and bound, but he succeeded in selling few copies. For the Slocums, times were hard. Late in 1892 a retired whaling captain offered Slocum a disused oysterman, the thirty-seven-foot *Spray;* for a year or more Slocum used his spare time to repair the sloop, and launched her at last in the summer of 1894. About then the idea came to him of sailing her around the world; he laid plans and made preparations and on April 24, 1895, set out from Boston Harbor on his great adventure, with just a dollar and a half in his pocket.

Three years, two months, and two days later, with 46,000 miles of ocean behind him, Slocum returned. Suddenly he was famous: Richard Wat-

Unlike Slocum's first wife, his second wife, Hettie, declined to share his vagabond life at sea. To judge by this 1902 photograph, however, she was willing to board his boat, so long as it was safely moored in the snug harbor of West Tisbury.

son Gilder bought the rights to publish his account of his epic voyage in the *Century* magazine, and his book *Sailing Alone Around the World* sold 10,000 copies in its first year. Many duplicates of the *Spray* were built. Mariners differed sharply, however, about her sailing properties, some declaring that the sloop, designed for oyster dredging in sheltered waters, was hopelessly ill-adapted to voyaging on the open sea and would unquestionably have tipped over had a seaman less skilled than Slocum been at the helm.

In the first years of the new century Slocum settled down on Martha's Vineyard to grow hops, but his brother's wife, a zealot for temperance, made such a fuss that he gave it up and went back to "hustling for the dollar" in the *Spray,* up and down the coast and occasionally to the West Indies. He spent less and less time at home, perhaps, if the rumors were true, because he didn't get on with Hettie. Early in the fall of 1909 he conceived the plan of an unusual voyage of discovery: he would, he told friends, sail up the Orinoco and thence, via the Río Negro, to the Amazon, which he would ascend to its unknown source and then follow out to the ocean. He would be gone, he estimated, about two years. And in November, as we have seen, he sailed south.

For most chroniclers of Slocum's story his subsequent fate remains a mystery, one that is made the more perplexing by suggestions in the record of deteriorating health, memory lapses, and a tendency to "black out" from time to time. Many possible denouements have been proposed: that Slocum finally met the gale that could sink him, or that the *Spray* caught fire; that he fell overboard, either accidentally or in consequence of a blackout spell; that he died a natural death and the sloop later foundered with his body still aboard. But for Edward R. Snow, surely the most prolific American recounter of true tales of the sea, the mystery of Slocum's disappearance was definitively solved some time in the 1950's by a story he heard from a master mariner, Captain Charles H. Bond of Wollaston, Massachusetts— a story Bond had, in turn, been told by a planter in the Lesser Antilles named Felix Meinickheim.

According to Meinickheim, Slocum spent a few days toward the end of 1909 at his house on Turtle Island. Two days after Slocum left for the mouth of the Orinoco the planter, waiting on his wharf for the five-hundred-ton steamer that ferried mail, freight, and passengers among the islands, noticed a gash in the approaching vessel's stem just above the water line. Boarding her, he asked the captain about it and was told that the steamer had run down a native boat the night before. How did the captain know it was a native? With a shrug, the captain asked, "Who else could it be?"

Upon inquiry, Meinickheim learned that the accident had occurred during the midnight-to-four-o'clock "grave-yard" watch, always taken by the second mate. That officer related that the night had been unusually dark but asserted that he was nevertheless sure there had been no one at the wheel of the vessel that was hit. But the mate's recollection of that vessel did not square with what the captain had said: "In the few seconds when I saw the other craft," he told Meinick-heim, "I made out that she was not a native of this area."

Since the chances were over-whelming that the *Spray* was the only stranger vessel anywhere in those then little-visited waters, Meinickheim concluded sorrowfully that his recent guest, the celebrated circumnaviga-tor Joshua Slocum, had been acci-dentally run down while he was sleeping, and drowned.

A sad end? Perhaps, but a merciful-ly sudden and quick one, and as such preferable, no doubt, to some of the alternatives.

The craft in which Slocum disappeared—and had earlier sailed around the world— was a humble oysterman. Was she, as some said, an ungainly vessel, unsuited to ocean trips, which only a sailor of Slocum's skills could have kept from capsizing?

MISSING IN THE ARCTIC

In 1815, when the defeat of Napoleon freed the British government from preoccupation with war for the first time in a generation, the Royal Navy turned again to the centuries-old search for a water route to the Orient across the top of North America. Earlier explorers, from Sir Martin Frobisher and Henry Hudson to Sir Alexander Mackenzie, had gradually established the contours of the large and small Arctic Ocean islands making up the continent's northern barrier; it remained to be determined whether a navigable way could be found through them to connect Davis Strait, the northward-reaching arm of the North Atlantic between Baffin Island and Greenland, with the open waters of the Arctic Ocean north of Alaska. To the British, the fact that Alaska was occupied by an expanding and potentially hostile imperial power, Russia, lent a certain urgency to this endeavor. The renewed quest for the Northwest Passage, which would continue for decades, spawned a mystery that for several years claimed the concern of the British people and of multitudes elsewhere: the disappearance, in the vast, island-cluttered seas of arctic Canada, of Sir John Franklin and his expedition of two ships.

Franklin, a veteran of Trafalgar and New Orleans, was well qualified for the task he undertook. Following his first voyage into arctic waters in 1818, he had led two overland expeditions across northwestern Canada in 1819–22 and 1825–27, accompanied by the explorer George Back; and he knew intimately the fellow officers whose discoveries had enriched

The Erebus, *one of Franklin's two ships, is about to become trapped in ice in Victoria Strait next to King William Island in this painting by François Musin.*

knowledge of the Canadian North: William Edward Parry, the first to winter there, in 1819–20; John Ross, who had returned to England from his second arctic expedition, in 1829–33, long after being given up for lost; and Ross's nephew James Clark Ross, the discoverer, in 1831, of the magnetic north pole. From 1836 to 1843 Franklin had served as governor of Van Diemen's Land (later Tasmania); and when in 1845 it was decided to send out another large expedition to the region, he was a logical choice to head it. (Actually, the sea lords considered Franklin, at nearly sixty, too old, and offered the command to James Clark Ross, but the latter, having promised his wife to give up polar exploring, declined, whereupon Parry urged them to appoint Franklin: "He is a fitter man to go than any I know," Parry wrote, "and if you don't let him go, the old man will die of disappointment.")

Besides the wish to find the Northwest Passage before the Russians or Americans could, the Admiralty had a technical motive in sending another expedition to northern Canada. The development of the screw propeller made it possible to contemplate converting the navy completely to steam, and the Arctic was the most rigorous testing ground anywhere.

Like Franklin, his ships, the *Terror* and the *Erebus,* were themselves veterans of arctic voyages; they were now not only equipped with engines and screw propellers but further reinforced against polar ice. The 128 officers and men under Sir John's command included, moreover, some of the finest in the queen's navy, and their proud countrymen saw them off confident that they would succeed.

When a second winter went by without word of them, however, a few people suggested that a relief expedition should be sent out, but the

LIEUT: LE VESCONTE.   LIEUT: COUCH. (MATE.)   LIEUT: DES VOEUX. (MATE.)   LIEUT: R.O. SARGENT. (MATE.)

LIEUT: FAIRHOLME.   CAPT. CROZIER. ("TERROR.")   — CAPT. SIR JOHN FRANKLIN.   COM: FITZJAMES. (CAPT. "EREBUS.")   LIEUT: GRAHAM GORE. (COM:)

JAMES REID. (ICE MASTER.)   H.D.S. GOODSIR. (ASST: SURGEON.)   S. STANLEY. (SURGEON.)   C.H. OSMER. (PURSER.)   H.F. COLLINS. (2ND MASTER.)

SAILED FROM ENGLAND 19TH MAY 1845 IN SEARCH OF THE NORTH-WEST PASSAGE.

Sir John Franklin, above center, is flanked, to left and right respectively, by the captains of his ships, the Terror *and the* Erebus. *Not one of the fourteen officers portrayed here, and not one of their 115 companions on the doomed expedition of discovery, was ever again seen alive. The poster at lower left spells out its own ominous story.*

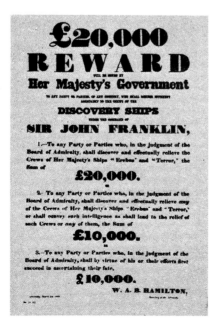

Admiralty, recalling John Ross's four-year "hibernation" and citing the fact that Franklin's ships carried provisions for a long voyage, rejected the suggestion as premature. But as more time passed, anxiety mounted steadily throughout the nation, and in the summer of 1848 two ships were dispatched to investigate. More than a year later the investigators returned to report that they had found no trace of Franklin or his expedition.

Now thoroughly alarmed, the British people and press clamored for decisive action: the government, in response, offered £20,000 for the discovery and relief of the missing men and £10,000 for the determination of their fate, and in the spring of 1850 ordered ten naval vessels to the northern rim of North America, three from the west and seven from the east. An appeal by Lady Franklin brought five more ships into the search, while the Hudson's Bay Company sent Dr. John Rae, an explorer, north overland. Altogether more than forty expeditions, governmental and private, would take part in the search before it ended, six by land and the rest by sea.

The first trace of the missing explorers came to light in August of 1851, when American searchers found crude gravestones bearing the roughly carved names of three of Franklin's men. By then, everyone knew, the expedition's stores must have long since been consumed, yet the search went on, year after year. In March, 1854, the Admiralty announced that Sir John and his men were officially presumed to have perished, and in October Dr. Rae, back from his protracted overland search, offered gruesome testimony as to how some of them had done so. A band of Eskimos, he reported, had told him of seeing white men heading south on foot a few years before, dragging their boats, and had led him to a place where those men had camped; there Dr. Rae found thirty bodies: "From the mutilated state of many of the corpses and the contents of the kettles," he wrote, "it is evident that our miserable countrymen had been driven to the last resources."

Dismayed though they were by this revelation of behavior scarcely in accordance with the Royal Navy's cherished traditions, the members of the Admiralty board paid Dr. Rae £10,000 for determining the fate of a large part of the expedition. But if they hoped thereby to write finis to the tragedy, they reckoned without Lady Franklin, by now the object of much popular sympathy and indeed something of a national heroine for her refusal, against the odds, to accept that her beloved husband would never again come home to her. Unable to induce the Admiralty to reopen the search, she again appealed for funds, purchasing and refitting a small steam yacht, the *Fox,* with the proceeds. With the help of Prince Albert she obtained from the navy the services of Captain Francis Leopold McClintock, who had taken part in three earlier expeditions in the search for Franklin. He sailed from England in 1857.

At least to some extent because he was readier to improvise than most naval officers, McClintock achieved the success that had eluded his colleagues. When in the winter of 1858–59 the *Fox* became locked in pack ice, he led a party to King William Island, where Dr. Rae had seen the half-eaten corpses, and there came

upon numerous relics of the lost expedition: uniform buttons, tools, pieces of wardroom silver. From Eskimos, moreover, he learned that two ships had years earlier been trapped in ice off the island's northern tip: one, crushed by the ice, had sunk, while the other had been cast ashore, badly smashed. Their people, the Eskimos said, had left them earlier and gone south on foot.

Leaving his second-in-command to explore the area, McClintock, with a few men, followed the shoreline south and then sledged across the frozen strait separating the island from the mainland; near the wide mouth of the Back River they found a skeleton they recognized as that of a young white man. And on regaining his base McClintock learned that his subordinate had found, in a cairn, a tin box containing a written record of the Franklin expedition: a message dated May 28, 1847, stating that the *Terror* and *Erebus* had ventured as far as 77 degrees north, wintered at Beechey Island, and had come south via Peel Sound to King William Island. The brief report ended "All well." Around the

margins of the sheet, however, was a longer message in another hand, written on April 25, 1848, which showed that by then all was very far from well, the provisions being exhausted: Franklin had died the previous June, eight more officers and fifteen men were also dead, and the 105 survivors, having abandoned the ships, were starting out the following morning for the Back River in the forlorn hope of crossing hundreds of miles of inhospitable wilderness, half-starving as they were, to civilization.

Although traces of the doomed expedition are even now still being found, McClintock's report ended the search for Sir John Franklin, a search which—although the fact can have been of scant consolation to his grieving widow—added immeasurably to geographical knowledge of the Canadian Arctic. Not one of Franklin's men was ever seen again. And when the Northwest Passage was at last transited by sea in 1903–6, the feat was accomplished, ironically, not by an Englishman, nor by a Russian or American, but by a Norwegian, the famed explorer Roald Amundsen.

Sailors in search of Franklin battle polar bears among icebergs that conform closely to the tenets of Victorian Gothic architecture in this aquatint by George Baxter.

SURVIVORS

Stories of disaster at sea exercise a powerful hold on the human imagination. Not surprisingly, therefore, shipwrecks have long been a favorite subject of artists. The paintings that follow, while faithfully recording the circumstances of individual wrecks, seem to be making statements about human suffering and survival that have more universal application.

The lesson to be learned from the scene at right is, surely, composure in the face of adversity. The painting was commissioned in 1865 by one Leopold Bamberger to commemorate his wife's rescue at sea seventeen years earlier. Mrs. Bamberger, at that time Teresa Littauer, had embarked on the packet *Ocean Monarch* at Liverpool, an emigrant ship bound for Boston and New York. Only hours after leaving port, the ship burned and sank, and nearly half of the passengers drowned. Miss Littauer, her coiffure not noticeably disarranged by immersion, was rescued by the *Shanunga*. She survived her ordeal, married Mr. Bamberger, a lace importer, and went on to become a well-known collector of art.

Clinging resolutely to an oar, Teresa Littauer awaits rescue by sailors from the Shanunga *in this painting by the sculptor and artist William Rimmer.*

The British East Indiaman Halsewell *left England in 1786 carrying 250 passengers. Only a few days into the voyage a severe gale blew the ship onto the rocks off the coast of Dorsetshire, and huge waves made it impossible to launch lifeboats. Seventy-nine passengers managed to make it to shore by clinging to the rocks until the storm subsided, as shown in the engraving above. Many of the others aboard, including Captain Richard Pierce and his two daughters, took shelter in the roundhouse at the stern (left). When it finally broke away and washed overboard, they were drowned.*

Captain Inglefield and several crew members of the sinking British warship Centaur struggle for places on a lifeboat in this aquatint based on a painting by James Northcote. In a published narrative of the incident, the captain relates that the Centaur was already "in leaky condition" when she left Jamaica in September of 1782. Soon afterward a gale struck, battering the ship for several days. The crew valiantly manned the pumps but were unable to save her. In his account Captain Inglefield describes the choice he faced, whether "to remain and perish with the ship's company, whom I could not be any longer of use to, or seize the opportunity which seemed the only way of escaping, and leave the people who I had been so well satisfied with . . . that I thought I would give my life to preserve them. . . . The love of life prevailed." In the mid-Atlantic, without a compass and with only a blanket for a sail, the twelve men could do little but run before the wind and hope to sight land or a passing ship. One man died of starvation; the others managed to stay alive on biscuits and rainwater until, sixteen days after leaving the Centaur, their boat washed ashore in the Azores.

Théodore Géricault's Raft of the Medusa *may well be the most dramatic shipwreck painting of all time. The men aboard the raft are survivors of the French frigate* Medusa, *which ran aground off the coast of Africa in 1816. Abandoned by the ship's officers, who could have saved them, they endured nearly two weeks on the raft in conditions so horrible that they were driven to murder and even cannibalism in their struggle to survive. Géricault here depicts the thirteenth day of their ordeal, when the survivors sighted a ship on the horizon and their despair was suddenly infused with hope.*

A lookout in the rigging sights a whale in this illustration from William M. Davis's novel Nimrod of the Sea, *published in 1874.*

On Distant Seas

A PERILOUS PASSAGE
It was at the suggestion of the poet William Butler Yeats that the young John Millington Synge, the future author of *Riders to the Sea*, *The Playboy of the Western World*, and other plays evoking Irish life and character, went in 1898 to live on the remote Aran Islands, off Ireland's west coast, to study the islanders' customs, language, and lore. He returned there for the next four summers. The following account of a short but never-to-be-forgotten trip in a curragh— the traditional Irish rounded boat of waterproof material stretched over a wicker or wooden frame— first appeared in a collection of Synge's sketches and impressions entitled *The Aran Islands*, published in 1907, just two years before his death.

My voyage from the middle island was wild. The morning was so stormy, that in ordinary circumstances I would not have attempted the passage, but as I had arranged to travel with a curagh that was coming over for the Parish Priest— who is to hold stations on Inishmaan—I did not like to draw back.

I went out in the morning and walked up to the cliffs as usual. Several men I fell in with shook their heads when I told them I was going away, and said they doubted if a curagh could cross the sound with the sea that was in it.

When I went back to the cottage I found the Curate had just come across from the south island, and had had a worse passage than any he had yet experienced.

The tide was to turn at two o'clock, and after that it was thought the sea would be calmer, as the wind and the waves would be running from the same point. We sat about in the kitchen all the morning, with men coming in every few minutes to give their opinion whether the passage should be attempted, and at what points the sea was likely to be at its worst.

At last it was decided we should go, and I started for the pier in a wild shower of rain with the wind howling in the walls. The schoolmaster and a priest who was to have gone with me came out as I was passing through the village and advised me not to make the passage; but my crew had gone on towards the sea, and I thought it better to go after them. The eldest son of the family was coming with me, and I considered that the old man, who knew the waves better than I did, would not send out his son if there was more than reasonable danger.

I found my crew waiting for me under a high wall below the village, and we went on together. The island had never seemed so desolate. Looking out over the black limestone through the driving rain to the gulf of struggling waves, an indescribable feeling of dejection came over me.

The old man gave me his view of the use of fear.

"A man who is not afraid of the sea will soon be drownded," he said, "for he will be going out on a day he shouldn't. But we do be afraid of the sea, and we do only be drownded now and again."

The crew carried down the curagh and then stood under the lee of the pier tying on their hats with string and drawing on the oilskins.

They tested the braces of the oars, and the oarpins, and everything in the curagh with a care I had not yet seen them give to anything, then my bag was lifted in, and we were ready. Besides the four men of the crew a man was going with us who wanted a passage to this island. As he was scrambling into the bow, an old man stood forward from the crowd.

"Don't take that man with you," he said. "Last week they were taking him to Clare and the whole of them were near drownded. Another day he went to Inisheer and they broke three ribs of the curagh, and they coming back. There is not the like of him for ill-luck in the three islands."

"The divil choke your old gob," said the man, "you will be talking."

We set off. It was a four-oared curagh, and I was given the last seat so as to leave the stern for the man who was steering with an oar, worked at right angles to the others by an extra thole-pin in the stern gunnel.

When we had gone about a hundred yards they ran up a bit of a sail in the bow and the pace became extraordinarily rapid.

The shower had passed over and the wind had fallen, but large, magnificently brilliant waves were rolling down on us at right angles to our course.

Every instant the steersman whirled us round with a sudden stroke of his oar, the prow reared up and then fell into the next furrow with a crash, throwing up masses of spray. As it did so, the stern in its turn was thrown up, and both the steersman, who let go his oar and clung ... to the gunnel, and myself, were lifted high up above the sea.

The wave passed, we regained our course and rowed violently for a few yards, when the same manoeuvre had to be repeated. As we worked out into the sound we began to meet another class of waves, that could be seen for some distance towering above the rest.

When one of these came in sight, the first effort was to get beyond its reach. The steersman began crying out in Gaelic "Siubhal, siubhal" ("Run, run"), and sometimes, when the mass was gliding towards us with horrible speed,

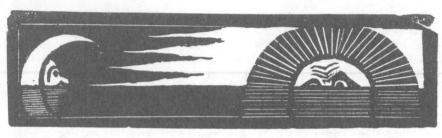

his voice rose to a shriek. Then the rowers themselves took up the cry, and the curagh seemed to leap and quiver with the frantic terror of a beast till the wave passed behind it or fell with a crash beside the stern.

It was in this racing with the waves that our chief danger lay. If the wave could be avoided, it was better to do so, but if it overtook us while we were trying to escape, and caught us on the broadside, our destruction was certain. I could see the steersman quivering with the excitement of his task, for any error in his judgment would have swamped us.

We had one narrow escape. A wave appeared high above the rest, and there was the usual moment of intense exertion. It was of no use, and in an instant the wave seemed to be hurling itself upon us. With a yell of rage the steersman struggled with his oar to bring our prow to meet it. He had almost succeeded, when there was a crash and rush of water round us. I felt as if I had been struck upon the back with knotted ropes. White foam gurgled round my knees and eyes. The curagh reared up, swaying and trembling for a moment, and then fell safely into the furrow.

This was our worst moment, though more than once, when several waves came so closely together that we had no time to regain control of the canoe between them, we had some dangerous work. Our lives depended upon the skill and courage of the men, as the life of the rider or swimmer is often in his own hands, and the excitement of the struggle was too great to allow time for fear.

I enjoyed the passage. Down in this shallow trough of canvas that bent and trembled with the motion of the men, I had a far more intimate feeling of the glory and power of the waves than I have ever known in a steamer.

THE GHOST OF COLUMBUS'S NAVIGATOR

Almost four centuries after Magellan, New Englander Joshua Slocum became the first person in history to circumnavigate the globe on his own. Like many another sailor Slocum was an inveterate reader, and although he had had little formal education, his account of his epic voyage, *Sailing Alone Around the World*, revealed him to be a lively writer with a sharp eye for detail, a narrative gift, and a natural, unstrained literary style.

I set sail from Horta early on July 24. The southwest wind at the time was light, but squalls came up with the sun, and I was glad enough to get reefs in my sails before I had gone a mile. I had hardly set the mainsail, double-reefed, when a squall of wind down the mountains struck the sloop with such violence that I thought her mast would go. However, a quick helm brought her to the wind. As it was, one of the weather lanyards was carried away and the other was stranded. My tin basin, caught up by the wind, went flying across a French school-ship to leeward. It was more or less squally all day, sailing along under high land; but

rounding close under a bluff, I found an opportunity to mend the lanyards broken in the squall. No sooner had I lowered my sails when a four-oared boat shot out from some gully in the rocks, with a customs officer on board, who thought he had come upon a smuggler. I had some difficulty in making him comprehend the true case. However, one of his crew, a sailorly chap, who understood how matters were, while we palavered jumped on board and rove off the new lanyards I had already prepared, and with a friendly hand helped me "set up the rigging." This incident gave the turn in my favor. My story was then clear to all. I have found this the way of the world. Let one be without a friend, and see what will happen!

Passing the island of Pico, after the rigging was mended, the *Spray* stretched across to leeward of the island of St. Michael's, which she was up with early on the morning of July 26, the wind blowing hard. . . . Since reaching the islands I had lived most luxuriously on fresh bread, butter, vegetables, and fruits of all kinds. Plums seemed the most plentiful on the *Spray*, and these I ate without stint. I had also a Pico white cheese that General Manning, the American consul-general, had given me, which I supposed was to be eaten, and of this I partook with the plums. Alas! by night-time I was doubled up with cramps. The wind, which was already a smart breeze, was increasing somewhat, with a heavy sky to the sou'west. Reefs had been turned out, and I must turn them in again somehow. Between cramps I got the mainsail down, hauled out the earings as best I could, and tied away point by point, in the double reef. There being sea-room, I should, in strict prudence, have made all snug and gone down at once to my cabin. I am a careful man at sea, but this night, in the coming storm, I swayed up my sails, which, reefed though they were, were still too much in such heavy weather; and I saw to it that the sheets were securely belayed. In a word, I should have laid to, but did not. I gave her the double-reefed mainsail and whole jib instead, and set her on her course. Then I went below, and threw myself upon the cabin floor in great pain. How long I lay there I could not tell, for I became delirious. When I came to, as I thought, from my swoon, I realized that the sloop was plunging into a heavy sea, and looking out of the companionway, to my amazement I saw a tall man at the helm. His rigid hand, grasping the spokes of the wheel, held them as in a vise. One may imagine my astonishment. His rig was that of a foreign sailor, and the large red cap he wore was cockbilled over his left ear, and all was set off with shaggy black whiskers. He would have been taken for a pirate in any part of the world. While I gazed upon his threatening aspect I forgot the storm, and wondered if he had come to cut my throat. This he seemed to divine. "Señor," said he, doffing his cap, "I have come to do you no harm." And a smile, the faintest in the world, but still a smile, played on his face, which seemed not unkind when he spoke. "I have come to do you no harm. I have sailed free," he said, "but was never worse than a *contrabandista*. I am one of Columbus's crew," he continued. "I am the pilot of the *Pinta* come to aid you. Lie quiet, señor captain," he added, "and I will guide your ship to-night. You have a *calentura*, but you will be all right to-morrow." I thought what a very devil he was to carry sail. Again, as if he read my mind, he exclaimed: "Yonder is the *Pinta* ahead; we must overtake her. Give her sail; give her sail! *Vale, vale, muy vale!*" Biting off a large quid of black twist, he said: "You did wrong, captain, to mix cheese with plums. White cheese is never safe unless you know whence it comes. *Quien sabe*, it may have been from *leche de Capra* and becoming capricious———"

"Avast, there!" I cried. "I have no mind for moralizing."

I made shift to spread a mattress and lie on that instead of the hard floor, my eyes all the while fastened on my strange guest, who, remarking again that I would have "only pains and calentura," chuckled as he chanted a wild song:

High are the waves, fierce, gleaming,
    High is the tempest roar!
High the sea-bird screaming!
    High the Azore!

I suppose I was now on the mend, for I was peevish, and complained: "I detest your jingle. Your Azore should be at roost, and would have been were it a respectable bird!" I begged he would tie a rope-yarn on the rest of the song, if there was any more of it. I was still in agony. Great seas were boarding the *Spray*, but in my fevered brain I thought they were boats falling on deck, that careless draymen were throwing from wagons on the pier to which I imagined the *Spray* was now moored, and without fenders to breast her off. "You'll smash your boats!" I called out again and again, as the seas crashed on the cabin over my head. "You'll smash your boats, but you can't hurt the *Spray*. She is strong!" I cried.

I found, when my pains and calentura had gone, that the deck, now as white as a shark's tooth from seas washing over it, had been swept of everything movable. To my astonishment, I saw now at broad day that the

Spray was still heading as I had left her, and was going like a race-horse. Columbus himself could not have held her more exactly on her course. The sloop had made ninety miles in the night through a rough sea. I felt grateful to the old pilot, but I marveled some that he had not taken in the jib. The gale was moderating, and by noon the sun was shining. A meridian altitude and the distance on the patent log, which I always kept towing, told me that she had made a true course throughout the twenty-four hours. I was getting much better now, but was very weak, and did not turn out reefs that day or the night following, although the wind fell light; but I just put my wet clothes out in the sun when it was shining, and lying down there myself, fell asleep. Then who should visit me again but my old friend of the night before, this time, of course, in a dream. "You did well last night to take my advice," said he, "and if you would, I should like to be with you often on the voyage, for the love of adventure alone." Finishing what he had to say, he again doffed his cap and disappeared as mysteriously as he came, returning, I suppose, to the phantom *Pinta*. I awoke much refreshed, and with the feeling that I had been in the presence of a friend and a seaman of vast experience. I gathered up my clothes, which by this time were dry, then, by inspiration, I threw overboard all the plums in the vessel.

XERXES ORDERS THE SEA FLOGGED
In this fragment from his *History*, Herodotus (fifth century B.C.) relates how the king of Persia reacted, in 480 B.C., to being temporarily prevented by bad weather from sending his army across the Hellespont to invade Greece.

Now between the cities of Sestus and Madytus in the Chersonesus upon the Hellespont there is a rough headland which cometh down into the sea over against Abydus. To this headland from Abydus they whose duty it was made two bridges, one with ropes of white flax and the other with ropes of paper reeds. (Now from Abydus to the land opposite is seven stades.) But when the strait had been spanned, a great storm arose and broke up and dissolved all their work. And when Xerxes heard thereof, he was wroth and commanded to lay three hundred stripes on the Hellespont with a scourge and cast down a pair of fetters into the deep. And I have heard ere now that he also sent branders with the other officers, to brand the Hellespont. Howsoever, he charged them, as they whipped the Hellespont, to say these barbarous, froward words: Bitter water, this punishment thy master layeth upon thee, because thou hast wronged him albeit he did no wrong to thee. King Xerxes will cross thee, whether thou wilt or whether thou wilt not; but it is right that no men sacrifice to thee, because thou art a salt and turbid river. Thus he charged them to punish the sea.

FIRST DAYS AT SEA

Herman Melville, the author of *Moby Dick* and one of the greatest of all American writers, was born in New York in 1819 into a well-to-do family, but in 1830 his father went bankrupt. The son worked as a bank clerk, salesman, farmhand, and schoolteacher, and at twenty went to sea. In this passage from *Redburn* (1849) he draws upon his own experience.

The second day out of port, the decks being washed down and breakfast over, the watch was called, and the mate set us to work.

It was a very bright day. The sky and water were both of the same deep hue. . . . There were little traces of sunny clouds all over the heavens; and little fleeces of foam all over the sea; and the ship made a strange, musical noise under her bows, as she glided along with her sails all still. It seemed a pity to go to work at such a time; and if we could only have sat in the windlass again, or if they would have let me go out on the bowsprit, and lay down between the *manropes* there, and look over at the fish in the water, and think of home, I should have been almost happy for a time.

I had now completely got over my seasickness, and felt very well; at least in my body, though my heart was far from feeling right; so that I could now look around me and make observations.

And truly, though we were at sea, there was much to behold and wonder at, to me, who was on my first voyage. What most amazed me was the sight of the great ocean itself, for we were out of sight of land. All round us, on both sides of the ship, ahead and astern, nothing was to be seen but water—water—water; not a single glimpse of green shore, not the smallest island, or speck of moss anywhere. Never did I realize till now what the ocean was: how grand and majestic, how solitary, and boundless, and beautiful and blue; for that day it gave no tokens of squalls or hurricanes, such as I had heard my father tell of; nor could I imagine how anything that seemed so playful and placid could be lashed into rage, and troubled into rolling avalanches of foam, and great cascades of waves, such as I saw in the end. . . .

While the stun'-sails were lying all tumbled upon the deck, and the sailors were fastening them to the booms, getting them ready to hoist, the mate ordered me to do a great many simple things, none of which could I comprehend, owing to the queer words he used; and then, seeing me stand quite perplexed and confounded, he would roar out at me, and call me all manner of names, and the sailors would laugh and wink to each other, but durst not go farther than that for fear of the mate, who in his own presence would not let any body laugh at me but himself. . . .

People who have never gone to sea for the first time as sailors, can not imagine how puzzling and confounding it is. It must be like going into a barbarous country, where they speak a strange dialect, and dress in strange clothes, and live in strange houses. For sailors have their own names, even for things that are familiar ashore; and if you call a thing by its shore name, you are laughed at for an ignoramus and a land-lubber. This first day I speak of, the mate having ordered me to draw some water, I asked him where I was to get the pail; when I thought I had committed some dreadful crime; for he flew into a great passion, and said they never had any *pails* at sea, and then I learned that they were always called *buckets*. . . .

At last we hoisted the stun'-sails up to the top-sail yards, and as soon as the vessel felt them she gave a sort of bound like a horse, and the breeze blowing more and more, she went plunging along, shaking off the foam from her bows like foam from a bridle-bit. Every mast and timber seemed to have a pulse in it that was beating with life and joy, and I felt a wild exulting in my own heart, and felt as if I would be glad to bound along so round the world. . . .

Yes! yes! give me this glorious ocean life, this salt-sea life, this briny, foamy life, when the sea neighs and snorts, and you breathe the very breath that the great whales respire! Let me roll around the globe, let me rock upon the sea, let me race and pant out my life with an eternal breeze astern and an endless sea before!

But how soon these raptures abated, when, after a brief idle interval, we were again set to work, and I had a vile commission to clean out the chicken coops and make up the beds of the pigs in the long-boat.

Miserable dog's life is this of the sea! Commanded like a slave, and set to work like an ass! Vulgar and brutal men lording it over me, as if I were an African in Alabama. Yes, yes, blow on, ye breezes, and make a speedy end to this abominable voyage!

THE NYMPHS OF TYPEE

In 1841 Melville embarked as a seaman in the whaler *Acushnet* for the Pacific, and a year and a half later jumped ship in the Marquesas Islands; he and a comrade were captured by cannibals, who treated them kindly, but after a few months they were rescued by the crew of an Australian whaler. Melville spent some time in Tahiti and the Hawaiian Islands before sailing home in 1844. The first fruit of these adventures was *Typee,* a romance (1846); the passage from it below, describing the narrator's arrival in the port of Nuku Hiva in the Marquesas, conveys the exotic (and erotic) flavor that won the book a wide audience.

As we slowly advanced up the bay, numerous canoes pushed off from the surrounding shores, and we were soon in the midst of quite a flotilla of them, their savage occupants struggling to get aboard of us, and jostling one another in their ineffectual attempts. Occasionally the projecting out-riggers of their slight shallops, running foul of one another, would become entangled beneath the water, threatening to capsize the canoes, when a scene of confusion would ensue that baffles description. Such strange outcries and passionate gesticulations I never certainly heard or saw before. You would have thought the islanders were on the point of flying at one another's throats, whereas they were only amicably engaged in disentangling their boats.

Scattered here and there among the canoes might be seen numbers of cocoa-nuts floating closely together in circular groups, and bobbing up and down with every wave. By some inexplicable means these cocoa-nuts were all steadily approaching towards the ship. As I leaned curiously over the side, endeavouring to solve their mysterious movements, one mass, far in advance of the rest, attracted my attention. In its centre was something I could take for nothing else than a cocoa-nut, but which I certainly considered one of the most extraordinary specimens of the fruit I had ever seen. It kept twirling and dancing about among the rest in the most singular manner: and as it drew nearer, I thought it bore a remarkable resemblance to the brown shaven skull of one of the savages. Presently it betrayed a pair of eyes, and soon I became aware that what I had supposed to have been one of the fruit was nothing else than the head of an islander, who had adopted this singular method of bringing his produce to market. The cocoa-nuts were all attached to one another by strips of the husk, partly torn from the shell, and rudely fastened together. Their proprietor, inserting his head into the midst of them, impelled his necklace of cocoa-nuts through the water by striking out beneath the surface with his feet.

I was somewhat astonished to perceive that among the number of natives that surrounded us, not a single female was to be seen. At that time I was ignorant of the fact that by the operation of the "taboo," the use of canoes in all parts of the island is rigorously prohibited to the entire sex, for whom it is death even to be seen entering one when hauled on shore; consequently, whenever a Marquesan lady voyages by water, she puts in requisition the paddles of her own fair body.

We had approached within a mile and a half perhaps of the foot of the bay, when some of the islanders, who by this time had managed to scramble aboard of us at the risk of swamping their canoes, directed our attention to a singular commotion in the water ahead of the vessel. At first I imagined it to be produced by a shoal of fish sporting on the surface, but our savage friends assured us that it was caused by a shoal of "whinhenies" (young girls), who in this manner were coming off from the shore to welcome us. As they drew

nearer, and I watched the rising and sinking of their forms, and beheld the uplifted right arm bearing above the water the girdle of tappa, and their long dark hair trailing beside them as they swam, I almost fancied they could be nothing else than so many mermaids:— and very like mermaids they behaved too.

We were still some distance from the beach, and under slow headway, when we sailed right into the midst of these swimming nymphs, and they boarded us at every quarter; many seizing hold of the chainplates and springing into the chains; others, at the peril of being run over by the vessel in her course, catching at the bob-stays, and wreathing their slender forms about the ropes, hung suspended in the air. All of them at length succeeded in getting up the ship's side, where they clung dripping with the brine and glowing from the bath, their jet-black tresses steaming over their shoulders, and half enveloping their otherwise naked forms. There they hung, sparkling with savage vivacity, laughing gaily at one another, and chattering away with infinite glee. Nor were they idle the while, for each one performed the simple offices of the toilet for the other. Their luxuriant locks, wound up and twisted into the smallest possible compass, were freed from the briny element; the whole person carefully dried, and from a little round shell that passed from hand to

hand, anointed with a fragrant oil: their adornments were completed by passing a few loose folds of white tappa, in a modest cincture, around the waist. Thus arrayed they no longer hesitated, but flung themselves lightly over the bulwarks, and were quickly frolicking about the decks. Many of them went forward, perching upon the head-rails or running out upon the bowsprit, while others seated themselves upon the

taffrail, or reclined at full length upon the boats.

Their appearance perfectly amazed me; their extreme youth, the light clear brown of their complexions, their delicate features, and inexpressibly graceful figures, their softly moulded limbs, and free unstudied action, seemed as strange as beautiful.

The *Dolly* was fairly captured; and never I will say was vessel carried before by such a dashing and irresistible party of boarders. The ship taken, we could not do otherwise then yield ourselves prisoners, and for the whole period that she remained in the bay, the *Dolly*, as well as her crew, were completely in the hands of the mermaids.

In the evening after we had come to an anchor, the deck was illuminated with lanterns, and this picturesque band of sylphs, tricked out with flowers, and dressed in robes of variegated tappa, got up a ball in great style. These females are passionately fond of dancing, and in the wild grace and spirit of their style excel everything that I have ever seen. The varied dances of the Marquesan girls are beautiful in the extreme, but there is an abandoned voluptuousness in their character which I dare not attempt to describe.

Our ship was now wholly given up to every species of riot and debauchery. The grossest licentiousness and the most shameful inebriety prevailed,

with occasional and but short-lived interruptions, through the whole period of her stay. Alas for the poor savages when exposed to the influence of these polluting examples! Unsophisticated and confiding, they are easily led into every vice, and humanity weeps over the ruin thus remorselessly inflicted upon them by their European civilizers. Thrice happy are they who, inhabiting some yet undiscovered island in the midst of the ocean, have never been brought into contaminating contact with the white man.

WE ENCOUNTER A GALE

Following the success of his *Typee*, Melville wrote another romance of the South Seas, which he called *Omoo* (1847), a Polynesian word meaning "rover." The chapter from it below makes it clear that then as now the Pacific Ocean, in its behavior, frequently gave the lie to its name.

The mild blue weather we enjoyed after leaving the Marquesas, gradually changed as we ran farther south and approached Tahiti. In these generally tranquil seas, the wind sometimes blows with great violence; though, as every sailor knows, a spicy gale in the tropic latitudes of the Pacific is far different from a tempest in the howling North Atlantic. We soon found ourselves battling with the waves, while the before mild Trades, like a woman roused, blew fiercely, but still warmly, in our face.

For all this, the mate carried sail without stint; and as for brave *Little Jule*, she stood up to it well; and though once in a while floored in the trough of a sea, sprang to her keel again and showed play. Every old timber groaned—every spar buckled—every chafed cord strained; and yet, spite of all, she plunged on her way like a racer. Jermin, sea-jockey that he was, sometimes stood in the fore-chains, with the spray every now and then dashing over him, and shouting out, "Well done, Jule—drive into it, sweetheart! Hurrah!"

One afternoon there was a mighty queer noise aloft, which set the men running in every direction. It was the main-t'-gallant-mast. Crash! it broke off just above the cap, and held there by the rigging, dashed with every roll, from side to side, with all the hamper that belonged to it. The yard hung by a hair, and at every pitch thumped against the cross-trees; while the sails streamed in ribbons, and the loose ropes coiled, and thrashed the air, like whip-lashes. "Stand from under!" and down came the rattling blocks like so many shot.

The yard, with a snap and a plunge, went hissing into the sea, disappeared, and shot its full length out again. The crest of a great wave then broke over it—the ship rushed by—and we saw the stick no more.

While this lively breeze continued, Baltimore, our old black cook, was in great tribulation.

Like most South Seamen, the *Julia's* caboose, or cook-house, was planted on the larboard side of the forecastle. Under such a press of canvas, and with the heavy sea running, the barque, diving her bows under, now and then shipped green glassy waves, which, breaking over the head-rails, fairly deluged that part of the ship and washed clean aft. The caboose-house—thought to be firmly lashed down to its place—served as a sort of breakwater to the inundation.

About these times, Baltimore always wore what he called his "gale-suit;" among other things, comprising a Sou'-Wester and a huge pair of well-anointed sea-boots, reaching almost to his knees. Thus equipped for a ducking or a drowning, as the case might be, our culinary high-priest drew to the slides of his temple, and performed his sooty rites in secret.

So afraid was the old man of being washed overboard, that he actually fastened one end of a small line to his waistbands, and coiling the rest about him, made use of it as occasion required. When engaged outside, he unwound the cord, and secured one end to a ring-bolt in the deck; so that if chance sea washed him off his feet, it could do nothing more.

One evening, just as he was getting supper, the *Julia* reared upon her stern like a vicious colt, and when she settled again forward, fairly *dished* a tremendous sea. Nothing could withstand it. One side of the rotten head-bulwarks came in with a crash; it smote the caboose, tore it from its moorings, and after boxing it about, dashed it against the windlass, where it stranded. The water then poured along the deck like a flood, rolling over and over pots, pans, and kettles, and even old Baltimore himself, who went breaching along like a porpoise.

Striking the taffrail, the wave subsided, and, washing from side to side, left the drowning cook high and dry on the after-hatch: his extinguished pipe still between his teeth, and almost bitten in two.

The few men on deck having sprung into the main-rigging, sailor-like, did nothing but roar at his calamity.

The same night, our flying-gib-boom snapped off like a pipe-stem, and our spanker-gaff came down by the run.

By the following morning, the wind in a great measure had gone down; the sea with it; and by noon we had repaired our damages as well as we could, and were sailing along as pleasantly as ever.

A RESCUE AT SEA

For many devotees of the genre the greatest of all writers about the sea in English is a Pole named Teodor Józef Konrad Korzeniowski, whose second language was French and who did not learn English until he was twenty. Orphaned at eleven, Joseph Conrad, as he was later known, was sent to Marseilles at sixteen to become a sailor, and after four turbulent years involving gun-running, an intense love affair, and an attempt at suicide, he shipped aboard a British freighter. In 1886 he earned his master's papers and became a naturalized British subject; he continued to command vessels—notably including a river steamer in the Belgian Congo—until 1895, when, with the publication of his novel *Almayer's Folly*, he left the sea to write. His best known works are the novels *The Nigger of the Narcissus, Lord Jim, Nostromo, The Secret Agent,* and *Under Western Eyes* and the novella *Heart of Darkness*, based on his Congolese experience. The passage below is taken from a work of reminiscence, *The Mirror of the Sea* (1906).

The most amazing wonder of the deep is its unfathomable cruelty. I felt its dread for the first time in mid-Atlantic one day, many years ago, when we took off the crew of a Danish brig homeward-bound from the West Indies. A thin, silvery mist softened the calm and majestic splendor of light without shadows—seemed to render the sky less remote and the ocean less immense. It was one of the days when the might of the sea appears indeed lovable, like the nature of a strong man in moments of quiet intimacy. At sunrise we had made out a black speck to the westward, apparently suspended high up in the void behind a stirring, shimmering veil of silvery blue gauze that seemed at times to stir and float in the breeze which fanned us slowly along. . . . "A water-logged derelict, I think, sir," said the second officer quietly, coming down from aloft with the binoculars in their case slung across his shoulders; and our captain, without a word, signed to the helmsman to steer for the black speck. Presently we made out a low, jagged stump sticking up forward—all that remained of her departed masts.

The captain was expatiating in a low, conversational tone to the chief mate upon the danger of these derelicts, and upon his dread of coming upon them at night, when suddenly a man forward screamed out, "There's people on board of her, sir! I see them!" in a most extraordinary voice—a voice never heard before in our ship; the amazing voice of a stranger. It gave the signal for a sudden tumult of shouts. The watch below ran up the forecastle head in a body, the cook dashed out of the galley. Everybody saw the poor fellows now. They were there! And all at once our ship, which had the well-earned name of being without a rival for speed in light winds, seemed to us to have lost the power of motion, as if the sea, becoming viscous, had clung to her sides. And yet she moved. Immensity, the inseparable companion of a ship's life, chose that day to breathe upon her as gently as a sleeping child. . . .

With the binoculars glued to his eyes, the captain said in a quavering tone: "They are waving to us with something aft there." He put down the glasses on the skylight brusquely, and began to walk about the poop. "A shirt or a flag," he ejaculated irritably. "Can't make it out . . . some damn rag or other!" He took a few more turns on the poop, glancing down over the rail now and then to see how fast we were moving. His nervous footsteps rang sharply in the quiet of the ship, where the other men, all looking the same way, had forgotten themselves in a staring immobility. "This will never do!" he cried out suddenly. "Lower the boats at once! Down with them!"

Before I jumped into mine he took me aside, as being an inexperienced junior, for a word of warning:

"You look out as you come alongside that she doesn't take you down with her. You understand?"

He murmured this confidentially, so that none of the men at the falls should overhear, and I was shocked. "Heavens! as if in such an emergency one stopped to think of danger!" I exclaimed to myself mentally, in scorn of such cold-blooded caution.

It takes many lessons to make a real seaman, and I got my rebuke at once. My experienced commander seemed in one searching glance to read my thoughts on my ingenuous face.

"What you're going for is to save life, not to drown your boat's crew for nothing," he growled severely in my ear. But as we shoved off he leaned over and cried out: "It all rests on the power of your arms, men. Give way for life!"

We made a race of it, and I would never have believed that a common boat's crew of a merchantman could keep up so much determined fierceness in the regular swing of their stroke. What our captain had clearly perceived before we left had become plain to all of us since. The issue of our enterprise hung on a hair above that abyss of waters which will not give up its dead till the Day of Judgement. It was a race of two ship's boats matched against Death for a prize of nine men's lives, and Death had a long start. We saw the crew of the brig from afar working at the pumps—still pumping on that wreck, which already had settled so far down that the gentle, low swell, over

which our boats rose and fell easily without a check to their speed, welling up almost level with her head-rails, plucked at the ends of broken gear swinging desolately under her naked bowsprit.

We could not, in all conscience, have picked out a better day for our regatta had we had the free choice of all the days that ever dawned upon the lonely struggles and solitary agonies of ships since the Norse rovers first steered to the westward against the run of Atlantic waves. It was a very good race. At the finish there was not an oar's length between the first and second boat, with Death coming in a good third on the top of the very next smooth swell, for all one knew to the contrary. The scuppers of the brig gurgled softly all together when the water rising against her sides subsided sleepily with a low wash, as if playing about an immovable rock. Her bulwarks were gone fore and aft, and one saw her bare deck low-lying like a raft and swept clean of boats, spars, houses—of everything except the ring-bolts and the heads of the pumps. I had one dismal glimpse of it as I braced myself up to receive upon my breast the last man to leave her, the captain, who literally let himself fall into my arms.

It had been a weirdly silent rescue—a rescue without a hail, without a single uttered word, without a gesture or a sign, without a conscious exchange of glances. Up to the very last moment those on board stuck to their pumps, which spouted two clear streams of water upon their bare feet. Their brown skin showed through the rents of their shirts; and the two small bunches of half-naked, tattered men went on bowing from the waist to each other in their back-breaking labour, up and down, absorbed, with no time for a glance over the shoulder at the help that was coming to them. As we dashed, unregarded, alongside a voice let out one, only one hoarse howl of command, and then, just as they stood, without caps, with the salt drying grey in the wrinkles and folds of their hairy, haggard faces, blinking stupidly at us their red eyelids, they made a bolt away from the handles, tottering and jostling against each other, and positively flung themselves over upon our very heads. The clatter they made tumbling into the boats had an extraordinarily destructive effect upon the illusion of tragic dignity our self-esteem had thrown over the contests of mankind with the sea. On that exquisite day of gently breathing peace and veiled sunshine perished my romantic love of what men's imagination had proclaimed the most august aspect of Nature. The cynical indifference of the sea to the merits of human suffering and courage, laid bare in this ridiculous, panic-tainted performance extorted from the dire extremity of nine good and honourable seamen, revolted me. I saw the duplicity of the sea's most tender mood. It was so because it could not help itself, but the awed respect of the early days was gone. I felt ready to smile bitterly at its enchanting charm and glare viciously at its furies. In a moment, before we shoved off, I had looked coolly at the life of my choice. Its illusions were gone, but its fascination remained. I had become a seaman at last.

ROUNDING CAPE HORN
In 1834, at the end of his second year at Harvard, Richard Henry Dana, Jr., shipped as a sailor for California via Cape Horn, returning a year later. In 1840, the year he was admitted to the Massachusetts bar, Dana published, anonymously, *Two Years Before the Mast,* a classic narrative of a sailor's life at sea, based on a diary he had kept. Of the two excerpts that follow, the first depicts an encounter with typically foul weather off the Horn.

Sunday, November ninth. To-day the sun rose clear, and continued so until twelve o'clock, when the captain got an observation. This was very well for Cape Horn, and we thought it a little remarkable that, as we had not had one unpleasant Sunday during the whole voyage, the only tolerable day here should be a Sunday. We got time to clear up the steerage and forecastle, and set things to rights, and to overhaul our wet clothes a little. But this did not last very long. Between five and six—the sun was then nearly three hours high—the cry of "All Starbowlines ahoy!" summoned our watch on deck, and immediately all hands were called. A true specimen of Cape Horn was coming upon us. A great cloud of a dark slate-colour was driving on us from the south-west; and we did our best to take in sail (for the light sails had been set during the first part of the day) before we were in the midst of it. We had got the light sails furled, the courses hauled up, and the topsail reef-tackles hauled out, and were just mounting the fore-rigging when the storm struck us. In an instant the sea, which had been comparatively quiet, was running higher and higher; and it became almost as dark as night. The hail and sleet were harder than I had yet felt them; seeming almost to pin us down to the rigging. We were longer taking in sail than ever before; for the sails were stiff and wet, the ropes and rigging covered with snow and sleet, and we ourselves cold and nearly blinded with the violence of the storm. By the time we had got down upon deck again, the little brig was plunging madly into a tremendous head sea, which at every dive rushed in through the bow-ports and over the bows, and buried all the forward part of the vessel. At this instant the chief mate, who was standing on the top of the windlass, at the foot of the spencer-mast, called out, "Lay out there and furl the jib!" This was no agreeable or safe duty, yet it must be done. John, a Swede (the best sailor on board), who belonged on the forecastle, sprang out upon the bowsprit. Another one must go. It was a clear case of holding back. I was near the mate, but sprang past several, threw the downhaul over the windlass, and jumped between the knight-heads out upon the bowsprit. The crew stood abaft the windlass, and hauled the jib down, while John and I got out upon the weather side of the jib-boom, our feet on the foot-ropes, holding on by the spar, the great jib flying off to leeward and *slatting* so as almost to throw us off the boom. For some time we could do nothing but hold on, and the vessel, diving into two huge seas, one after the other, plunged us twice into the water up to our chins. We hardly knew whether we were on or off; when, the boom lifting us up dripping from the water, we were raised high into the air and then plunged below again. John thought the boom would go every moment, and called out to the mate to keep the vessel off, and haul down the staysail; but the fury of the wind and the breaking of the seas against the bows defied every attempt to make ourselves heard, and we were obliged to do the best we could in our situation. Fortunately no other seas so heavy struck her, and we succeeded in furling the jib "after a fashion"; and coming in over the staysail nettings, were not a little pleased to find that all was snug, and the watch gone below; for we were soaked through, and it was very cold. John admitted that it had been a post of danger, which good sailors seldom do when the thing is over. The weather continued nearly the same through the night.

LOSS OF A MAN
In this passage from his *Two Years Before the Mast* Dana records a tragedy that took place just ten days after the events chronicled above.

Monday, November nineteenth. This was a black day in our calendar. At seven o'clock in the morning, it being our watch below, we were aroused from a sound sleep by the cry of "All hands ahoy! a man overboard!" This unwonted cry sent a thrill through the heart of every one, and hurrying on deck, we found the vessel hove flat aback, with all her studding-sails set; for, the boy who was at the helm leaving it to throw something overboard, the carpenter, who was an old sailor, knowing that the wind was light, put the helm down and hove her aback. The watch on deck were lowering away the quarterboat, and I got on deck just in time to fling myself into her as she was leaving the side; but it was not until out upon the wide Pacific, in our little boat, that I knew whom we had lost. It was George Ballmer, the young English sailor, whom I have before spoken of as the life of the crew. He was prized by the officers as an active and willing seaman, and by the men as a lively, hearty fellow, and a good shipmate. He was going aloft to fit a strap round the maintopmast-head, for ringtail halyards, and had the strap and block, a coil of halyards, and a marline-spike about his neck. He fell from the starboard futtock shrouds, and, not knowing how to swim, and being heavily dressed, with all those things round his neck, he probably sank immediately. We pulled astern, in the direction in which he fell, and though we knew that there was no hope of saving him, yet no one wished to speak of returning, and we rowed about for nearly an hour, without an idea of doing anything, but unwilling to acknowledge to ourselves that we must give him up. At length we turned the boat's head and made towards the brig.

Death is at all times solemn, but never so much so as at sea. A man dies on shore; his body remains with his friends, and "the mourners go about the streets"; but when a man falls overboard at sea and is lost, there is a suddenness in the event, and a difficulty in realising it, which give to it an air of awful mystery. A man dies on shore—you follow his body to the grave, and a stone marks the spot. You are often prepared for the event. There is always something which helps you to realise it when it happens, and to recall it when it has passed. A man is shot down by your side in battle, and the mangled body remains an object and a real evidence; but at sea, the man is near you—at your side—you hear his voice, and in an instant he is gone, and nothing but a vacancy shows his loss. Then, too, at sea—to use a homely but expressive phrase—you *miss* a man so much. A dozen men are shut up together in a

little bark upon the wide, wide sea, and for months and months see no forms and hear no voices but their own, and one is taken suddenly from among them, and they miss him at every turn. It is like losing a limb. There are no new faces or new scenes to fill up the gap. There is always an empty berth in the forecastle, and one man wanting when the small night watch is mustered.

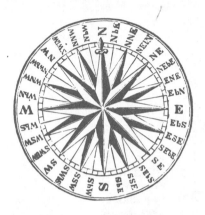

There is one less to take the wheel, and one less to lay out with you upon the yard. You miss his form and the sound of his voice, for habit had made them almost necessary to you, and each of your senses feels the loss.

All these things make such a death peculiarly solemn, and the effect of it remains upon the crew for some time. There is more kindness shown by the officers to the crew, and by the crew to one another. There is more quietness and seriousness. The oath and the loud laugh are gone. The officers are more watchful, and the crew go more carefully aloft. The lost man is seldom mentioned, or is dismissed with a sailor's rude eulogy—"Well, poor George is gone! His cruise is up soon! He knew his work, and did his duty, and was a good shipmate." Then usually follows some allusion to another world, for sailors are almost all believers in their way; though their notions and opinions are unfixed and at loose ends. They say, "God won't be hard upon the poor fellow," and seldom get beyond the common phrase which seems to imply that their sufferings and hard treatment here will be passed to their credit in the books of the Great Captain hereafter—"*To work hard, live hard, die hard, and go to hell after all, would be hard indeed!*" Our cook, a simple-hearted old African,

who had been through a good deal in his day, and was rather seriously inclined, always going to church twice a day when on shore, and reading his Bible on a Sunday in the galley, talked to the crew about spending the Lord's-day badly, and told them that they might go as suddenly as George had, and be as little prepared.

Yet a sailor's life is at best but a mixture of a little good with much evil, and a little pleasure with much pain. The beautiful is linked with the revolting, the sublime with the commonplace, and the solemn with the ludicrous. . . . As is usual after a death, many stories were told about George. Some had heard him say that he repented never having learned to swim, and that he knew that he should meet his death by drowning. Another said that he never knew any good to come of a voyage made against the will, and the deceased man shipped and spent his advance, and was afterwards very unwilling to go, but, not being able to refund, was obliged to sail with us. A boy, too, who had become quite attached to him, said that George talked to him, during most of the watch on the night before, about his mother and family at home, and this was the first time that he had mentioned the subject during the voyage.

The night after this event, when I went to the galley to get a light, I found the cook inclined to be talkative, so I sat down on the spars, and gave him an opportunity to hold a yarn. I was the more inclined to do so, as I found that he was full of the superstitions once more common among seaman, and which the recent death had waked up in his mind. He talked about George's having spoken of his friends, and said he believed few men died without having a warning of it, which he supported by a great many stories of dreams, and of unusual behaviour of men before death. From this he went on to other superstitions, the *Flying Dutchman*, etc., and talked rather mysteriously, having something evidently on his mind. At length he put his head out of the galley and looked carefully about to see if any one was within hearing, and, being satisfied on that point, asked me in a low tone,—

"I say! you know what countryman 'e carpenter be?"

"Yes," said I; "he's a German."

"What kind of a German?" said the cook.

"He belongs to Bremen," said I.

"Are you sure o' dat?" said he.

I satisfied him on that point by saying that he could speak no language but the German and English.

"I'm plaguy glad o' dat," said the cook. "I was mighty 'fraid he was a Fin. I tell you what, I been plaguy civil to dat man all the voyage."

I asked him the reason of this, and found that he was fully possessed with the notion that Fins are wizards, and especially have power over winds and storms. I tried to reason with him about it; but he had the best of all arguments, that from experience, at hand, and was not to be moved. He had been to the Sandwich Islands in a vessel in which the sail-maker was a Fin, and could do anything he was of a mind to. This sail-maker kept a junk bottle in his berth, which was always just half-full of rum, though he got drunk upon it nearly every day. He had seen him sit for hours together, talking to this bottle, which he stood up before him on the table. The same man cut his throat in his berth, and everybody said he was possessed.

He had heard of ships, too, beating up the Gulf of Finland against a head wind, and having a ship heave in sight astern, overhaul, and pass them, with as fair a wind as could blow . . . and find she was from Finland.

"Oh, oh!" said he; "I've seen too much o' dem men to want to see 'm 'board a ship. If dey can't have der own way, dey'll play the d——l wid you."

As I still doubted, he said he would leave it to John, who was the oldest seaman aboard, and would know, if anybody did. John, to be sure, was the oldest, and at the same time the most ignorant, man in the ship; but I consented to have him called. The cook stated the matter to him, and John, as I anticipated, sided with the cook, and said that he himself had been in a ship where they had a head wind for a fortnight, and the captain found out at last that one of the men, with whom he had had some hard words a short time before, was a Fin, and immediately told him if he didn't stop the head wind he would shut him down in the fore-peak. The Fin would not give in, and the captain shut him down in the fore-peak, and would not give him anything to eat. The Fin held out for a day and a half, when he could not stand it any longer, and did something or other which brought the wind round again, and they let him up.

"Dar," said the cook, "what you tink o' dat?"

I told him I had no doubt it was true, and that it would have been odd if the wind had not changed in fifteen days, Fin or no Fin.

"Oh," says he, "go 'way! You tink, 'cause you been to college, you know better dan anybody. You know better dan them as 'as seen it wid der own eyes. You wait till you've been to sea as long as I have, and den you'll know."

DR. JOHNSON ON "THE WRETCHEDNESS OF A SEA-LIFE"

With, as usual, a prod or two from his indefatigable interrogator, that most confirmed of landsmen, Samuel Johnson, dismisses shipboard life in a few words in this snippet from James Boswell's *Life of Samuel Johnson*.

I again visited him on Monday. He took occasion to enlarge, as he often did, upon the wretchedness of a sea-life. "A ship is worse than a gaol. There is, in a gaol, better air, better company, better conveniency of every kind; and a ship has the additional disadvantage of being in danger. When men come to like a sea-life, they are not fit to live on land."—"Then (said I) it would be cruel in a father to breed his son to the sea." JOHNSON: "It would be cruel in a father who thinks as I do. Men go to sea, before they know the unhappiness of that way of life; and when they have come to know it, they cannot escape from it, because it is then too late to choose another profession; as indeed is generally the case with men, when they have once engaged in any particular way of life."

MAROONED

In this article, written in 1713 by Richard Steele for his magazine *The Englishman*, that famous essayist considers the case of a certain gentleman—*not* an Englishman, by the way, but a Scot —whose solitary sojourn on a remote Pacific island was to inspire one of the most popular books of all time, Daniel Defoe's novel *Robinson Crusoe*, which would appear in print six years later.

Under the title of this paper I do not think it foreign to my design to speak of a man born in Her Majesty's dominions and relate an adventure in his life so uncommon that it's doubtful whether the like has happened to any other of human race. The person I speak of is Alexander Selkirk, whose name is familiar to men of curiosity, from the fame of his having lived four years and four months alone in the island of Juan Fernandez. I had the pleasure frequently to converse with the man soon after his arrival in England, in the year 1711. It was matter of great curiosity to hear him, as he is a man of good sense, give an account of the different revolutions in his own mind in that long solitude. When we consider how painful absence from company for the space of but one evening is to the generality of mankind we may have a sense how painful this necessary and constant solitude was to a man bred a sailor and ever accustomed to enjoy and suffer, eat, drink and sleep, and perform all offices of life in fellowship and company. He was put ashore from a leaky vessel, with the captain of which he had had an irreconcilable difference; and he chose rather to take his fate in this place than in a crazy vessel under a disagreeable commander. His portion were a sea chest, his wearing clothes and bedding, a firelock, a pound of gunpowder, a large quantity of bullets, a flint and steel, a few pounds of tobacco, a hatchet, a knife, a kettle, a Bible and other books of devotion, together with pieces that concerned navigation, and his mathematical instruments. Resentment against his officer, who had ill-used him, made him look forward on this change of life as the more eligible one, till the instant in which he saw the vessel put off; at which moment, his heart yearned within him and melted at the parting with his comrades and all human society at once.

He had in provisions for the sustenance of life but the quantity of two meals, the island abounding only with wild goats, cats and rats. He judged it most probable that he should find more immediate and easy relief by finding shellfish on the shore than seeking game with his gun. He accordingly found great quantities of turtles, whose flesh is extremely delicious and of which he frequently eat very plentifully on his first arrival, till it grew disagreeable to his stomach except in jellies. The necessities of hunger and thirst were his greatest diversions from the reflection of his lonely condition. When those appetites were satisfied the desire of

society was as strong a call upon him and he appeared to himself least necessitous when he wanted everything; for the supports of his body were easily attained, but the eager longings for seeing again the face of man during the interval of craving bodily appetites were hardly supportable. He grew dejected, languid and melancholy, scarce able to refrain from doing himself violence, till by degrees, by the force of reason and frequent reading of the Scriptures and turning his thoughts upon the study of navigation, after the space of eighteen months he grew thoroughly reconciled to his condition. When he had made this conquest, the vigor of his health, disengagement from the world, a constant, cheerful, serene sky and a temperate air made his life one continual feast, and his being much more joyful than it had before been irksome. He, now taking delight in everything, made the hut in which he lay, by ornaments which he cut down from a spacious wood, on the side of which it was situated, the most delicious bower fanned with continual breezes and gentle aspirations of wind, that made his repose after the chase equal to the most sensual pleasures. . . .

The precautions which he took against want, in case of sickness, was to lame kids when very young, so as that they might recover their health but never be capable of speed. These he had in great numbers about his hut, and when he was himself in full vigor he could take at full speed the swiftest goat running up a promontory and never failed of catching them but on a descent.

His habitation was extremely pestered with rats, which gnawed his clothes and feet when sleeping. To defend him against them he fed and tamed numbers of young kitlings, who lay about his bed and preserved him from the enemy. When his clothes were quite worn out he dried and tacked together the skins of goats, with which he clothed himself, and was inured to pass through woods, bushes and brambles with as much carelessness and precipitance as any other animal. It happened once to him that running on the summit of a hill he made a stretch to seize a goat, with which under him he fell down a precipice and lay senseless for the space of three days, the length of which time he measured by the moon's growth since his last observation. This manner of life grew so exquisitely pleasant that he never had a moment heavy upon his hands; his nights were untroubled and his days joyous from the practice of temperance and exercise. It was his manner to use stated hours and places for exercises of devotion, which he performed aloud in order to keep up the faculties of speech and to utter himself with greater energy.

When I first saw him I thought, if I had not been let into his character and story I could have discerned that he had been much separated from company, from his aspect and gesture; there was a strong but cheerful seriousness in his

look, and a certain disregard to the ordinary things about him, as if he had been sunk in thought. When the ship which brought him off the island came in he received them with the greatest indifference with relation to the prospect of going off with them, but with great satisfaction in an opportunity to refresh and help them. The man frequently bewailed his return to the world, which could not, he said, with all its enjoyments, restore him to the tranquillity of his solitude. Though I had frequently conversed with him, after a few months' absence he met me in the street, and though he spoke to me I could not recollect that I had seen him; familiar converse in this town had taken off the loneliness of his aspect and quite altered the air of his face.

This plain man's story is a memorable example that he is happiest who confines his wants to natural necessities, and he that goes further in his desires increases his wants in proportion to his acquisitions; or to use his own expression, "I am now worth eight hundred pounds, but shall never be so happy as when I was not worth a farthing."

THE CASTAWAY
The story of the shipwrecked Peter Serrano's seven-year stay on a desolate island off Peru was recorded by Garcilaso de la Vega (1539–1616), a Peruvian historian known as *el Inca* to distinguish him from an earlier Spanish poet of the same name, in *Royal Commentaries of Peru,* from which it was translated into English in 1688 by Sir Paul Rycant.

Peter Serrano escaped from shipwreck by swimming to that desert island which from him received its name, being, as he reported, about two leagues in compass. It was Peter Serrano's misfortune to be lost upon these places and to save his life on this disconsolate island, where was neither water, wood, grass or anything for support of human life, at least not for maintenance of him so long a time as until some ship passing by might redeem him from perishing by hunger and thirst; which languishing manner of death is much more miserable than by a speedy suffocation in the waters. With the sad thoughts hereof he passed the first night, lamenting his affliction with as many melancholy reflections as we may imagine capable to enter into the mind of a wretch in like extremities.

So soon as it grew day he began to traverse his island and found on the shore some cockles, shrimps and other creatures of like nature which the sea had thrown up and which he was forced to eat raw because he wanted fire to roast them.

With this small entertainment he passed his time, till observing some turtles not far from the shore, he watched until they came within his reach, and then, throwing them on their backs (which is the manner of taking that sort of fish), he cut the throat, drinking the blood instead of water. And, slicing out the flesh with a knife which was fastened to his girdle, he laid the pieces to be dried and roasted by the sun. The shell he made use of to rake up the rainwater, which lay in little puddles, for that is a country often subject to great and sudden rains.

In this manner he passed the first of his days, by killing all the turtles that he was able, some of which were so large that their shells were as big as targets or bucklers. Others were so great that he was not able to turn them or stop them in their way to the sea; so that in a short time experience taught him which sort he was able to deal with and which were too unwieldly for his force. With his lesser shells he poured water into the greater, some of which contained twelve gallons; so that having made sufficient provisions both of meat and drink, he began to contrive some way to strike fire, that he might not only dress his meat with it but also make a smoke to give a sign to any ship which was passing.

Considering of this invention (for seamen are much more ingenious in all times of extremity than men bred at land), he searched everywhere to find out a couple of hard pebbles instead of flints, his knife serving in the place of a steel. But the island being all covered over with a dead sand and no stone appearing, he swam into the sea and, diving often to the bottom, he at length found a couple of stones fit for his purpose, which he rubbed together until he got them to an edge, with which, being able to strike fire, he drew some thread out of his shirt, which he worked so small that it was like cotton and served for tinder. So that, having contrived a means to kindle fire, he gathered a great quantity of seaweeds thrown up by the waves, which, with the shells of fish, and the planks of ships which had been wrecked on those shoals, afforded nourishment for his fuel. And lest sudden showers should extinguish his fire he made a little covering like a small hut with the shells of the largest turtles or tortoises that he had killed, taking great care that his fire should not go out.

In the space of two months and

sooner he was as unprovided of all things as he was at first, for with the great rains, heat and moisture of that climate his provisions were corrupted. And the great heat of the sun was so violent on him, having neither clothes to cover him nor shadow for a shelter, that when he was, as it were, broiled in the sun, he had no remedy but to run into the sea.

In this misery and care he passed three years, during which time he saw several ships at sea and as often made his smoke; but none turned out of their way to see what it meant, for fear of those shelves and sands which wary pilots avoid with all imaginable circumspection. So that the poor wretch, despairing of all manner of relief, esteemed it a mercy for him to die.

Being exposed in this manner to all weathers, the hair of his body grew in such manner that he was covered all over with bristles, the hair of his head and beard reaching to his waist, so that he appeared like some wild and savage creature.

At the end of three years Serrano was strangely surprised with the appearance of a man in his island, whose ship had, the night before, been cast away upon those sands, and who had saved himself on a plank of the vessel. So soon as it was day he espied the smoke and, imagining whence it was, he made towards it.

As soon as they saw each other it is hard to say which was the most amazed. Serrano imagined that it was the Devil who came in the shape of a man to tempt him to despair. The newcomer believed Serrano to be the Devil in his own proper shape and figure, being covered over with hair and beard. In fine they were both afraid, flying one from the other. Peter Serrano cried out, as he ran, "Jesus, Jesus, deliver me from the Devil." The other, hearing this, took courage; and, returning again to him, called out, "Brother, Brother, don't fly from me, for I am a Christian, as thou art." And because he saw that Serrano still ran from him he repeated the Credo or Apostles' Creed in words aloud. Which, when Serrano heard, he knew it was no Devil that would recite those words, and thereupon gave a stop to his flight. And returning with great kindness, they embraced each other with sighs and tears, lamenting their sad estate, without any hopes of deliverance. Serrano, supposing that his guest wanted refreshments, entertained him with such provisions as his miserable life afforded. And, having a little comforted each other, they began to recount the manner and occasion of their sad disasters.

For the better government of their way of living they designed their hours of day and night to certain services. Such a time was appointed to kill fish for eating; such hours for gathering weeds, fish bones and other matters which the sea threw up, to maintain their constant fire; and especial care had they to observe their watches and relieve each other at certain hours, so that they might be sure their fire went not out.

In this manner they lived amicably together for certain days. But many did not pass before a quarrel arose between them, so high that they were ready to fight. The occasion proceeded from some words that one gave the other that he took not that care and labor as the extremity of their condition required. This difference so increased (for to such misery do our passions often betray us) that at length they separated and lived apart one from the other. However, in a short time, having experienced the want of that comfort which mutual society procures, their choler was appeased. And so they returned to enjoy converse and the assistance which friendship and company afforded, in which condition they passed four years, during all which time they saw many ships sail near them. Yet none would be so charitable or curious as to be invited by their smoke and flame. So that, being now almost desperate, they expected no other remedy besides death to put an end to their miseries.

However, at length a ship, venturing to pass nearer than ordinary, espied the smoke; and, rightly judging that it must be made by some shipwrecked persons escaped to those sands, hoisted out their boat to take them in. Serrano and his companion readily ran to the place where they saw the boat coming. But as soon as the mariners approached so near as to distinguish the strange figure and looks of these two men they were so affrighted that they began to row back. But the poor men cried out and, that they might believe them not to be Devils or evil spirits, they rehearsed the Creed and called aloud on the name of Jesus. With which words the mariners returned, took them into the boat and carried them to the ship, to the great wonder of all present, who with admiration beheld their hairy shapes, not like men but beasts, and with singular pleasure heard them relate the story of their past misfortunes.

The companion died in his voyage to Spain but Serrano lived to come thither; from whence he traveled into Germany, where the Emperor then resided. All which time he nourished his hair and beard to serve as an evidence and proof of his past life. Wheresoever he came the people pressed as to a sight, to see him for money. Persons of quality, having the same curiosity, gave him sufficient to defray his charges. And his

Imperial Majesty, having seen him and heard his discourses, bestowed a rent upon him of four thousand pieces of eight a year, which make 4,800 ducats in Peru. And, going to the possession of this income, he died at Panama without further enjoyment.

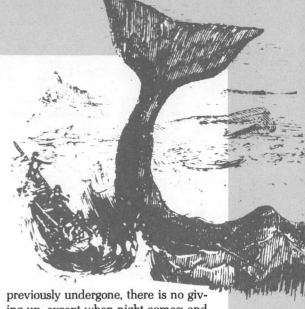

THE MAORI BEMBO HARPOONS A WHALE
In *Omoo* Herman Melville describes an extraordinary character, a Polynesian New Zealander, or Maori, presumably modeled on some person he himself had encountered in the South Seas.

There was a man among us who had sailed with the Mowree on his first voyage, and he told me that he had not changed a particle since then.

Some queer things this fellow told me. The following is one of his stories. I give it for what it is worth; premising, however, that from what I know of Bembo, and the foolhardy, dare-devil feats sometimes performed in the sperm-whale fishery, I believe in its substantial truth.

As may be believed, Bembo was a wild one after a fish; indeed, all New Zealanders engaged in this business are; it seems to harmonize sweetly with their blood-thirsty propensities. At sea, the best English they speak, is the South Seaman's slogan in lowering away, "A dead whale, or a stove boat!" Game to the marrow, these fellows are generally selected for harpooners; a post in which a nervous timid man would be rather out of his element.

In darting, the harpooner, of course, stands erect in the head of the boat, one knee braced against a support. But Bembo disdained this; and was always pulled up to his fish, balancing himself right on the gunwale.

But to my story. One morning, at daybreak, they brought him up to a large lone whale. He darted his harpoon, and missed; and the fish sounded. After a while, the monster rose again, about a mile off, and they made after him. But he was frightened, or "gallied," as they call it; and noon came, and the boat was still chasing him. In whaling, as long as the fish is in sight, and no matter what may have been

previously undergone, there is no giving up, except when night comes; and nowadays, when whales are so hard to be got, frequently, not even then. At last, Bembo's whale was alongside for the second time. He darted both harpoons; but, as sometimes happens to the best men, by some unaccountable chance, once more missed. Though it is well known that such failures *will* happen at times, they nevertheless occasion the bitterest disappointment to a boat's crew, generally expressed in curses, both loud and deep. And no wonder. Let any man pull with might and main for hours and hours together, under a burning sun; and if it do not make him a little peevish, he is no sailor.

The taunts of the seamen may have maddened the Mowree; however it was, no sooner was he brought up again, than, harpoon in hand, he bounded upon the whale's back, and for one dizzy second was seen there. The next, all was foam and fury, and both were out of sight. The men sheered off, flinging overboard the line as fast as they could; while a-head, nothing was seen but a red whirlpool of blood and brine.

Presently, a dark object swam out; the line began to straighten; then smoked round the loggerhead, and, quick as thought, the boat sped like an arrow through the water. They were "fast," and the whale was running.

Where was the Mowree? His brown hand was on the boat's gunwale; and he was hauled aboard in the very midst of the mad bubbles that burst under the bows.

Such a man, or devil, if you will, was Bembo.

"OH, MY GOD! WHERE IS THE SHIP?"

Having witnessed and survived an astonishing disaster—an attack on his ship by an infuriated whale that was sufficiently forceful to smash his vessel to pieces and send it to the bottom of the Pacific—harpooner Owen Chase was moved to write in 1821 a *Narrative of the Most Extraordinary and Distressing Shipwreck of the Whaleship Essex of Nantucket,* from which the passage below is excerpted. Two of the *Essex*'s three boats were eventually picked up by ships; eight men survived the long and terrifying voyage, during which they killed and ate one of their number.

On the 20th of November (cruising in latitude 0° 40′ S. longitude 119° 0′ w.) a shoal of whales was discovered off the lee-bow. The weather at this time was extremely fine and clear, and it was about eight o'clock in the morning, that the man at the mast-head gave the usual cry of, "there she blows." The ship was immediately put away, and we ran down in the direction for them. When we had got within half a mile of the place where they were observed, all our boats were lowered down, manned, and we started in pursuit of them. The ship, in the mean time, was brought to the wind, and the main-top-sail hove aback, to wait for us. I had the harpoon in the second boat; the captain preceded me in the first. When I arrived at the spot where we calculated they were, nothing was at first to be seen. We lay on our oars in anxious expectation of discovering them come up somewhere near us. Presently one rose, and spouted a short distance ahead of my boat; I made all speed towards it, came up with, and struck it; feeling the harpoon in him, he threw himself, in an agony, over towards the boat (which at that time was up alongside of him), and giving a severe blow with his tail, struck the boat near the edge of the water, amidships, and stove a hole in her. I immediately took up the boat hatchet, and cut the line, to disengage the boat from the whale, which by this time was running off with great velocity. I succeeded in getting clear of him, with the

loss of the harpoon and line; and finding the water to pour fast in the boat, I hastily stuffed three or four of our jackets in the hole, ordered one man to keep constantly bailing, and the rest to pull immediately for the ship; we succeeded in keeping the boat free, and shortly gained the ship. The captain and the second mate, in the other two boats, kept up the pursuit, and soon struck another whale. They being at this time a considerable distance to leeward, I went forward, braced around the main yard, and put the ship off in a direction for them; the boat which had been stove was immediately hoisted in, and after examining the hole, I found that I could, by nailing a piece of canvass over it, get her ready to join in a fresh pursuit, sooner than by lowering down the other remaining boat which belonged to the ship. I accordingly turned her over upon the quarter, and was in the act of nailing on the canvass, when I observed a very large spermaceti whale, as well as I could judge, about eighty-five feet in length; he broke water about twenty rods off our weather-bow, and was lying quietly, with his head in a direction for the ship. He spouted two or three times, and then disappeared. In less than two or three seconds he came up again, about the length of the ship off, and made directly for us, at the rate of about three knots. The ship was then going with about the same velocity. His appearance and attitude gave us at first no alarm; but while I stood watching his movements, and observing him but a ship's length off, coming down for us with great celerity, I involuntarily ordered the boy at the helm to put it hard up; intending to sheer off and avoid him. The words were scarcely out of my mouth, before he came down upon us with full speed, and struck the ship with his head, just forward of the fore-chains; he gave us such an appalling and tremendous jar, as nearly threw us all on our faces. The ship brought up as suddenly and violently as if she had struck a rock, and trembled for a few seconds like a leaf. We looked at each other with perfect amazement, deprived almost of the power of speech. Many minutes elapsed before we were able to realize the dreadful accident; during which time he passed under the ship, grazing her keel as he went along,

came up alongside of her to leeward, and lay on the top of the water (apparently stunned with the violence of the blow), for the space of a minute; he then suddenly started off, in a direction to leeward. After a few moments' reflection, and recovering, in some measure, from the sudden consternation that had seized us, I of course concluded that he had stove a hole in the ship, and that it would be necessary to set the pumps going. Accordingly they were rigged, but had not been in operation more than one minute, before I perceived the head of the ship to be gradually settling down in the water; I then ordered the signal to be set for the other boats, which, scarcely had I despatched, before I again discovered the whale, apparently in convulsions, on the top of the water, about one hundred rods to leeward. He was enveloped in the foam of the sea, that

his continual and violent thrashing about in the water had created around him, and I could distinctly see him smite his jaws together, as if distracted with rage and fury. He remained a short time in this situation, and then started off with great velocity, across the bows of the ship, to windward. By this time the ship had settled down a considerable distance in the water, and I gave her up as lost. I however ordered the pumps to be kept constantly going, and endeavoured to collect my thoughts for the occasion. I turned to the boats, two of which we then had with the ship, with an intention of clearing them away, and getting all things ready to embark in them, if there should be no other resource left; and while my attention was thus engaged for a moment, I was aroused with the cry of a man at the hatchway, "here he is—he is making for us again." I turned around, and saw him about one hundred rods directly ahead of us, coming down apparently with twice his ordinary speed, and to me at that moment, it appeared with tenfold fury and vengeance in his aspect. The surf flew in all directions about him, and his course towards us was marked by a white foam of a rod in width, which he made with the continual violent thrashing of his tail; his head was about half out of water, and in that way he came upon, and again struck the ship. I was in hopes when I descried him making for us, that by a dexterous movement of putting the ship away immediately, I should be able to cross the line of his approach, before he could get up to us, and thus avoid, what I knew, if he should strike us again, would prove our inevitable destruction. I bawled out to the helmsman, "hard up!" but she had not fallen off more than a point, before we took the second shock. I should judge the speed of the ship to have been at this time about three knots, and that of the whale about six. He struck her to windward, directly under the cathead, and completely stove in her bows. He passed under the ship again, went off to leeward, and we saw no more of him. Our situation at this juncture can be more readily imagined than described. The shock to our feelings was such, as I am sure none can have an adequate conception of, that were not there: the misfortune befell us at a moment when we least dreamt of any accident; and from the pleasing anticipations we had formed, of realizing the certain profits of our labour, we were dejected by a sudden, most mysterious, and overwhelming calamity. Not a moment, however, was to be lost in endeavouring to provide for the extremity to which it was now certain we were reduced. We were more than a thousand miles from the nearest land, and with nothing

but a light open boat, as the resource of safety for myself and companions. I ordered the men to cease pumping, and every one to provide for himself; seizing a hatchet at the same time, I cut away the lashings of the spare boat, which lay bottom up, across two spars directly over the quarter deck, and cried out to those near me, to take her as she came down. They did so accordingly, and bore her on their shoulders as far as the waist of the ship. The steward had in the mean time gone down into the cabin twice, and saved two quadrants, two practical navigators, and the captain's trunk and mine; all which were hastily thrown into the boat, as she lay on the deck, with the two compasses which I snatched from the binnacle. He attempted to descend again; but the water by this time had rushed in, and he returned without being able to effect his purpose. By the time we had got the boat to the waist, the ship had filled with water, and was going down on her beam-ends: we shoved our boat as quickly as possible from the plank-shear into the water, all hands jumping in her at the same time, and launched off clear of the ship. We were scarcely two boat's lengths distant from her, when she fell over to windward, and settled down in the water.

Amazement and despair now wholly took possession of us. We contemplated the frightful situation the ship lay in, and thought with horror upon the sudden and dreadful calamity that had overtaken us. We looked upon each other, as if to gather some consolatory sensation from an interchange of sentiments, but every countenance was marked with the paleness of despair. Not a word was spoken for several minutes by any of us; all appeared to be bound in a spell of stupid consternation; and from the time we were first attacked by the whale, to the period of the fall of the ship, and of our leaving her in the boat, more than ten minutes could not certainly have elapsed! God only knows in what way, or by what means, we were enabled to accomplish in that short time what we did; the cutting away and transporting the boat from where she was deposited would of itself, in ordinary circumstances, have consumed as much time as that, if the whole ship's crew had been employed

in it. My companions had not saved a single article but what they had on their backs; but to me it was a source of infinite satisfaction, if any such could be gathered from the horrors of our gloomy situation, that we had been fortunate enough to have preserved our compasses, navigators, and quadrants. After the first shock of my feelings was over, I enthusiastically contemplated them as the probable instruments of our salvation; without them all would have been dark and hopeless. Gracious God! what a picture of distress and suffering now presented itself to my imagination. The crew of the ship were saved, consisting of twenty human souls. All that remained to conduct these twenty beings through the stormy terrors of the ocean, perhaps many thousand miles, were three open light boats. The prospect of obtaining any provisions or water from the ship, to subsist upon during the time, was at least now doubtful. How many long and watchful nights, thought I, are to be passed? How many tedious days of partial starvation are to be endured, before the least relief or mitigation of our sufferings can be reasonably anticipated. We lay at this time in our boat, about two ship's lengths off from the wreck, in perfect silence, calmly contemplating her situation, and absorbed in our own melancholy reflections, when the other boats were discovered rowing up to us. They had but shortly before discovered that some accident had befallen us, but of the nature of which they were entirely ignorant. The sudden and mysterious disappearance of the ship was first discovered by the boat-steerer in the captain's boat, and with a horror-struck countenance and voice, he suddenly exclaimed, "Oh, my God! where is the ship?" Their operations upon this were instantly suspended, and a general cry of horror and despair burst from the lips of every man, as their looks were directed for her, in vain, over every part of the ocean. They immediately made all haste towards us. The captain's boat was the first that reached us. He stopped about a boat's length off, but had no power to utter a single syllable: he was so completely overpowered with the spectacle before him, that he sat down in his boat, pale and speechless.

THE CHARACTER OF THE WEST WIND

Like the passage from the writings of Joseph Conrad given above under the heading "A Rescue at Sea," this one is taken from his book of reminiscences, *The Mirror of the Sea*.

The southwesterly weather is the thick weather *par excellence*. It is not the thickness of the fog; it is rather a contraction of the horizon, a mysterious veiling of the shores with clouds that seem to make a low-vaulted dungeon around the running ship. It is not blindness; it is a shortening of the sight. The West Wind does not say to the seaman, "You shall be blind"; it restricts merely the range of his vision and raises the dread of land within his breast. . . . I arose suddenly and staggered up on deck. The autocrat of the North Atlantic was still oppressing his kingdom and its outlying dependencies, even as far as the Bay of Biscay, in the dismal secrecy of thick, very thick, weather. The force of the wind, though we were running before it at the rate of some ten knots an hour, was so great that it drove me with a steady push to the front of the poop, where my commander was holding on.

"What do you think of it?" he addressed me in an interrogative yell.

What I really thought was that we both had had just about enough of it. The manner in which the great West Wind chooses at times to administer his possessions does not commend itself to a person of peaceful and law-abiding disposition, inclined to draw distinctions between right and wrong in the face of natural forces, whose standard, naturally, is that of might alone. But, of course, I said nothing. For a man caught, as it were, between his skipper and the great West Wind silence is the safest sort of diplomacy. Moreover, I knew my skipper. He did not want to know what I thought. Shipmasters hanging on a breath before the thrones of the winds ruling the seas have their psychology whose workings are as important to the ship and those on board of her as the changing moods of the weather. The man, as a matter of fact, under no circumstances, ever cared a brass farthing for what I or anybody else in his ship thought. He had had just about enough of it, I guessed, and what he was at really was a process of fishing for a suggestion. It was the pride of his life that he had never wasted a chance, no matter how boisterous, threatening, and dangerous, of a fair wind. Like men racing blind-fold for a gap in a hedge, we were finishing a splendidly quick passage from the Antipodes, with a tremendous rush for the Channel in as thick a weather as any I can remember, but his psychology did not permit him to bring the ship to with a fair wind blowing—at least not on his own initiative. And yet he felt that very soon indeed something would have to be done. He wanted the suggestion to come from me, so that later on, when the trouble was over, he could argue this point with his own uncompromising spirit, laying the blame upon my shoulders. I must render him the justice that this sort of pride was his only weakness.

But he got no suggestion from me. I understood his psychology. Besides, I had my own stock of weaknesses at the time (it is a different one now), and amongst them was the conceit of being remarkably well up in the psychology of the Westerly Weather. I believed—not to mince matters—that I had a genius for reading the mind of the great ruler of high latitudes. I fancied I could discern already the coming of a change in his royal mood. And all I said was:

"The weather's bound to clear up with the shift of wind."

"Anybody knows that much!" he snapped at me, at the highest pitch of his voice.

"I mean before dark!" I cried.

This was all the opening he ever got from me. The eagerness with which he seized upon it gave me the measure of the anxiety he had been labouring under.

"Very well," he shouted, with an affectation of impatience, as if giving way to long entreaties. "All right. If we don't get a shift by then we'll take that foresail off her and put her head under her wing for the night."

I was struck by the picturesque character of the phrase as applied to a ship brought-to in order to ride out a gale with wave after wave passing under her breast. I could see her resting in the tumult of the elements like a sea-bird sleeping in wild weather upon the raging waters with its head tucked under its wing. In imaginative precision, in true feeling, this is one of the most expressive sentences I have ever heard on human lips. But as to taking the fore-sail off that ship before we put her head under her wing, I had my grave doubts. They were justified. That long-enduring piece of canvas was confiscated by the arbitrary decree of the West Wind, to whom belong the lives of men and the contrivances of their hands within the limits of his kingdom. With the sound of a faint explosion it vanished into the thick weather bodily, leaving behind of its stout substance not so much as one solitary strip big enough to be picked into a handful of lint for, say, a wounded elephant. Torn out of its bolt-ropes, it faded like a whiff of smoke in the smoky drift of clouds shattered and torn by the shift of wind. For the shift of wind had come. The unveiled, low sun glared angrily from a chaotic sky upon a confused and tremendous sea dashing itself upon a coast. We recognized the headland, and looked at each other in the silence of dumb wonder. Without knowing it in the least, we had run up alongside the Isle of Wight, and that tower, tinged a faint evening red in the salt wind-haze, was the lighthouse of St. Catherine's Point.

My skipper recovered first from his astonishment. His bulging eyes sank back gradually into their orbits. His psychology, taking it all round, was really very creditable for an average sailor. He had been spared the humiliation of laying his ship to with a fair wind; and at once that man, of an open and truthful nature, spoke up in perfect good faith, rubbing together his brown, hairy hands—the hands of a master-craftsman upon the sea.

"Humph! that's just about where I reckoned we had got to."

The transparency and ingenuousness, in a way, of that delusion, the airy tone, the hint of already growing pride, were perfectly delicious, But, in truth, this was one of the greatest surprises ever sprung by the clearing-up mood of the West Wind upon one of the most accomplished of his courtiers.

This engraving, showing whaling in Greenland, illustrated a history of the island by the missionary Hans Egede, published in 1750.

5

MYSTERIOUS CREATURES

Iuitas syrie que nunc tyrus dicit. olim ſerra uocabat̄ a piſce quodam qui illic abundabat. quem ſua lingua ſar apellāt ex quo diriuatū eſt huʼ ſimilitudinis piſciculos ſardas. ſardinaſ q: uocari.

The Grace Line's *Santa Clara* was off the North Carolina coast on a fine December day in 1947, sailing south to the old fortress city of Cartagena, Colombia. Suddenly the third officer cried out, pointing off to starboard. The other mates saw what he had seen, watched it as it passed close astern. Shortly afterward the wireless operator of the *Santa Clara* tapped out a message:

LAT 34.34 N LONG 74.07 W 1700 GCT STRUCK MARINE MONSTER EITHER KILLING IT OR BADLY WOUNDING IT PERIOD ESTIMATED LENGTH 45 FEET WITH EEL LIKE HEAD AND BODY APPROXIMATELY THREE FEET IN DIAMETER PERIOD LAST SEEN THRASHING IN LARGE AREA OF BLOODY WATER AND FOAM . . .

The reaction, at the dawn of the atomic age when science seemed particularly unshakable, was skeptical. Journalists interviewed those aboard ship on the liner's return, leery of a hoax. One went to an expert at the New York Zoological Society, who thought that the animal involved could have been a large porpoise or oarfish—a long ribbon of a creature which might, to the uninitiated, look monsterish. That was that.

Not quite, though. The incident went into the files of a French-born zoologist and sometime jazz singer named Bernard Heuvelmans. A passionate pursuer of unknown animals, Heuvelmans spent years collecting and analyzing reports of marine unaccountables. His book, which appeared in English under the title *In the Wake of the Sea-Serpents*, is almost as long as its subjects. Heuvelmans gave two reasons for carrying on so. "Firstly I wanted to be able to base my conclusions on the greatest possible number of sightings. Sir Arthur Conan Doyle has shown how the human mind is disposed to believe in something in proportion to the number of witnesses." Secondly, Heuvelmans felt that by "publishing indiscriminately and impartially all the evidence that can be collected," he would be serving the needs of objectivity.

All told, Heuvelmans came up with 587 reported

SEA MONSTERS IN FABLE AND FACT

by William H. MacLeish

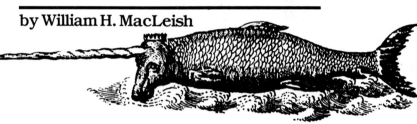

Reports of strange creatures seen by seamen gave rise to fanciful illustrations: on the opposite page, a flying fish as depicted in a twelfth-century English bestiary, and above right, a narwhal, a small whale with a long tusk. The engraving on the preceding pages was based on reports by officers of the British ship Daedalus, *who saw a sea monster while sailing in the South Atlantic in 1848.*

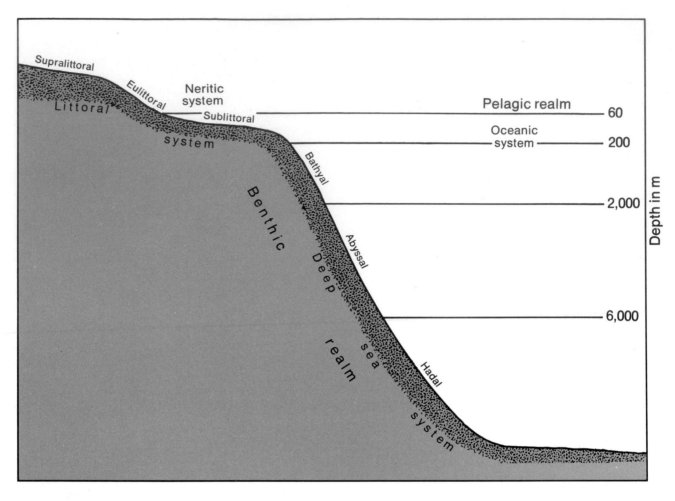

Biological oceanographers divide the sea into two general realms of life. The pelagic realm is the home of the water-dwelling creatures, including those that live in the seas above the continental shelf (the neritic system) and those that live in deep water (the oceanic system). The benthic realm is the home of the bottom dwellers, including those that live in the shallows (the littoral system) and those that live in successive layers of the deep sea system (bathyal, abyssal, and hadal).

sightings of sea monsters between the mid-seventeenth and the mid-twentieth centuries. Of these, 121 seemed vague or doubtful. Fifty or so more were hoaxes, many identifiable by their excessive detail (one overheated account described a 200-foot specimen sporting a bright green handle-bar mustache; another gave precise co-ordinates placing the observer in the Libyan desert). And another fifty looked like mistaken identities—a train of playing porpoises, a flight of skimming sea birds, a mass of seaweed or, if the sighting was of a stranded, rotting carcass, a basking shark. Heuvelmans settled down with 358 sightings that he considered fairly reliable.

They came from most parts of the sea but seemed

concentrated along the Scandinavian, British, and American coasts and grouped together in certain apparently random time periods. As is so often the case when measuring the unknown with the calipers of the known, witnesses saw what they had been conditioned to see. They would call the great creatures "serpents" and describe vertical undulatory motions of which serpents are incapable. Some of the animals moved in "flexuous hillocks," some at the flank speed of a destroyer. Fear was in most descriptions—the awful size, the snake's evil. But there were other emotions. A steamer reported encountering a sea-giraffe in 1913 off Newfoundland, a creature with a twenty-foot neck, liquid blue eyes that "took in the ship with a surprised, injured and fearful stare," and a wail like a baby's. There were several sightings around Victoria Island, British Columbia, of huge animals that the local residents regarded as "lovable and homely." And for years the Scots have had their elusive and alluring "Nessie."

Heuvelmans' work convinced him there was not one type of monster swimming the seas but several.

Comparing data from the most likely sightings, he arrived at seven: an animal as long as the largest whale but shaped much like an otter; an elongated, whale-sized creature with a row of humps along its spine; a many-finned wonder with a head like a walrus; a merhorse with huge eyes and a mane; a long-necked variety with a massive blubbery body. These might be mammals. Then there were the super-eel, less than fifty feet long, and the marine saurian, a seagoing crocodile of about the same size.

Belief in sea creatures of almost any shape and size came easier in the ancient days when the unknown was all about and creations of the imagination were less terrifying than the emptiness of ignorance. Then, there could be a great catfish at the bottom of the sea under Japan. There could be multieyed, web-footed pigs swimming in the scud alongside 600-foot fanged whales. "Canst thou draw out Leviathan with a hook?" asked the Book of Job. "Who can open the doors of his face? His teeth are terrible round about . . . his eyes are like the eyelids of the morning." And the kraken, the squidlike terror described by Bishop Erik Pontoppidan of Norway as having an "upper part which seems . . . about an English mile and a half in circumference, (some say more, but I chuse the least for greater certainty)." And the mermaids, bishop fishes, monk fishes—all manner of ichthyomorphic versions of terrestrial and terrified man.

Disbelief grew as sailors learned to venture far from the coasts and as the spiritual masochism of the Dark Ages receded. Too many folk had been taken in by the whoppers and the hoaxes. Thoreau claimed that Daniel Webster spied a huge sea creature near Plymouth and enjoined his companion: "For God's sake, never say a word about this to anyone." In 1893, three journalists aboard a ship off the southeast coast of Africa witnessed a violent volcanic upheaval that sent cold bottom water to the surface. In the roil were two huge beasts, one in its death struggles. The journalists noted what they saw but two of them tore up their reports. "Truth," one of them remarked, "is a naked lady, and if by accident she is drawn up from the bottom of the sea, it behooves a gentleman either to give her a print petticoat or to turn his face to the wall and vow he did not see." The third witness tried to publish his account but found that it would be accepted only as fiction.

What is particularly interesting about Heuvelmans is that his work is that of a modern scientist working with the tools of pre-science. Biological oceanography, the study of sea creatures and their environment, is not much more than fifteen decades old. There are reports that Aristotle may have run marine research stations on the island of Lesbos, and surely there were attempts for centuries after to understand sea life. But during those centuries, students of the sea depended heavily on the accounts of mariners home from months or years of voyaging. They could discount, disbelieve, question, compare, rearrange. But they could not in the main fish for themselves in blue water, could not until quite recently do more than work the shallows of their chosen world. Hypotheses were constructed on what evidence could be found, but the casualty rate was high. For example, one nineteenth-century theory argued that animal life dwindled with depth and that there was none at all below 300 fathoms. Another held that a gelatinous substance found in samples of calcareous ooze dredged from deep bottoms was living matter—bathybius, it was called.

The voyage of the British corvette *Challenger* (1872–76) was the first intensive, interdisciplinary research expedition of marine science. The ship explored all the oceans except the Arctic, brought home enough material and data (4,717 animal species new to science) to keep investigators busy for more than two decades. By the time the expedition's fifty volumes had been published, bathybius had been reduced to the product of chemical interactions between preservatives and samples. The theory of the dead deeps dissolved, along with numberless others.

Marine biology has burgeoned since *Challenger*. Roughly $100,000,000 is spent annually on all its ramifications in the United States, much of this by the federal government. Some work is done in shore-based laboratories—in tanks, culture dishes, Formalin-filled jars, under incredibly powerful microscopes. Seagoing equipment has moved well beyond the made-over vessel, the yacht on loan. Oceanographic vessels, ships that spend three days out of four at sea, are designed to meet the professional needs of scientists from every pertinent discipline. For the biological oceanographer, there are nets capable of fishing the water layer by layer. There are arrays of "fish"—towable, streamlined tubes loaded with sensors. There are corers, grabs, dredges for the bottom.

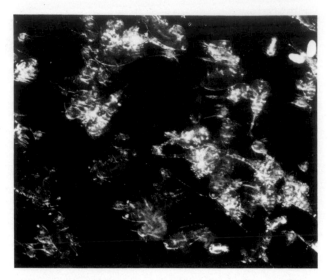

Plankters, the tiniest forms of floating oceanic life, show great variety of shape and function. The translucent salps on this page are among the largest. Coccolithophores (opposite page) are so small that scanning electron microscopy must be used to study them. Their skeletons drop to the bottom; in very deep water they tend to dissolve (bottom, far right).

There are baited cameras used by such inventive folk as John Isaacs of the Scripps Institution of Oceanography in California to capture the images of otherwise uncapturable deep sea life. Side-scan sonars range on school fish. Submersibles dive to the bottom of the deepest trench more than 35,000 feet down, or nose along the wall of a coral reef. Measuring devices borrowed from other disciplines plot salinity, temperature, and depth profiles. Computers crammed into every corner do their binary best to assimilate. All to shed light on the questions central to the art: What lives in the sea? By what means? How are organisms distributed and what accounts for their distribution patterns?

Scientists have identified much of sea life, though surprises are still not surprising. But for all that, there are some senior practitioners of the art who are not happy with the pace of discovery. In the mid-1970's, a report by the National Academy of Sciences argued that while sampling techniques could produce the qualitative data needed in the study of evolution, they performed less satisfactorily in providing the numbers we must have to understand the dynamics of sea life (and to estimate accurately how much of it man can safely harvest). "After a century of extensive collecting," said the N.A.S. committee, "we know something about what species live in the oceans, but we have only a nebulous idea of the temporal and spatial variations of these species."

Considering the stomachs of the larger ocean predators as collectors, the committee found that they can contain kinds and sizes of animals quite different from those captured in the sampling nets. Porpoises yield ear bones of fish much larger than those of the same species taken by net; diving birds feed on larval tuna, comparatively few of which turn up in nets built specifically to catch them. Said the committee, "fast-swimming animals such as the squid are rarely caught by present sampling methods, yet sperm whales may annually capture a quantity of them approaching the total amount of fish man takes from the sea. . . . Oceanographers have never been outstandingly successful fishermen. In large part, they have been content with nets that catch mostly 'the weak, the blind, and the unlucky.'" One result: estimates of marine food potential, which are based in large part on sampling, may be off by a factor of ten.

The fault, if there is one, lies not in the attempt.

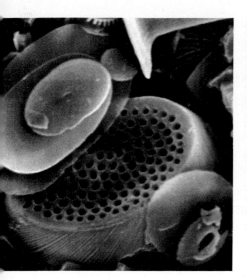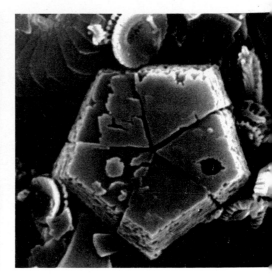

Biological oceanographers in the main lead lives dominated by the rigors of any scientific discipline overlaid by the demands and dangers of going to sea—the tedium of long cruises, seasickness, the riskiness of the dives, and of working on a rolling fantail with heavy equipment and straining cable. The obstacle is the sea itself. Sea water is viscous, eight hundred times denser than air. It is the common component of the earth's surface, covering more than half of it to a depth of at least 4,000 meters. The volume of the oceanic biosphere, the region where life is found, is three hundred times that of the terrestrial biosphere. Living things comprise less than a millionth part of the whole at the surface, where organisms tend to be concentrated. In the great depths, the ratio may be on the order of one to one billion. Not much of a

target, even if the specimen is waiting patiently for capture. But since creatures as small as copepods, the bugs of the sea, and as large as fish or mammals—or monsters—seem capable of evading nets with frustrating frequency, the job can seem disheartening.

L ife in the sea is less exposed to extremes than is a tree, a deer, a man. Temperatures range only between about −2°C and 40°C. Particularly in the deeps, temperature and salinity readings remain quite constant. There is an abundance of light right at the surface—too much of ultraviolet length for some species. In particularly clear water, light can penetrate to below 200 meters, but in more turbid conditions—particularly in coastal waters—illumination is much more limited. Sea water is so dense that it buoys its

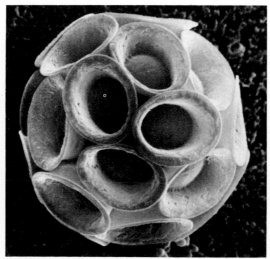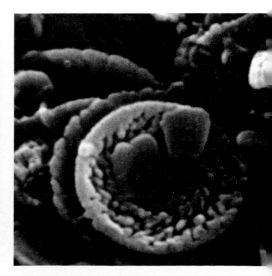

swimmers and floaters, lessening the need for strong—and heavy—skeletons; even whales are lightweights in this medium. It is a solvent in constant motion, supplying dissolved gases, minerals, and other essentials to plants and animals. It is a buffered liquid that can carry abundant supplies of carbon (as dissolved carbon dioxide) and other foundation elements of life without causing dangerous shifts in its slightly alkaline state.

Not that all is sweetness in the salt. Pressure is a factor to be contended with, increasing one atmosphere (one kilogram per square centimeter) with each ten meters of depth. Whales can dive deeper than 100 atmospheres, or 1,000 meters, and porpoises, seals, and penguins to sizable fractions of that depth. Many organisms that do not have swim bladders for buoyancy—such as crustaceans, squids, sharks, and swordfish—can move up and down in the water

This monstrous-looking creature is in fact only eight inches long and spends its days at depths of 2,000 meters. Its cavernous mouth and large teeth make it an efficient predator at depths where food is sparse.

column, but other organisms must stay within narrower boundaries. Relatively stable as it is, the sea has its provinces of life, each set off by tolerances of light, salinity, temperature, density, turbidity, chemical composition. So close do some organisms stick to home that oceanographers use them to establish the provenance of the waters they are studying.

When tolerances are narrow, exposure to variations in vital properties of sea water have their effect. A rise of 10°C in sea water temperature can produce a two- or threefold rise in metabolism. An increase in nutrients can bring on a riotous bloom of life. Shifts in weather patterns can shunt aside coastal waters in some areas and bring deep, rich waters welling up to the surface. Off Peru, upwelling sustains a productive anchovy fishery. But when conditions change, warm water moves in and upwelling ceases. The tiny plants and animals on which the anchovies graze dwindle away. The fish die or move to other waters. Sea birds starve and fishermen suffer. In any area of the open ocean, a severe storm can mix the upper waters, dragging light-dependent organisms too deep to survive.

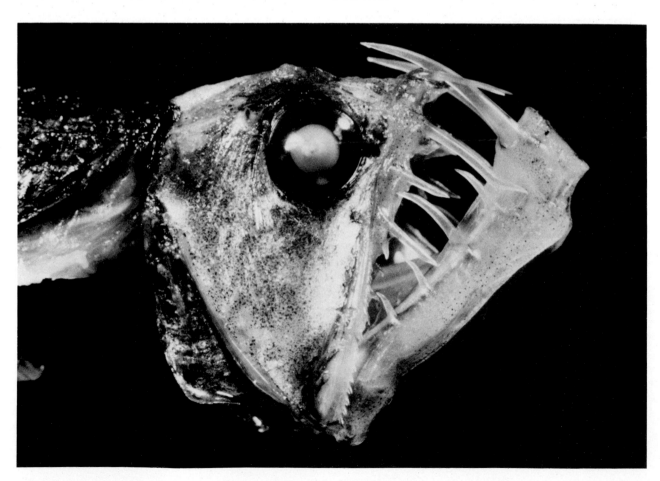

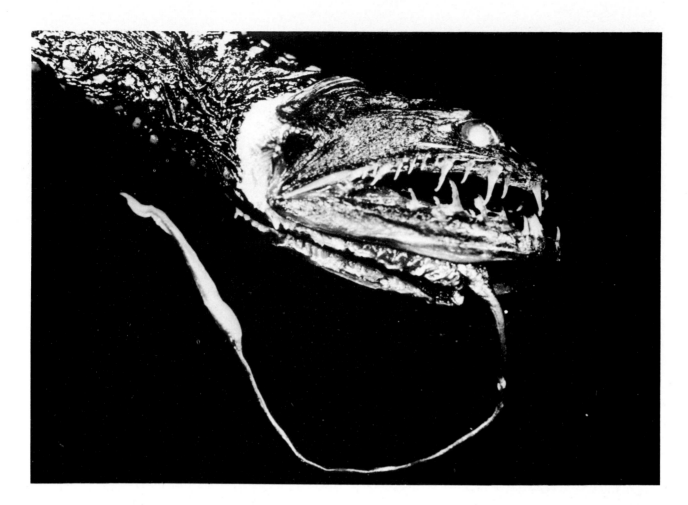

Bioluminescence is common in the depths. This Pacific blackdragon carries a light at the end of its barbel, the appendage on its chin, probably to attract mates and prey.

Nowhere is death more demonstrably part of life than in the place where life began. An oyster can lay up to 500 million eggs in a year, a cod 90 million. All but a relative few of the ocean's young die young. Most are ingested by other organisms, digested, egested, ingested again, egested. Soon or late, bacteria in the water column or bottom sediments break down what is left into essential nutrients, some of which find their way back to the primary producers.

Biological oceanographers divide their world into two general zones of life—pelagic, or water-dwelling, and benthic, or bottom-dwelling. Within each realm are subgroupings. The pelagic comprises neritic life, the concentrations in waters overlying the continental shelves, and oceanic life, in blue water. Benthic communities start close to the tide line; they encompass a littoral system, extending to 200 meters, and a deep sea system that takes in the bathyal (200–2,000 meters) and abyssal (2,000–6,000 meters) environments and the deep trenches of the hadal area (6,000–11,000 meters).

In relative terms, the populations of the benthos, the

bottom dwellers, shift with depth away from plant and toward animal life. Sea grasses and the other true rooted plants grow only in depths penetrated by sufficient sunlight—usually to less than 50 meters. Most of the algae and other plants have a difficult time of it at depths of much more than 200 meters. Here, at the edge of the continental shelves, are the great bottom fishing grounds. On beyond and below, higher plant life pinches out, though bacteria continue in force. Animal diversity and numbers tend to shrink as light disappears, pressure rises, and temperature falls (the latter decreases much more slowly in the depths than at the thermocline, the zone of rapid drop-off which is generally found in the top 200 meters of the open sea). This is the abyssal world, the largest and least known environment on earth. Above the bottom and on the mud, animals feed on the drizzle of fecal

Seals maintain their body temperature while moving back and forth between air and water. In extreme cold they can reduce or cut off blood circulation to exposed parts of their bodies.

among the most productive areas of the ocean. Plants and fish larvae abound in the upper waters; great schools of fish flash below them. In blue water, the oceanic province, productivity drops. Life is farther apart: tuna, dolphins, whales, the ubiquitous shark, pelagic fish, strong swimmers, and epic wanderers.

Between 500 and 1,000 meters down in the open sea, remarkable things can happen. Organisms ranging from small crustaceans to squid and lantern fish spend daylight hours at these depths, rising toward the surface at night to feed. Concentrations are dense enough to trigger depth recorders into signaling a false bottom and are thus called deep scattering layers. One type is known to oceanographers as Alexander's Acres, named for an individual doubtless long at sea who was reminded by the layer's multicurved signature on the recording chart of acres of bosoms.

Every phylum of animals in the world is represented in the sea. Dry land seems to offer plants the best opportunities for diverse development. But consider this: marine plants, in terms of sheer mass, are several orders of magnitude scarcer than the trees, grasses, and crops of land, yet they contribute roughly the same amount to global food production. Sea plants are therefore many times more productive than land plants. Yet most are so small that they cannot be studied with the naked eye.

Most sea plants are planktonic—small and single-celled, rootless and leafless, yellow-green algae. Of these, the most important in terms of abundance are the diatoms, tiny pillboxes of silica. Next come the dinoflagellates, some of which appear animallike in their eating habits, all of which have hairlike tails giving them a modicum of mobility. Dinoflagellates, like other phytoplankton, can undergo blooms, or enormous increases in population, when conditions are right. Some of them are responsible for the red tides, the blooms during which shellfish feeding on them can be poisonous to humans. The shellfish do not seem to be affected, but in some waters fish grazing the blooms suffer massive die-offs.

Among the smallest of the small are the coccolitho-

pellets from the upper waters or the occasional corpse of a fish or mammal. Plantlike animals put down their holdfasts and fish the gelid currents. Sea cucumbers, brittle stars, and other crawlers leave their trails. Worms and other small life work and rework the sediments. Given the comparative scarcity and the types of food, the benthos should not include large predators. But cameras have caught large sharks coming to the bait at great depth. There may be others.

The pelagic realm is more familiar to us, at least in part. Its inshore, or neritic, division has become an open laboratory for skin-diving scientists and those working from coastal craft. These waters are apt to be

The sense of sight manifests itself in strange places. Scallops (opposite page, top) have developed rows of eyes just inside the edges of their shells. The fan worm Sabella crassicornis *(bottom) is equipped with paired eyespots along the ribs of radioles it uses to capture plankton.*

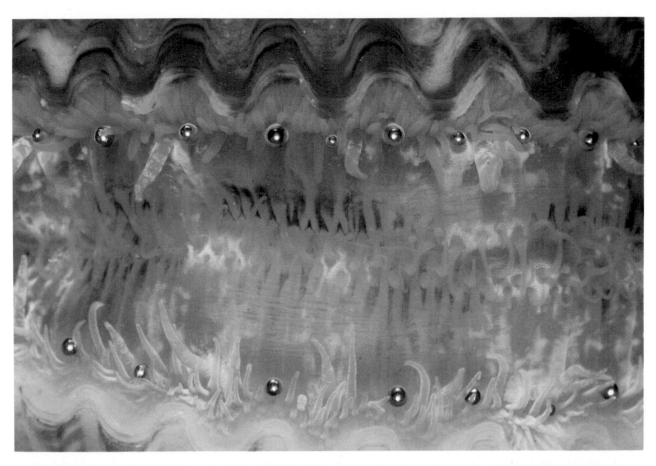

phorids, first remarked on by geologists studying oozes composed chiefly of their remains—calcareous shells as startling in symmetry as any snowflake (diatoms and many other plankters, plant and animal, contribute similarly to the sediments).

Plankters are mostly floaters, drifters ("plankton" comes from the Greek term for "one made to wander"). Some can move, but all are subject to the motion of their medium. Phytoplankton are the primary producers of the sea. They and some of the bacteria floating with them are capable of turning inorganic into organic material. The plants, like their terrestrial relatives, rely on sunlight for energy to power photosynthesis, the process of more than one hundred chemical steps whereby carbon dioxide and water are converted into carbohydrates and oxygen—in a pinhead.

Zooplankton graze the patchy meadows of floating plants. Most numerous are the copepods, tiny crustaceans which—it has recently turned out—are quite choosy about which morsel to fan into their mouth parts. There are other vaguely shrimplike animals past numbering; in rich antarctic waters, clouds of krill feed on phytoplankton. There are single-celled protozoa, such as the foraminifera and radiolaria. And there are the larvae of fish and of animals who will spend their adult lives fixed to the bottom.

Herring and other fish feed on the zooplankton. Tuna and other large predators feed on them. Man takes his toll—some sixty million tons annually, mostly of the larger species. Seals and porpoises probably equal man in their fishing. Some scientists are of the opinion that sperm whales take roughly 100 million tons of deep sea squid, the kind biologists find so hard to capture in their nets.

In all the killing, survival depends to a large degree on the ability to distinguish prey from predator from mate from fellow and to act or react accordingly. Here as elsewhere in their development, the animals of the sea show variety and sophistication that continue to astound researchers trying to understand the mysteries of senses in the sea.

Humpback whales, like the one breaching in Alaskan waters at left, roam the world's oceans, and as they migrate they sing mysterious songs. Scientists have detected repetition within the songs but have not deciphered their meaning, nor are they sure why whales make their spectacular leaps.

The ability to hide, to dissemble, is often a key to survival. Shown above, left to right, are three stages of the process by which the white sea urchin Lytechinus variegatus *creates a shield of shells held by its tube feet.*

How, for example, do marine animals see? Light fades fast with depth to ghostly blues and grays to an abyssal black that astonished those who first looked on it from behind the thick glass ports of the earliest submersibles. Mid-water and deep sea fish often have outsized eyes. Some are so large that they would not fit in the head but for their being elongated and mounted like old-fashioned headlights. Some have no lenses, sacrificing focus so that the few photons of light encountered at depth can pass through without attenuation to the retina. Some sharks and other species have developed eye tissues that act as mirrors to intensify available light. The octopus boasts a particularly well-developed optical system. So does the blue-eyed scallop of the shallows, which has mirroring tissues and two retinas.

The swordfish has been discovered by Frank Carey of the Woods Hole Oceanographic Institution in Massachusetts to come equipped with an eye warmer, heavily vascularized tissues that maintain the predator's visual apparatus at peak performance levels. The lowly horseshoe crab rearranges its retinas for day and night vision, and this circadian rhythm continues even when the animal is placed in an isolation chamber. Its night vision is triggered into extra sensitivity by two tiny "eyes" on the top of its head; the heightened acuity may help male find female on mating nights.

Most incredibly, a dinoflagellate, one-celled plankter though it may be, has organized materials in its body so that an oil droplet is used as a lenslike device and is backed by light absorption and pigment layers. Nobody knows how it works, but in physical terms it is an eye. Perhaps it is used to help the organism orient effectively to sunlight.

Light is emitted as well as received by some organisms. Bioluminescence, the eerie glow in a boat's wake on a summer night, is the work of planktonic creatures. In the abyss, some fish have come to an arrangement with luminescent bacteria: a safe home, encapsulated in a light organ, in return for a glow that can be focused, shuttered, and otherwise manipulated to illuminate, identify, and—in the case of the angler fish, which dangles an elongated and luminescent fin ray before its mouth—lure.

Hearing-sensing sound underwater is a fascinating blend of detections. Sound moves about five times faster in the sea than in the air. Since most sea creatures are mostly water, they tend to be transparent to sound. But there are ingenious ways of receiving signals. Herring and other fish equipped with gas-filled swim bladders use those bladders as vibrators. Sound waves cause vibrations of the bladder which are picked up by small bones and carried through a fluid-filled canal to the ear itself. That the system works can be shown by placing a small rubber balloon under an obliging flounder, a fish without a swim bladder. The fish's hearing improves measurably.

A cross between hearing and touch is the lateral line, a canal running along the sides of a fish, connected by pores to the surface of the skin. Movement in the water—a predator, a fellow member of the school—sends a pressure wave against the body, inducing movement in the fluid of the canal. Tiny

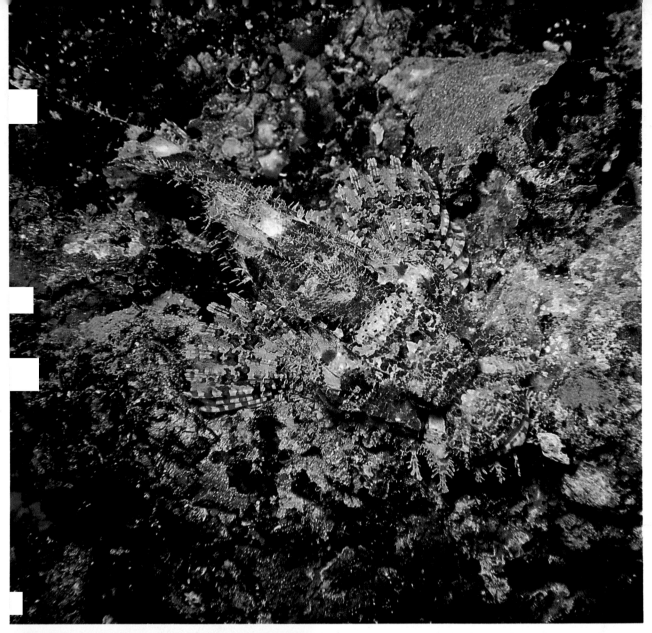

The Death Mask, a scorpionfish (above), blends in with the bottom, waiting for food to swim by. Its camouflage is accomplished by a combination of coloration, body shape, and appendages. The butterfly fish at left has a false eye, a black spot near the tail. There is evidence that the marking is a ruse, diverting predators from the animal's vitals.

hairs, or cilia, mounted inside gelatinous flaps along the canal, register the flow and alert the brain.

We are not sure what fish hear, but hydrophones record noises enough to keep any ear busy—pops of shrimp, crackles and snaps from fish, clicks from porpoises, seals, walruses. And the glorious songs of the whales. The humpback is the ocean's minstrel, lying at ease, great flippers drooping, putting the birds to shame.

Experiments with squirrelfish off Hawaii show that at least in some cases the lateral line is for close work and loses much of its efficiency when the source is, say, more than a few meters away. But the pressure waves of sound, as opposed to its near-field displacement effect, can be far-reaching indeed. It is clear that whales can signal to each other over considerable reaches of ocean space.

The senses of smell and taste in the sea might seem redundant. Why would a fish in its bath of chemicals need both to tell him: this is your prey, your young, your mate, your competition, your killer? But two there are. Fishes' nostrils are not used for breathing. They are blind sacs rich in sensors connected to the olfactory bulb in the brain. Lining the mouth and lips are taste buds, anatomically similar to those of a cow, bird, man, or any other vertebrate. Certain freshwater catfish have taste sensors all over the body, sensitive enough to direct the animal to distant food.

Jelle Atema of the Marine Biological Laboratory at Woods Hole has spent a good deal of time on the redundancy question. He feels that taste in every case serves the feeding behavior. Smell, too, is important. It alerts the fish to the presence of food—but it doesn't account for the final decision to eat. Taste is what the fish relies on to tell it whether the food in its mouth should be taken or not. Atema's work with tuna has convinced him that these cruising predators use smell to trigger a chemical "search" that tells them what to look for. Sight then leads them in. "The olfactory part of the brain," says Atema, "may be telling the fish what sensory modality to use next."

Touch is a part of the marine sensory array, linked to the others. It comes into play, along with taste, as bottom feeders sort through the mud to find their food, as the sea robin probes the bottom with the front rays of its pectoral fins. And touch of a long-distance variety is observable when lateral lines are activated.

Beyond these familiar senses is another. Sharks and rays can and do sense the weak electrical emissions of other animals. Adrianus Kalmijn of Woods Hole has demonstrated that sharks will attack electrodes mim-

Two decorator crabs (below) survey each other's disguise. Each has taken a sponge on its back for camouflage. The clownfish on the opposite page makes its home in a sea anemone, whose tentacles are poisonous to most other species. The clownfish sometimes feeds the anemone but at other times steals food right out of the anemone's mouth.

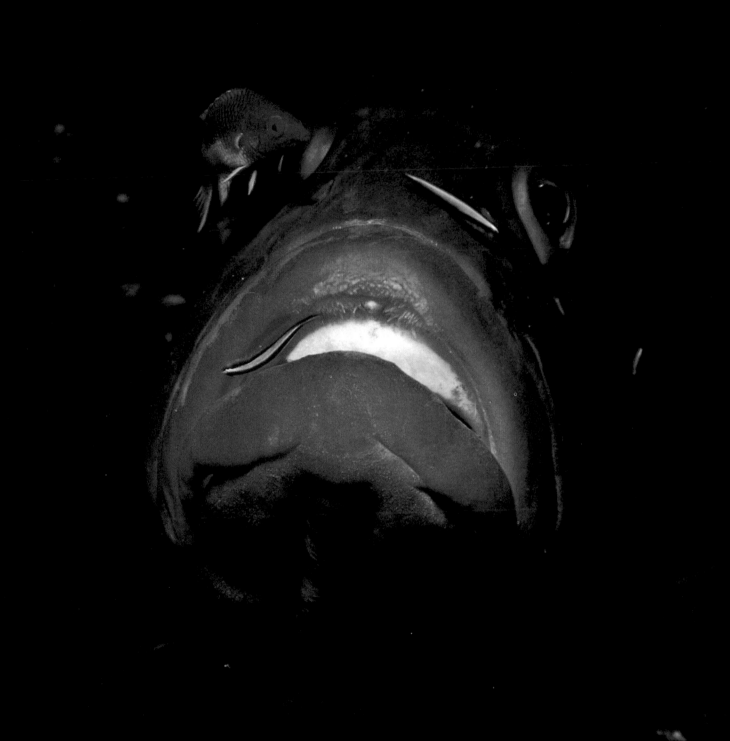

Little black-striped cleaner wrasses provide a parasite-removal service for goatfishes, who line up like patients in a doctor's waiting room.

Saber-toothed blennies pretend to be cleaner wrasses. But when a bigger fish comes along looking for cleaning service, the blennies take bites out of it.

icking the signals of prey. There is also evidence that sharks may be able to read electromagnetic fields, to place themselves in the sea in somewhat the same way that a navigator reads a compass.

What superb predation! The big pelagic shark smells a trace of blood in the water. He begins to circle. Vision joins in. He closes, his elegant lateral line system helping him to track true. Then his electrical receptors function and he bites. His taste buds give the go-ahead. He swallows.

It is this sort of adaptation to the environment, this net of responses, this behavior, that determines the success of species over time. Certainly the sharks are successful. They have survived in their direct, well-wired way for hundreds of millions of years. There are as many scenarios for survival as there are species, and the task of studying even the most accessible is difficult.

Marine mammalogists, for instance, are just beginning to understand how their subjects function. Echolocation—using high-pitched sound to size up objects underwater—draws the greatest public atten-

Co-operation for mutual benefit is no rarity in the sea. Three gobies and a young Spanish hogfish (opposite page) feed on parasites and other matter adhering to a grouper. These are not random encounters but part of interspecific behavior.

tion. But considerable work has been done on the ability of seals and other mammals to regulate the heat in their bodies during deep cold dives or during intensive work in warmer waters. Researchers can trace the blood routes to and from the heat-exchanging flippers, the blubber, and the thick skin, circulatory systems that can support a skin temperature of 35°F and an internal temperature of 99°F. They have learned something of the ways in which diving birds and mammals can shut off blood flow to peripheral areas, preserving it for the vitals. They study kidneys unusually efficient in ridding the body of excess salt. They spend years training porpoises and orcas, always hoping for new information on levels of intelligence, on communication.

Among organisms of cooler blood, some opt for gathering food by stinger and tentacle, like the colony of animals that make up the Portuguese man-of-war. Some, like the grouper, lie in wait and suck in their prey. Some, like the trumpetfish, position themselves so as to fade into the background. Others alter their pigmentation to mimic the coloration of their ambient sands. Many deep sea fish tackle prey much larger than they are, while the baleen whales plow through antarctic seas sieving small krill by the ton. The electric ray stuns his prey, the sea otter cracks open his shellfish on a flat stone he takes from the bottom and holds on this chest. Certain wrasses maintain cleaning stations for other fish, which come to let these parasite-eaters search their skins for food. Noting this, the blenny poses as a wrasse and takes a bite out of his customers. The damselfish, partial to wrasse eggs, has developed the ability to sense when they are about to be laid; it follows the female wrasse to the surface and times its arrival perfectly for its purpose. A nudibranch, one of the surrealistically colored naked snails of the sea, grazes on organisms that use stinging cells as a defense. Unperturbed, the nudibranch reuses the stinging cells in its own body to ward off predators.

Often behavioral relationships develop between species that improve the chances for survival of one or both. A case of mutual benefit involves the hermit crab, which is a favorite food of octopuses, and the sea anemone, whose stinging cells the octopuses generally avoid. Scientists have observed hermit crabs approaching anemones and stroking them. The anemone loosens its hold on the substrate, transfers itself to the borrowed shell the crab lugs around as a home, and the two move off together. The crab evidently gets extra protection, the anemone mobility and more food. Similarly, coral polyps and algae co-operate in a way that aids the polyp in the formation of its calcareous cup. It seems likely that the algae benefits through an assured food supply.

Not all relationships are so mutualistic. Remoras and pilot fish attached to or riding the bow waves of certain sharks get a free ride, but the shark appears to be neither helped nor harmed by the commensalism. Parasitism, on the other hand, can be harmful or fatal to the host. One type of barnacle invades the bodies of crabs, rendering them incapable of reproduction.

From the properties of skin that make the porpoise so speedy to the schooling habits of herring to the behavior of bacteria, knowledge is accumulating. The business of turning threads into fabric, observations into theories and models that will test them—this is what occupies the minds of many who are thinking of the future of the science.

Laboratory and field experiments at times seem to indicate that there is not enough food in the oceans to support the organisms living there. What is happening,

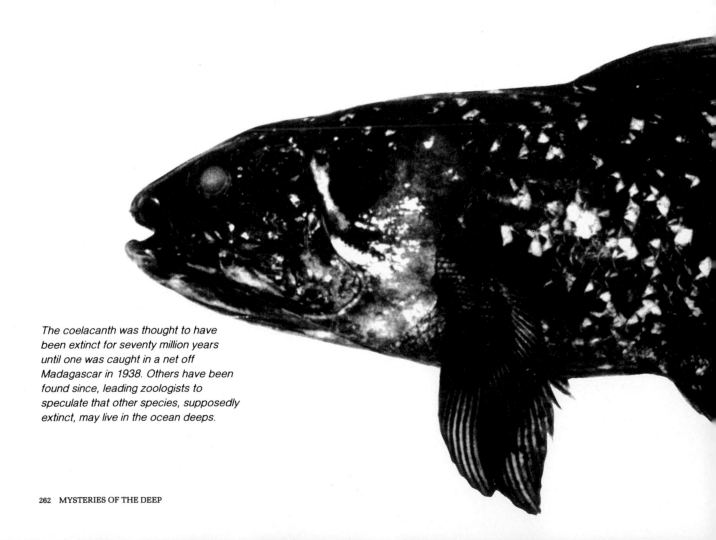

The coelacanth was thought to have been extinct for seventy million years until one was caught in a net off Madagascar in 1938. Others have been found since, leading zoologists to speculate that other species, supposedly extinct, may live in the ocean deeps.

of course, is that sampling programs are not sophisticated enough to measure the marked differences—the vertical and horizontal patchiness—of food distribution. Information from the microscale, where readings are in centimeters, will be increasingly important in precisely defining the areas of the sea where plankton is sufficiently concentrated to support larger forms of life. In addition, we will need to know more of how species become species in a medium in which it is difficult to identify barriers to genetic transfer, such as those that occurred on land when the continents drifted apart and life developed differently on each segment. Obviously, barriers do exist in the sea, separating one group of organisms from another long enough to permit evolution of new species. Otherwise there would be far less variety. But what and where are they?

And what is the carrying capacity of the oceans in terms of pollution? Clearly, the seas are not dead. There is evidence that they may be able to absorb safely more of man's wastes than previously thought. But what wastes, and how much? Can we implant high-level radioactive wastes deep in mid-ocean sediments without undue risks to the marine biota and to ourselves? What effect will oil filming have on the surface layer of the sea? What effect will the present decrease in atmospheric ozone have on surface life? It is fairly clear that the oxygen produced by phytoplankton is not essential to our immediate survival (much of it is consumed in the plants' own respiration). But what about plankton's role in processing carbon dioxide and other compounds, whose balance is of more immediate concern?

There is, there always will be, an unsettling ratio of questions to answers. Many deal with the function of bacteria and protozoa; it could be that these microscopic nanoplankton constitute a little understood but basic link in the food chain from sun to swordfish. Other questions focus on the enormous variations in fish populations, the generations, or "year classes," and subsequent dwindling of man's favorite food fishes. Still others address the large creatures of the sea, those that come to an abyssal baited camera

A monster at last? This strange-looking creature was hauled up, in decaying condition, by a Japanese fishing boat in 1977. It stank so badly that after photographing it the fishermen threw it back. Cautious biologists point out that other rotting carcasses have proved, on examination, to be fairly common species, such as the basking shark.

out of nowhere, those never seen, those we cannot catch.

There may be monsters of a kind among these last, creatures of a size and shape that appear out of keeping with what our senses and prejudices tell us life should be. Consider the coelacanth, the large stodgy fish presumed long extinct until the first one was caught a few decades ago. Surprises like these keep alive hopes of cryptozoologists that other finds will occur in time. If the Loch Ness monster exists, is it another relict—perhaps a plesiosaur or Heuvelmans' long-necked mammal? It is possible that a blue-eyed creature as long as a Grand Banks trawler may some day surface beside an oceanographic research vessel, wailing like a baby. If so, and if the biological oceanographers aboard have anything to say about it, the creature will be studied from eyetooth to anus, admitted to the scientifically ordered ranks of creation. The name "monster" will drop away, and with it the fascination it held for our imaginations when its existence was only a possibility.

This famous photograph, taken by a British surgeon in 1934, is accepted by true believers as a picture of the Loch Ness monster. Skeptics think it may show a log or a waterfowl.

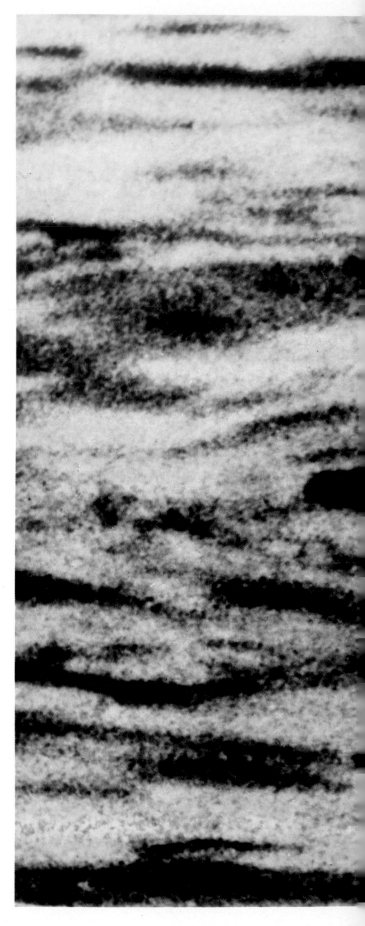

NONE DIVINER
THAN THE DOLPHIN

Man, mythic and modern, has made more of the porpoise, or dolphin, than of any other marine animal. Perhaps it is the set of the jaws in an eternal smile. Perhaps it is the friendliness, the availability of the creature, in captivity or in the wild. Whatever the reason, there seems to be deep in the human mind an expectation, a belief in a coming together—in a companionship, if you will—that informs legend and resists the efforts of science to set the record straight.

"Diviner than the dolphin is nothing yet created," wrote the Greek poet Oppian. "For indeed they were aforetime men and lived in cities along with mortals, but by the devising of Dionysus they exchanged the land for the sea and put on the form of fishes." It is a lovely tale, that of Dionysus, god of wine and frenzy, sailing incognito to the island of Naxos: how the crewmen conspired to sell him into Asian slavery; how the god changed the oars into serpents and caused grape vines to sprout from his loins and music from invisible flutes to fill the ship; how the crazed seamen jumped into the sea; and how the sea-god Poseidon saved them from drowning by turning them into dolphins, earning their undying gratitude and loyalty.

Friendship of dolphins for humans figures in many legends. The poet and musician Avion, cast into the sea by pirates, is said to have been borne up by a dolphin and carried ashore. Many are the tales of boys and dolphins, the children riding on the backs of the creatures as they sported in the sea. Pliny, who figures strongly as a propagator of marine legend, tells of a dolphin living in the days of Augustus Caesar who carried his young friend to school and back. Ronald Lockley, in his *Whales, Dolphins and Porpoises,* has this from Pliny:

"When the boy was falne sick and dead, yet the Dolphin gave not over his haunt, but usually came to the wanted place, and missing the lad, seemed to be heavie and mourne again, untill for verie griefe and sorrow (as it is doubtless to be presumed) he was also found dead on the shore."

From Aristotle onward there were accounts, some of them quite factual, of the behavior of dolphins, their ways of supporting young or weak members of their group so that they could breathe easier at the surface, their curious partnership with men in driving schools of fish to the nets or spears.

Some people who have reported seeing sea serpents may have been fooled by a line of dolphins like the one at the top of this photograph, taken in mid-Atlantic.

Porpoises use high-pitched sound to locate, identify, track, and capture underwater objects. At Marineland of the Pacific the blindfolded animal above, relying on echolocation, easily slips its snout through a series of rings. Below, a porpoise emits a stream of bubbles for some purpose that scientists have yet to explain.

Said Plutarch: "It is the only creature who loves man for his own sake." A dog, he wrote, is tame because man feeds him. "To the dolphins alone, beyond all others, nature has granted what the best philosophers seek: friendship for no advantage. Though it has no need at all of any man, yet it is a genial friend to all, and has helped many." Perhaps. But mammalogists have noticed that though the dolphin may not need man, he is curious and quite possibly gets as much pleasure from watching our antics as we do his.

A good deal of research has been undertaken on the intelligence of the dolphin or porpoise. (The names are almost interchangeable; many marine biologists prefer "porpoise," since "dolphin" also refers to the brilliantly colored, heavy-browed pelagic fish sometimes called the dorado.) The porpoise's brain is roughly the same size as the human brain and is, like ours, highly convoluted. How it is used is, of course, an extraordinarily difficult question to answer. Investigators agree that porpoises are quick studies, that they appear to register a number of feelings or levels of interest, that they remember. Beyond that, few experts are willing to ascribe an intelligence level to the porpoise much higher than that of a dog or, at best, the smarter apes.

In at least one area, however, porpoises and others of the odontocetes, or toothed whales, have abilities that go well beyond the sensing limits of ape—or man. One of the first to uncover evidence of this was the curator of Florida's Marine Studios, Arthur McBride. A sharp-eyed fisherman who for years had been netting porpoises for McBride's tanks told him that when fine-mesh nets were used, the animals would jump over the net's floating cork line and escape— this at night and in turbid water that would render visual sense all but inoperative. When coarse mesh was used, porpoises would strike at and become entangled in the net; but when its corkline was pulled below the

The tale of Dionysus and the dolphins is depicted on the inside of a Greek wine cup. When mutineers tried to seize his boat, the god terrified them by causing grapevines to writhe around the mast. The seamen jumped into the sea and were turned into dolphins.

surface by the impact, those still free would instantly make for the breach.

McBride was not satisfied that his information was solid enough to make public. But in one unpublished paper, dated July 1947, he put the question that has kept an appreciable number of biologists, physiologists, behaviorists, acousticians, and naturalists hard at work ever since:

"This behavior calls to mind the sonic sending and receiving apparatus which enables the bat to avoid obstacles in the dark. In view of the enormous development of the cerebral cortex of the porpoise and its probable dependence on the penetrations of large numbers of sensory impulses into this region . . . and because of the obvious importance of the acoustic sense to the porpoise, might we not suspect that the above described behavior is associated with some highly specialized mechanism enabling the porpoise to learn a great deal about his environment through sound?"

William Schevill and his wife, Barbara Lawrence—of the Woods Hole Oceanographic Institution and Harvard, respectively—were among the first to provide solid evidence that McBride's question should be answered in the affirmative. Their earliest experiments indicated that porpoises could sense high frequencies at about ten times the upper limit of man's normal, air-coupled auditory system. (Through "bone conduction" we, too, can sense the presence of high-frequency sound; but unlike porpoises, which depend on bone or body conduction of sound from water to ear, we cannot tell the pitch of the sound much above fifteen kilocycles.)

Later they were able to show that their subjects could navigate around obstacles in murky water and find food beyond. The sounds they heard from the reconnoitering porpoises were like those emitted by a rusty hinge.

Schevill and Lawrence, and Winthrop Kellogg, of Florida State University, thought that porpoises might be equipped with some sort of animal sonar. More work needed to be done to test the idea. For example, might not the animals have eyesight acute enough to account for their unusual navigational powers? Kenneth Norris, now at the University of California, worked with an Atlantic bottle-nosed porpoise named Kathy to check out that possibility. The problem was finding a way to blindfold Kathy. Eye covers attached to a clamp of spring steel didn't work, not even with eyecups fashioned from a pair of junior-teen-sized falsies. Finally Norris and his colleagues came up with suction-cup devices that did the job. Blind as a bat, Kathy located and took

her food rewards. She emitted a series of the rusty-hinge noises, each composed of hundreds of clicks of about one thousandth of a second in duration. As Kathy neared her fish the clicks came faster, and she began to waggle her head vigorously. As Norris described it in his book The Porpoise Watcher, "she looked for all the world like a miner peering into the crevices of a mine shaft with his head lamp."

The head lamp throws quite a beam. Working with an old navy porpoise named Alice, Norris found that after considerable training the blindfolded animal could tell the difference, most of the time, between a 2½-inch and a 2¼-inch sphere from several feet away. "While our work with Alice did not prove how she performed her remarkable discrimination," wrote Norris, "it showed the rich possibilities she had for learning about her world from sound alone. Echoes allowed her to glean information about the shapes, sizes, textures, compositions, and speeds of objects, perhaps to a very refined degree.''

Demonstration of echolocation was difficult enough, given the frustrations of running convincing experiments on intelligent and complex animals placed in an artificial environment. Explaining how echolocation

Playing to an audience on the beach, seven porpoises fish in the surf off the southern California coast.

works is equally difficult. Sam Ridgway of the navy's Ocean Systems Center in San Diego says that the porpoise's clicks are produced ''in the nasal tract of the animal by compression of the nasal passages and sacs through the action of a number of large muscles and a fibro-muscular apparatus called the nasal plug.'' Ridgway thinks that the sounds may come from vibrating membranes, but he is not sure yet.

Some researchers feel that the sounds are in some way focused by the ''melon,'' the fatty tissues lying behind the bulging forehead of the porpoise. Since the echolocating spectra of clicks are picked up by hydrophones most clearly when the animal emitting them is head-on to the sensor, it is clear that the sounds are directional.

Then there is the matter of bubbles. Porpoises can make a good deal of

them by exhaling underwater. Sometimes they let go a bubble train with a whistle, sometimes they whistle without bubbling. Karen Pryor, who has worked with porpoises in Hawaii and elsewhere, dove on groups of them surrounded by purse seines set for the tuna that so often accompany them. She saw some porpoises making screens of bubbles, some making toruses (underwater "smoke rings"). Why? Air bubbles underwater are easily detected by sonar. Do the porpoises use them in conjunction with echolocation? To confuse? Communicate?

Guesswork, intuition, and unproven theories abound. Most scientists tend to shy away from theories that porpoises and whales are at least our equal in intelligence. They are not comfortable with accounts of extrasensory communication between man and porpoise, such as that given by Frank Robson, a porpoise trainer in New Zealand. Robson insists that he found himself able to issue silent commands to his captive animals. He says he once willed a group of them to dance the twist; he and his astonished boss joined in. But—as so often happens with these smiling, affectionate, and mysterious creatures—the two men found themselves outtwisted, bested at their own game. Ah, the lure of dolphin lore!

THE DEEP SURPRISE

The big frame sled had a simple name, ANGUS, for its complicated function—Acoustically Navigated Geophysical Underwater System. It squatted on the fantail of the research vessel *Knorr* in the dusk of a February evening in 1977, some 200 miles northeast of the Galápagos Islands and 400 miles west of Ecuador. The sea was calm, but there was a fairly strong current setting to the west. It was time to lower.

One of the *Knorr*'s sophisticated winches swung Angus up, out, and down. Forty-five minutes later its camera began taking pictures by strobe light, one every ten seconds. For twelve hours the sled's operators sweated and swore, flying it at less than five meters above sea bottom covered with pillows and ropes of rock, lava that had spilled out on the Galápagos Rift valley and cooled almost instantly in the 2°C water. Part of a worldwide system of mid-ocean ridges, where the sea floor pulls apart a few inches each year and new ocean crust is formed, the Galápagos Rift contains several warm-water vents. The *Knorr*, the small submersible *Alvin*, and its tender, *Lulu*, had come from their base at the Woods Hole Oceanographic Institution on Cape Cod to investigate those thermal springs, jets of seawater that had filtered down through cracks deep in the lava to be heated by the hot magma below and returned, rich in minerals, to the surface.

Back aboard the *Knorr*, Angus was

Resembling overgrown lipsticks, these red-tipped tube worms, some more than three meters long, crowd around a warm-water vent on the sea floor west of the Galápagos Islands. Scientists also found huge clams and an organism shaped like a dandelion.

relieved of its color-film roll. Hours later scientists gathered for a remarkable slide show. For veterans of previous ocean ridge surveys such as Robert Ballard of Woods Hole, things looked fairly normal—a desert of lava old and new. But there was expectation. As Angus had made its run some one and a half miles deep, sensors had telemetered a large temperature anomaly to the ship. A vent? The time registered in the corner of each frame of film was creeping up to midnight, when the temperature rise had been noted. And suddenly there it was.

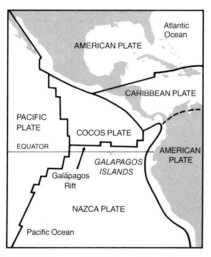

The Galápagos Rift (above) is part of a system of mid-ocean ridges where the sea floor cracks and separates as new ocean crust is formed. As the floor pulls apart (below), cold sea water seeps into the cracks, is heated, and then rises again rich in minerals.

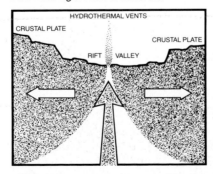

Not just a vent. The photographs showed something else: life, in abundance never before seen in the deep sea. Thirteen frames were filled with hundreds of outsized white clams and brown mussels, mats and bunches of other organisms. Then nothing, just the barren lava.

The *Alvin* went down for a look, carrying its three occupants from the routine to the unknown in ninety minutes. As Ballard wrote in the Woods Hole magazine, *Oceanus:*

"Coming out of small cracks cutting across the lava terrain was warm, shimmering water that quickly turned a cloudy blue as manganese and other chemicals in solution began to precipitate out . . . and were deposited on the lava surface, where they formed a brown stain. But even more interesting was the presence of a dense biological community living in and around the active vents. The animals were large, particularly the white clams (up to thirty centimeters, or twelve inches). This oasis of life was only fifty meters across and totally different from that of the surrounding area. What were the organisms eating? They were living on solid rock in total darkness."

There was no one around competent to answer the question. The expedition had come to investigate the vents, not living colonies. Without biologists, all that the geologists, chemists, and other specialists aboard could do was observe and describe. One vent, which they called Clambake II, had apparently closed off; the clams and mussels surrounding it were all dead, unable to move to an active vent only 225 meters to the east. At another site, the Dandelion Patch, golden globes floated, moored by radiating fiber elements to the floor. The Oyster Bed contained

Mineral-darkened sea water spews from the bottom at temperatures of more than 350°C. These vents form oases for life on otherwise barren sea floor.

shellfish but no oysters ("What's a geologist to know?" cracked Ballard). The Garden of Eden grew in rings of life; at the rim were "dandelions" and white crabs. Closer in were worms, limpets, pink fish, and tube worms with flaming red tips.

Two years later, a follow-up expedition with a biological team returned to the Galápagos Rift. They had the *Alvin* with them and a much-improved Angus, capable of taking pictures of a half-acre of bottom from a height of eighteen meters. An advanced, miniaturized television camera system enabled scientists to view the behavior of vent organisms almost as easily as a naturalist might turn his binoculars on a flight of shore birds.

Some of the mysteries began to come clear. The "dandelions" of the geologists turned out to be benthic siphonophores, relatives of the Portuguese man-of-war. They had been

known since the *Challenger* expedition a century earlier but had been thought to be residents of the deep, not the bottom. Mats of slender white filaments—called spaghetti by the geologists—were identified by the chief biologist, J. Frederick Grassle of Woods Hole, as "wormlike relatives of the early ancestors of vertebrates, normally found living in sediments." The red-tipped worms, creatures whose white, hoselike housings grow as long as three meters, live only in the warm water close to the vents. They have no gut and probably use dissolved organic material in the vent water as food. Hemoglobin accounts for the red color of the worms and of the flesh of the huge clams nearby.

The discoveries piled up: new species of whelks, barnacles, leeches, and other animals; a growth rate among clams approximately 500 times that of smaller relatives found

on deep and ventless bottoms; a small shrimplike creature with combs at the end of its eyestalks, apparently for scraping food off the rocks—a modification never seen before.

What accounts for these rings of thronging life—life that is distributed sparsely if at all in regions of the deep where there are no vents? Microbiologists of the Galápagos team wrote in *Oceanus* that they found the shimmering vent water to be rich in bacteria. "Bacterial oxidation of the hydrogen sulfide to elementary sulphur and sulphate," they suggested, "could produce the basic food source for the entire community in the form of bacterial cells." Tests showed bacterial productivity at the vents to be two to four times higher than in the productive surface waters above the rift, and up to a thousand times higher than that in a control sample taken on the bottom away from the vents.

Most laymen are familiar with nature's normal way of producing organic material, the base of the food chain. In the sea, tiny plants and some bacteria utilize energy from the sun to turn carbon dioxide into carbohydrate in a complex process called photosynthesis. What the microbiologists were describing is chemosynthesis, a process which scientists theretofore had thought contributed an insignificant amount to total organic production. The discoveries at the vents had shattered that supposition. Here were untold numbers of bacteria—more than two hundred strains were isolated for study—floating in the benthic black, using energy liberated by the oxidation of hydrogen sulfide and other compounds and metals to produce the organic substances they needed as food. Indications are that the mussels around the vent, and presumably other organisms as well, were able to feed on the bacteria directly. A simple food web, but an efficient one.

The study of the vents goes on. Animals similar to those in the Galápagos Rift valley were found 1,800 miles

to the northwest, in a different rift system in the East Pacific Rise. There—and in another location on the rise farther to the north, dark water spews from chimneylike "smokers" at more than 300°C, and the minerals with which it is laden precipitate out in what might be minable amounts. The question of how animals find their way from oasis to oasis across the deep barrens is still unanswered, though possibly enough long-lived larvae may drift in the benthic currents to assure propagation. Since there is evidence that most vents function for only a few decades, it is clear that an extraordi-

nary balance must be struck in these bleak valleys as the old fountains die and new ones beckon to the larval founders of new colonies.

There are practical implications of the research, some of considerable potential. Holger Jannasch, a member of the team led by Grassle, has been working with strains of vent bacteria at Woods Hole. He and his co-workers are developing an experimental pilot plant to see if a chemosynthetic system similar to that operating around the vents might be useful in aquaculture at the surface. If it works, the system could make use of sulfur compounds now regarded as

Returning from a dive to the Galápagos Rift, the submersible Alvin *is hoisted aboard its tender,* Lulu.

hazardous or useless waste products.

In 1981 Jannasch will return to the vents and try to bring back mussel larvae to see, among other things, if they can adapt to surface life. "We don't know what will happen," he says with proper scientific caution. "They may grow smaller, or not at all. Or they could grow faster and bigger than the surface species." If those giant clams of the Galápagos Rift are any indication, they could indeed.

THE GLOUCESTER SERPENT

"I wish to refute the unjust imputations cast on the inhabitants of the villages in the vicinity of Gloucester Bay, for their want of courage and enterprize; to which his escape has been sometimes attributed. Nothing can be further, from the truth. . . . Many boats, completely manned by the inhabitants of Gloucester, and properly equipped for offence and defence, were constantly patroling the harbour in search of him, during his continuance in it. He never came within striking distance. Strong hooks, used for catching sharks, with still stronger apparatus, baited with various kinds of fish and flesh, were set for him in all directions. . . . Nets were fixed almost all over the bay. . . . On the evening of the twenty-seventh of August, he was seen within a few rods of the mouth of one of them. Yet, although they took especial care not to alarm him with any noise, he went off without entering."

So wrote David Humphreys from Boston in September of 1817 to the Right Honorable Sir Joseph Banks, president of the Royal Society of London. Humphreys, a fellow of that prestigious organization and a former aide-de-camp to General Washington, was winding up his report on the appearances off the Massachusetts coast of one or more huge animals—appearances that occurred almost every summer for more than a decade and that were witnessed by hundreds of people, lubbers and salts alike. Few if any sightings of "monsters" have been so well documented, discounted, and defended.

This engraving of the Gloucester sea serpent, which bears the inscription "taken from life . . . August 23, 1817," incorporates the white neck stripes that were reported by some witnesses.

It was a fine year for herring, and they may have drawn the creature in. First to see it—or to have the courage to say he saw it—was the skipper of a coaster down from Maine. The weather was making up that day in early August of 1817, and the vessel put in at Gloucester as a precaution. Upon landing, the captain told bystanders in W. Lipple's auction room that he and his crew had come upon a terrible-looking creature at the entrance to the harbor, a serpentine thing that must have been at least sixty feet long. But, wrote Humphreys to Sir Joseph, "so extraordinary and improbable a story, told by a person who was unknown, appearing to gain no credit: he, in disgust, quitted his hearers and sailed as soon as the wind permitted."

About four or five days later, a Mrs. Story ("a woman held in high estimation for her veracity," reported Humphreys) told her husband, Amos, that she had seen what looked like a great log move from the beach at Ten Pound Island out into deeper water. Amos went looking and saw something large and alive off Ten Pound. He got the same treatment from his listeners as the skipper from Maine and decided to keep his mouth shut. But when other accounts began to surface, Amos changed his mind. Gloucester's justice of the peace, Lonson Nash, had been asked by the Linnaean Society of New England, a well-respected scientific organization, to take depositions on the matter. When Nash, who himself was a witness to the outsized goings-on offshore, asked Story to come forward, the seaman made a statement under oath, from which we have the following excerpt:

"On the 10th of August, 1817, I saw a strange animal, that I believe to be a Serpent, in the harbor of Gloucester. He continued in sight for an hour and a half. I was about twenty rods from him. His head appeared shaped much like the head of a sea-turtle, and he carried it about a foot above the surface of the water. At that distance,

his head appeared larger than that of any dog I ever saw. [He] moved rapidly through the water, a mile in two or at most three minutes. Also on the 23d instant, in the morning a little after sunrise, I saw him. He lay perfectly still, extended on the surface of the water, and at this time, I saw fifty feet of him at least. For half an hour, I was looking at him with a good spy-glass; his colour a dark brown, and about the size of a man's body."

On August fourteenth, Matthew Gaffney fired at a "strange marine animal resembling a serpent, in the harbor in said Gloucester. I was in a boat and was within thirty feet of him. His head appeared full as large as a four-gallon keg, his body as large as a barrel, and his length that I saw, I should judge forty feet, at least. . . . I had a good gun and took good aim. I aimed at his head, and I think I must have hit him. He turned towards us immediately after I had fired, and I thought he was coming at us; but he sunk down and went directly under our boat and made his appearance about a hundred yards from where he sunk." Answering Nash's questions, Gaffney said that the creature seemed uninjured and "continued playing as before."

There was a $5,000 bounty on the beast, and Banks fishermen and Nantucket whalemen joined the locals in netting, harpooning, shooting, and just plain fishing for the money. It was no go. The Gloucester monster was watched by a crowd as he sported one whole afternoon under Windmill Point. He was seen both from the shore and from nearby ships, and that is a thorny point for those who would put the whole thing down to mass hallucination.

The Linnaean Society, having taken pains to structure Nash's interrogation of witnesses, came to conclusions that seemed at odds with the accounts. Bernard Heuvelmans, the careful researcher of unknown animals, found that though witnesses differed somewhat, most described

the creature as undulating in a vertical plane. When it surfaced, it sometimes exhibited a number of small humps along the spine, sometimes not. Its motion in tight turns at the surface was that of an animal with a solid thorax rather than the fully articulated body of a serpent. It sounded precipitately, an indication that it had flippers. None of these characteristics are remotely serpentine. Yet the society's committee of inquiry seemed to show all the preconceptions of our deep fears— the ones that equate the unknown with evil and evil with the serpent. The committee pointed to the overall snakelike appearance of the beast, noted its coil-like humps and its undulations (ignoring the fact that both were in the wrong plane for a snake), and declared the creature a sea serpent. They decided further that the sea serpent probably had come ashore to lay eggs. The search was on for its progeny.

One was found, in a field east of Cape Ann close by the sea: a small blackish serpent with bumps on its spine. The thing was pitchforked and sent off to the Linnaean Society, which dissected it, prepared detailed anatomical plates for its journal, and gave it the name *Scoliophis atlanticus,* or Atlantic humped snake. Though the society did find that its three-foot specimen resembled a local garden variety of reptile, it gave it and the giant of Gloucester harbor membership in the same species "until more close examination of the great Serpent shall have disclosed some difference of structure, important enough to constitute a specific distinction."

Then disaster struck. The respected biologist Alexandre Lesueur reported that he had dissected a portion of *Scoliophis* and found it to be from a common black snake badly deformed by some accident.

To the public the whole thing looked like an invention of hoaxers and hysterics. And there was more than enough evidence to support that suspicion. One captain told of bounc-

A Monstrous Sea Serpent,

The largest ever seen in America,

Has just made its appearance in Gloucester Harbour, Cape Ann, and has been seen by hundreds of Respectable Citizens.

The Editor of the Salem Gazette, says:—We have in our possession an extract of a letter from John Low, Esq. to his son in this town, dated Gloucester, Thursday afternoon, August 14, 1817.

"There was seen on Monday and on Tuesday morning playing about our harbor, between Eastern Point and Ten pound Island, a SNAKE with his head and body about eight feet out of water, his head is in perfect shape as large as the head of a horse, his ———— ed to be about FORTY-FIVE or FIF————
it is thought h———
and hi—

of Gloucester, and has been seen by hundreds of people. He is declared by some persons who approached within 10 or 15 yards of him, to be 60 or 70 feet in length round, and of the diameter of a barr——
his length variously, fr—— 50 ——
tions are ——
ly ——

A broadside published in Boston carried this illustration of a boatload of men trying to gun down the beast.

ing a cannon ball off the hide of a 130-foot creature. Another claimed he saw a sea serpent beating a whale with its tail.

Yet seemingly reliable people kept seeing the thing and risking ridicule by reporting on what they saw. In 1819 about two hundred people watched a serpentlike animal off the resort town of Nahant; Boston newspapers fed so steadily on accounts of his doings that summer that one called it quits: "The existence of this fabulous animal," said an editor, "is now proven beyond a shadow of a doubt."

Matching up accounts, a picture appears of an animal more mammal than snake. That, at least, was the way Heuvelmans looked at it. And the humps? They could be folds of fat. That agrees with a report of a sighting off Gloucester in 1819 from a distance of ten yards:

"His head was elevated from three to five feet. The distance was about six feet from his neck to the first bunch (hump). We counted about twenty bunches, and we supposed them on an average about five feet apart, and his whole length could not be less than one hundred and twenty feet. . . . His head was of a dark brown color, formed like a seal's, and shined with a glossy appearance."

The years went by, the creature—or creatures—abandoned its Gloucester grounds, scared off perhaps by the pot shots and publicity. Some scientists had been convinced of its existence. "To us it seems as matter of surprise," wrote Yale's distinguished geologist Benjamin Silliman, "that any person who has examined the testimony, can doubt the existence of the Sea serpent." But the skeptics were not to be silenced, and because there were no more sightings to undercut their disbelief, they eventually drove the monster back to the preternatural periphery from which it had come. Caustic couplets like this were written in epitaph:

But go not to Nahant, lest men
should swear
You are a great deal bigger than
you are.

A QUESTION OF KRAKEN

It was the first one seen in Massachusetts since 1908, a great chomped cigar of a thing lying on the beach at Plum Island, north of Boston, in February of 1980. What was left of it weighed 430 pounds. Its original length, depending upon how you measured, might have been between twenty-five and thirty feet. The brick-red outer skin was mostly gone; the flesh was milky-white. They lugged it off to the New England Aquarium, where scientists from Harvard and the Smithsonian Institution pronounced it a giant squid, genus *Architeuthis,* probably a female. Not much more than that could they say, for architeuthids, though thought to be plentiful, are so seldom seen that they remain mysteries, veiled by the myths they inspired centuries ago.

Squids are the most numerous of cephalopods, a class of the huge phylum Mollusca, whose 75,000 species include snails, octopuses, and the chambered nautilus. A layman lucky—or unlucky—enough to approach a giant squid in mint condition might remark on the reddish color, the huge eyes, the eight stout arms and two much longer and thinner tentacles that can shoot out like snakes to grab prey and bring it to the parrotlike beak emerging from the oral opening. He might record the comparatively soft

The illustration opposite, published in 1802, dramatizes a real incident in which a giant squid attacked a ship off the coast of Angola. The size of the squid, which is shown winding its tentacles around the rigging in an effort to sink the ship, is no doubt exaggerated. According to reports, the sailors prayed to Saint Thomas, grabbed axes and swords, and were able to cut through the squid's arms to free the ship.

texture of the mantle, or body, of the creature.

For a more scientific appraisal one might turn to Kenneth Boss of Harvard, a respected mollusk man:

"Giant squids . . . over twenty species described but status uncertain, probably fewer than half a dozen. Body rounded, elongate, pointed posteriorly. Size gigantic, largest invertebrate animal; length including tentacles to twenty meters; mantle length to four meters; perhaps weighing a ton . . . eight arms and two tentacles; arms thick; powerful and long with two rows of suckers; tentacles long; . . . all suckers with toothed chitinous ring. . . . Fins extensive, long, ovate and terminal. . . . Eyes largest in animal kingdom with diameter to 400 millimeters. . . . Luminescent organs lacking. Most records of these gigantic squids come from stranded specimens or those found moribund, floating at surface; also from whale stomachs. . . . Probably living at intermediate water depths between 500 and 1,000 meters, rising nocturnally; voracious predators."

In the early times, when myth and reality lived in the same mirror, there were legends of giant, many-armed sea creatures. The Hydra, vanquished by Hercules, could have been modeled on a cephalopod. So, surely, was Homer's Scylla, each of whose "six lank, scrawny necks" bore "an obscene head, toothed with three rows of thickset crowded fangs blackly charged with death."

In the north was the kraken, the name taken from the word for a stunted tree. Olaus Magnus, a Catholic ecclesiastic exiled from Sweden in 1523, wrote a history of his lost land in which he spoke of monstrous fish.

"Their Forms are horrible, their Heads square, all set with prickles,

and they have sharp and long horns round about, like a Tree rooted up by the Roots. . . . One of these Sea-Monsters will drown easily many ships provided with many strong Mariners."

Two centuries later a Norwegian bishop, Erik Pontoppidan, set out to describe what he thought was "incontestably the largest Sea-monster in the world." Fishermen unanimously affirmed, he wrote, that the monster "looks at first like a number of small islands, surrounded by something that floats and fluctuates like seaweed . . . at last several bright points or horns appear, which grow thicker and thicker the higher they rise above the surface of the water, and sometimes they stand up as high and as large as the masts of middle-sized vessels."

It was hard to find much truth in these accounts as the years rolled by and reality came into fashion. Two scholars in the mid-nineteenth century did bolster dying interest in the kraken by bringing to light remains of giant cephalopods long forgotten in European museums. But it was not until 1861 that scientists and public alike were jolted into reviewing what they were ready to reject as tall tales. A French warship, the *Alecton,* reported that it had come upon and attempted to capture something that could only be a real kraken, a giant squid.

In his well-crafted book *Kingdom of the Octopus,* Frank W. Lane presents a translation of the *Alecton*'s report. The ship, according to the captain, was close to the Canary Islands when it encountered "a monstrous creature which I recognized as the 'Giant Octopus,' the disputed existence of which seems to have been relegated to the realm of fable." The *Alecton* closed, fired at the animal, harpooned

Crew members of the Alecton *attempt to capture a giant squid in this engraving, made shortly after the event. At first some scientists discredited the crew's report, but when other squids washed up in Newfoundland, even skeptics were convinced.*

charged with electric effluvia."

There were no electric effluvia observable when another giant squid surfaced off Portugal Cove, Newfoundland, in 1873. But the animal did precisely what Lieutenant Bouyer had feared his adversary would do. A fishing boat rowed over to it and a fisherman, thinking it dead, hit it with a boat hook. The squid charged the boat, bit the gunwale with its beak, wrapped a tentacle and an arm around the small craft, and began to drag it down. A boy on board grabbed a hatchet from the floorboards and freed the boat. The squid darkened the water with its ink and sounded— without its prize.

The boy-hero, one Tom Piccot, later sold the tentacle—or rather a section of it nineteen feet long—to the Reverend Moses Harvey of St. John's, Newfoundland, described in *The Kingdom of the Octopus* as "a keen naturalist with a special interest in kraken lore."

For Harvey and the scientific world, the 1870's marked the emergence of the giant squid as a biologically acceptable animal. More evidence of its reality came to light then than in any decade since. Dozens of the big squid were found dead or dying on the surface off Newfoundland in the next few years. Many were chopped up for bait or dog food. One, stranded in Tickle Bay, must have measured about fifty-five feet overall. Clearly, something had shifted in the squid's environment, something that produced a noticeable rise in mortality.

What do we know now about *Architeuthis*? Kenneth Boss's terse summary covers a good deal of what scientists can say with any degree of certainty. Clyde Roper, of the Smithsonian Institution, a mollusk expert called in with Boss to have a look at the Plum Island specimen at the New England Aquarium, explained some of the current scientific thinking about what the animal is and does. Architeuthids generally are regarded as midwater animals, part of the huge squid

it, lassoed it—and lost it. Left behind was a part of the tail fin weighing over forty pounds. The thing had enormous eyes flush with its head, a mouth like a parrot's beak that opened half a meter, eight arms, and two tentacles. The estimated weight of the entire animal was a couple of tons.

There were some grounds for skepticism when the report and attending documentation was studied by French scientists. Particularly troubling was a statement by the captain, Lieutenant Frédéric-Marie Bouyer, that he was not willing to pursue the escaping architeuthid lest it "fling out its long tentacles armed with long suckers on the side of the boat, make it capsize, and perhaps strangle some of the sailors in its fearful lashes populations occupying the water column between, say, one hundred and several hundred meters down. Their life span is probably on the order of five years or so. They appear to have worldwide distribution, though most of the sightings and strandings have been in the higher latitudes, with concentrations off the Canadian Maritime Provinces, Scandinavia, and Japan in the northern hemisphere, and New Zealand in the southern. They may prefer the water above fairly rough bottoms (they are not bottom creatures themselves), such as those found along continental shelves.

Since most of the stranded animals have had empty stomachs—probably the result of the diseased state that weakened them enough to cause their stranding—it is difficult to know what giant squid feed on. There are indications that medium-sized fish—herring and the like—make up the bulk of the diet.

Legends of Scylla and the Hydra to the contrary, architeuthids are not remarkably powerful. Their musculature is not tough and compact like the voracious squid inhabiting the Humboldt Current off western South America. The muscles are actually infused with ammoniac substances, perhaps for buoyancy. The animal, says Roper, is "a slow cruiser, not one to zing around like a torpedo." The flat fins at its pointed tail end act as a rudder for steering and stabilizing. A flexible siphon (common to squids and octopuses), through which water is ejected, allows the giant squid to swim backward or forward with true jet propulsion.

If fish are prey, the sperm whale is predator, and a dedicated one. Not that the giant squid is singled out for special attention; the sperm whale is expert at feeding on squids of many sizes in the mid-water zone. But *Architeuthis* is not gently taken. There have been a number of eyewitness reports, some of them undoubtedly exaggerated, of whale and squid

fighting, the sperm chomping away, the squid throwing his sharp-suckered arms around the great body.

There is evidence that strandings of the giant squid recur about every third decade. Roper admits that the cyclic shifts in current and eddy patterns might cause more squid than usual to be swept far into cold-water masses that weaken them and eventually leave them dying on the surface or the shore. But he has a counter-theory of his own. It is possible, he says, that the cycle is more of mind than matter. Every three decades, at least for the past century or so, a biologist has come along who takes up with the kraken. It may be his or her interest that brings *Architeuthis* to

public view, not an errant eddy.

The mystery remains. If we are to know more about the giant of many arms, we must trap him alive where he lives. How? Well, perhaps with the right lure—and a very tough cable. Frederick Aldrich, a zoologist in Newfoundland and a dedicated student of the giant squid, plans to try his luck with a five-foot version of the New-foundlanders' conventional squid jigger, fished with an array of lights and bait. Jigger and lights will be red, the color local fishermen are convinced will bring the monster in. Clyde Roper is of a different opinion. He'd like to see a cable-mesh net fished over the rough bottoms where—he thinks—*Architeuthis* may live.

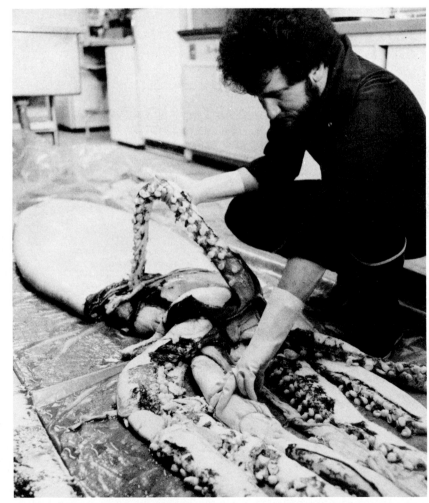

A giant squid, the first to come ashore in Massachusetts since 1908, is examined by a scientist. Little is known of the huge creatures, since none has been taken alive. What was left of this one weighed more than 400 pounds.

A MARINE
BESTIARY

Since ancient times man has feared unknown and mysterious creatures of the oceans. In the sixteenth century a number of books on the nature of the universe appeared in print, books that recognized the existence of these monsters and gave definite shape to what had previously been amorphous fears.

One of the most influential of these works, and the source of the illustration at right, was *Cosmographia*, published in 1550 by the German cartographer Sebastian Münster. By the end of the century the illustrations had been reprinted so often on maps and in books that they had gained almost universal acceptance. Accompanying Münster's picture are the following notations:

A   Huge fish the size of mountains are sometimes seen close to Iceland. They overturn ships unless frightened away by the sound of trumpets, or they may play with empty barrels thrown in the water, a game which amuses them greatly. . . .

B   There is a fearful species of whale called physeters, mentioned by Pliny and Solinus. When it stands erect this monster of the sea can sink even a large ship by sucking in water and then blowing it out again in clouds through holes in its forehead.

C   These hydrae or serpents, 200 or 300 feet in length, are found in northern waters. They throw themselves on ships with the purpose of turning them over. . . .

D   One of these enormous sea monsters has terrible tusks, the other is horrifying with horns, flames, and huge eyes sixteen or twenty feet across. . . .

H   This is a horrible sea monster, called a Ziphius, which devours seals.

I   The fruit of certain trees produces ducks.

K   A sea monster resembling a pig was sighted in 1537.

L   The Norwegians call this a Spring whale because of its agility. It has a broad, high hump on its back.

M   There are crabs so large and strong that they can kill a swimmer who is caught in their claws.

N   A creature resembling a rhinoceros is able to devour a crab twelve feet long. . . .

P   The pelican, a bird at least as large as a goose, can fill its throat with water and let out a noise as loud as the braying of a donkey. Under its beak it has a sack-like swelling.

Having by now scared his readers nearly to death, Münster comes up with the species marked *S*, creatures "noted for their kindness, for they save swimmers from being eaten by sea monsters."

These prints give specific suggestions for warding off attacks by sea monsters. The ship in the sixteenth-century Dutch print at left and in the detail below carries at least eight bells, placed at strategic places around the hull. Seafarers believed the sound of ringing bells would keep monsters at bay. Above, in an illustration from Olaus Magnus's Historia de gentibus septentrionalibus, *beleaguered sailors toss empty barrels overboard to distract their attackers.*

Many legends of the sea describe creatures that have the upper body of a man or woman and the tail of a fish. The Chaldean sea god Ea and the Phoenician god Dagon were divine merpersons, as were the Greek Tritons and Sirens. As myth evolved into folk tale, mermen and mermaids took on a beguiling character. Usually friendly to man initially, they often made trouble later, causing shipwrecks or luring sailors to their deaths.

This fifth-century mosaic adorns a church in Ravenna, Italy.

Throughout history promoters have found ways to combine the lower bodies of fish with the upper bodies of monkeys—or sometimes women—and have presented the resulting creatures as mermaids. The illustrations below depict mermaids exhibited in the late eighteenth century.

MERMAID.

Scientists over the years have tried
to dispel the myths about mermaids,
claiming that what people saw
were manatees, an explanation this
artist found difficult to credit.

Popular legends during the Middle
Ages held that earthly personages
had undersea counterparts, such as
the bishop fish and monk fish (right)
from Guillaume Rondelet's 1558
work L'Histoire entière des poissons.

Eastern cultures produced sea monsters in their own characteristic styles. In the thirteenth-century Japanese scroll above, depicting the founding of the Kegon sect of Buddhism in Korea, a sea dragon carries the monk Gishō to Korea. The dragon is actually a beautiful Chinese girl who fell in love with the monk. When she learned of his holy mission, she resolved to help him. Turning herself into a dragon, she carried his ship on her back. Another Japanese artist gave the baleen whale at right a benevolent and almost human expression.

Hanuman the monkey (opposite page) leaps over the ocean and a collection of monsters including a sea dragon, a sea camel, and a sea elephant in this eighteenth-century illustration of a tale from the Indian epic Ramayana. Hanuman is on his way to rescue the hero Rāma's wife, Sītā, who has been kidnapped.

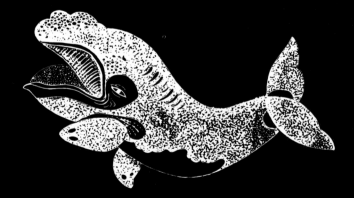

6

LAND BELOW, SEA ABOVE

...cast off from the Jetty in Falmouth Harbor, and with steam
...menced our voyage of Scientific exploration and circumnavigati...
...a wonder the sun shone out just as we started and remained out
...we discharged our Pilot and a few friends to the Tug which had
...panied us out as far as Spithead — These good people did
...best to enliven our departure — and we were greeted with three
...rs as they shoved off, and immediately afterwards we proceed...
...the Needles. The lively propensities of the ship were soon to be
...loped, for even before we reached the Needles — signs of motion
...observable, and made me anxious to get everything secured
...ickly as possible — precautions which were soon to be found
...essary, as a falling Barometer and awkward looking sunset
...very indication of a gale from the sea. In the first watch it
...ame thick — and plenty of drizzle — at 2.30 am. we got a glimpse
...the Start Light abeam — and lost
...of him 2 hours afterwards.
...22nd opened with a fine
...sunshine — the wind having
...led gradually from West
...to the Southward
...moderate breeze — to which
...made all Plain Sail
...pt Royals and F. Jib.
...ing course to W'S. to keep
...good Westing in case of falling
...with the expected SW. gale — At midnight the wind and sea
...to increase — and necessitated a gradual shortening of sail
...til 4am found us under Topsails on the Cap and Courses — There
...a nasty confused sea — and the Ship was uncommonly uneasy
...ing 22° to Starboard and 14° to Port, with a few hints that she could
...would ultimately do more — The Barometer still fell steadily
...the ship was kept rap full on the Port Tack to make Westing in
...fin slip to the SW — A lively day promised — under close reefed
...ails and gaff sails with heads hauled in — a fresh gale from
...SSW. the ship rolling 35° to leeward — During the day
the Bar. fell and the wind rose. Were in the hope
of getting wind from NW. but "Breas would n't"
The wind never getting farther round than from
SW to WSW. a heavy Sea running and ship knocking about a great
...l. The first night in a gale of wind always produces a few mishaps.
...ately ours were confined to those at which one could well

In 1520 in the Tuamotu Archipelago, on his way across the Pacific, Magellan had two of the longest ropes he had—each six hundred feet—spliced together and lowered to measure the depth in the new ocean he had discovered. They failed to reach bottom, and Magellan is said to have concluded that he was over the deepest part of the ocean. This was less than a century after a Portuguese expedition had finally rounded Cape Bojador in West Africa, a wholly innocuous piece of real estate before which a score of earlier expeditions had fled, fearing that ahead the seas boiled and irresistible currents would draw them over the edge of the world. One might fault Magellan's reasoning, but he tried to probe the ocean as well as cross it, and early in this century two distinguished oceanographers, Sir John Murray and Johan Hjort, recorded the attempt in their history of oceanography as the first at deep-sea research.

Despite a few promising ideas, it was four hundred years before what Magellan tried was actually accomplished. It was too difficult. The appropriate equipment was easily conceived, but either could not be built or could not be made to work. Exploration into the oceans did not begin in earnest until well into the nineteenth century. The nineteenth-century explorers set out to dispel mystery beneath what had become by that time well-traveled seas; but they also found some mysteries that have remained to our own day. In sailors' fancy the depths of the sea were hell, Davy Jones's locker, or Fiddler's Green where the seal-folk and mer-people lived. It was also common belief that the ocean was bottomless, and though to a practical nineteenth-century mind such an idea was anathema, early soundings in the ocean could not find a bottom. "Could it be more difficult to sound out the sea than to gauge the blue ether and fathom the vaults of the sky?" wrote the pioneer oceanographer Matthew Fontaine Maury.

From the most ancient times, sailors measured the depth of the waters they sailed with a rope and lead weight called a sounding line. Finding depth was called sounding, the depths measured were called

EXPLORING THE OCEAN FLOOR

by William Wertenbaker

A page from Lieutenant Pelham Aldrich's journal (opposite) records a day in the Challenger's *voyage of discovery. That expedition began the scientific study of the ocean realm, from the frothing tide line on the continental margins (preceding pages) to the deep trenches of the sea floor.*

soundings, and regions that had been or could be measured were called on-soundings. For the mariners were well aware that a few tens or hundreds of miles from land the bottom of the sea drops below the reach of any rope or combination of ropes that ships carried. This was "off-soundings," nearly the entire ocean, most of the earth—the unknown. Nineteenth-century mariners came to it armed with mile upon mile of rope, and winches to lower the rope and bring it back. Yet still they failed. In the early 1840's a Lieutenant Berryman of the American brig *Dolphin* made a sounding in the Atlantic of 39,000 feet and reported no bottom. A Captain Denham of H.M.S. *Herald* did report finding bottom in the South Atlantic—at 46,000 feet—but a Lieutenant Parker of the frigate *Congress* ran out 50,000 feet of rope in the same area without finding bottom. Is there anything difficult about letting a lead weight drop down at the end of a rope and waiting until it hits? In the depths of the sea there is.

An accurate measurement of the depth of an ocean—the first—was made in 1840 by Sir James Ross, who was making a voyage with H.M.S. *Erebus* and *Terror* "to the utmost navigable limits of the Antarctic ocean." The method employed was not one to inspire imitation. Two ship's longboats were tied together. One held four miles of rope on a reel. The other held oarsmen, who rowed constantly against wind and current to hold the first boat on station for the six hours—during which it might otherwise have drifted several miles—that the lead took to reach bottom. The rope was marked at regular intervals and its descent was timed; when it slowed down, very slightly, Ross concluded correctly that he had reached bottom, though the rope kept on running out. The depth was 14,550 feet, "a depression, of the bed of the ocean beneath its surface, very little short of the elevation of Mont Blanc above it," Sir James observed respectfully. At the turn of the century Sir John Murray singled it out as the first "abysmal" sounding, and in the 1960's, in the British journal *Nature*, oceanographers reported accurate sonar measurements in the area confirming Sir James's figure.

Had soundings remained so cumbersome and slow, the ocean could never have been explored. Devising

Meditation by the Sea is the title of this folk painting by an anonymous American artist of the mid-nineteenth century.

On August 27, 1873, the Challenger *tied up to St. Paul's Rocks, a cluster of rugged islets in the Atlantic. Scientists on board concluded that the stony outcrops were "the last trace of some vast district lost by submergence," but later research identified them as part of the Mid-Atlantic Ridge.*

a better way of making soundings preoccupied Matthew Maury for several years (Maury was superintendent of the navy's Depot of Charts and Instruments, the forerunner of the Hydrographic Office and the Naval Observatory); and a variety of other men turned their hands to the problem for more than a century. In fact, the problem of depth has bedeviled oceanographers right up to our own time. "The most ingenious and beautiful contrivances for deep sea soundings were resorted to," Maury wrote. "By exploding petards or ringing bells in the deep sea, when the winds were hushed and all was still, the echo or reverberation from the bottom might, it was held, be heard, and the depth determined from the rate at which sound travels through water. But though the concussion took place many feet below the surface, echo was silent and no answer was received from the bottom." Maury himself devised a rotor that

would measure and record distance as it was lowered to the bottom. But no rope was strong enough to hold it. Later, scientists tried to establish the depth of the ocean from variations in the strength of gravity; one tried to establish the average depth of the Pacific from the characteristics of tsunamis, or tidal waves. Depth was calculated from measurements of water pressure, which increases with depth. Maury made the first line of soundings across an ocean, from the United States to Europe, by timing the descent of common baling twine weighted with cannon balls; the twine went down straighter than rope did, and when it reached bottom it could simply be snipped off and abandoned, saving the time spent hauling up rope, an early demonstration of the American genius for disposability.

For the next survey voyage, having begun to find the depth of the sea, Maury revised the device to bring back a sample, to find out what the deep sea floor was like and what was on it and in it. These questions fascinated him and many of his contemporaries. "The wonders of the sea," he proclaimed, "are as marvelous as the glories of the heavens. Among the revelations which scientific research has lately made concerning the crust of our planet, none are more interesting to the student of nature, or more suggestive to the Christian philosopher, than those which relate to the bed and bottom of the ocean." For a while during the nineteenth century, the curiosity to know what the depths were like may have been even greater than the present-day fascination with space.

In 1841 Edward Forbes, the leading British naturalist of the day, made dredgings in the Mediterranean on Her Majesty's survey ship *Beacon*, bringing up living things from as deep as 1,380 feet. He formed a picture of the depths of the sea that lasted in qualified form to the present day. "As we descend deeper and deeper," he wrote, "the inhabitants become more and more modified, and fewer and fewer, indicating our approach toward an abyss where life is extinguished or exhibits but a few sparks to mark its lingering presence." Everything below 1,800 feet was the "azoic zone," a void. Indeed, sunlight cannot penetrate that far, and without light there is no plant life; the abyss is cold as well, and its pressure will buckle steel. Forbes's idea was accepted by many naturalists.

But deeper dredging kept turning up living creatures. In 1868 Forbes's successor at the University of Edinburgh, Sir Charles Wyville Thomson, found in a dredge haul a little animal, a kind of sea urchin, that had never been seen alive before, though it was well known as a fossil. Another idea of the depths of the sea emerged, quite different from Forbes's: that the depths harbored living things that in the rest of the world had become extinct—living fossils. The idea was elaborated by some of the century's greatest minds. Louis Agassiz believed the deep sea preserved some of the conditions of the atmosphere of the ancient earth; Thomson wrote that there should be more primitive creatures in greater depths, just as there are more primitive fossils in older rocks. The German biologist Ernst Haeckel wrote that the floor of the abyss might contain the original, formless protoplasm from which all life originally sprang. He called it the urschleim. If the azoic zone had a flavor of Davy Jones's locker and Hell, this had a touch of Fiddler's Green and the Elysian Fields. But in 1870 the great Thomas Huxley announced he had actually found urschleim, in sample bottles from an earlier expedition.

In 1872 an expedition on the British ship *Challenger* sailed to investigate for the first time "the conditions of

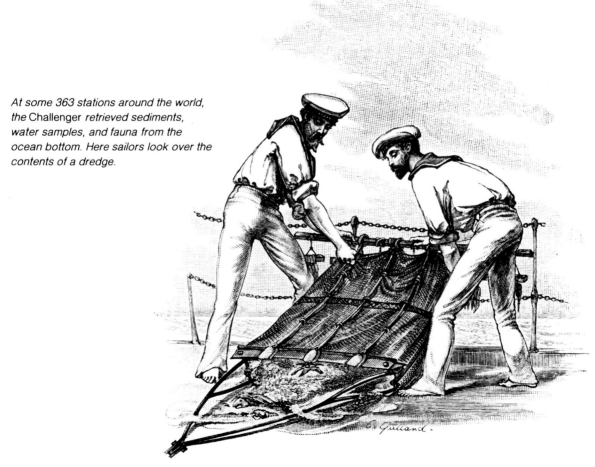

At some 363 stations around the world, the Challenger *retrieved sediments, water samples, and fauna from the ocean bottom. Here sailors look over the contents of a dredge.*

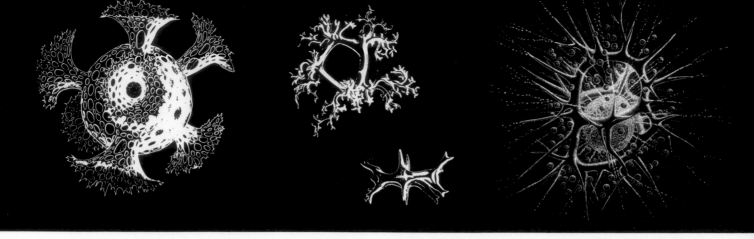

Delicately patterned radiolaria, shown above in the original drawings from the Challenger *report, are minute animals whose remains drift down to carpet much of the ocean floor.*

the Deep Sea throughout all the Great Oceanic Basins," under the direction of Wyville Thomson. England was first to send out such an expedition, Germany second; it was the space race of the day and the newspapers reported the findings. The *Challenger* was gone four years, circumnavigating the world. It laid the foundations of scientific knowledge of the deep sea: its life, from the floating plankton to the creatures of the bottom (marine biology); the motions and composition of the water, from the surface to the bottom (physical oceanography); and the shape and composition of the bottom (marine geology). Every 200 miles, on the average, sails were furled, the auxiliary steam engine fired up, and the ship was brought into the wind and held steady for a "station." Winches rumbled and lines carrying lead sinkers, dredges, thermometers, and water-sampling bottles went over the side. At each station the following measurements were made: depth; the rate and direction of any current at the surface and, occasionally, beneath the surface; temperature at various depths; and meteorological conditions. Dredges sampled the bottom and its life, and nets gathered plants and animals of the surface and intermediate levels. The work was exhaustive, and exhausting. Maury had got a few small samples, but what the *Challenger* brought back from the deep sea took twenty years of work by experts—seventy-six of them, from many countries—to digest, and then occupied fifty volumes.

Although Thomson had eagerly examined each dredge haul, as it came up, for living fossils, and the *Challenger* did find over 13,000 species that were new to science, few of these species were living fossils, or even very antique. There was life to the very greatest depths of the sea all over the world, and no azoic zone, though the idea that life is sparse in the deep sea has persisted to this day. There was no urschleim; Huxley's discovery turned out to be slime indeed, chemical in nature, not biological. The floor of the abyss was covered instead with different types of ooze, composed of the mostly microscopic corpses and debris that filter down from above in what writers from Maury to Rachel Carson have described as an endless snowfall. The Dover Cliffs are a part of a 1,600-foot layer of one such type of ooze, hardened into rock. Muffled in sediments, the bottom was thought to be pretty much the same everywhere, and unchanging, an idea that was not finally dispelled until our own generation.

In the lifetime of an animal, the floor of the abyss is indeed unchanging, and the lack of change makes it one of the best places in the sea to live, and one of the most heavily—not sparsely—populated, according to recent findings. The scientists who studied the *Challenger* samples did not imagine that most of the living creatures in the samples had washed out of the dredges on the way up to the ship. In the 1960's, with new self-closing dredges, biologists at the Woods Hole Oceanographic Institution brought up more animals from the deep sea floor in a single dredge than the *Challenger* had collected from there in four years.

As soon as soundings began to accumulate (often in advance of the first submarine telegraph cables), the shadowy lines of an abyssal landscape began to emerge, giving much aid and comfort to believers in Atlantis and other lost continents. In the middle of the North Atlantic there was an area of bottom several miles higher than the ocean basin to either side, and only a mile below the surface. In Maury's 1854 chart of the North Atlantic, the first ever made of the floor of an ocean (there were 180 deep soundings to base it on),

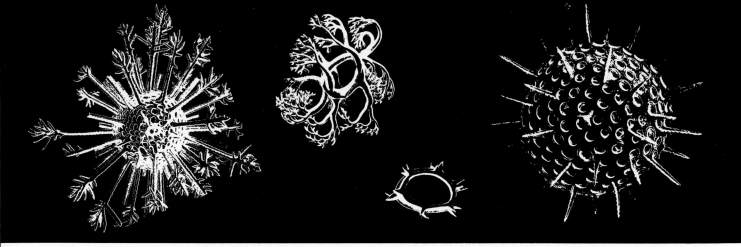

it is called Telegraphic Plateau, and Middle Ground. Expeditions in the 1870's, including the *Challenger's*, found that high ground runs from Iceland almost to the Antarctic down the middle of both the North and South Atlantic oceans. It became known as the Mid-Atlantic Ridge, or Rise, or Swell (no one was very certain what it was) and included, or at least abutted, Iceland and the Azores. Tristan da Cunha, Ascension, and St. Paul's Rocks in the South Atlantic emerge out of it. In size it compared with some continents (though no continent is so long and thin). One theory was that it was a new, growing continent only just beginning to emerge as dry land—but not a lost continent. In the 1930's echo soundings showed mountains along the ridge in the South Atlantic—so perhaps it was a mountain range like the Alps.

To a man, oceanographers and geologists had no use for Atlantis. Everywhere there was evidence that the deep sea had been deep a long time. But some did have sound scientific reasons for believing that continents that had sunk millions of years ago lay beneath the oceans. The Appalachian Mountains were built up out of sediments that originally washed in from some land to the east; geologists concluded that there had been a continent east of the present coastline and named it Appalachia. European geologists had another continent on their side, and in the Pacific there were Cascadia, and Mu, and Melanesia (whose highest mountains were the South Sea Islands). Sampling the ocean floor, oceanographers found traces of sand—a product of erosion on dry land—in dozens of places, though never on the heights of the Mid-Atlantic Ridge. The sand was interpreted as evidence that the ocean basins had once been dry land, in some cases several times, since some samples contained several layers of sand. As late as the 1950's an expedition in the Atlantic found the skeletons of fresh-water plankton in recent sediments on the deep sea floor and concluded that

the area had been dry land. But such planktonic remains have also been collected in dust storms blown out from Africa.

In January 1934, Sunday science pages reported—breathlessly—the discovery of a lost continent. A navy captain on a routine voyage from Hawaii to Japan had made and recorded regular echo soundings on the way—17,230 of them—and they showed mountains, and were thought to show valleys, former river beds, and other dry-land features (though in fact they did not). In hindsight, the exciting thing about the soundings is the way they were made. There were more soundings from the one voyage than had been made with rope, line, wire, or cable by all the world's oceanographers in the course of a century. Electronic echolocation, SONAR (for SOund NAvigation and Ranging), had been invented shortly after the *Titanic* sank, and its first use was for finding icebergs without running into them. Echo sounders were used for many years in the continental shelves, with great success, but only occasionally in the deep ocean.

Then after World War II a few men went out with echo sounders, and other instruments improved or developed for the war, and began to explore the floor of the deep sea. The postwar echo sounders drew a continuous outline of the land below, and between the sparse soundings of earlier years a new landscape materialized. The machines had a few weaknesses—if the ship's cook opened his refrigerator door, a canyon might appear in the sea floor, while other shipboard electrical events produced ridges and other phantom land forms—but oceanographers quickly built better machines. From the restlessly moving pens of these instruments emerges a profile of the sea floor directly below the ship, almost as if, in the words of Matthew Maury, the waters of the ocean had been drawn aside, exposing to view the earth below.

By the late 1950's the shape of the new landscape had appeared, awesome and astonishing, not muffled in a snow of sediments but raw and unworn, wild and ragged. Submerged volcanoes pepper the ocean floor. Here and there are guyots, seamounts with flat tops as much as a mile below the surface; guyots were islands that sank tens of millions of years ago. Through the 1950's scientists tracked a series of mountainous cliffs out across the Pacific Ocean floor from the California and Mexican coasts to the longitude of Hawaii. The fracture zones, as they are called, are thousands of feet high, cutting arrow-straight—and parallel—for thousands of miles across the sea floor, huge areas of which are higher on one side of the fracture zone than the other. These great areas of ocean floor appeared to have shifted many miles, but how or why no one could tell. "The origin and history of these great fracture zones are not becoming more obvious as additional

The movement of gigantic plates of the earth's crust slowly changes the shape and position of the continents. The lines where the plates meet are areas of instability, marked by earthquakes and volcanoes. The buckling of plates throws up mountains such as the Alps (left); their grinding together causes cracks such as the San Andreas Fault (opposite).

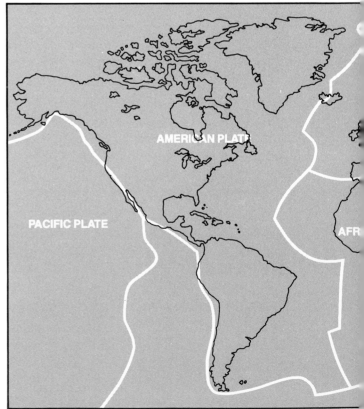

facts accumulate," wrote H. W. Menard in the 1960's, after almost twenty years of exploration.

Out of the sea floor the continents rise like mesas. Off many coastlines the edge of the continent is a sheer cliff dropping twenty to thirty thousand feet into deep troughs called trenches (the deepest parts of the ocean are all close to land). Slicing through the edges of the continent are submarine canyons. The Hudson Canyon becomes a colossal gorge wider and deeper than the Grand Canyon; the Congo Canyon is deeper still. Out from the foot of the continent stretch abyssal plains. In 1947 Maurice Ewing and other scientists from Columbia University on the research ship *Atlantis* sailed over such a plain 17,400 feet deep, a depth which scarcely varied a fathom for two and a half days. More investigation showed that the abyssal plains are formed by turbidity currents, towering submarine avalanches of churned-up mud, sand, and silt that occasionally sweep down the submarine canyons and spread out on the plains. The sand on the deep sea floor is carried there by turbidity currents. A turbidity current that occurred after an earthquake in Newfoundland in 1929 was reconstructed by Ewing and a colleague, Bruce Heezen, from telegraph cable records and sea floor samples. It had reached a cable

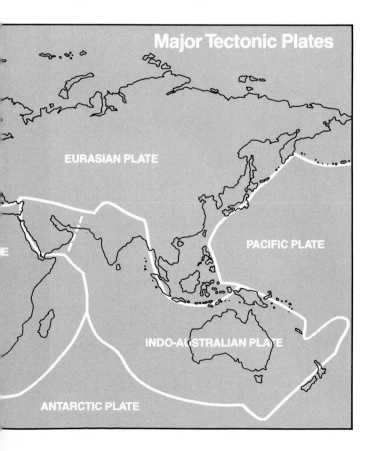

An earthquake on the northern margin of the Pacific plate in 1964 caused a block of the business section of Anchorage, Alaska, to drop twenty feet.

fifty miles out on the abyssal plain just under an hour after the earthquake, and cables as far as 400 miles out to sea broke, one after another, during the following twelve hours. The turbidity current reached the last cable, which had a breaking strength of 10.5 tons, with enough force to carry away 200 miles of it. The turbidity current appeared to be more than 800 feet high, and it dropped 100 cubic kilometers of sediment on the abyssal plain.

Far out from land, hills begin to sprout through the abyssal plain like islands from the ocean, rising and clustering into the foothills of the Mid-Atlantic Ridge. The ridge is a forest of volcanic mountains, a place of abrupt chasms, earthquake-shattered rocks, and fresh lava flows, the wildest of all the landscape of the sea floor. From where it rises out of the abyssal plains on either side, it is over a thousand miles wide in the ocean between North America and North Africa. Its highest peaks tower miles above the abyssal plain and rise within a few hundred feet of the surface, and sometimes above it. The ridge is constantly shaken by earthquakes and regularly builds up new peaks.

Of sunken continents on the sea floor there was not a sign. Yet exploration had only made it more certain that something monstrous was afoot on the ocean floor. But what was it? Why was the Pacific Ocean encircled with volcanoes, trenches, growing mountain ranges, and zones of regular, shattering earthquakes? What vast wrenching of the sea floor did the fracture zones record? Why have islands sunk en masse, and others risen? Some of the first postwar research, by Maurice Ewing and Frank Press, a student of Ewing's (later presidential science adviser under Jimmy Carter), found that the sea floor everywhere is only about three miles thick, whereas continents are about thirty miles thick. Also, the sea floor is made of basalt, while the continents are made of granite and other rocks much lighter than basalt. Aside from making retired continents on the sea floor a geological impossibility, this distinction between sea floor and continent is as important for the earth as the idea of mutation is for life. But its meaning was not realized through the fifties and early sixties, even as the face of the sea floor took on clarity and detail like a developing picture.

For centuries men tried, and failed, to explain how the features of the earth were made. Several hundred years ago scholars tried to reconcile the observable world and the text of the Bible in a belief called diluvialism. Diluvialism explained everything about the earth with the biblical Flood, and in some versions, many floods. In one, for example, the great rush of waters tore North and South America from Europe and Africa and created the Atlantic Ocean. In the late nineteenth century Sir George Darwin, impressed with the fact that the moon is getting steadily farther away from earth, wondered if the moon might not have been torn out of the earth when the earth was young, leaving a wound of which the great, almost round basin of the Pacific Ocean, the largest of the oceans, was the scar. The reverberations of the cataclysm might have opened up the Atlantic. Another idea appeared in 1961 in the journal *Nature*: that the ocean basins were originally formed by the impact of huge meteors, as the maria on the moon were. Like the moon idea, this could only have happened at a time that even in the scale of geology was very long ago; but one of the most unexpected discoveries about the ocean floor is that it is, geologically, very young. A stranger explanation, though one supported by equations of quantum physics, was that the earth is expanding (because gravity in the universe is weakening), and the Mid-Atlantic Ridge is the new growth.

In the 1920's Alfred Wegener published a book

The mapping of the ocean floor has been one of the major scientific achievements of our time. Tens of thousands of echo soundings, made by research vessels around the world, were reported back to the Lamont-Doherty Geological Observatory, where they were translated into a picture of the bottom by Bruce Heezen and Marie Tharp. An artist's rendition of their world map appears on pages 308–309.

The segment on the opposite page shows the Atlantic basin with the Mid-Atlantic Ridge snaking down the center. At the crest of the ridge is the rift through which lava periodically rises and spreads out to either side. Along the edges of the mesalike continents are deep trenches, where slabs of the earth's crust are drawn down into the underlying mantle to be melted in the unending cycle. At a few places, including Iceland, the Azores, and Ascension Island, the ridge breaks the surface. Other islands, such as the Canaries, the Cape Verdes, and Bermuda, are the tops of former volcanoes, as are the subsurface rises called seamounts.

As shown in the world map on the following pages, the Mid-Ocean Ridge curves southeast around Africa and then splits, one branch going north to the Red Sea, the other continuing through the Indian Ocean, south of Australia, and on up through the Pacific to the coast of California. Running at right angles to the ridges are fracture lines, consisting of parallel scarps and trenches, where bands of the crust have moved sideways, displacing the line of the ridge.

3 383 ▲

ICELAND

FAER
ISLAN

LOUSY
BANK

ROCKALL
BANK

HUDSON
BAY

REYKJANES RIDGE

· 2 853

— 250 ·

· 340 ·

PORCUPINE
BANK

NORTH AMERICA

CAPE
FAREWELL

MID OCEAN CANYON

CONTINENTAL RISE

LABRADOR

GIBBS FRACTURE ZONE

— 60 ·

· 4 500

FLEMISH
CAP

NEWFOUNDLA

ST. LAWRENCE

— 12 ·

GRAND
BANKS

· 51

· — 102

— 4 780

LAURENTIAN
CONE

SOHM ABYSSAL PLAIN

OCEANOGRAPHE

MISSISSIPPI

HUDSON CANYON

CORNER
RISE

APPALACHIAN MTS.

HATTERAS ABYSSAL PLAIN

BERMUDA RISE

BERMUDA

· 4 500

ATLANTIS

· 5 445

BLAKE
PLATEAU

NARES
ABYSSAL
PLAIN

KANE FRACTURE ZONE

CANARY ABYSSAL PLAIN

MADEIRA

CANARY
ISLANDS

BAHAMA
ISLANDS

MISSISSIPPI
CONE

— 3 500

CUBA

— 5 500

HAITI

▲ 5 386

PUERTO RICO TRENCH

CAPE VERDE
ISLANDS

5 125 ·

COLOMBIA
ABYSSAL PLAIN

DEMERARA ABYSSAL PLAIN

AMERICA TRENCH

ORINOCO

MT. IRAZU
▲ 3 500

DEMERARA
PLATEAU

— 170

AMAZON
CONE

CEARA ABYSSAL PLAIN

SIERRA LEON
RISE

RIDGE

MAUDELO

CARNEGIE RIDGE

GALAPAGOS
ISLANDS

AMAZON

— 4 435

FRACTURE ZO

SOUTH AMERICA

PERNAMBUCO
A.P.

ASCENSION

ANDES

MATO
GROSSO

STOCKS
SMT.

PERU

NAZCA RIDGE

COLUMBIA
SMT.

— 8 055

▲ 6 613

SAN ESS

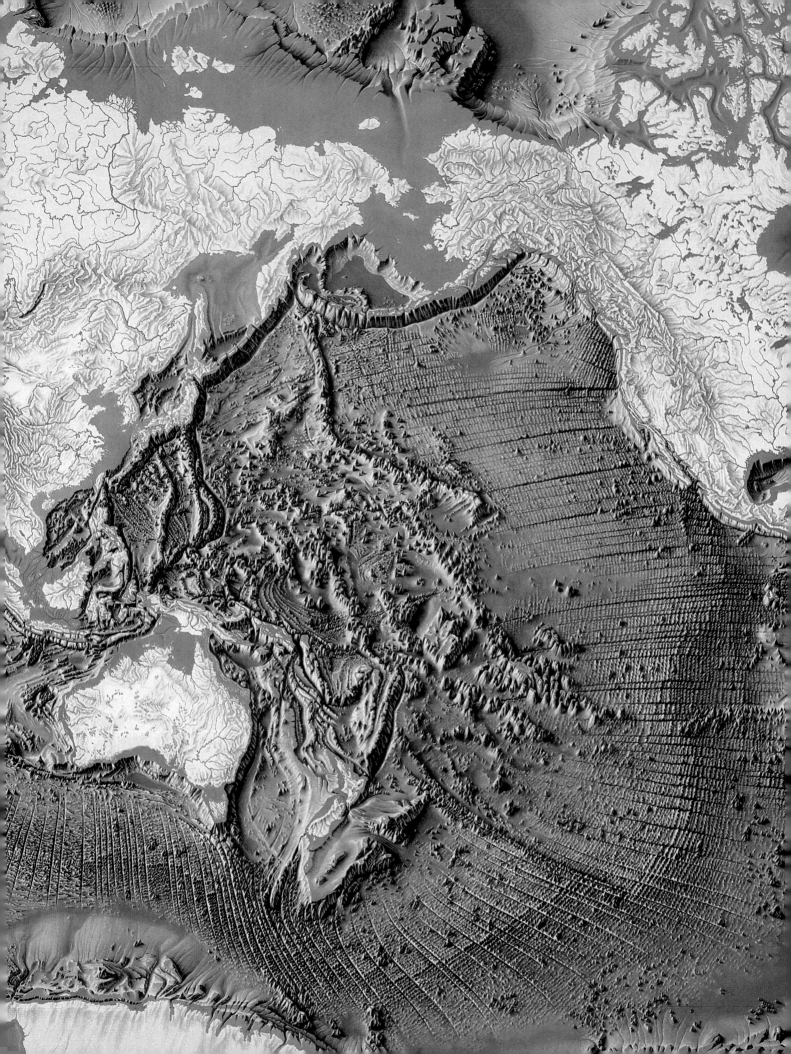

called *The Origin of Continents and Oceans*, in which he collected a mass of evidence that the continents once were all in one piece, then split apart and slowly moved to their present positions, crumpling up the sea floor before them into mountains and leaving new sea floor behind. But within a decade or so geologists had firmly rejected continental drift—so firmly, in fact, that according to the crystallographer Sir Lawrence Bragg, the only time he ever saw a man actually foam at the mouth was when he showed a geologist some of Wegener's work. Today most geologists believe that continental drift has occurred. The acceptance in the late 1960's of the concept of continental drift by nearly everyone who was working in the earth sciences is one of the most remarkable events in the history of science. From time to time it is reported that the discovery of some fossil here or there has proved continental drift; but this is only the sort of evidence which Wegener collected so much of, and which almost no one believed when it was all the evidence there was.

It is the floor of the sea, and two discoveries in particular, that finally convinced most geologists of continental drift. In 1956 Heezen and Ewing announced that the Mid-Atlantic Ridge was merely a segment of a Mid-Ocean Ridge that went all the way around the world. A few years earlier Heezen and Marie Tharp were transforming echo sounder profiles into a North Atlantic sea floor map, and they concluded that the Mid-Atlantic Ridge is split down its center by a rift valley. Earthquakes from the ocean floor had been recorded for years, and when their locations were calculated they formed a narrow line that was also at the center of the ridge—in fact it ran down the rift valley. Beyond the North Atlantic and into the South Atlantic, the narrow line of earthquakes continued down the center of the ridge. A rift valley was subsequently discovered there too. Then the earthquakes curved east around Africa and went north through the Indian Ocean, where the line split, sending a spur into the Red Sea and East Africa—

In 1971 divers observed and photographed for the first time what happens when lava erupts underwater (opposite page). The surface of the red-hot lava is cooled by the sea, making a brittle tube through which the molten lava continues to flow. The resulting shapes are called pillow lava and have recently been photographed on the Mid-Atlantic Ridge (above, right).

where there are rift valleys. It continued out of the Indian Ocean south of Australia, made a great sweep across the Pacific and up the Gulf of California (one end of the San Andreas Fault), re-emerging at sea at Cape Mendocino (the other end), and continued to Alaska.

Ewing and Heezen predicted that a ridge like the Mid-Atlantic Ridge would be found on the ocean floor wherever their line of earthquakes ran, and so it happened. A few oceanographers went out to prove that there was nothing like the Mid-Atlantic Ridge in one part of the Pacific, and certainly no rift valley; but every expedition, including theirs, has shown that there is a Mid-Ocean Ridge, as it is now called, in every ocean, wherever the earthquake line goes, although the ridge is not as high or spectacular everywhere as it is in the Atlantic. It is larger than all the continents together, 40,000 miles long, volcanically active, shaken by earthquakes. But no one knew then what—besides something totally new—it was. "There were a few marvelous years there," says an oceanographer, "knowing the ridge was there, cooking, knowing we were on the verge of something big, and that the next time at sea might find it."

The second great discovery was a pattern. One of the gadgets that oceanographers started taking to sea after the war measured magnetism—submarines are magnetic, and so are many rocks, especially volcanic ones—but a decade of towing magnetometers at sea only showed that rocks on the sea floor are magnetic too. One group of oceanographers, who almost had not bothered to put their magnetometer on a ship starting a survey in the Pacific, discovered when they got their data back that it resolved into a pattern of stripes, areas of sea floor (some wide, some narrow) with high magnetic intensity interleaved with others of low magnetic intensity. In a few years the striped pattern was also found in the Atlantic, at the crest of the ridge. The pattern on each side of the ridge was the same, the mirror of the other. In 1963 Fred Vine, a graduate student, and Drummond Matthews, his tutor at Cambridge University, realized in a leap of imagination what the pattern meant. Ashore, scientists had been studying magnetism too, and had demonstrated that the earth's magnetic field periodically reverses itself. Seven hundred thousand years ago, and for most of a million years before that, the north magnetic pole was in Antarctica. Still earlier it was in the Arctic, earlier yet in the Antarctic, and so on, and on, as deep into the past as rocks preserve a record. Vine and Matthews saw that the sea floor magnetic pattern embodies sea floor spreading, a revised version of continental drift in which the continents, instead of plowing their way across the sea floor, are carried with it as it spreads away from the Mid-Ocean Ridge, where it is constantly created.

The sea floor magnetic pattern records both the reversals of the earth's magnetic field and the spreading of the sea floor. Lava rising in the rift valley is magnetized as it cools. After a few tens or hundreds of thousands of years of this, there would be a band of recently magnetized rock at the center of the ridge, running the length of it through all the oceans. If then the poles flipped, a new, differently magnetized band would begin to form. Ultimately there should be a sequence of stripes, and a pattern. If the sea floor is spreading, its magnetic pattern should match the sequence of magnetic pole reversals known from rocks on land, and it does.

The same pattern is found along the Mid-Ocean Ridge continuously, in every ocean, all over the world. It stretches out from the crest of the ridge across the sea floor to the edges of the continents. Each stripe represents a span of time, each stripe out from the rift valley is older than the last one. The sea floor is young near the ridge and gets older farther from it (in recent years, drilling the sea floor has provided samples that confirm its age). In fact, what were originally called the ridge and the sea floor are the same, except that near the rift valley the sea floor is hot and swollen like a wound, and farther away it is older and cooler and buried in sediments; the ridge is in the sea floor, and the sea floor is the ridge. The sea floor is continuously created at the rift valley, was being created two hundred million years ago when the oldest parts of the oceans were new, and is still being created as this page is written and read, though so gradually that at most only a few inches are added in a year—ten to twenty square miles over the entire length of the ridge.

Written in the sea floor and its magnetic pattern is the story of the breakup of the continents and their travels across the face of the world. Even some of their future can be divined. Two hundred million years ago (there is no ocean floor older than two hundred million years) what is now India was nestled against Antarctica. Antarctica itself was tropical. The south pole was in central Africa. The future Confederate States of America were attached to West Africa (the "lost continent of Appalachia" was Africa). You could have walked from Newfoundland to Algiers across Spain in a few days without wetting your feet. Buenos Aires would have been almost a suburb of Capetown, had those cities existed. There was one great continent then, and a single, encircling ocean. The continent has been called Pangaea. (Some scientists believe that the land was divided by a narrow sea into two supercontinents, Laurasia and Gondwanaland.) Since that supercontinent, or super-continents, started to break apart some two hundred million years ago, when dinosaurs were beginning to dominate the world, the continents that remain have been dispersing about the world, carried along with the sea floor.

North and South America, along with the half of the Atlantic Ocean floor that is west of the Mid-Atlantic Ridge, are headed west at speeds of about an inch a year. (These great sheets of both continent and ocean floor are called "plates.") Almost the entire Pacific ocean basin is moving northwest at several inches a year. The Pacific plate includes the southwestern part of California, which is being dragged past the advancing front of North America along the line of the San Andreas Fault. In a million years or so, the Pacific will have brought Los Angeles within the city limits of San Francisco. Another part of a continent that is leading a life of its own is East Africa, but here a rift valley is growing within the continent, as rift valleys must have started to grow within the ancient super-

continent. Given enough time, East Africa will become a small continent the size of Madagascar, and its rift valley will be a small ocean like the Red Sea, which geologists regard as similar to the early stages of the Atlantic.

Earthquakes mark the borders of the great plates that trundle across the world, scraping and bumping. Plates move as slowly as ice but neglect to stop or pause. India is still moving northeast into Asia, and as land distorts to accommodate it, there are earthquakes. The whole Pacific moves a quarter of a foot a year. If the edges stick, eventually something gives. The longer it holds, the harder it breaks. In the Anchorage earthquake of 1964, the coast of Alaska rose twelve feet. After the Chile earthquake two years earlier, the entire planet vibrated like a bell for twenty-four hours.

Wherever two plates collide, there are mountains. An ocean floor that once lay between India and Asia remains, in part, in the Himalayas. The Franciscan structures of the Coast Ranges of California are composed of slabs of old sea floors; ancient abyssal plains and the deposits of turbidity currents even crop

The submersible Alvin, *built especially to carry out deep sea research for the Woods Hole Oceanographic Institution, rests on the bottom of the Pacific near the Galápagos Islands. Mounted on the front is a remote-controlled claw that picks up samples and dumps them into a revolving basket.*

out in San Francisco itself. There are marine fossils in the tops of the Andes (as Charles Darwin observed and wondered over as naturalist on the *Beagle*). Thus, while the floors of the oceans are continually renewed and kept always young by sea floor spreading, the mountains of the world preserve ancient sea floors from earlier oceans and record the distant comings and goings of the continents that bordered them—not only the Andes and the Himalayas, but the Alps, the Appalachians, the Urals, the Adirondacks, and others themselves so ancient they remain only as flat stumps, whose tilted layers are still-older sea floors. The Appalachians encompass great areas that are the floor of an ocean that grew by sea floor spreading when crinoids and trilobites dominated the bottom world. Later a trench formed along its margin; the ocean then shrank and the sea floor was raised into mountains,

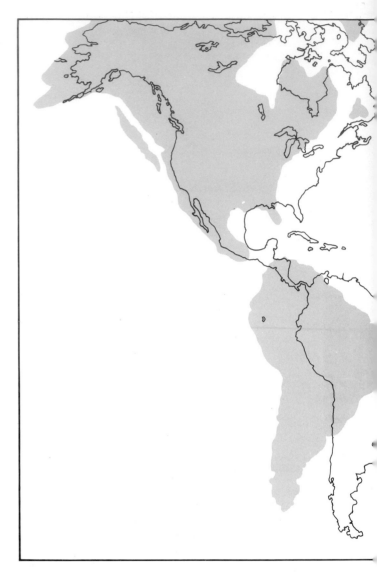

The theory of continental drift, now generally accepted, proposes that all the land mass of the earth was once a single continent, which geologists call Pangaea. The map above shows how the present continents originally fitted together. According to the theory, the Atlantic Ocean is still widening. The map at right shows where the continents will end up fifty million years from now (dark gray).

higher by far than the Alps, during the collision of its bordering continents, an early North America that included northern parts of Scotland and Scandinavia, and an Africa that included the southeastern part of the United States. The very oldest rocks that have been found in the world, 3,500 million years old, are the remains of ancient mountains, and are made of the debris of still older rocks and mountains; and they carry the record of continental drift.

While new sea floor is created in the rift valley of the Mid-Ocean Ridge, old sea floor is consumed. Partly it is uplifted in mountains, which largely consist of old sea floors; but chiefly it is, in the current language of geology, subducted, in the oceans' trenches, where it dives down into the molten interior of the earth, the mantle. That it does not do so willingly is indicated by some of the world's most devastating earthquakes, in the trenches of the coasts of Chile, Japan, and Alaska, and other places as well. The descending slabs can be traced several hundred miles down in the earth by analyzing earthquake waves. The mantle is both the source of lava for new sea floor and the repository for old sea floor. Many geologists have supposed that some sort of convection (a circulation impelled by heat) within the mantle is the force behind continental drift and sea floor spreading. The mantle also is

thought to contain "hot spots," which produce lines of volcanoes within the plates on the earth's surface, far from the rift valley or trenches. The hot spots remain fixed while the plates drift over them, producing formations like the Hawaiian Islands, which along with some seamounts make a straight chain several thousand miles long. From Hawaii, in the southeast, the islands and seamounts get steadily older to the northwest—as they would if the plate had moved northwest over a fixed source of lava. Some of the other Pacific islands form such lines too, and some geologists believe that there is a hot spot under Yellowstone Park. Virtually nothing is known of hot spots, however, except for what can be seen on the surface. Direct information about the mantle is fairly sparse, and it remains somewhat mysterious. There may be several layers within it, according to investiga-

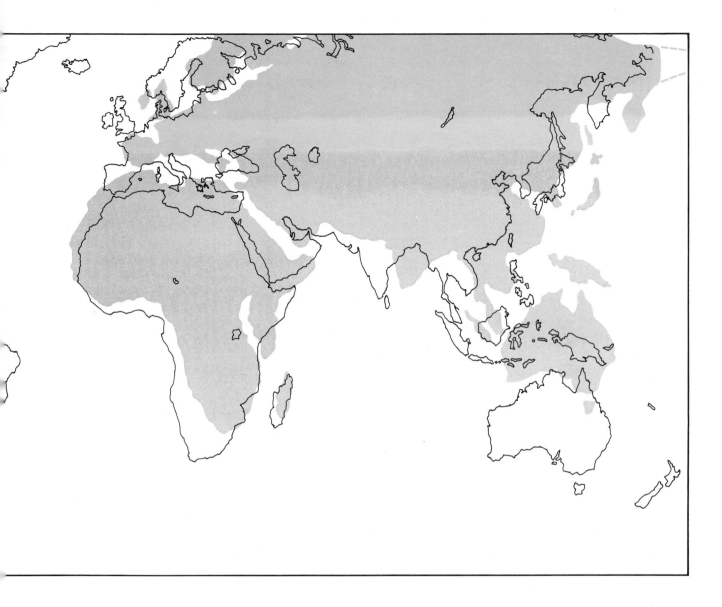

tions published in 1979, and geologists are having a harder time conceiving of convection in it.

Out of the exploration of the sea have emerged new mysteries, at least as tantalizing, and even unsettling, as some of the old ones. Can earthquakes be predicted, now that their origins are largely understood? Could the deadliest ones be diluted? What huge churnings go on in the interior of the earth to move the continents and ocean basins about, and why has the process speeded up in some ages and slowed down in others, first making fertile conditions for life, then destroying them? Why does the earth's magnetic field reverse? Why have species become extinct at some of these very times? Is the earth's magnetic field—which has been weakening for one hundred and fifty years—working up to a new reversal?

In this diagram of sea floor spreading, molten rock rises from the lower part of the earth's crust (the asthenosphere) to emerge at the ridge. From the ridge the lithosphere spreads toward the continental edges, where it is subducted back into the mantle.

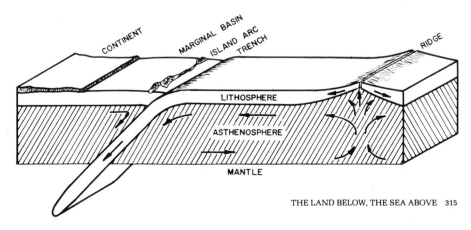

"RIVERS IN THE OCEAN"

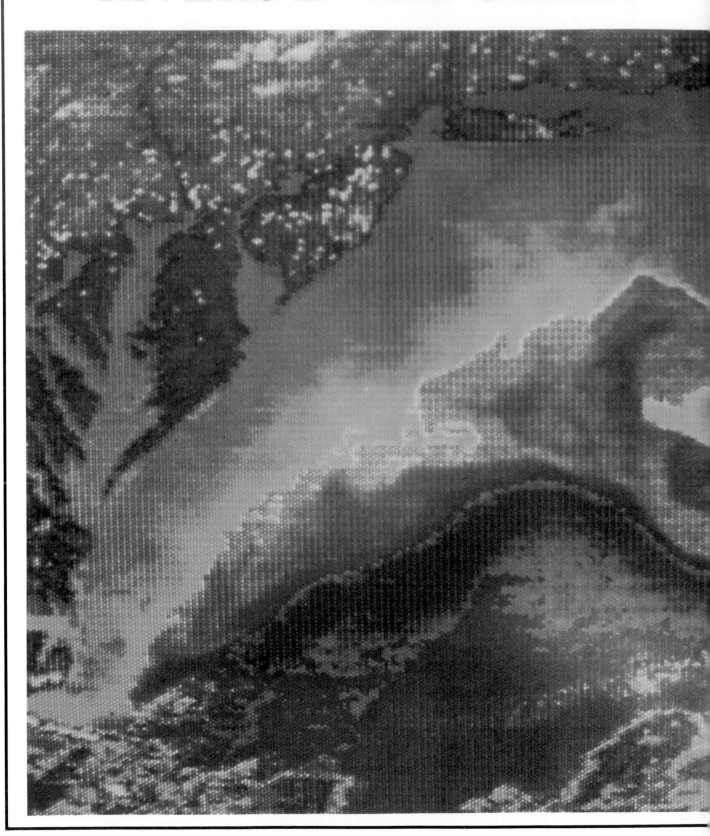

In this color-enhanced infrared satellite photograph of the Gulf Stream, the warmest water is purple, with cooler eddies and swirls appearing in red, orange, and blue.

"There is a river in the ocean," Matthew Maury wrote in Chapter Two of *The Physical Geography of the Sea.* "In the severest droughts it never fails, and in the mightiest floods it never overflows. . . . It is the Gulf Stream." The most famous phrase in oceanography, however, is not strictly true, by the discoveries of modern oceanography.

The Gulf Stream was one of the first discoveries in the New World. Columbus observed its beginnings heading out of the Caribbean, but although he had gotten a lift on the way over from another current, he never realized that he could have gotten a ride all the way home as well. John and Sebastian Cabot encountered the current along the coast of North America, and Sebastian Cabot remarked on the unusual warmth in the hold of his ship and the spoiling of the beer stored there. The Florida Current, where the Gulf Stream emerges into the Atlantic, was first described by Ponce de León when he visited the coast in 1513, and a few years later Spanish ships were riding the Equatorial Current to the New World and the Gulf Stream home.

Benjamin Franklin, the Gulf Stream's most famous student, learned about it in 1769 from his cousin Timothy Folger, the captain of a Nantucket whaling ship. Franklin was then postmaster general for the colonies and was vexed to learn that it took a mail ship two weeks longer to reach the colonies than it took merchant ships. Folger told him why, explaining that whales liked to lounge around the edges of the stream but not inside it, so the whale men knew well where the stream was and how fast it went. He added they had often met British mail packets fighting the current, and advised them to get out of it; "but they were too wise to be councelled by simple American fishermen!" Franklin fared little better with the British, though he published a famous map of the stream with his cousin's help. When the Revolution came he suppressed the map to keep it from the British. Not until 1980 did a scientist at the Woods Hole Oceanographic Institution uncover two original copies, of which he observed that Franklin's account of the stream still could not be much improved on. During the war the canny Franklin also proposed diverting the Gulf Stream and freezing the English into submission; but the engineering for such a project would not be available for another hundred years.

The Gulf Stream emerges through the Florida Straits at speeds as high as seven miles an hour. This is an enormous flow—on the average twenty-five times more water than emerges from all the rivers in the world added together. The stream is saltier than the local waters it passes, bluer, and of course warmer. Along its edge there may be not only whales but large schools of small fish and tuna, herds of turtles, innumerable seabirds, and forests of loose wood. In a northerly breeze, there can be large waves within the Gulf Stream, while the water outside is quite calm. Because of the stream, palm trees can grow in Scotland, and North American wildflowers have seeded themselves in Ireland. The Gulf Stream also delivers European eels to Europe. (They are born, and later return to spawn, in the Sargasso Sea.)

In 1913, C. L. Riker, reported to be

Sargassum weed (above) is sparsely distributed over two million square miles of the mid-Atlantic. It provides a unique refuge for marine life in the open ocean, and a number of species have become specifically adapted to it.

an able engineer, proposed not to divert but to boost the Gulf Stream toward Europe with a 200-mile jetty out from Newfoundland. The frigid Labrador Current (which makes the water as far away as Maine so cold) sweeps around Newfoundland over the shallow Grand Banks, and from it the Gulf Stream, as Riker wrote, "receives a staggering blow from which it never recovers." Riker's ingenious idea was to divert the Labrador Current around the Grand Banks to deep water into which it could subside and presumably be felt no more. The Gulf Stream then would sweep unimpeded on toward Europe. The most ingenious part of the plan

was a way of inducing the Labrador Current to deposit sediment and build the jetty itself. Eminent men endorsed the scheme, but the First World War put an end to it; and the long-term effects on climate might not have been just what was hoped for.

As early as the seventeenth century it was realized—but not widely accepted, and often forgotten—that the Gulf Stream is only a part of a huge revolution of surface waters of the entire ocean, rather than the traditional "river." Oceanographers now call this more or less round turning a gyre, and there are gyres also in the South Atlantic Ocean (the gyres are counterclockwise in the southern hemisphere), and in the Indian and Pacific oceans—separate gyres in each hemisphere—as well as lesser gyres in small bodies of waters like the Gulf of Maine.

Currents—and gyres—are driven primarily by winds, by differences of temperature and salinity, and by the

rotation of the earth, which imparts a twist known as Coriolis force; and they are further directed by land. The greatest drivers of currents are the trade winds blowing westward just to the north and south of the equator; beneath them in the Atlantic, Pacific, and Indian oceans flow the great streams called the North and South Equatorial Currents. (Along the equator in each ocean, between the North and South Equatorial Currents, runs an equatorial countercurrent returning some of the water that constantly flows westward.) In the Atlantic, the North Equatorial Current runs from the neighborhood of the Canary Islands to Barbados; to the merchant ships that used to sail down to the Canaries to catch the trade winds across the ocean, and to the yachts that still do, the North Equatorial Current has given an extra lift ever since Columbus first noticed it. The current is split into two by the Caribbean islands. As the Antilles Current it continues northeast of the islands, and it emerges above the Bahamas heading northeast on its way back to Europe as part of the Gulf Stream. The part of the North Equatorial Current that enters the Caribbean is joined by a large part of the South Equatorial Current, which is deflected north by the coast of Brazil. These two currents pile an enormous amount of water into the Caribbean (sea level is always higher at the western ends of the equatorial currents than at the eastern), and, deflected north and east by the Yucatán Peninsula, it comes squirting out between Cuba and Florida as the Florida Current. The Florida and the Antilles currents become the Gulf Stream.

Once in the Atlantic, the current begins, like any jet, to slow down, spread out, and break up. South of Newfoundland it is deflected and cooled by the Labrador Current (which it deflects west to the New England coast); it reaches the European side much spread out as the Azores Current, the Portugal Current (both of which turn south to join the Equatorial Current, completing the gyre), and as the North Atlantic Drift, which passes north of Scotland, and the Irminger Current, which warms Iceland.

Far from being a great sedate river confined as though between banks, the Gulf Stream meanders and eddies and shifts itself a hundred miles to one side or another. There are even cold streaks down the middle of it. The kinks in the Gulf Stream often break off from it, forming independent loops like miniature gyres that continue swirling about for weeks or months. Tropical fish are often carried into New England in these loops, and navigators deceived by them. The shape and size and position of the stream's meanders and loops change in just a few days, and oceanographers doing their work often watch merchant ships bucking a current while carefully keeping courses that should give them a boost from it. The regular use of a good

thermometer remains the only reliable way to keep a ship in the stream.

The still interior of the turning Atlantic gyre is the Sargasso Sea, whose thin scattering of seaweed struck fear in the hearts of early mariners. They imagined their ships were being slowed down by it and feared they might get stuck altogether in a mass of impenetrable floating weed. Ships were supposed to have sat unmoving in the tropic sun until their crews died of thirst or starvation and the ships themselves finally rot-

ted. This specter was disproved as soon as it arose, by Columbus, but it kept springing up as fast as it was put down, as the most perfect of gruesome ideas do. Even Matthew Maury stated that ships are impeded by the weed. It is possible that a few sailing ships were actually slowed down in the Sargasso. There is a phenomenon called dead water, which was explained by Walfried Ekman at the end of the last century after observations made on the Norwegian ship *Fram,* which was doing research in

This depiction of a weed-clogged Sargasso Sea is based on legend that persisted well into the twentieth century. The ship is shown stranded in a tangle of seaweed so thick that even the rowboat is making little progress.

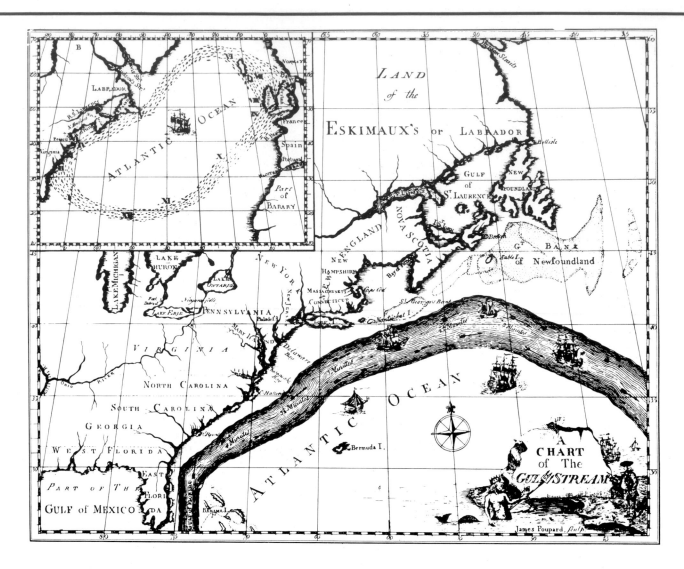

the Arctic. Where the ocean is covered by a thin layer of warm or—in the case of the arctic ice pack—fresh water, drag develops on a moving ship. The *Fram,* not a fast vessel for her day but perhaps the equal of the caravels of Columbus's, was so slowed by the dead water that she could be sailed full tilt toward floating pack ice and yet bump only gently.

The floating weed often collects in large rafts, so that from the low vantage of a small sailboat the sea looks like a balding lawn, but the rafts would scarcely discommode a toy sailboat. The Sargassum weed is kept afloat by little air sacs like clusters of small grapes. It reproduces by breaking off fronds that grow into new plants, each of which is a little

ecosystem in itself. Small algae on the weed provide some of the nutrients it needs. Barnacles and other small shellfish grow on the stems. The weed supports an astonishingly varied population of minuscule fish, crabs, shrimps, and other animals and larvae. The sargassum fish has come to look precisely like a frond of the weed; it lurks waiting for little shrimps, equally camouflaged, to come into view. The plant produces fewer air sacs as it ages, and finally it sinks under the weight of the creatures attached to it, carrying with it all that cannot swim.

The Atlantic gyre and pattern of currents is closely matched in the Pacific. A powerful stream, the Japan Current, or Kuroshio, pours out of the

tropics, carrying warm water north and east across the ocean, warming Japan, Alaska, and the west coast of North America. In 1951 scientists discovered a new current in the Pacific, an enormous one, the second largest in the ocean and half as large as the Gulf Stream; yet there had been not a hint of it before. "It seems incredible," the oceanographer C. P. Idyll has written, "that a current transporting forty million tons of water a second—as massive as thousands of Mississippi Rivers—could escape the notice of men for so long." Scientists of the U.S. Fish and Wildlife Service had been looking for tuna 1,200 miles south of Hawaii in the South Equatorial Current. They lowered their gear to about 150 feet, and

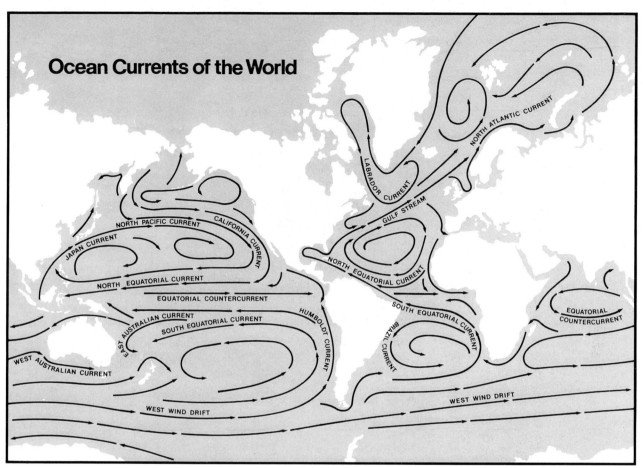

Ocean Currents of the World

Benjamin Franklin is credited with being the first to map the Gulf Stream, with the help of his whaling captain cousin, Timothy Folger. On his chart (opposite page) he recorded the velocity of the current in "minutes," roughly equivalent to nautical miles per hour. The Gulf Stream is one of a number of currents that carry water in a great circle in the North Atlantic. This and gyres in other seas are connected in a worldwide system of oceanic currents (above).

to their amazement the surface buoys attached to it started moving eastward against the surface current. They concluded that beneath the surface current there was another current going in the opposite direction. The Cromwell Current, as it has been called after the oceanographer who first charted it, lies below the depth of sixty-five feet, an amazingly thin ribbon of water with none of the Gulf Stream's irregularities. It is about 600 feet thick from top to bottom and 250 miles wide, and it is at least 3,500 miles long and may be as long as 8,000. It ends near the Galápagos Islands and may start as far away as the Solomon Islands.

There is as complex a web of currents within the sea as on its

surface. The coldest (twenty-nine degrees) and saltiest water in the oceans is formed in the Weddell Sea in Antarctica as ice freezes on the surface; the water sinks to the bottom and creeps north along the sea floor, reaching as far north as the latitude of Puerto Rico. In the Arctic, a smaller (about four million tons a second) and somewhat warmer flow of water sinks and drifts southward, most or all of it as a countercurrent under the Gulf Stream. About 100,000 tons of water evaporates every second from the Mediterranean, leaving warm salty water that sinks and pours out beneath the surface at the Strait of Gibraltar, reaching as far west as the Bahamas and to the north and south also. Mixing the oceans' waters,

these and other currents modify extreme temperatures and keep the planet pleasant to live on.

Finally, there are the gaudiest currents of all, cold bottom waters, rich in minerals and nutrients, which rise from the depths to the surface near Walvis Bay, Southwest Africa, and off the coast of Peru. These currents cause all forms of marine life to flourish (as well as fishermen) until an influx of warm water urges the flourishing too far, the oxygen in the water is all used up, and everything dies. Rotting corpses stink; the hydrogen sulphide in the water makes it more poisonous, and often brightly colored, and will cause a ship's paint to turn black—for which in Peru the current is called the Callao Painter.

VOLCANOES OF
THE MID-OCEAN RIDGE

An account of the voyages of Saint Brendan during the sixth century describes his passing a barren island whose "inhabitants" came out and hurled at "the servants of Christ" rocks which made the ocean hiss and steam where they fell; "then they returned to their forges, which they blew up into mighty flames, so that the whole island seemed one globe of fire and the sea on every side boiled up and foamed like a cauldron set on fire. . . . Then Saint Brendan [said] 'We are now on the confines of hell.' "

Early in the morning of November 14, 1963, a fishing boat called the *Isleifur II* set out its lines several miles west of Geirfuglasker, the southernmost of a group of islands that straggles south from Iceland. These Westman Islands are small blocks of basalt which look when the sun is high like icebergs, or full-rigged ships scudding before the wind; only one, Heimaey, has a settlement. It was a still, hazy, ordinary morning—though there was an odd smell about. The crew had a cup of coffee and went to sleep. About 7:15 Olafur Vestman, the cook, who was on watch on deck, had a strange sensation, as if the boat were being carried along in a current. He also saw something in the haze along the horizon. It looked at first like a rock, but there was no rock in that location and he realized that he was looking at smoke. He woke the captain. To any seaman even the thought of fire at sea is terrible. The captain radioed the coast guard and asked if there had been distress calls. None. He focused his binoculars on the smoke and saw dark pillars and white clouds boiling out of the sea itself. Then, guessing what he had

A towering column of smoke and ash rose 50,000 feet in the air above Surtsey in the early days of the eruption (opposite page). A few months later, in April 1964, a lava flow began and continued for more than a year (below).

seen, he took the *Isleifur II* in for a closer look at the eruption, but the sea was so turbulent that half a mile was as close as he could get. Even there the ocean itself was nine degrees warmer than normal.

The violence of the submarine explosions was increasing. Jets of ash, cloud, and stone were shooting high in the sky, as though from some colossal rocket engine. Bombs of lava fell hissing beside the boat. The smoke rose to 12,000 feet by mid-morning and to 20,000 by afternoon and was seen in Reykjavík seventy miles away, later turning pink in the rays of the setting sun. The explosions went on through the night; sometime after dark the volcano rose above water and an island was born out of the sea. Surtsey—as it was later named after a mythical Norse giant—was thirty-three feet high. Few children are so intently observed in the first hours, days, and years of their lives. The first volcanologists were overhead at 11 A.M.

The Mid-Ocean Ridge was growing and showing itself off in its most spectacular style. The new island had a wide opening on one side, and the ocean poured through it onto molten lava; the island shook with the explosions. Fountains and sheets of ash shot up, some fanning out in all directions, some—vast upheavals a quarter of a mile across—reaching a quarter of a mile high. Lightning cracked back and forth; tornadoes appeared briefly between the clouds. Dense roiling smoke rose in columns that looked like hardened foam. Ash fell thickly on the island and sea.

In four days Surtsey was 200 feet high; in two weeks it was the second largest of the islands in its group— and gulls were landing on it in calm moments, ''warming their feet,'' as an observer remarked. The sea recoiled from the new land, frothing about its shores. Duncan Blanchard, a scientist who was among the first to visit, wrote in his book *A Volcano at the Surface of the Sea* :

''At times the eruptions would cease, as if Surtsey were resting from its strenuous exercises. The bottom of the crater filled with sea water, and sea birds swooped low over the now quiet surface. Only a gentle steaming disturbed the surface, and we approached to within 300 feet of the crater. But no closer, for the giant was only slumbering. Surtsey would awaken suddenly, the water in the center of the crater beginning to bubble, and within a second or two ash and cloud would be hurled upward and outward at speeds of up to 200 miles per hour. . . . From the surface of these clouds secondary explosions hurled huge feathered spears of cloud and ash that fanned outward and finally arched earthward in long exquisite streamers silhouetted against the clear blue sky. . . .''

In April lava began to flow out of Surtsey, armoring it against the sea and ensuring its survival. It flooded down the island's slopes at fifty miles an hour; rivers of it ran red into the ocean and split into smaller streams that writhed through the rough landscape like cadaverous fingers ending in a small bulge at the water's edge. Already microbes had found their way to Surtsey, and by summer flies and butterflies and spiders were in residence; seals basked on the shore. In June 1965 a flower bloomed on the beach, and more soon followed. Mosses and lichens, too, came, but only several years later. Surtsey stopped erupting in May 1965, just a year and a half old.

A few days later the sea heaved and churned nearby, and in June Syrtlingur was born. Syrtlingur grew to 160 feet high and 1,600 feet across before October 17, when the eruption stopped; in one week the ocean washed it away. The day after Christmas there were more eruptions half a

In 1973 Iceland's island port of Heimaey was threatened with extinction by a volcanic eruption lasting three months.

mile to the south, and Jólnir, Christmas Island, appeared. Jólnir erupted for six months and stopped; a week later there was a new eruption on Surtsey. All these eruptions fell along parallel lines whose direction was that of the rift valley of the Mid-Ocean Ridge. In 1973 Heimaey erupted, and some of the streams of lava oozed into the streets of the village, which was evacuated. The village was resettled within a year, and a way was devised of piping winter heat for the houses out of the lava field.

Volcanic eruptions raising new islands or enlarging old ones are typical of the Mid-Ocean Ridge in the Atlantic, where sea floor spreading is slow and the ridge high, and are a glimpse of the ridge itself, the factory from which the earth's crust emerges and is pushed about the earth. Recently, the author spent some time near the edge of the Red Sea where the growing ocean floor has raised up a piece of itself as large as the state of Kansas. It is called the Afar, or

Molten lava glows within the crater of a continuously erupting volcano in the Afar's dried-out oceanic ridge.

Danakil, Depression, after the nomadic people who live there. The Afar is the eastern part of Ethiopia and includes the French protectorate of Djibouti; it is several hundred miles long and over a hundred wide. Much of the interior of the Afar is still well below sea level, the ocean being blocked off by a coastal range of mountains. Salt flats stretch for miles. Here and there out of the flat plain rises a single, strange conical mountain with a perfectly flat top. These appear to have been guyots. Except along a few stream and river beds and in some small dots of irrigation, the Afar is desert and is fiercely hot; the sun feels like a roaring fire, and ninety-five degrees in the shade is like a deliciously cooling breeze.

The Afar has not only been sea floor, it is also part of the Mid-Ocean Ridge. In fact, three rift valleys meet there, one emerging from East Africa, one from the Red Sea, and one from the Gulf of Aden and the Indian Ocean. Even on the scale of men's lifetimes, the spreading of the earth's crust is visible in the region. On my way into the Afar by the main highway from Addis Ababa to the sea, I passed within a few feet of a large hill that was sliced cleanly down the middle, with

one half shifted twenty feet to the side. The fault that had divided the hill so neatly continued on as far as I could see—the better part of a mile—as a low cliff across which the land dropped a dozen feet or so. The road also crossed a great field of lava that had swept down from the shoulder of some hills to the edge of a lake. Farther on I found myself looking down at a strange green field that I suddenly realized was the tops of young trees—perhaps a dozen years old—growing out of the same rough, black lava in a small volcanic crater. Between the towns of Awash and Gewani the rift valley is a magnificent plain, twenty or thirty miles across, bounded by thousand-foot cliffs. At the center, behind Gewani, rises the single six- or eight-thousand-foot cone of Ayelu. Bordering Lake Abbaye in Djibouti, through which the rift passes, the earth lies heaved up in slabs the size of mountains. Deeper in the Afar the terrain is a jumble sliced by faults every few yards. Out of some of them lava oozes in sheets. Open cracks run across flat plains. A new volcano erupted near Asal in 1978, and the rift there, broken by many small faults, widened by about six feet in the course of five years.

The cone of this extinct volcano was formed when the Afar region was under the Red Sea. By the time it emerged from the water it was already dormant, but volcanic activity in the rest of the mountain range is still intense.

Salt beds thousands of feet deep lie in the enclosed sea basin of the northern Afar region. Erosion from wind and occasional rainfall has sculpted the salt into bizarre shapes.

GREAT WAVES

Lituya Bay is a large, still body of water north of Sitka, near the top of the Alaskan panhandle; it is perfectly sheltered from the Pacific, and it is uninhabited. Early geologists exploring Alaska found high-water marks several hundred feet above sea level on the wooded slopes of the mountains that rise out of Lituya Bay. High up, the forests were old, while below the water lines the woods were relatively recent; the Tlingit Indians had a legend of a village in Lituya Bay whose men returned from hunting to find it completely destroyed. The usual explanation was that tidal waves had washed in from the ocean, though the high-water lines were higher than even the greatest known tidal wave. But in 1936, and again in 1958, eyewitnesses survived to tell what happened in Lituya Bay.

On July 9, 1958, there was a major earthquake along the Fairweather Fault, one of the lines along which the floor of the Pacific Ocean is edging northward past North America; by later measurements a segment of the Alaska coast moved instantaneously twenty-one feet horizontally and three feet vertically. In Lituya Bay the side of a mountain, some 400 million cubic yards of rock, dropped into one arm of the bay. Water from the bay

The associated disasters of tsunami and earthquake struck the Portuguese capital of Lisbon on All Saints' Day, 1755, while most of its devout citizens were in church. Much of the city was destroyed, including thirty churches, and a quarter of the population left dead. So heavy was the blow to Christian optimism that theologians and philosophers debated its meaning for years after.

Storm waves, like this one engulfing a lighthouse off Land's End, England, can reach awesome proportions.

washed up the mountain on the opposite shore to a height of 1,740 feet, rebounded, and sloshing back and forth from shore to shore, resolved itself into a towering wave, from 50 to 110 feet high by various accounts, which roared out toward the mouth of the bay. There were three fishing boats, forty to sixty feet in length, anchored in Lituya Bay, which is still prized as the only sheltered anchorage in a hundred miles. Two of the boats upped anchor and headed for the entrance of the bay as the wave started toward them; one of them was never seen again. The wave

rushed down the bay, shaving whole forests off the shores like a barber's razor. It lifted one of the surviving boats across a two-hundred-foot-wide spit, eighty feet above the tops of the trees, according to her owner's account, into the ocean where she subsequently broke up and sank. The owner of the third boat also described looking down on trees from a great height. Subsequent investigations confirmed the size of the Lituya Bay wave, and the fact that a wave sweeps the bay when there is an earthquake on the fault, about every twenty years.

Waves, like fish, are apt to get larger with every telling, but waves of towering height, and other perhaps stranger things, are documented. Winter storm waves have washed

right over the top (seventy-five feet high) of the Minots Ledge lighthouse off Hingham, Massachusetts, and a bell one hundred feet up on the Bishop lighthouse off Cornwall was hit by a wave whose breaking crest went even higher. Surface waves are raised up by the wind, but exactly how it happens remains something of a mystery. One might suppose that the drag, or friction, of the wind on the water would be responsible, but in fact it seems that the wind travels over waves more easily than it would if the water were flat, at least at speeds of twenty miles or less. However they manage it, winds do raise waves, and while there is a theoretical limit to the size of the waves that a wind can make, if these proportions are not noble enough, several waves may briefly coalesce to make one enormously large one. The odds are that every thirtieth wave will be twice the average height, every thousandth, three times; and every three hundred thousandth, four times the average height. Waves more than 200 feet high are possible theoretically, though it is doubtful whether one will ever be reported.

The tallest recorded sea wave was measured from the U.S.S. *Ramapo.* The *Ramapo* was a navy tanker nearly 500 feet long making regular runs between San Diego and Manila. In 1933 during one passage from Manila to San Diego, the *Ramapo* was overtaken by a series of low-pressure areas that finally merged into a single fierce storm. Winds averaged sixty knots, with higher gusts. The waves had thousands of miles of unobstructed water over which to build up. They were passing the *Ramapo* at speeds close to fifty-five knots, almost the speed of the wind, and they were so long—1,100 to almost 4,000 feet—that the *Ramapo* slid down them quite comfortably. At one point the officer on watch on the bridge observed that he was able to sight a horizontal line across the ship's crow's-nest—which was much higher than the bridge—to the top of an approaching wave. At the same instant, the angle of the ship was measured with a sextant. Simple trigonometry on a series of these sightings showed that the waves had been 107, 112, and 119 feet high. Because the observations and calculations were precisely done and carefully checked, they are generally accepted as the highest sea waves ever sighted.

Just as waves can build up to enormous heights under the right conditions, it appears that the troughs between them can drop into seemingly bottomless pits. This even more unnerving phenomenon has only been reported in the last few decades, perhaps because earlier mariners failed to survive it, and thus far it has been reported only from the waters south and east of the Cape of Good Hope. In August 1964 the *Edinburgh Castle,* a ship 750 feet long, was steaming easily into a heavy swell between Durban and Capetown. Suddenly the sea dropped from under her bow and she was surging down the back side of a wave at an angle of thirty degrees into a hole in the ocean. The next wave swept over her as solid water fifteen or twenty feet higher than her decks. The *Edinburgh Castle* came through little damaged; but in 1974 the 132,000-ton tanker *Wilstar* lost over forty feet of her bow in a giant trough, in the same area.

Yet another potentially lethal sort of wave is the internal wave. Entirely within the sea and never reaching its surface, an internal wave normally passes unnoticed by all but oceanographers. But to a submarine moving at high speed, deeply submerged, encountering an internal wave would be like a plane striking an air pocket; and many authorities believe that such a wave sank, or helped to sink, the U.S. submarine *Thresher,* which disappeared in 1963 between Cape Cod and Nova Scotia during a submerged run. Sailing at high speed near her depth limit, and ballasted to equilibrium with the water at that depth, she could suddenly have been hurtling down along the face of the invisible wave instead of sailing horizontally. In seconds she could have been more than 100 feet deeper.

Other waves are simply eerie when they strike. On December 9, 1970, at 11:35 P.M., the liner *Bergensfjord*—on her way from Peru to Panama—began to shake. A passenger reported "a loud, bumping, rasping sound" as if the ship "had hit something hard and was skidding over a rough surface." The ship listed, then righted. Engines were stopped and signs of grounding or collision damage searched for; as none could be found, she continued on her voyage.

Steel hull plates were torn like paper when the oil tanker Wilstar *lost her bow to a giant wave off South Africa.*

In 1846 inhabitants of Jamestown, St. Helena, were astounded when a huge wave suddenly appeared 500 yards from shore and smashed thirteen ships in the harbor to kindling. Boats farther out to sea were unaware of the tsunami.

Four years earlier another ship was shaken so violently she began to leak, and back in 1941 a ship off Mexico began to vibrate so hard that a deck load of steel, parts of which weighed as much as six tons, jumped six inches up and down on its blocks.

These ships had been shaken by waves from seaquakes on the Mid-Ocean Ridge and in the trenches that border the Pacific. Such waves are called pressure, or P, waves, and are the same ones that destroy buildings on land, but at sea they have not received the attention that other sea waves or earthquake waves have.

The most chilling of all the phenomena of the sea, to those who know its meaning, is the sudden withdrawal of the water from the shore. The sea drops far below the lowest tide level.

Harbors dry out. Ships lie stranded. Land is exposed that no living person has ever seen before, and occasionally old wrecks. Sometimes people wander out curiously to explore, but they are never seen again. There is a hissing and sucking and rattling of stones as the water leaves. As the waves recede farther and farther, there is an eerie silence. When the sea returns, it comes in at a hundred or more miles an hour. Sometimes it simply rises, frothing and churning, dozens of feet higher than it ever has;

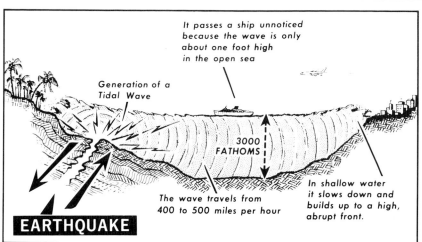

The drawing above shows the progression of a tsunami from its principal cause, a submarine earthquake, to its towering finale.

and sometimes it comes as a cresting, towering wave, sweeping and crashing over everything. These are tsunamis (the Japanese word is generally preferred to "tidal waves," since they have no relation to tides).

In 1883 the Indonesian island of Krakatoa blew up (it lies at the juncture of several plates of the earth's crust), leaving depths of 1,000 feet where there had been peaks reaching as high as 2,623 feet above sea level. The tsunami from that explosion rose into a crest 135 feet

high along the nearby coasts of Java and Sumatra and swept away thousands of villages, killing 36,380 people, according to a thorough investigation done immediately afterward by the British Royal Society. There are older reports of still larger waves, but none is so well documented as this one. The wave destroyed 6,000 ships in Calcutta, and it was recorded, much diminished, in England. The sound of the explosion was heard 3,000 miles away.

Most tsunamis are caused by earthquakes, or by submarine landslides caused by earthquakes; they cross the oceans at tremendous speeds, and until they reach shallow water are so long and low they cannot be detected except by instruments. In 1946 there was an earthquake in the Aleutian Trench. Less than five hours later a series of tsunamis struck the Hawaiian Islands 2,000 miles away, killing several hundred people. The waves were about thirty feet high at Hawaii and more than fifty feet high at Molokai. At Hilo the part of the city around the harbor was demolished. Yet the captain of a ship a mile offshore was unable to detect the waves as they went by under his ship.

Tsunamis have not been wholly without redeeming virtue—though almost. As a child I heard from my

grandmother the story of her uncle by marriage, who as a young naval officer was aboard the U.S.S. *Wateree,* which was anchored in the harbor at Arica, Chile, in August 1868, when a tsunami struck. The *Wateree* was a 205-foot, steel, flat-bottomed side-wheeler gunboat. She was carried right over the town and some of its tallest buildings and set down undamaged and upright among sand dunes a mile inland, where she sat looking as though the tide had just gone out. Here the family story diverges from the written accounts, and has it that the ship landed on the front lawn of the British consul. Photographs do not confirm this conjoining, but the consul's daughter did sweep the young man away all over again, and he married her and became an admiral. The *Wateree* was sold at auction after several months for $2,775. In the meantime, she remained commissioned, and naval routine continued with only a few modifications. If the captain "went ashore," a boatswain's mate piped and ordered the captain's gig. A coxswain ran out on the ship's boat boom, slid down a rope, and unmoored a donkey. The captain saluted the colors, descended the boarding ladder (lengthened to reach ground), and rode off.

THE WEALTH OF THE SEA

Is there great wealth in or beneath the ocean? Men have always believed so, and generally they have been wrong. Oceanographic exploration during the last half century has shown that a number of the "riches" of the sea were illusory, though on the whole more resources have been discovered than have proved to be mirages. There is gold in sea water, for example; the percentage is minute, but the total is very large. During the twenties the great German chemist Fritz Haber decided that it could be extracted profitably. Had he succeeded, the supply of gold would have been limitless; but he failed, and later research, including samples and measurements taken on the German ship *Meteor,* which spent several years doing oceanographic research in the South Atlantic during the 1930's, showed that the amount of gold in sea water is several hundred times less than had been believed.

But the greatest disappointment of recent ocean research concerns the often repeated promise that the oceans will feed mankind when the land can do no more. Exploration has shown that the open ocean, the vast majority of the surface of the oceans, is a biological desert, in which little lives or grows. The nutrients in the water are highly diluted, and if the waters did not circulate, all growth would stop. Even in the Sargasso Sea there are at most times only enough nutrients in the water to support about ten minutes' of plant growth, according to Dr. John Teal, as compared to half a day's growth in the richest parts of the ocean. The great productive areas of the oceans are all near the

Twin oil rigs in the Gulf of Mexico tap the rich deposits of fossil fuel that lie beneath the floor of the sea.

coasts, and they have been both overexploited and badly reduced in size and productivity by pollution. The promise of more food from natural production in the sea has been quietly dropped by the prophets of the ocean. Great promise remains in aquaculture—the cultivation of food in water—and much ingenuity has been shown in recent years in developing different schemes of cultivation, in which many kinds of seafood have been raised successfully. But that promise should not be exaggerated as the other was. Much of the commercial production of aquaculture thus far has been of specialty foods and not of cheap bulk protein; moreover, in the ocean, aquaculture will be confined to coastal areas and will be affected by their problems, especially pollution, perhaps even more than are natural stocks.

The greatest wealth of the high seas may be on the sea floor, in homely little hamburgers of various minerals called manganese nodules, which have several dozen of the world's largest corporations in a scramble to mine the deep sea. Manganese nodules contain about forty different minerals, and they carpet the sea floor all over the world, in almost endless numbers. In fact they are reported to cover more of the earth's surface than any other salable resource. Fields of nodules cover millions of square miles in every ocean, and sea floor photographs often show them packed so thickly they completely cover the bottom. For the most part they are small, potato-shaped or round, or like bunches of grapes—or like nothing in particular. There is enough copper in nodules on the Pacific floor alone to supply the world's needs for 6,000 years, versus 40 years' supply on land, according to one authority on them; enough nickel

for 50,000 years, versus 100 on land; and aluminum for 20,000 years, versus 100.

Manganese nodules were discovered during the voyage of the *Challenger.* They are dark and soft and crumbly, and when sliced through show rings of growth rather like a tree's. They can grow around a shark's tooth, a whale's ear bone, a piece of another nodule or of pumice, or some other piece of sea floor detritus. One theory is that some of the microscopic organisms of the sea floor play a role in precipitating or extracting minerals from sea water or sediments and depositing them in manganese nodules. In any case, they grow extremely slowly, about one millimeter per hundred thousand years—or per million years, by other estimates—so they are not truly a renewable resource. It has been estimated that all the nodules of the ocean collectively are growing faster than mankind could use them—or, by less enthusiastic calculations, at the more modest rate of sixteen million tons a year. But most of the nodules of the world are not concentrated enough, or rich enough in the valuable minerals, to be worth mining.

It was the discovery, during the fifties, of a per cent or so of cobalt, a high-priced metal used for alloys and other metallurgical applications, in nodules in the Pacific that inspired the idea of mining them. There is a belt of sea floor that sweeps across the Pacific from somewhere off Mexico to a region south of the Hawaiian Islands where nodules are both thickly concentrated and particularly rich in cobalt and in nickel. These two metals are the economic basis of sea floor mining. (Copper would be a profitable but relatively unimportant by-product of the extraction of cobalt and nickel, while manganese would not even be

produced by some processes.) Four consortia of American, British, and Japanese companies—Lockheed, U.S. Steel, British Petroleum, Kennecott, International Nickel, Mitsubishi, Sun Oil, Amoco, and Shell, among them—have explored the sea floor in that area intensively, and one outfit even filed a claim for mining rights on a square mile of sea floor with the secretary of state (since the claim was not in territorial waters).

Operating equipment four or five miles beneath a ship on the high seas seems a tenuous prospect (it has been compared to standing on the World Trade Center with a long piece of spaghetti trying to snag something on the sidewalk), but the companies have used newly developed methods at sea and brought up sample quantities of nodules. Generally the equipment is a variety of suction dredge, armed with television cameras for the benefit of the operators on shipboard; but hoppers on immensely long cables strung between two ships have also been used. While the companies perfect their equipment, the government has been investigating whether such mining would significantly affect life in the ocean—either surface life, including fishes, which might be harmed by clouds of sediment brought up from the bottom with the nodules, or the life of the bottom itself, whose great quantity and potential value is only now being realized.

Energy could be the most attractive resource of the oceans today, and not merely the offshore oil deposits that the oil companies have recently realized are there in plenty. The ocean itself is a far greater reservoir of energy sources. In waves, in currents, in tides, in temperature, and in its saltiness are stored enormous

Manganese nodules are strewn across the ocean floor in an almost continuous layer. They are valued more for the small quantities of copper, nickel, cobalt, and zinc they contain than for their primary component, manganese.

amounts of energy derived originally from the sun, winds, the earth's rotation, or geologic processes. There are also submarine hot springs that might be used, and even submarine volcanoes, embodying more energy than a hydrogen bomb and just as dangerous. A single iceberg towed from the Antarctic to the tropics would supply not only fresh water but, by means of heat exchangers, several thousand megawatt-years of energy, as well.

Ocean energy is already in use in a few cases. A tidal power plant on the Rance River in France, where there is a tide that averages over twenty-five feet, produces over 500,000 megawatt-hours. There is another tidal plant in the Soviet Union, and there have been plans for one in Passamaquoddy Bay, Maine, for half a century. More than half a dozen other areas in the world could support tidal plants. Also, harbors could be engineered to dredge themselves through tidal currents. Tidal energy is not strictly a renewable resource. Tidal friction slows the rotation of the earth and lengthens the day by 1.5 thousandths of a second per century; but if all the electrical energy needed in the twenty-first century could be gotten from tides, the day would only get thirty thousandths of a second longer per century, or five minutes per million years.

Wave power has been used for years to power navigational buoys, and a power plant based on this principle was reportedly under construction in Japan in 1980. Usually there is more energy in the up and down motion of a ship than is being used by its engines, and this energy could be employed to help move it. A recent invention called the anisotropic towline reportedly harnesses wave power with a series of flexible umbrella-shaped flaps attached to the towrope, and when tested multiplied the pulling power of a tow almost twenty times. Other new and promising wave power devices have such colorful

names as Salter's Duck, Savonius Rotors, the dynamic breakwater, and Arthur's Island.

Currents like the Gulf Stream represent a large source of energy to the few areas where they come in reach of shore. The temperature differential between surface water and cold deep water could be mined and used in heat exchangers to produce electricity or fuel; the same water used in aquaculture would be even more productive of animal protein, and this latter technique is already in use. Curiously, the greatest energy potential of the ocean is salt, though as yet there is no technology for making use of the salinity differentials in the oceans. (The process could be like that of a battery, or might employ membranes, as in osmosis.) There is more potential energy in the salt of an offshore salt dome—salt domes are among the most common of oil-bearing geologic structures—than there is in its oil, by several hundred times, according to recent investigations.

The ocean is so huge that it was once assumed, by scientist and layman alike, that whatever was dumped into it would simply disappear, virtually without a trace. But in the early seventies scientists from several different laboratories found comparatively large and possibly harmful amounts of the lethal chemical PCB in ocean life—codfish, for example—thousands of miles from land or civilization. PCB, which was produced in amounts that were tiny on an industrial scale (compared, for example, to DDT), had never been dumped in the ocean (though it was dumped in some rivers—the Hudson, for one). It had never even been purposefully introduced anywhere in the environment, as DDT was; but it was just as widespread in the oceans as was DDT. It was found, for example, in the far South Atlantic. It was especially worrisome that some of the highest levels of PCB were measured in plankton, which are directly or indi-

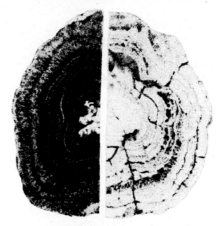

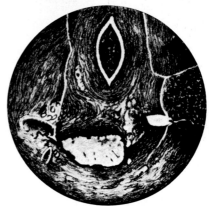

Illustrations from the Challenger *report show a manganese nodule in cross section (top) and in microscopic detail.*

rectly the food of all other creatures of the oceans' surface, and of many from the depths as well. If PCB accumulated in marine creatures as it and similar chemicals do in birds and mammals, increasing with each step in a food chain, the effects could have been catastrophic. Instead, it appears that the highest concentrations of PCB in ocean plant life and in animals with gills coincide with very high concentrations in the water; when there is less PCB in the water there is less in the marine life. Birds and mammals are still affected, but the fish can partially purge themselves, if they find cleaner water. A decade earlier, strontium 90, a radioactive isotope produced in atom bomb tests in Nevada and elsewhere, was traced in antarctic ice and the flesh of antarctic penguins; it had even penetrated water thousands of

feet below the surface, though it had not, as yet, reached the bottom waters. Fallout was quickly forgotten in many quarters, and bomb fallout in the oceans was considered a special case of pollution; but the experience with PCB showed finally that the oceans are no longer infinite with respect to man's ability to scatter harmful substances.

Oil pollution also became a major problem in the oceans in the 1960's, especially along the shorelines, where nearly all ocean life is concentrated— but also out in the middle of the open ocean, thousands of miles from any land. Oil from tanker accidents, and an even vaster quantity from intentional dumping during routine oil industry procedures, reached millions of tons a year during the sixties and continued to rise. In the Sargasso Sea oceanographers found oil slicks, floating tar balls, and gummy deposits in all stages of decomposition, in quantities that were reported to exceed the amount of surface life there; far from being in danger of being caught in the seaweed, the modern sailor stands a greater risk of getting stuck in the tar that br'er oil company has left behind. Even enormously diluted oil (twenty to fifty parts

Eighty-five per cent of the world's aquaculture production comes from Asia. Fish farms in Laguna de Bay, the Philippines, raise milkfish in bamboo-and-weed enclosures (left) and send them to Manila, one of the world's largest fish markets, for distribution (right, above). At right, a large catch of squid dries in the sun in Thailand before it is sent to market.

per billion) causes subtle—and not so subtle—inhibitions in living tissues, so that animals and plants reproduce less, for example, and forms of plankton that are better food for fish and other larger organisms, including man, are replaced by other forms of plankton that are less good food.

What then of the oceans' future? Or do the oceans have a future? A few authorities already believe not, that damage by mankind can no longer be stopped before it becomes irreversible; and most independent authorities agree that the problems are threatening and intractable. The ocean has always been the poet's symbol of the eternal and the inexhaustible. It is ironic that when man knows more than ever about the oceans their future is most in doubt. Things have come to such a pass largely out of overconfidence, and fail to improve because no one will forgo anything until everyone else has agreed to do so too.

On November 1, 1967, the delegate from Malta, Dr. Arvid Pardo, rose in the General Assembly of the United Nations and, in one of the most influential speeches ever made there, reminded his colleagues of the many resources of the ocean, and of the threats to them, and to life in the ocean, and to human life as well. Pardo was especially concerned with the sea floor, and he raised the issue of its military use. He pointed out that submarine depots could be established on the flat tops of guyots, and that very complex technology could be placed on the ocean floor itself, or floated in the mid-depths, and that there was—and is—no international sanction against such installations. Pardo spoke of the wealth of the sea bed, and of the loopholes in existing international law regarding it. The law was—and still is—the Geneva Convention of 1958, whose establishment of limits of national sovereignty, a compromise that seemed effective at the time, has been rendered totally meaningless by technology. It gives maritime nations sovereignty over the sea floor off their shores out to a depth of 200 meters, not an unreasonable boundary—"or beyond that limit, to where the depth of the superjacent waters admits of the exploitation of the natural resources of the said areas." In other words, a nation owns anything it can get. Since it is now possible to drill—and mine—in depths of four or five miles, the United States could claim from its shores across to Europe and Asia, and countries there could claim all the way back to ours—if they had the technology. "We could see a scramble for land like the one in Africa in the last century," Pardo told me after his speech; he called on the U.N. to establish the sea floor as a "common heritage of mankind," and in 1970 the U.N. passed a resolution doing so, and another declaring the resources of the sea bed off limits to mining until further notice. (The United States voted for the first but not the second.)

In 1973, the Law of the Sea Conference convened to write new laws governing use of the oceans, embodying the knowledge and capabilities that exist today—laws pertaining not only to the sea bed and mining, but to the surface waters and waters between as well, regulating fishing, pollution, research, and passage of vessels through waters once considered international and now claimed by some nations as theirs. The negotiations have been difficult, and occasionally rancorous; and the most intractable issue of all has been the mining of the sea floor (progress has been even slower than the growth of the nodules themselves, the head of a mining company remarked after one session). In 1977, when many people thought an agreement was near, the chairman of the negotiating committee for the sea floor scrapped critical portions of the negotiated text and substituted new wording of his own. Third-world countries have insisted on a share in the mining of the common heritage, and a share in policy and profits, generally a much larger share than those with the technology for mining would willingly concede. Metal exporting countries saw threats to their markets (five ocean mining sites would produce the entire world consumption of cobalt), while metal importers saw an opportunity to make supplies independent of local politics.

Elaborate policies have been worked out to govern operations on the sea floor, and to help developing countries have a share in future activities. Mining companies would pay fees and taxes to an international sea bed authority which, during a twenty-year project, could amount to $200 million for an economically marginal project, and $2 billion for a profitable one. Impatient with the U.N., some mining companies, and some legislators, have urged that the United States enable its companies to start mining without waiting for the U.N. But slow as progress has been, the goal of lawful regulation of the seas is worth waiting and working a long time for. The oceans' future is at stake, but the greatest problem is man's reluctance to change his own habits and expectations. The wealth of the sea can be lost in a generation, or its food, its minerals, and its energy can last for centuries and ages to come for all humanity.

ACKNOWLEDGMENTS AND CREDITS

The editors wish to thank the following individuals and institutions for their help in preparing this book: Robert Wolk of the Joseph Conrad Library, Seaman's Church Institute of New York; Helga Moody and Donald Petty of the Morris Raphael Cohen Library, City College, New York; Mercantile Library, New York City; New York Public Library; New York Society Library.

Text Permissions

CHAPTER TWO 86—excerpt from article in *Life*, May 5, 1961: "Sea Search Into History at Caesarea" by Ken MacLeish, *Life* © 1961 Time Inc.; reprinted with permission.

ANTHOLOGY I 114—"A World of Color": reprinted by permission of G. P. Putnam's Sons from *Beneath Tropic Seas* by William Beebe; copyright 1928 by William Beebe. 115—"Sharks": abridged from pp. 230–33 in *The Silent World* by Capt. Jacques-Yves Cousteau with Frédéric Dumas, copyright ©1953 by Harper & Row, Publishers, Inc.; reprinted by permission of the publisher. 116—"Attacked by a Big Fish": reprinted from *The Sun Beneath the Sea* by Jacques Piccard, translated from the French by Denver Lindley, copyright © 1971 by Charles Scribner's Sons. 117—"God's Little Underwater Acre": reprinted by permission of *Sports Illustrated* from the September 16, 1957 issue, © 1957 Time Inc. "Part II, God's Little Underwater Acre: The Reef and its Treasure" by Clare Boothe Luce. 119—"Death of a Young Diver": abridged from pp. 63–64 in *The Living Sea* by Capt. Jacques-Yves Cousteau with J. Dugan, copyright © 1963 by Harper & Row, Publishers, Inc.; reprinted by permission of the publisher. 119—"A Flash in the Deep": reprinted by permission of Elsevier-Nelson Books from *Half Mile Down* by William Beebe, © 1934, 1951 by William Beebe. 120—"Hunting for Bodies": excerpted from *The Treasure Divers of Vigo Bay* by John S. Potter, Jr., copyright © 1958 by John S. Potter, Jr.; reprinted by permission of Doubleday & Company, Inc. 122—"Laughing Sea Cows": reprinted from *Diving For Pleasure and Treasure* by Clay Blair, Jr. ©1960, World Publishing Company. Reprinted by permission of the author. 123—"Cave Diving": abridged from pp. 69–80 in *The Silent World* by Capt. Jacques-Yves Cousteau with Frédéric Dumas, copyright ©1953 by Harper & Row, Publishers, Inc.; reprinted by permission of the publisher. 127—"The Deepest Trench": reprinted from *Seven Miles Down* by Jacques Piccard and Robert S. Dietz, © 1961 by Jacques Piccard and Robert S. Dietz; reprinted by permission of Curtis Brown, Ltd.

ANTHOLOGY II 225—"A Perilous Passage": reprinted from *The Aran Islands* by John Millington Synge, published by George Allen & Unwin, Ltd.; by permission of the publishers. 227—"Xerxes Orders the Sea Flogged": reprinted from *Herodotus*, translated by J. Enoch Powell, The Clarendon Press, Oxford, 1949; by permission of the publishers. 230—"A Rescue at Sea," and 240—"The Character of the West Wind": both reprinted from *The Mirror of the Sea* by Joseph Conrad, © 1906, 1933 by Jessie Conrad; by permission of J. M. Dent and Sons Ltd., Publishers.

Picture Credits

Credits for illustrations from left to right are separated by semicolons; from top to bottom, by dashes.

END PAPERS Paolo Curto.

TITLE PAGE From *Monsters of the Sea*, by John Gibson, 1887.

CHAPTER ONE 8, 9,—Peter Stackpole, *Life* © 1959 Time Inc. 10—Museo Naval, Madrid. 12, 13—all, Bibliothèque Nationale, Paris. 15—courtesy of the Hispanic Society of America, New York. 16, 17—National Maritime Museum, Greenwich. 18—William L. Clements Library, University of Michigan, Ann Arbor. 20, 21—Museo de America, Madrid, photo: Oronoz. 22, 23—The Dietrich Brothers Americana Corporation of Philadelphia, Pennsylvania, photo: Will Brown. 24, 25—David Doubilet. 26—John Launois/Black Star—American Numismatic Society, New York. 26, 27—Flip Schulke/Black Star. 28, 29, 30, 31—all, Peter Stackpole, *Life* © Time Inc. 32, 33—reproduced by permission of the British Library, London. 34—National Maritime Museum, Greenwich. 35—The Mansell Collection—Department of Coins and Medals, British Museum, London. 36, 37—all, courtesy of Seaquest International, Inc. 38, 39, 40, 41—all, Jonathon Blair/Woodfin Camp and Associates. 42, 43—National Maritime Museum, Greenwich. 44—Museo del Prado, Madrid—G. Tyrwhitt-Drake, Bereleigh, Petersfield. 44, 45—National Maritime Museum, Greenwich. 46, 47—Private Collection. 47—Robert Sténuit. 48—Marc J. Jasinski—Robert Sténuit. 50—Bibliothèque Nationale, Paris. 51—reproduced by permission of the British Library, London, photo: Robert Marx. 52—Delaware Art Museum, Wilmington, Howard Pyle Collection. 53—both, Flip Schulke/Black Star. 54, 55—Bibliothèque Nationale, Paris. 56, 57—The Mariners Museum of Newport News. 57—The Bettman Archive. 58—bottom, New York Public Library; The Bettman Archive. 59—Electric Boat Division of General Dynamics; United Press International—New York Public Library. 60, 61—Collection of Davis Allen.

CHAPTER TWO 62, 63—Michael L. Katzev. 64—The Bettman Archive. 66, 67—Peter Throckmorton. 68—Peter Throckmorton. 68, 69—Harold E. Edgerton. 70—Peter Throckmorton. 71—Musei Vaticani, Rome, photo: Alinari/Editorial Photocolor Archives. 73—Peter Throckmorton/Nancy Palmer Photo Agency. 74—Peter Throckmorton. 76, 77—both, Peter Throckmorton/Nancy Palmer Photo Agency. 78—Flip Schulke/Black Star. 79—John G. Cassils, courtesy American Institute of Nautical Archeology. 80—Flip Schulke/Black Star. 81—John Veltri. 82—Susan Womer Katzev. 83—Michael L. Katzev. 84, 85—The Bettman Archive. 86, 87—© 1979 The Mobius Group. 88—Hassia—Harold E. Edgerton. 89—Professor R. Schoder, S.J.—drawn by Joseph W. Shaw, courtesy of University of Chicago, Indiana University Excavations at Kenchreai for the American School of Classical Studies. 90, 91—Museo Nazionale, Naples, Scala/Editorial Photocolor Archives. 91—Anderson/Editorial Photocolor Archives. 92—Joseph Shaw. 94, 95—F. Patellani. 95—Harold E. Edgerton. 96, 97—National Archeological Museum, Athens. 98, 99—Leonard von Matt/Photo Researchers Inc. 99—John Ross. 100, 101, 102, 103—all, The Illustrated London News Picture Library. 104—National Archeological Museum, Athens, photo: Alison Frantz. 105—Peter Throckmorton/Nancy Palmer Photo Agency. 106, 107—both, National Archeological Museum, Athens, photo: Hirmer Verlag. 108—both, Guido Ucelli. 109—National Archeological Museum, Athens, photo: Hirmer Verlag. 110—Musée Alaoui, Le Bardo, Tunis; The J. Paul Getty Museum. 111—Fotosub Maltini, Solaini, Rome.

ANTHOLOGY I 112—Electric Boat Division of General Dynamics.

CHAPTER THREE 130, 131—David Hiser. 132—illustration courtesy Bibliothèque Nationale, Paris. 134, 135—Geoffrey Clements. 136, 137—Erich Lessing/Magnum. 138—both, Rene Noorbergen/Camera Press via Pictorial Parade. 138, 139—Fred Maroon/Photo Researchers Inc. 140—courtesy of Stift Klosterneuburg, Austria, photo: Erich Lessing/Magnum. Museo Cristiano, Brescia, photo: Scala/Editorial Photocolor Archives. 142, 143—both, Erich Lessing/Magnum. 145—Vatican Museum, photo: Hirmer Verlag. 147—British Museum, photo: Michael Holford. 148—© Nordbok, Gothenburg, Sweden. 152, 153—Erich Lessing/Magnum. 153—British Museum, London, photo: Michael Holford. 154—Erich Lessing/Magnum. 155—American Heritage Publishing Company—Erich Lessing/Magnum. 156—Erich Lessing/Magnum—Metropolitan Museum of Art, New York, Fletcher Fund. 157—Erich Lessing/Magnum. 158, 159—all, Erich Lessing/Magnum. 160—David Hiser. 161—Shensi Provincial Museum, Sian. 162—American Heritage Publishing Company. 163—Bibliothèque Nationale, Paris. 164—both, *Chronica Botanica*, Vol. 14, No. 6. 164, 165—Nicholas De Vore III/Bruce Coleman Inc. 166—National Maritime Museum, Greenwich. 167—David Hiser. 168, 169—Bibliothèque Nationale, Paris. 170—University Library, Heidelberg University. 172—Library of Congress. 174—Biblioteca Estense, Modena. 174, 175—Map Division, New York Public Library. 177—Ian Yeomans/Woodfin Camp and Associates. 178—American Heritage Publishing Company. 178, 179—Norman Brouwer Collection. 180—Norman Brouwer Collection. 181—Bath Marine Museum. 182—from *The Report of the Scientific Results of the Exploring Voyage of HMS Challenger during the years 1873–1876, Narrative, Part Two*—Norman Brouwer Collection. 183—both, Norman Brouwer Collection. 184—Instituto dela Patagonia—both, Norman Brouwer Collection. 184, 185—Norman Brouwer Collection.

CHAPTER FOUR 186, 187—Courtesy of the Fogg Art Museum, Harvard University, Washington Allston Trust. 188—The Bettman Archive. 189—from *A History of Lloyd's*, by Charles Wright and Ernest C. Fayle, Macmillan, 1928. 190, 193, 195—all, Peabody Museum of Salem. 196—Williams College Museum of Art, Williamstown. 197—New York Public Library, Rare Book Room. 198—Keystone Press Agency. 201—Lewis Walpole Library. 202, 203—Peabody Museum of Salem. 205—The Mariners Museum of Newport News. 206—United Press International. 207—National Maritime Museum, Greenwich. 208—The Mystic Seaport Museum, Mystic. 210—Peabody Museum of Salem. 212—from *Joshua Slocum*, by Walter Teller, Rutgers University Press, 1971. 213—Peabody Museum of Salem. 214, 215—National Maritime Museum, Greenwich. 216—National Maritime Museum, Greenwich—Royal Geographical Society, London. 217—The Mariners Museum of Newport News. 218, 219—Private Collection. 220, 221—National Maritime Museum, Greenwich. 222, 223—The Louvre Museum, Paris.

CHAPTER FIVE   242, 243—Culver Pictures. 244—The Pierrepont Morgan Library, New York. 246—from *Introduction to Oceanography* by David A. Ross, Appleton Century Croft, 1970. 248—James H. Carmichael, Jr.—both, L. P. Madin. 249—all, Susumu Honjo, Woods Hole Oceanographic Institution. 250, 251—both, Ken Lucas. 252—Jen and Des Bartlett/National Audubon Society Collection, Photo Researchers Inc. 253—James H. Carmichael, Jr.—Jack Dermid. 254, 255—Betty and Neil Johannsen. 256—both, Jack Dermid. 257—both, Douglas Faulkner. 258—James H. Carmichael, Jr. 259, 260, 261—all, Douglas Faulkner. 262, 263—courtesy of Dr. N. A. Locket and the Royal Society, London. 264—Taiyo Fishery Co./Michihiko Yano. 264, 265—Keystone Press Agency. 266, 267—J. J. Languepin/National Audubon Society Collection, Photo Researchers Inc. 268—Tom McHugh/National Audubon Society Collection, Photo Researchers Inc.—Ralph Silva III, Scientific Research, Dedicated Vessel. 269—Staatliche Antikensammlungen, Munich. 270, 271—Scott Preiss. 272—Dudley B. Foster, Woods Hole Oceanographic Institution. 273—both, American Heritage Publishing Company. 274—Dudley B. Foster, Woods Hole Oceanographic Institution. 275—Dr. John A. Whitehead, Jr., Woods Hole Oceanographic Institution. 276, 277—Peabody Museum of Salem. 279—The Boston Athenaeum, Boston, photo: George Cushing. 280—The Bettman Archive. 282—Culver Pictures. 283—New England Aquarium, Boston. 284, 285—Culver Pictures. 286, 287—New Bedford Whaling Museum, New Bedford. 287—from *Historia de gentibus septentrionalibus*, by Olaus Magnus. 288—San Giovanni Evangelista, Ravenna—both, Photo Quest. 289—The Bettman Archive—both, Culver Pictures. 290, 291—Sekai Bunka Photo. 291—The Rietberg Museum, courtesy of the Asia Society.

CHAPTER SIX   292, 293—Photo Quest, The Sea Library/Woodfin Camp and Associates. 294—Royal Geographical Society, London, photo: Derrick Witty. 295—from *Book of Pirates*, by Henry K. Brooke, 1847. 296, 297—Museum of Fine Arts, Boston, M. and M. Karolik Collection. 298—Radio Times Hulton Picture Library. 299—Michael Holford Library. 300, 301—from *The Report of the Scientific Results of the Exploring Voyage of HMS Challenger during the years 1873-76*, Volume 18. 302—The Swiss National Tourist Office. 302, 303—The American Heritage Publishing Company. 303—George Hall/Woodfin Camp and Associates. 304, 305—Ward W. Wells. 307, 308, 309—© Hachette—Guides Bleu. 310—Richard W. Grigg. 311, 313—both, Woods Hole Oceanographic Institution. 314, 315—American Heritage Publishing Company. 315—M. N. Toksöz in *Oceanus*, Volume XVII, Winter 1973-74. 316, 317—National Environmental Satellite Service, N.O.A.A., Department of Commerce. 318—David Doubilet. 319—Culver Pictures. 320—The Franklin Institute, Philadelphia. 321—American Heritage Publishing Company. 322—Solar Film, Reykjavik. 323—Ragnar Larusson/Photo Researchers Inc. 324, 325—ZEFA. 326—Georg Gerster/Photo Researchers Inc. 327—Georg Gerster/Photo Researchers Inc.—Victor Englebert/Photo Researchers Inc. 328, 329—The Bettman Archive. 330—United Press International. 331—Wide World Photos. 332, 333—courtesy of Kenneth M. Newman, The Old Print Shop. 333—Wide World Photos. 334—Exxon Corporation, photo: David Moore. 336—courtesy of the Lamont-Doherty Geological Observatory of Columbia University, photo: Larry Sullivan. 337—both, Michael Holford Library. 338, 339—Robert Ketchum/F.I.O.I., 1977. 341—Chuck Nicklin © 1980.

BIBLIOGRAPHY

Chapter 1   SUNKEN TREASURE

Burgess, Robert F., and Carl J. Clausen. *Gold, Galleons and Archaeology*. Indianapolis: Bobbs-Merrill, 1976.

Earle, Peter. *The Treasure of the Concepción: The Wreck of the Almiranta*. New York: Viking Press, 1980.

Martin, Colin. *Full Fathom Five: Wrecks of the Spanish Armada*. New York: Viking Press, 1975.

Marx, Robert F. *Shipwrecks of the Western Hemisphere, 1492-1825*. New York: David McKay Co., 1975.

Parry, J. H. *The Spanish Seaborne Empire*. New York: Alfred A. Knopf, 1966.

Peterson, Mendel. *The Funnel of Gold*. Boston: Little, Brown, 1975.

Chapter 2   UNDER ANCIENT SEAS

Bascom, Willard. *Deep Water, Ancient Ships*. Garden City, New York: Doubleday, 1976.

Bass, George Fletcher. *Archaeology Under Water*. Ancient Peoples and Places. New York: Praeger, 1966.

————, ed. *A History of Seafaring, Based on Underwater Archaeology*. New York: Walker, 1972.

Casson, Lionel. *Ships and Seamanship in the Ancient World*. Princeton, New Jersey: Princeton University Press, 1971.

Flemming, Nicholas C. *Cities in the Sea*. Garden City, New York: Doubleday, 1971.

Galanopoulos, A. G., and Edward Bacon. *Atlantis: The Truth Behind the Legend*. Indianapolis: Bobbs-Merrill, 1969.

Latil, Pierre de, and Jean Rivoire. *Man and the Underwater World*. Translated by Edward Fitzgerald. New York: Putnam, 1956.

Throckmorton, Peter. *Shipwrecks and Archaeology: The Unharvested Sea*. Boston: Little, Brown, 1970.

Chapter 3   MYSTERIOUS VOYAGES

Arciniegas, Germán. *Amerigo and the New World: The Life and Times of Amerigo Vespucci*. Translated by Harriet de Onís. New York: Knopf, 1955.

Bradford, Ernle. *Ulysses Found*. New York: Harcourt, Brace & World, 1963.

Casson, Lionel. *The Ancient Mariners: Seafarers and Sea Fighters of the Mediterranean in Ancient Times*. New York: Macmillan, 1959.

Lewis, David. *The Voyaging Stars: Secrets of the Pacific Island Navigators*. New York: W. W. Norton, 1978.

Morison, Samuel Eliot. *The European Discovery of America*. 2 vols. New York: Oxford University Press, 1971-74.

Stanford, William B., and J. V. Luce. *The Quest for Ulysses*. New York: Praeger, 1974.

Chapter 4   MYSTERIOUS DISAPPEARANCES

Fay, Charles Edey. *Mary Celeste: The Odyssey of an Abandoned Ship*. Salem, Massachusetts: Peabody Museum, 1942.

Snow, Edward Rowe. *Ghosts, Gales and Gold*. New York: Dodd, Mead & Co., 1972.

Stackpole, Edouard A., ed. *Those in Peril on the Sea*. New York: Dial Press, 1962.

Teller, Walter Magnes, ed. *The Voyages of Joshua Slocum*. New Brunswick, New Jersey: Rutgers University Press, 1958.

Villiers, Alan. *Posted Missing: The Story of Ships Lost Without Trace in Recent Years*. New York: Scribner, 1974.

Chapter 5   MYSTERIOUS CREATURES

Borgese, Elisabeth Mann. *The Drama of the Oceans*. New York: Abrams, 1975.

Cousteau, Jacques-Yves and Frédéric Dumas. *The Silent World*. New York: Harper & Row, 1953.

Heuvelmans, Bernard. *In the Wake of the Sea-Serpents*. Translated by Richard Garnett. New York: Hill & Wang, 1968.

Idyll, C. P. *Abyss: The Deep Sea and the Creatures that Live in It*. 3d ed. New York: T. Y. Crowell, 1976.

Jensen, Albert C. *Wildlife of the Oceans*. New York: Abrams, 1979.

Matthews, Leonard Harrison, et al. *The Whale*. New York: Crescent Books, 1975.

Chapter 6   LAND BELOW, SEA ABOVE

Corliss, William R. *Mysteries Beneath the Sea*. New York: T. Y. Crowell, 1970.

Heezen, Bruce C., and Charles D. Hollister. *The Face of the Deep*. New York: Oxford University Press, 1971.

Idyll, C. P., ed. *Exploring the Ocean World: A History of Oceanography*. rev. ed. New York: T. Y. Crowell, 1972.

Linklater, Eric. *The Voyage of the Challenger*. Garden City, New York: Doubleday, 1972.

Menard, H. William and Jane L. Scheiber, eds. *Oceans: Our Continuing Frontier*. Del Mar, California: Publisher's Inc., 1976.

Wertenbaker, William. *The Floor of the Sea: Maurice Ewing and the Search to Understand the Earth*. Boston: Little, Brown, 1974.

INDEX

Numbers in boldface refer to illustrations or captions.

A

abyssal zone, **246,** 251, 303–6
Actium, Greece, 89
Acushnet, 228
Adams, Richard, 44
Admiral Karpfanger, 209
Aeetes, King of Colchis, 146
Aegean Islands, 75
Aeschylus, 146
Afar (Danakil) Depression, 316, **326–27**
Africa, 176
Agassiz, Louis, 299
Alaska, 161, 215
Albemarle, Duke of, 33, 35
Alberti, Leon Battista, 101
Aldrich, Frederick, 283
Aldrich, Lt. Pelham, journal of, **295**
Alecton, 281–82, **282**
Alexander's Acres, 252
Alexander the Great, 54, 67
Alexandria, Egypt, 85, 87
Alps, **302**
Alston, Theodosia Burr, 199, **201**
Alston, Washington, painting by, **188–89**
Alvin, 273–74, **275, 313**
Amazon River, 212
Ambassador, **178**
Ambrosian Bank, 34
America, 161, 177
Amundsen, Roald, 217
Ancient Mariners, The, 89
anemone, **258**
ANGUS (Acoustically Navigated Geophysical Underwater System), 273–74
animals of the sea, 254
    behavioral relationships among, **261,** 262
    cold-blooded, 261–62
    senses of, 256–61, **252**
Antikýthēra, 68, 70–72, 89, 108
Antiquities of the Jews, 141
Apollonia, Cyrene (Libya), 91
Apollonius of Rhodes, 146
aquaculture, 275, 335, 337, **339**
Aquidneck, 211
Aran Islands, The, 225–26
archaeology, marine, **57,** 72, 74–75, 77–80, **80,** 83, 99
Archaeology Beneath the Sea, 80
Arctic Ocean, 215
Argentina, 176
Argo, 146–49
Argonautica, 146
Argus, 197
Aristotle, 151, 247
Armenia, 141
art:
    damaged, 68, 75
    recovered, 68, 71, 97, 103–4, **107–8, 110**
Ashdod, Israel, 86
Asherah, **78**

Ashurbanipal, King of Assyria, 136
Atalanta, 207–9
Atema, Jelle, 258
Athenaeus, 98
Athens, Greece, 70, 89
Atlantic Ocean, 89, 96, 151, 161, 169, 171, 195, 209, 211
Atlantis, 93, 96–97, 300–301, 303
Augustus, Emperor of Rome, 89
Australia, 201, 209
Azores, 151, 176, 189, 191, 194, 208–9

B

Back, George, 215
Back River, Canada, 217
Baffin Island, 215
Bahamas, 199
Baiae, Italy, 89, 93
Baker, Janet, 149
Ballard, Robert, 273–74
Bamberger, Mrs. *See* Littauer
Banks, Sir Joseph, 277–78
Barbados, 201, 203, 207–8
Bardo Museum, Tunis, 72
Barkman, Lars, 75
Bartley, James, 142–43
Bass, Ann, **74, 76**
Bass, George, 72, **76,** 77–78, 80, 83
Baths of Ocean, 144, 146
bathyal zone, **246,** 251
Baxter, George, 217
Beacon, 299
Beebe, William, 114, 119–20
Beechey Island, 217
benthic zone, **246,** 251
Bérard, Victor, 144
Bergensfjord, 331
Berlitz, Charles, 204–5
Bermuda, 16–17, 29, 31, 194, 204, 207
Bermuda Triangle, 204–5, 211
Bermuda Triangle, The, 204–5
Bermuda Triangle Mystery, The, 204–5
Berryman, Lieutenant, 297
biological oceanography, **246,** 247–64, 273–75
bioluminescence, **251,** 256
blackdragon, **251**
Blair, Clay, Jr., 122–23
Blanchard, Duncan, 324
blennies, **261**
Blue Grotto, Capri, Italy, **111**
Bonaparte, Napoleon, 196, 215
Boss, Kenneth, 281–82
Boswell, James, 234
Bounty, 195
Bouyer, Lt. Frédéric-Marie, 282
Bowden, Tracy, 39, **39**
Bradford, Ernle, 153, 155
Bragg, Sir Lawrence, 311
Brazil, 162, 174, 177
Brendan, 177, **177**
Briggs, Benjamin, 191–93, **193**
Bristol, England, 178
Bryan, George S., 193
Bryce, Sir James, 141
Bullitt, John, 86

Burr, Aaron, 199, 201
Burr, Theodosia, 199, **201**
butterfly fish, **257**

C

Cabot, John, 168, 173, 177, 317
Cabot, Sebastian, 168, 317
Cádiz, Spain, 39, 175
Caesarea, Israel, 86
California, 161
Caligula, Emperor of Rome, 101–2, 108
Calypso, 145
camouflage, **256–58**
Cannes, France, 74
Cape Artemisium, Greece, 72, 104, 107
Cape Breton Island, Nova Scotia, 168
Cape Canaveral, Florida, 16
Cape Circeo, Italy, 145
Cape Gelidonya, Turkey, 72, **72,** 74, 76–78, 80
Cape Hatteras, 175, 203
Cape Horn, 178, 180, 182, 203, 209
Cape of Good Hope, 149, 203, 209, 211
Cape Reef, Florida, 16
Carey, Frank, 256
Caribe Salvage, 39
Caribbean, 14, 33
Caroline Islands, 165
Carrera de Indias, 11–21, 29
Carroll A. Deering, 203, **205**
Cartagena, 12, 14–15, 17, 19
Carthage, 149–51
Case for the UFO, The, 203
Casson, Lionel, 89
Centaur, **221**
Ceram, C. W., 104
Cerne, 150
Challenger, 247, 274, **298–300,** 299–301, 335, 337
Champlain, Samuel de, 29
Charles II, King of England, 33
Charles Cooper, 182, **182**
Chase, Owen, 238–39
Chaumareix, Capt. Duroys de, 196–97
chemosynthesis, 274–75
China, 161–64, 178
Ch'in Shih Huang Ti, Emperor of China, 162
Churchill, Winston, 201
circumnavigation, 149–50, 226
clownfish, 258
Club Alpin Sous-Marin, 74
coccolithophores, **248**
coelacanth, **262**
Colossus of Rhodes, **65**
Columbus, Christopher, 11, 14, 172–77, 227, 317, 319
Congo Canyon, 303
Conrad, Joseph, 21, 205, 230–32, 240
continental drift, 311–12, **314–15**
Cook Islands, 166
coral, 19, 26, **27,** 33–39, 53
Coral Sea, 200
Corinth, Greece, 95
Correard, Alexandre, 196–97
Cosmographia, 284, **284–85**
Cosmographiae Introductio, 177
Costa Rica, 175

Cousteau, Jacques-Yves, 71–72, 75, 115–16, 119, 123–27
Crates, 143–44
Crete, 93, 97
Critias, 96
Cromwell Current, 320–21
crusades, 76, 83–86
Cuba, 14, 175
curragh, 169, 171, **177,** 225–26
    See also shipbuilding, Irish
currents, 318–21, **321**
Currier, Nathaniel, 202
Cutty Sark, 178
Cyclops, 201–2
Cyprus, 65

D

da Gama, Vasco, 149
Dana, Richard, Henry, Jr., 232–34
Danish East Asiatic Company, 209
Darwin, Sir George, 306
Daughters of the American Revolution, 171
Davis, William M., **224**
Davis Strait, 215
Davy Jones, 198
dead water, 319–20
Death Mask, **257**
decorator crabs, **258**
Deepest Trench, The, 119–20
Defoe, Daniel, 194, 197, **197,** 234
de Guignes, Joseph, 161
Dei Gratia, 189–95, **190–91**
deities, 65–68, 70, 75, 88, 95, **107,** 142, **142,** 145, 166, 188–89, 194, 196
de Las Casas, Bartolemé, 173–75
de la Vega, Garcilaso, 235–37
Denham, Captain, 297
Denmark, 207, 209
de Orscelar, Marianus, 151
de Parville, Henri, 143
depth sounding, 295–98
derelicts, 197, 231
Descent into the Maelstrom, A, 128, **129**
Deveau, Oliver, 189, 191–92
Diamond Shoals, 203
diluvialism, 306
dinoflagellates, 252, 256
Diodorus of Sicily, 151
divers, 10, **11,** 24, 29–31, **54, 57, 59–61,** 68–72, **112**
    and diving gear, **54, 57,** 58, **59,** 67–72, 86, **111**
    and equipment, 68–72
    helmeted, 67, **67,** 85
    Indian pearl, 19, 33–34
    modern scientist, **24,** 48, **53,** 65, **65,** 80, 85, 86
    scuba, 49, 72, 86, 95, **111**
    slave, 19
    sponge, 60–61, 65, 71–72, 104, **104,** 108
    treasure, 39, 76
    West Indian, 53
Diving for Treasure and Pleasure, 122–23
dolphins, 267–71, **267–70**
Drake, Sir Francis, 17, 35
Dugan, James, 119
Dumas, Frédéric, 75, 80, 115–16
Dutch West India Company, 18

E

earthquakes, 51, 95, 99, 311, **302, 305,** 314–15, **329,** 333, **333**
echolocation, 261, **268,** 270–71
   electronic, 301
echo soundings, **306**
Edgerton, Harold, 95
Edinburgh Castle, 331
Egede, Hans, 241
Egypt, 71, 150
El Gran Grifon, 49
Elizabeth I, Queen of England, **44**
Emerson, Ralph Waldo, 173
energy resources of the oceans, 336–37
England, 44, 173, 215, 217–18
   British Royal Navy, 215, 217
English Channel, 43
Englishman, The, 234–35
Eratosthenes, 95, 143
Erebus, **214,** 215–17
Ericson, Leif, 172, **172,** 173
Eric the Red, 173
Eric the Red, 172–73
Eskimos, 217
Essex, 195
Etruscans, 98
Etymologies, 141
Euripides, 146
Eurydice, 207
Ewing, Maurice, 303, 306, 311

F

Fair Isle, 49
Falkland Islands, 178, 180, **180**
fan worm, **252**
faults, 93
Fay, Charles Edey, 193
Fell, Barry, 151
Ferdinand, King of Castile, 174–76
Figuier, Louis, 97
Firth of Forth, 43
Fisher, Mel, 20–21, **24,** 26
Fitzwilliam, William, 47
Flemming, Nicholas, 91
Flood, 134, 136, 306
Florida, 175
Florida Keys, 16, 18, 20
Florida Straits, 14, 16, 18, 23
flota, 12, 14, 23, 29
Flying Dutchman, 197
Folger, Timothy, 317, **321**
food potential, 248
   See also aquaculture
Forbes, Edward, 299
Forbidden Mountain, The, 141
Fox, 217–18
fracture zones, 302, 306
Fram, 319–20
Franklin, Benjamin, 317, **321**
Franklin, Sir John, 215–17, **216**
Frobisher, Sir Martin, 215
Fusang, 161
Fu- Sang, Land of, 161–62

G

Gaddis, Vincent H., 204
Gades (Cádiz), Spain, 151
Gaeta, Gulf of, 155
Gaffney, Matthew, 278
Gage, Thomas, 14, 29
Gagnan, Emile, 72, 115
Galápagos Rift valley, 273–75, **273, 275, 313**
Galli Islands, Italy, 156–57
General Archive of the Indies, 23
Genoa, Italy, 173, 191–92
geological theories, 93
Georgetown, South Carolina, 199
Géricault, Théodore, 197, **223**
Giant's Causeway, 49
Gibraltar, 144, 191–95
   Strait of, 96, 144
Gilbert Islands, South Pacific, 211
Gilder, Richard Watson, 211–12
Gilgamesh epic, 136–41
Girona, 47–49
Gloucester monster, 277–79, **277**
goatfishes, **261**
gobies, **261**
gold, 335
Golden Hind, 35
Gondwanaland, 312
Gordon, Cyrus, 151
Grand Bahamas, 21
Grand Congloué, France, 75, 119
Grassle, J. Frederick, 274–75
Graveyard of the Atlantic, 199
Great Britain, 178
Great Mary Celeste Hoax, The, 192
Greece, 144, 146, 149, 194
Greenland, 172, 215
Greenwich, England, 178
Guadalupe, 14
Gulf of Mexico, 17, 19, 175
Gulf Stream, 16, 204, 317–21, **317, 321**
Günther, Robert Theodore, 93
guyots, 302
gyres, 318–20, **321**

H

hadal zone, **246,** 251
Haeckel, Ernst, 299
Hakluyt, Richard, 172
Half Mile Down, 114
Halifax, Nova Scotia, 207
Halsewell, **220**
Halut, Remigny de, 49
Hamburg-America Line, 209
Hamilton, Sir William, 93
Hampshire, 201
Hanno, 150–51
harbor structures, sunken, 85–86, **86–91,** 91
Harrisse, Henry, 175
Harvey, Rev. Moses, 282
Havana, Cuba, 15–18, 24
Hawaii, **165,** 166
Heezen, Bruce, 303, **306,** 311

R

Rackham, Arthur, **129**
radiolaria, **300**
Rae, Dr. John, 216–17
Raft of the Medusa, The, 197, **223**
Raiatea, 165–66
Ramapo, 331
Ramayana, **290**
Real Eight Company, 26
Recife, Brazil, 176
Redburn, 228
Red Rock, 200
Rhodes, Greece, 71
Ridgway, Sam, 270
rift systems, 273–74
Riker, C. L., 318
Robinson Crusoe, 194, 197, 234
Robson, Frank, 271
Rockport, Massachusetts, 208
Rodin, Auguste, 210–11
Roman Empire, 169, 194
Rondelet, Guillaume, **289**
Roper, Clyde, 282–83
Ross, Sir James, 297
Ross, James Clark, 215
Ross, John, 215–16
Royal Commentaries of Peru, 235–37
Royal George, 57
Royal Society of London, 93, 277

S

Sailing Alone Around the World, 212, 226–27
St. Augustine, Florida, 24
Saint Brendan, 169–71, **171, 177,** 323
Saint Mary, **180**
Salem, Massachusetts, 195
Salerno, Gulf of, 156
salt, **327,** 337
salvaging, 30, 34–36, 53, 70, 72, 80, 85–86, 95–96, 104
Samoa, 162, 164
San Andreas Fault, **302**
San Antonio, 31
San Martin, 43
San Pedro, 31
Santa Clara, 245
Santa Maria de la Rosa, 49
Sargasso Sea, 204, 319, **319,** 335, 338
sargassum weed, **318–19,** 320
Sataspes, 149–50
Savigny, Henri, 196–97
scallops, **252**
Schevill, William, 269
Schliemann, Heinrich, 74
Scotland, 43–44, 47, 49
Scripps Institution of Oceanography, 248
Scylla and Charybdis, 153, 281, 283
"Sea Beggars," 43
Sea Diver, 53, 86
seafaring, **161,** 162, **163,** 164, 169, 171–73
seals, **252**
sea monsters, **47,** 67, 142, **171,** 245–47, **245,** 263–64, 277–79, **277,** 281–91, **288–91**

Seaquest International, 36
sea urchins, **256**
Selkirk, Alexander, 194
Senegal, West Africa, 196–97
Senegal River, 150
Serapis, Temple of, Pozzuoli, Italy, **91,** 93
Serçe Liman, Turkey, 83
serpents. *See* sea monsters
Serranilla Bank, 15, 19
Severin, Timothy, 171
Seville, Spain, 12, 14, 17, 19–21, **21,** 23, 176
Shakespeare, William, 194
Shanunga, 218, **218**
Shetland Isles, 49
shipbuilding, 80, **83**
   American, 89
   Greek, 89
   Hawaiian, **165**
   Irish, 169–71
   Phoenician, 86, **147–48**
   Polynesian, **133,** 164–66, 169
   prehistoric, **161**
   Roman, 72, 89, 91, 101–2
shipping, 76, 78, 83, 98
shipwrecks, 75, 80, 196–97, **218–23**
Sicily, 43
Sidon, Phoenician (Lebanon), 85, 91
Siebe, Augustus, 57, 69
Silent World, The, 115–16, 123–27
Silliman, Benjamin, 279
Silver Bank, 34–35
Sinbad the Sailor, 194–95
Sirens, 67, 153, 156, **156,** 171, 194, **290**
Skeleton in Armor, The, 172
Slocum, Mrs. Henrietta, 211, **212**
Slocum, Joshua, 204, **210–12,** 211–13, 226–27
Smithsonian Institution, 151
Snow, Edward R., 212–13
Soderini, Piero, 177
SONAR (SOund NAvigation and Ranging), 301
Sophocles, 146
South America, 209
Southey, Robert, 172
South Pacific sea lanes, 209
South Seas, 195
South Street Seaport Museum, New York City, 182
Spain, 11, 14, 43, 47
Spanish Armada, 43, **43,** 47–49
Spice Islands, 173, 194
Spotswood, Alexander, 24, 27
Spray, 211–12, 226
squid, 248, 250, 254, **281–83, 339**
   See also kraken
Stadiatis, Elias, 70
Star of the East, 142
Steele, Richard, 234–35
Stein, J. W., 176
Sténuit, Robert, 48–49, 120–22
Stevenson, Robert Louis, 133–34
Stick, David, 199
Stirling, Captain, 207–8
Stockholm, Sweden, 75
Story, Mr. and Mrs. Amos, 278
Strabo, 98, 144, 146, 151
Strait of Magellan, 178, **178, 185**
Strait of Messina, 153
Strange Sea Mysteries, 200